THIEF WITH
NO SHADOW

THIEF WITH NO SHADOW is set in an extraordinary
world where nightmarish creatures live alongside
men, and magic runs in the blood of mortals. It is
the story of Melke, a wraith who possesses the
ability to walk unseen. In order to break a curse
and save her brother's life, she is forced, against her
wishes, to use her magical talent to enter a den of
fire-breathing salamanders. Full of engaging
characters, this is a compelling tale rich in emotion.

THIEF WITH NO SHADOW

Emily Gee

SOLARIS

First published 2007 by Solaris
an imprint of BL Publishing
Games Workshop Ltd, Willow Road
Nottingham, NG7 2WS
UK

www.solarisbooks.com

ISBN-13: 978 1 84416 469 1
ISBN-10: 1 84416 469 1

A CIP catalogue record for this book is available from the
British Library.

Designed & typeset by BL Publishing

For my parents, Maurice and Margareta,
and my sister Abi.

CHAPTER ONE

MELKE CROUCHED IN the dying tree. Thirst was painful in her throat. The sun beat down, heating her hair until it almost burned on her scalp, and sweat prickled beneath her eyes. Yet the stolen necklace was cold, as if drops of icy water lay against her skin.

She released the branch with stiff fingers and wiped her face, and the beast below her growled.

The sound raised fine hairs on her skin, made her shiver in spite of the heat. How did it know she'd moved? She was a wraith. No living creature could see her, and yet every time she shifted, the hound's lips drew back and it growled, deep in its chest. Black hackles stood stiff down its spine and the sharp teeth were strong and white.

Melke took hold of the branch again and drew in a shallow breath. *Go away*, she thought. *You cannot see me, I am not here.*

The hound growled. Its pale wolf-eyes stared up at her.

The fierce sun inched across the sky. Heat burned through her ragged shirt and trousers. The tree was almost leafless, with thin and brittle branches. Splashes of blood showed dark on the parchment-pale bark, from where the snapping teeth had nipped her calf. The wound stung and her trousers were ripped from knee to ankle.

The skeleton shadow of the tree shifted on the ground, lengthening as noon passed. Desperation grew with each minute that slid away, each inhaled breath, each beat of her heart. *I am coming, Hantje. I will not let you die.*

There was a knife at her belt, thin and sharp, a few inches long. Melke fingered the hilt. Dare she attack the beast with so small a blade?

All morning the answer had been *No.* It was a knife for paring fruit, not killing savage hounds. Melke shifted cautiously on the branch. The beast growled again, showing its teeth. "Go away," she said, out loud. "I don't want to kill you." *I don't know if I can.*

Her voice, hoarse with thirst, set the creature leaping and scrambling, trying to reach her. She flinched back as strong claws tore at the bark. The hound began to bay, a fearsome sound, and the dying tree trembled beneath the onslaught.

Melke gripped the branch tightly. She closed her eyes and didn't move, scarcely daring to breathe, and the hound's baying became less frantic. It no longer scrambled to reach her, shaking the tree. The ululation became single deep barks, and then a low and menacing growl.

Melke opened her eyes. She saw a bright and cloudless sky and thin, twisted branches. Sunlight scorched her skin and hot air burned in her throat. She dared not look down at the hound.

I am coming Hantje, I promise.

The river was close. She almost heard the whisper of flowing water, almost smelled its damp scent. Trees stood lush and green on the far bank, beyond the edge of the dry meadow. So close. So far. The pain in her throat became more intense. She tried to swallow, but couldn't. Her throat cracked inside, peeling as the pale bark of the tree peeled.

The waterskin lay hidden a mile or more upstream, beneath the bridge. A loaf of bread was there too, and the map that had led her to this place. The bread and map were unimportant, she could survive without them, but the water—

The beast whined, a sound so unexpected that Melke looked down.

It whined a second time. The black ears twitched. The wolfish head turned.

A whistle sounded, high and faint and thin. Hope leaped beneath Melke's breastbone. Her heart beat faster. The whistle was repeated, louder and more imperatively. The hound shifted its weight.

Go, she urged it silently. *Go! Your master calls you.* She held her breath.

A man's voice shouted, impatient. The hound bared its teeth at her. A growl rumbled deep in its chest, and then it turned and ran swiftly across the meadow.

Melke peered through the thin branches. The beast was gone. *Gone.*

She scrambled out of the tree in sliding haste, tearing skin from her palms and leaving more blood on the bark. Dust puffed as her feet hit the dry ground.

The meadow was as threadbare as her clothes, the grass sun-bleached and the dirt the color of old bone. To the west—no more than quarter of a mile distant—stood a man, a thin, dark scarecrow figure against the white glare of the sun. The hound ran toward him, a blurring black shape.

Fear shrieked in her blood—*run run run*—but her legs were stiff and cramped. They wouldn't bend, wouldn't straighten, and she stumbled and fell heavily to the stone-hard dirt. The jarring pain was nothing, fear swamped it—*run run run*—and Melke pushed herself up, staggering and breathless, and snatched a glance behind her.

The hound stood with its master at the far edge of the parched meadow. The man had his hand on the beast's head and they both looked at her.

At her. The man looked *at* her.

Terror clenched in her chest. For a second, her heart failed to beat. Melke jerked her gaze down, certain she was visible. But no. Nothing, not even a shadow. No eyes could see her.

And yet the man knew she was there.

He shouted, and the hound began to bark.

Melke ran as she'd run that morning: for her life, pushing past pain, aware only of fear. Desperation whimpered in her throat. *Hantje*. The river was close. She heard it. The air that she gasped so frantically smelled of moss and mud, of dripping vegetation. Her throat burned, her chest burned, the muscles in her legs and arms burned. Each breath was a sob. The hound bayed behind her—close, too close—and the river bank was there, *right there*.

The water rushed in swift currents, thick and brown and swollen with spring rains.

There was a moment when she could have stopped, where dry ground ended and the river began, but the danger behind her—the hound with its snapping teeth and the man who'd take the necklace from her—was more frightening than any water could be. And so Melke jumped.

She plunged deep. Muddy water pressed down on her, filling her mouth and closing her eyes, making her blind. She thrashed against the downward pull, clawing at the water, and then there was sweet air and the glare of the sun. The river tossed her around as she coughed water from her lungs. High on the bank behind her was the black hound.

The current took her, spun her, as she gulped for air and tried to stay afloat. She twisted her head to see the hound. It stayed on the bank, growing smaller. The rush and hiss of water swallowed the sound of barking. And then its master was there, alongside it, tall.

The river swept around a bend, and hound and man were gone.

Branches snared Melke's clothes and hair. Water tumbled and choked her. Her shoes were heavy, dragging her feet down and pulling her under. She kicked hard, her heartbeat spiky with panic. One shoe came off, then the other. She spat water and gasped for air and fought the river with hands and feet. The far bank, green with ferns and trees, came closer.

The river curved again, widening. There was a moist brown scar where the floodwater had eaten into the ferny bank and the current doubled back on itself in a fat, slow eddy. Melke swam as her father had taught her, pulling with her hands and kicking with her feet. The rush of speed slowed as she slipped into calmer water.

A tree stripped of leaves lay heavily in the eddy. Melke grabbed a slippery branch and floated with it, coughing, and knew that her brother would live.

Her gulped breaths became easier, her heartbeat less urgent. She shivered in the cold water and, now that she was no longer fighting for her life, became aware of the sound.

She heard singing. Not one voice but many, no louder than the rustle of wind in long grass. The voices were as high as a skylark's song and as low as the rushing murmur of the river. They wept and sighed and laughed. A hundred different songs intertwined, melodies weaving and lacing with each other.

The singing grew louder, a whispered clamor. It was more than mere sound; it was sensation too, sliding over her skin, stinging slightly. It was inside her. It rushed in her blood, tingling, filling her lungs and vibrating in her bones. As her heartbeat grew louder, faster, the sound grew in her ears. It surrounded and engulfed her, more terrifying than either river or hound.

Melke pushed away from the tree, a scream building in her throat, and flung herself at the bank. Water splashed beneath her flailing arms. She scrambled ashore on hands and knees, gasping shallow, panicky breaths.

The voices faded as she left the water, muting to a whispered song that she heard faintly in her ears and felt tingling at her throat.

Her throat.

Melke knelt in the mud, shivering, panting. She raised a trembling hand to the necklace.

The eerie voices grew louder as she touched the smooth, cool stones. Sound stroked over her skin. She felt it in the bones of her hand, in her forearm. It pulsed in her blood.

Melke snatched her fingers away. Sound and sensation faded abruptly.

She shuddered, deeply. Instinct cried out to rip the necklace off and throw it as far from her as she could. But if she did that, Hantje would die.

"Moon, give me strength," she whispered.

MELKE FOLLOWED THE river, running fast. In contrast to the dry meadows of the farm, the eastern bank was lush with vegetation. Shiny ferns and dark-leaved creepers tangled on the ground and saplings fought for space beneath tall trees.

Humus squished under her bare feet. The necklace murmured faintly at her throat. Its song crawled over her skin and whispered in her ears, making her shiver and stagger as she ran, but as hair and skin and clothes dried, the sound quieted and the sensation eased. Eventually there was a faint tingle at her throat, nothing more. Other noises filled her ears: the hum of dragonflies and small flying insects, the call of birds, the swift rushing of the river, her own ragged panting and the swish of her legs through the ferns. Her arms and legs ached and her chest burned. She didn't know whether she was running so desperately to her brother, or from the hound, or both.

The ground rose to her left and she veered toward it; she needed to climb the ridge before dark and find the road. The ferns became less luxuriant and the ground stonier, steeper. The hiss of water was audible long after the river vanished from sight. Melke climbed with scrambling urgency, leaning forward. Dead branches snapped beneath her feet, jagged. Undergrowth tore her clothes and scratched her face and pulled strands of hair sharply from her plait.

Afternoon slid toward dusk and still she hadn't reached the ridgeline. She climbed slowly now, grabbing at rough rocks to steady herself, stumbling, limping, her breath whistling harshly in her throat. Fear built inside her as daylight faded, the familiar night-terror growing beneath her breastbone.

The ground became rockier and steeper. Trees grew in gnarled twists, stunted and hung with gray lichen. Then there was lightness ahead, a sense of space. The ridge.

At the crest, swaying exhaustion forced Melke to stop. She closed her eyes, panting, dizzy. The necklace with the songs trapped inside it was cold around her throat. Her feet throbbed with each beat of her heart, their pain sharp and raw. She dared not sit for fear she'd never stand again.

Melke opened her eyes. She wiped the sweat from her face with a hand that trembled. Each breath was a sob.

Distant mountains basked in the rose-pink blush of the setting sun. Everything was still, silent. Low rays of light touched stone and bark and leaf, deepening the colors and making them glow. Darkness would follow swiftly.

Darkness. She couldn't hide as she'd done last night, beneath the bridge, snatching nightmare-filled moments of sleep. If the hound pursued, it would find her. Tonight she must run.

Fear prickled across Melke's skin and knotted in her throat. Her heartbeat was loud and frightened in her ears. She wanted to hide, *needed* to hide, to creep into a crevice and make herself small and wait for the darkness to pass.

She dared not. For Hantje's sake she must run.

"Shine for me, Moon," she whispered as night gathered above the mountains. "I beg you."

CHAPTER TWO

RAGE FUELLED BASTIAN, roaring in his chest. He would kill the thief. He would flay her, tear her limb from limb, shred her and toss the pieces away. Her. Endal said the thief was a "her". A wraith.

Loathing made him shudder. Loathing, and fear. A wraith. A creature of evil, an aberration that shouldn't exist.

"Are we closer to her?" he asked aloud. The night air was cool against his sweat-damp face.

Endal trotted ahead of him up the steep, rutted road, a wolf-like dark shape in the moonlight. *Closer*, he agreed, the words whispering in Bastian's head. *She bleeds.*

She'll bleed more once I've caught her, Bastian promised grimly.

The dog made no reply.

Exhaustion hovered at the edge of Bastian's aware-ness, pushed aside by rage. Rage was everything. Rage and fury, and beneath those a stark core of ter-ror. If he didn't reclaim the necklace—

No. He *would* find the thief. He'd hold the necklace in his hand again. Too many people had died, too many lives been ruined, for him to fail.

And he would kill the filthy, verminous creature.

The moon was on the wane, a thick and misshapen crescent. Opalescent. Evil. No clouds obscured it. Bastian shivered and pulled the collar of his work-shirt higher at his throat. She travelled well, the filthy wraith, with the moon guiding her steps. Moon time. Wraith time. Time for slinking shadows, for wraiths and bandits and others with darkness in their souls.

The road crested the ridge and flattened. "We'll run again."

Endal made no comment, but lengthened his stride into a slow lope.

Bastian ran, refusing to acknowledge that his limbs ached with weariness. The road was rough. Night shadows gathered in the dips and hollows. The fierce-ness of his rage and urgency of his fear grew with each panted breath. *If he didn't catch her*—

The road descended again. Trees grew taller and shadows darker. The ground was more difficult to see, but still he ran. His breathing was harsh and labored, his lungs and legs burning, but still he ran. *Are we gaining on her?* he asked Endal.

An owl hooted.

Yes.

He wanted to ask how far ahead the wraith was, to know in terms of miles, of yards and feet and inches, but the dog didn't understand such measurements. *Will we catch her?* he asked instead.

Yes.

By sunrise?

Maybe, said Endal.

Bastian concentrated on his rage, on the need to keep running. Every step, each breath, brought him closer to the wraith.

The road became level and the forest grew close around them, hiding the sly face of the moon. The shadows were dark and thick. Bastian stumbled as he ran, kicking stones and scuffing his boots in the dirt. The road was something he no longer saw, merely sensed. It was a wideness, a shade of black slightly less dark than the forest around him.

The crossroads, Endal said.

Bastian slowed to a stop, gulping air. Sweat dripped from his face. He strained to see the white stones that marked the crossroads.

He reached out for Endal and the dog came to him in the dark. "Which road does she take?" he asked, steadying himself, his fingers clenched gently in Endal's silky-rough coat. "Which town?"

No town.

Alarm sparked in Bastian's chest. "What?"

She takes the road to the fire creatures.

Horror closed his throat. For a moment he couldn't breathe. *No.*

Yes, said the dog.

Bastian released his grip on Endal's coat and pushed the dog away from him. Fear gave him the strength to run again. *Fast. Faster.* If she gave the necklace to the salamanders—

He stumbled on the rough, dark road and caught himself before he fell. *Endal, we must catch her before she reaches—*

He stumbled again and fell heavily, hitting the ground hard, knocking the air from his lungs. He raised his head and gasped for breath.

Bas. Endal was a solid blackness in the dark, whining, touching a wet nose to his cheek. *Bas.*

"Fine," said Bastian hoarsely, spitting blood and dust as he pushed himself upright. He staggered, and then found his balance. "Fine." He took a step, and another, aware of Endal alongside, unseen in the darkness. The dog's anxiety was a silent touch in his mind.

He began to run again, clumsily, slowly. Pain didn't matter. Exhaustion didn't matter. What mattered was the necklace. He had to take it from the wraith before she reached the salamanders' den.

He concentrated on moving his feet one after the other, on inhaling and exhaling, on running as fast as he could. *Faster. Faster.* Minutes passed. Hours. The black sky turned gray. Endal became less shadow and more dog.

"How far ahead is she?" Bastian's voice was ragged. His pulse was high and hard in his throat, his head curiously light. He wiped stinging perspiration from his eyes.

Very close. We'll catch her soon.

Bastian had no breath left to speak aloud. *Good.* He pushed himself to lift his feet, to move his legs, to run. He would catch the wraith.

And when he'd caught her, he would kill her.

CHAPTER THREE

MELKE REACHED THE valley in the thin gray light of predawn. The nightmares that had kept pace with her drew back. She had survived the darkness, the memories.

Exhaustion blurred her eyesight, but even if she'd been blind she would have known she had arrived. The sounds were normal—the drowsy, stuttering song of birds rousing to a new day and the whisper of leaves moving in the breeze—but the scent was wrong. There was an extra something in the cool morning air: a spiciness, a hint of sulphur.

The narrow valley was unforested. Trees hung back, clinging to the hillsides as if they too were afraid of the salamanders. Grass grew thickly on the valley floor. Yellow and white and pink wild-flowers waited for the sun's touch, their petals loosely furled.

Her weary eyes mistook the salamanders' den for an outcrop of boulders, lumpy and irregular, squatting in the middle of the valley. She blinked, and blinked again, and saw the den for what it was: a fortress, asymmetric, a rough structure of red rock and baked mud. It looked organic, as if it had grown without design or forethought.

Melke shivered. Within those high red walls were an adult salamander and her kits. And Hantje, captive in the darkness and the heat.

The track through the meadow was overgrown; only the most foolhardy of humans approached a salamander's den. Or the most desperate. The long grass didn't dull the pain of her feet. She flinched from each step, lurching, her breath catching in her throat. The smell of sulphur became stronger. The grass began to grow less thickly.

Dawn broke as Melke stepped onto the bare red earth that ringed the den. She halted, swaying. Exhaustion almost dragged her to her knees.

She let her eyelids close. Her head hung heavily on her neck. "Moon, guide me," she whispered, and concentrated deep within herself. There was a moment of dizziness and nausea, when her skin turned inside out, then she opened her eyes, staggering, and clutched at the air with clumsy hands.

She could *see* her hands.

She saw scratched arms, bare and flecked with mud. Filthy trousers, bloody at one knee, and her feet... The bandages that she'd fashioned from her shirtsleeves were red with blood.

Seeing the blood made it worse. Tears stung her eyes and her breath came in short gasps.

Hantje. Help me.

The thought of Hantje steadied her. Her feet didn't matter, nor did the exhaustion, if only her brother lived.

Melke blinked back the tears. The necklace was wound twice around her throat. She fumbled to unfasten the catch. Her fingers were stiff and slow and shaking with fatigue.

The necklace slid into her hands, cool. The stones held the colors of the sea, rich blues and intense greens, smoky grays and glints of gold. Fifty, perhaps sixty teardrops, set in a delicate filigree of dark metal.

Melke inhaled deeply. The scent of salamander choked in her throat, heavy and spicy. She raised her chin. "Salamanders," she called.

The misshapen mass of red clay and rough rock towered above her. She had walked around it two days ago when she'd come to find Hantje. She'd seen no windows, only half a dozen narrow, irregular fissures and a stinking midden. It had taken no more than a few minutes to circumnavigate the den and realize there was only one entrance.

Melke closed her fingers around the necklace. "Salamanders," she cried again, and took an agonizing step toward the den. A second step. A third. "Salamanders!" She stood so close to the entrance that her breath brushed the heavy iron door.

Silence.

Melke cast a fearful glance behind her. Had the birds stopped singing because the hound and its master approached?

The door swung inward and she stumbled back, her heart thudding hard in her chest. Panic flared inside her. Lizard eyes. Bright eyes in which flames seemed to burn. A sense of something that wasn't human, wasn't animal, wasn't anything but... *other*. She took another involuntary step backwards, heedless of pain.

"Ssss."

Salamanders crowded in the doorway, lithe and slender. They stood no taller than her shoulder, with blood-red skin and burning eyes and spiny crests ridging their skulls.

"You have the necklasss?" asked the one in front.

The words were sibilant. The hiss of flames was audible in the creature's voice.

She counted them in the shadowy doorway. Four kits, not fully grown. Their mother wasn't with them. She'd chosen to stay inside the hot darkness of her den.

Melke swallowed the tight fear in her throat. She forced herself to breathe, inhaling the creatures' thick odor. "I have it."

The young salamanders hissed their glee. They crowded closer in the doorway. Heat radiated from them. The sinuous eagerness and the gleaming suppleness of their skin, the flame-bright lizard eyes, the choking scent, the nearness, the otherness... Panic beat loudly in her chest.

Melke took another lurching step backwards. She clenched the necklace in her hands and gasped to breathe, gasped to stand her ground and not flee. "Where's my brother?"

"Ssshow usss."

Melke opened her hands.

"Ssss." It was a hissed exhalation of air, hot and excited. The sound raised hairs on Melke's arms and the nape of her neck. She shivered.

One of the salamanders stepped from the shadow of the doorway. She saw it fully, the sharp fan of its crest and the slender snaking tail—her eyes flinched from the strangeness of it. A creature of legend. Not lizard, not man, but something else.

The salamander's carriage was proud. Her eyes wanted to call it man—two arms, two legs, an upright posture—but no human moved with such agile grace. The creature was young, half-grown. In adulthood it would stand taller than her, but now its bright eyes were only level with her shoulder. It was naked and asexual, lithe and bold. "Give it to me."

Melke felt the heat of salamander's breath. She thought her skin might blister from it. "No." The word was a dry croak. "Give me my brother."

The creature blinked its bright eyes lazily. Sharp, carnivorous teeth showed in a smile. "Asss you wisssh."

The shadowy doorway was suddenly empty. She hadn't seen or heard them move, but the other salamander kits were gone.

Melke shivered again, despite the heat that came off the salamander's skin. The creature's odor caught in her throat. She averted her eyes and struggled to breathe, clutching the necklace tightly, grateful for its chill. Hope swelled beneath her breastbone. *Hantje.*

The salamander yawned. The sound, so human and ordinary, caused Melke's heart to lurch in terror. Her pulse hammered in her throat. *Fool. Relax. It's only a child.*

A dangerous child. A creature of fire, of cruelty and greed and hedonism. And no child in human terms. How old was it? Thirty years? Forty? Salamanders lived for centuries.

Curiosity overcame fear for a quick second and she glanced at it. What sex would it choose when it reached adulthood?

As if it felt her gaze, the salamander's eyelids raised, snake-quick. Eyes as bright as flames stared at her, fierce and intelligent. It yawned again, showing white, sharp teeth. Its breath flickered across Melke's bare arm, as hot as if she stood before a fire.

She'd not heard the other salamanders leave, but she heard them return. There was a faint swell of sound, a susurration of hissed breaths, and the dark doorway was full again. The three blood-red kits carried a limp and awkward shape. She saw black hair, a charcoal gray cloak, and a dangling hand.

"Hantje!" She tried to step forward but the young salamander barred her way.

"The necklasss." The creature met her eyes again. Flames flared in the glowing irises. It held out a sharp-clawed hand.

The kits placed Hantje roughly on the ground. He lay utterly still, wrapped in his cloak. Melke couldn't see his face.

Her fingers clenched around the necklace. "Is he alive?"

The salamander hissed a laugh, showing its teeth again. "Yesss."

Melke opened her hands. The necklace lay cupped in her palms.

There was a moment of silence, of stillness and expectation and heat, and then she let the necklace fall into the salamander's hand.

The creature flinched slightly, as if the coldness of the stones stung. It inhaled sharply. "Ahhh..."

It turned away from her so fluidly and swiftly that her eyes almost missed the movement. The rust-pitted metal door closed with a grating *clang*, and the salamanders were gone.

"Hantje!"

He lay on the ground, unmoving.

Melke dropped to her knees and pulled at the cloak that wrapped him. It was torn and filthy and stank of burned wool and something foul. A thick, noisome substance caked the fabric. Hantje's hair fell black and tangled onto the bare dirt. His face, when she saw it—

Her throat constricted. Tears filled her eyes and spilled fast down her cheeks, running salty into her mouth. "Hantje..."

He lay as if dead. Swelling distorted his face. Beneath the soot and blood his skin was dark with bruises. A deep, raw burn slashed across cheek and jaw, the skin black and peeling at the edges. His mouth was torn and bloody, his eyelids swollen shut.

Melke bent her head to listen for his breath. She heard nothing. "Hantje," she whispered. "Please, Hantje, please don't—" Hot tears fell into his hair and blinded her as she fumbled to unfasten the cloak. Charred and stinking wool flaked at her touch.

She bared her brother's throat and laid trembling fingers on his skin, seeking a pulse. "Please live," she whispered, begging. "Please don't leave me..."

A hound barked, deep-throated, at Melke's back. Her body clenched in terror. She jerked around on her knees. Fear strangled breath and scream. The beast stood on the bare red dirt, as tall as she was. Taller. Huge.

The tears were gone from her eyes. Her heart pounded fast and hard in her chest. She saw pricked ears and raised hackles of stiff, black fur and fierce, pale wolf-eyes.

Melke reached for her knife. The hound pulled its lips back, showing sharp teeth. It took a stiff-legged step toward her.

CHAPTER FOUR

B ASTIAN STAGGERED TO a halt. The first gleams of sunlight touched the hilltops. He took it as a sign of hope, although fear that he was too late twisted in his belly. *Is that her?* he asked, gulping for air. His pulse hammered in his ears.

Endal growled. *Yes.*

Like the scum she was, the wraith crouched on the ground. The body of a man lay behind her. She stared wide-eyed at Endal. Black hair straggled from a long braid. Her face was filthy and scratched, streaked with blood and mud.

Rage filled Bastian's lungs and blurred his vision. It knotted in his muscles and vibrated in his chest. He reached for the wraith. Her gaze flicked to him and she flinched away, too slowly. He fisted his hand at the scruff of her neck, grasping shirt and plaited hair, and hauled her roughly to her feet.

"Where is it?" He shook her hard.

The wraith tried to jerk away from him.

Bastian tightened his grip. He shook her again, more fiercely, making her stumble. "*Where is it?*"

She raised her eyes and met his gaze boldly. "Where is what?" Her voice was unafraid.

"The necklace, you filthy vermin."

The wraith's chin rose slightly. She stood swaying in his grip and said nothing.

"*Where?*" He bared his teeth at her, snarling.

She tried to pull away.

Bastian shook her a third time, making her head snap back on her neck.

"I don't have it," she said hoarsely.

Fear stabbed in his chest, sharp and cold, and he pushed her from him. He heard the outrush of her breath as she fell hard on the dirt. "What have you done with it? *What?*" But even as he asked the question, he knew.

The wraith raised herself on one hand. She turned her head. Her eyes were like chips of gray stone, the eyes of a creature with no soul. "I gave it to the salamanders."

The utterness of the catastrophe stunned Bastian for several seconds. As well to have cast the necklace off the edge of the world. No one, common man or king or magical beast, could make the salamanders give it back.

He was blind and deaf. He heard nothing. Saw nothing. He was aware only of horror. No. It couldn't be happening. It couldn't. *No.*

Bastian inhaled a shuddering breath and blinked. Vision came back more clearly than before, sound more loudly. He saw a beetle scurry across the bare dirt, its carapace shining blackly. He heard the wraith breathe with quick and shallow inhalations. He saw her with the clarity of hatred: the scratches on her pale skin beaded with dried blood, the smears of mud and dust, the ragged clothes, the filthy, bloodstained bandages around her feet, the bold defiance in her eyes.

The wraith scrambled to stand.

"Do you know what you've done?" He clenched his hands. "Do you have *any idea*?"

She raised her chin and stood as haughtily as a queen in her rags and her dirt.

"You have destroyed us." His voice was hoarse with fear.

The wraith shrugged lightly.

"*You*—" Bastian snatched at her hair, knotting his fingers in the tangled braid. He twisted it tightly, baring his teeth at her... and could go no further. He couldn't hit her, couldn't punish her as she deserved.

She. Smaller and shorter and lighter than him. A woman. A wraith.

Bastian saw the silvery dried tracks of tears on her dirty cheeks.

He spat. The wraith flinched slightly as the spittle hit her ragged shirt, landing over her heart. He released his hold on her hair and she staggered and almost fell. Her chin rose high as she regained her balance. Her stance was proud and unrepentant.

"My parents died for that necklace." His voice choked on the words.

The wraith's mouth tightened. She shrugged again, a tiny movement of her shoulders.

Her utter lack of remorse or compassion drove the air from his lungs. Bastian turned away, breathless. His hands trembled with the need to hit her.

"You will steal it back," he said harshly, to the meadow.

The wraith made no reply.

He turned swiftly, almost stumbling, but the wraith was still there, still visible. She knelt on the bare dirt, bent over the man's body, her fingers touching his throat. Endal stood at her back.

"You will steal it from the salamanders," Bastian told her, more loudly.

The wraith didn't bother to turn her head. "No." Her voice was flat.

"Yes!" He crossed the distance between them in one stride and clenched his hand in her plait again, jerking her head up and around to look at him.

She met his gaze unflinchingly. "Nothing you can do to me will make me steal it back." She articulated the words slowly and coldly. "*Nothing.*"

He read the truth of the words in her eyes, in her expression. She was unafraid of him, unafraid of his size and strength, his rage, his hatred. Unafraid of Endal standing behind her.

Bastian released her hair.

The wraith turned her attention again to the man's body. "Go away," she said, dismissing him.

Bastian swayed on his feet. Failure pressed so heavily on him that he almost fell to the ground. The edges of his vision were dark with exhaustion and despair. "Did you get paid well?" His voice was slurred, rasping, nearly unintelligible. The farm. His parents. So many deaths, so much suffering. For nothing.

The wraith's dirty fingers curved protectively over the man's black hair. "Yes. Go away and leave us."

Understanding was slow to come. He stood stupidly for a moment. "You bartered the necklace for him."

She didn't look at him. "It was the price."

"The price of your thieving is my sister's life!" Liana's life. Or perhaps his own.

The wraith made no sign that she'd heard his words. Her attention was wholly on the man. She stroked the hair back from his face.

Bastian's gaze flinched from the man's injuries, the peeling, charred skin, the livid bruises, the swollen and blackened eyes. *Does he live?* he asked Endal.

He smells of death. He will die soon.

"Your thieving is for nothing," Bastian told her, the words bitter in his mouth. "He dies."

The wraith's fingers clenched in the man's hair. "No." Her voice was fierce. She didn't turn her head to look at him. "He will live."

Bastian shook his head, but she didn't see. He took a clumsy step backwards, away from her, and shook his head again.

Endal whined. His anxiety pressed into Bastian's mind.

The salamanders have the necklace, Bastian told him. *We are too late.* He pressed the heels of his hands to his eyes. Blackness.

Endal barked.

Bastian lowered his hands and opened his eyes. Endal stood at the heavy door to the salamanders' den. He barked again, loudly, futilely.

"No."

Endal gave another deep-throated bark.

"No! Endal, don't!"

Bastian made it to the door in fast, stumbling steps. He grabbed the leather collar around the dog's neck and pulled him back.

Too late.

Metal scraped against stone. Heat billowed out at him and peppery musk gagged in his throat. He saw shadows and sleek red skin and fiery eyes.

"Yesss?"

The salamander was smaller than he was, much smaller, and yet Bastian trembled to hold his ground. His heart beat hard, urging him to run. Endal whimpered. He pressed against Bastian's leg.

Bastian had read the tales. He'd heard storytellers speak of salamanders, had seen sketches drawn by those who'd encountered the creatures and lived, but reality was no match for second-hand description. The domed skull with its needle-sharp crest of spines, the elongated jaw and slitted nostrils, the lipless mouth, the eyes... so bright, like staring into the heart of a fire.

Bastian struggled to breathe.

"Yesss?"

Words choked on his tongue. It was useless to utter them, hopeless. Salamanders didn't give back their treasures. The necklace was lost.

Endal nudged his leg. He whined again.

Courage. For his sister Liana, he had to have courage. He swallowed. "The necklace she gave you." The words came out in a rush. "I'd like it back. Please."

The salamander uttered a gleeful, hissing sound, like steam rising from the spout of a kettle. A tiny wisp of flame licked from its mouth. "And what do you offer in exssschange?" it asked.

Bastian's mouth was dry. The sharp scent of the creature's skin choked in his throat. Sulphur stung his nostrils. He had no gold coins, no jewels, nothing that might tempt a salamander. The silver signet ring on his finger was too plain. "Her." He gestured at the wraith. Out of the corner of his eye he saw her head rise swiftly. "I offer her."

The salamander laughed its hissing laugh again. Its eyes narrowed in delight. "We do not want her," it said.

Bastian inhaled a shallow breath of musk and sulphur. "I have nothing else to offer."

The ember-bright eyes blinked slowly. The creature smiled, showing teeth that were small and neat and sharp. "You are male."

He'd heard the tales in the taverns, had laughed and scoffed outwardly, and recoiled inside himself. He didn't need to be told what the salamander meant. It was legend. It was horror.

Bastian trembled. *For Liana.* Fear knotted in his belly. There was perspiration on his skin. His pulse beat fast and loud in his ears. "No," he said hoarsely. "I... I can't."

The salamander shrugged sinuously. "Then the necklasss isss oursss." It turned away, into the hot shadows of the den.

"Please." Bastian swallowed his pride and begged,. holding his hands out to the creature. "I must have it. I need it to lift a curse."

The salamander looked back over its shoulder. It blinked burning eyes at him, uncaring, and closed the door.

CHAPTER FIVE

A CURSE. MELKE clenched one hand in Hantje's matted hair. What had she done to this man and his family?

She'd thought the harm was only to herself. She had stolen, had crossed a line burned in her soul that she'd sworn never to breach. She had become the creature she never wanted to be. Wraith. Thief.

If her actions ruined this man, if anyone died because of her...

She felt for Hantje's pulse. *Live. Let the sacrifice be worth it.*

The man stepped close to her. Melke tensed, her head bent.

"He's as good as dead."

She knew it from the way Hantje's pulse faltered beneath her fingertips. She shook her head.

Her grief was too huge, her shame too over-whelming, to admit he was right.

"Yes!" The man gripped the nape of her neck, jerking her head sharply back, forcing her to meet his gaze.

Melke struggled not to flinch from him. His face was as hard and brutal as those of the mercenaries she'd seen in the northern ports. He wanted to hurt her. It showed in the twist of his mouth and the tight furrows that bracketed it, in the flaring of his nostrils.

"I'll give you his life in return for the necklace." She heard hatred in his voice, and she heard the truth of his words.

"How?"

"A healer."

She stared at him. A healer. A chance for Hantje to live.

What was her brother's life worth? Her own death? Hantje had tried and failed. How could she hope to succeed?

Melke spoke the truth carefully, "The salamanders... I don't think it's possible to steal from them. Not even a wraith can do it."

The man's fingers pinched tighter at the nape of her neck. "If you want him to live, you will do it!"

"My brother tried," she said, her voice thin and slightly breathless. Could he hear her pain? "You see the result."

Breath hissed between his teeth. He released her abruptly. His face contorted in loathing. "Another wraith." He spat at the ground by Hantje's feet. "You have destroyed us because of a stinking, thieving piece of *scum!*"

His hands clenched into fists. Fury pulled his lips back from his teeth. She saw in his eyes that he trembled on the brink of violence. He wanted to injure her as she had injured him.

I am sorry, she wanted to say, but the sheer inadequacy of the words gagged her. No apology she could make would be sufficient. She turned her face away from his rage. *I did not mean to harm you. It was not my intention.*

She touched light fingers to Hantje's hair. How long before he died? How many minutes, hours, before she was alone?

"If my sister dies, I will kill you," the man said. Emotion was thick in his voice.

If someone dies because of me, I will not want to live.

She laid her fingers on Hantje's skin, bloodied and bruised and burned. How precious life was, how fragile, how easily destroyed. If Hantje died, if this man's sister died...

I will not want to live.

"I will try to do it," she whispered.

The man said nothing. She turned her head and looked up at him, tall and hard-faced. His eyes shone strangely in the dawn light. The hound stood, large and black, at his side.

"I will try," she said again. Better to die than to live without Hantje, to live with someone else's blood on her hands. "Take us to the healer. I will do my best to recover the necklace."

"Your best." His mouth twisted into a sneer. "And what is *that* worth, wraith?"

The man's contempt was as sharp and stinging as a slap. Melke lifted her chin. She met his eyes. "If it is possible to recover the necklace, I will do so. You have my word of honor."

"You!" His laugh was harsh. "Filthy vermin. You have no honor."

He was correct. She had no honor. She was a thieving wraith. She was worthless, she was nothing. Melke raised her chin higher. "You have my word. Give me yours."

He didn't trust her. She saw it in his eyes. They were the color of the ocean, green and cold. His mouth tightened. There was silence, in which birdsong and the hum of insects were loud. He fisted his hands so that the knuckles whitened, then unclenched them. "You have my word of honor. *Wraith*."

CHAPTER SIX

BASTIAN SHOVED THE inn door, pushing with his shoulder when it didn't swing open quickly enough. He paused inside, breathing heavily. This early in the morning, the large room was empty except for a barmaid mopping the flagstones. The stale smell of spilled ale was welcome and human after the hot, peppery scent of the salamanders.

The girl stopped mopping. She shook back sandy hair and smiled at him. "Good morning."

"Where's Ronsard?"

"In the stable yard. Would you like an ale? I can—"

Bastian pushed back outside. The battened oak door smacked against the wall and quivered on its hinges. He strode around the corner of the building, his boots sliding on the cobblestones. The smell of freshly-baked bread mingled with the familiar town scent of drains, and hunger cramped in his belly. "Ronsard!" he called as he entered the inn stable yard.

Sparrows pecking for grain took flight at his voice. The stableman sweeping straw lifted his head.

Ronsard emerged from an open stable. The innkeeper was a large man, heavy with food and wealth. Joviality creased his face, but the smile rarely reached his eyes. "Bastian. Good morning."

"I need to hire a horse and cart," Bastian said, brushing civilities aside. His muscles trembled with tension and exhaustion.

"Of course, of course." Ronsard smiled and nodded and clasped his hands together. He made no move to fetch either horse or cart.

Bastian fought the urge to shout at the man, to shake him as he'd shaken the wraith. "I'm in a hurry."

"Of course." Ronsard's smile didn't falter. He turned and called to the stableman. "A horse and cart for Bastian sal Vere."

Was it his imagination, or was there a faint sneer in Ronsard's voice as he uttered the words *sal Vere*? Bastian shook his head, too tired to think.

"Quickly!" Ronsard clapped his hands.

Bastian's stomach tightened again in a painful knot of hunger. "Some loaves of bread too, if you have them. And water."

"Of course." Ronsard nodded. "Excuse me." His voice was polite, smooth.

Bastian watched as the innkeeper crossed the stable yard to the kitchen entrance. He clenched his teeth together and looked away. The man's deliberate unhurriedness grated.

He leaned against the wall with his arms folded across his chest, rigid, while the stableman led a roan mare from a stable and harnessed her to a cart. The rough blocks of stone were hard against his shoulders. Ronsard's voice came faintly through the open kitchen window, ordering someone to tip two loaves of bread from their tins and fill waterskins quickly.

"Where's that big black dog of yours?"

Bastian swung his head around.

The youth strolling in from the street had his father's insincere smile. "We don't often see you without him."

"He's busy," Bastian said, shortly. *Guarding wraiths*. He turned his attention back to the stableman. *Hurry up, curse you*.

The innkeeper's son leaned against the wall alongside Bastian. "Women," he said. "More trouble than they're worth, don't you think?"

Bastian grunted and pushed away from the wall. "Ready?" he asked the stableman. He received a nod in reply.

A maid bustled out from the kitchen, plump-cheeked and breathless, clutching two loaves of bread and several bulging waterskins. Ronsard followed at a leisurely pace.

Bastian swallowed his pride. "I have no money with me," he said, pulling the signet ring from his finger. "I'll pay when I return. Take this."

"It's not necessary," Ronsard said smoothly, smiling. "I would never doubt the word of a sal Vere."

"Take it," Bastian said, his voice hard. *I am not a beggar and I do not need your charity*.

Ronsard's smile didn't change. "If you insist," he said, and allowed the ring to be pressed into his soft palm.

Bastian swung himself up into the cart. "Good day." He nodded curtly to Ronsard, and to the man's son.

"Good day," came the polite reply, followed by an undertone barely heard as the horse and cart clattered into the street, "high and mighty sal Vere."

Bastian ignored the words. He wasn't sure who'd uttered them, and he didn't care.

HIS HAND FELT light and naked without the ring. The skin was pale where the thick band had circled his finger. It had been his father's signet ring and his father's father's before that. The last item of value that he owned, precious because of those who'd worn it before him rather than the silver from which it was wrought. It was another wrong to be chalked on the slate against the wraith.

Bastian glanced behind him. The wraith sat cross-legged on the hard, bare boards of the cart, holding the man's hand. Her brother, she'd said. Another wraith like herself. A thief. She didn't look at the road, didn't close her eyes and sleep, although she had to be as exhausted as he was. She did nothing but watch her brother's face, hold his hand, and occasionally trickle water between his torn lips.

They had the same black hair and pale skin, the same thieving hearts. Vermin.

Bastian clenched his jaw and looked ahead again. He knew the wraith was using him. She had no intention of braving the salamanders' den. She would see her brother healed, and then vanish into the night.

She reckoned without Endal.

Bastian bared his teeth in a grim smile. He'd see her dead before he allowed her to renege on their bargain.

A bargain with a wraith. Was he mad?

The road was as endless as it had been in the dark. Daylight made it no shorter. He wanted to be home almost as urgently as he'd wanted to catch the wraith. Liana had spent the night alone, without any protection. It was no use telling himself that the farm had nothing to tempt either wolf or bandit. No use telling himself that Liana was sensible, that she'd have bolted the door. No use to lean forward on the seat as if his silent tension could make the horse move faster.

The air was warm and heavy with moisture. Clouds gathered in the distance, thunderheads piling slowly higher and higher. The cart lurched roughly over the ruts. Bastian felt each jolt in his bones. Old men must ache like this. He rubbed his face. Stubble was coarse on his cheeks and chin, and his eyes were gritty with tiredness.

Bread sat in his belly. He'd fed Endal, and the wraith too. *Yet another thing you owe me, wraith.* Two waterskins lay flaccid and empty in the cart, two more sloshed with each jolt of the wheels. He had taken care not to touch the skins the wraith used. He'd surely vomit if he put his mouth to the same spout as her.

Afternoon was lengthening toward evening when at last they reached the river. Bastian urged the horse forward. It flicked its ears and stepped reluctantly onto the narrow bridge. The warped timbers creaked as the cart rumbled slowly across.

The river was high and brown and running swiftly, swollen with rain. Bastian twisted his mouth. Did the wraith notice the difference between the spring growth they'd come through and the parched dryness of the farm? There had been no rain on Vere. Not this year, nor the last. The ground was hard and cracked, the grass colorless.

He wanted to stop the cart and jerk the wraith from it, to push her to her knees and grind her face into the dirt. *This is what you've done to us*, he wanted to shout. *We'll never get the rain back now.*

He let the horse walk on. Heat beat up from the hard ground. Brittle stems of grass snapped beneath the cart wheels. Dust rose behind them. The air was no longer humid, but dry. Desert-dry, furnace-dry, so dry it stung in his nose and throat. No clouds gathered in the sky here.

With each step the horse took and each turn of the wheels, weight settled on him. The dying trees, the dead grass, the few starving animals... they pressed down on him until he thought the cart seat would buckle beneath the weight of his responsibility, his failure. *And when the psaaron comes and I admit defeat, how heavy will I be then? Will I sink into the earth? Will it close over me? Will I lie in my grave without it having to be dug?*

"Endal." He looked back over his shoulder to where the dog lay asleep. Stretched out, he was almost as long as the male wraith. *Endal, wake up.*

Endal slitted his eyes open.

We're home.

The dog yawned hugely, showing teeth that were every bit as sharp as a salamander's. His tail thumped once on the timber.

Will you let Liana know we're back? Unspoken were the words: *And see that she is well.*

Endal rose to his feet and shook himself, shedding black hairs. The wraith watched warily. Her hand spread to shield her brother's face. *Be afraid*, Bastian wanted to tell her. *He has less restraint than I do.*

The dog stretched, and shook himself again. His movements were stiff as he leapt from the cart. He looked very black against the sun-bleached grass.

Bastian watched him run and felt tired. He wanted to peel off his clothes and fall exhausted onto his mattress, to sleep for long hours and then wake and find the necklace where it should be, in the chest under his bed.

The wraith had been in his bedchamber. She'd walked through his home. She had trespassed and stolen and *ruined*. Bastian couldn't look at her. Loathing filled him, as blood and breath filled him. It was in every pore of his skin and every fiber of his body. He wanted her on her knees. He wanted tears in her eyes. He wanted to her beg, to plead for his forgiveness, to abase herself before him. He wanted her to have conscience and soul and heart.

I may as well want to fly. She was a wraith. She had no conscience, no heart or soul, no honor. There was nothing but darkness inside her.

The farmhouse came into sight, sparse meadows before it, rising ground behind. Dead trees. *Home.* He saw it through a stranger's eyes for a moment, as the wraith must see it, and his mouth tightened.

The farm had once been prosperous, that much was obvious. The size of the house, the gables and ornate stonework, the many windows, spoke of wealth. But most of the high-ceilinged rooms were disused now. There were no curtains at the windows; the panes of glass were cracked. Paint flaked from the woodwork, leaving it bare. The great house was crumbling.

What words would the wraith use to describe his home? Shabby? Pitiful? Something knotted in Bastian's chest, as if a fist was clenched there, and he looked behind him. The wraith no longer watched her brother's face. Her gaze was on the farmhouse. Her face was utterly expressionless.

He jerked his head around as Endal barked. Liana stood in the kitchen doorway. Her hair shone white-gold in the sunlight.

The hatred in Bastian's chest dissolved. Moisture pricked in his eyes and he blinked. Tiredness, he told himself.

Endal barked again, wagging his tail in great sweeps. Liana ran across the dusty yard, holding up her skirt.

"Whoa," said Bastian, thrusting the reins aside as the horse obediently halted. He jumped down from the cart.

"Bastian!"

He put his arms around his sister and lifted her off her feet, hugging her. "Are you all right?" he asked, his voice rough. He kissed her hair and inhaled its rosemary scent.

"Yes." Her arms were warm around his neck.

"I was worried—"

"I'm fine, Bastian."

He closed his eyes and held her tightly. She was childlike in his arms.

"Did you get it?" Anxiety trembled in her voice.

Bastian opened his eyes.

"Bastian?"

He set Liana gently back on her feet and released her. He ignored the wraith. "Are you certain you're all right?"

"Yes."

She was as pretty as their mother had been, as fragile, as easily broken. Bastian looked at her, at the white-blonde hair and the delicate beauty of her face, and thought that he would forgive the wraith everything if only Liana could be saved.

"Bastian, who's that?" Liana asked in a low voice.

He turned to the cart and was struck by the contrast between the wraith and his sister. It was more than black hair and blonde, more than the difference in height, more than travel stains and cleanness. It was the contrast between soft and hard, between open and closed, sunlight and darkness. Liana had a mouth that laughed and a heart that cared. She had a sweetness and an innocence that the wraith utterly lacked.

"That's the wraith," he said flatly.

"Oh." Liana darted a glance at the wraith sitting haughtily in her dirt.

"Liana." He waited until she looked at him, a silent, anxious question in her eyes. He smoothed the shining hair back from her brow. "The wraith gave the necklace to the salamanders."

He said the words gently, but even so Liana flinched as if he'd struck her. The color drained from her face. "No," she whispered.

"Yes."

She shook her head, and he saw in her eyes all the horror that he felt. His rage and hatred flared anew. He should kill the wraith for making Liana look so frightened. He *would* kill her if Liana was harmed.

"Liana…" He stroked her hair with fingers that wanted to clench into fists. "It may be possible to get the necklace back. The wraith will try, if we can save her brother."

"Her brother?" Liana sent another wary, darting glance at the wraith.

"He's in the cart. He's… badly injured."

Liana swallowed. He saw the muscles move in her throat, saw her hesitation and uncertainty, saw her fear, and in the tightening of her mouth, her determination. "I can do it."

Bastian looked at her. Too young. Too fragile. And yet this was their only hope.

He lowered his hand from her hair and turned to the cart. "Get down," he ordered the wraith.

The wraith looked down her dirty, scratched nose at him. Then she stood. There was nothing cowed about her.

Bastian gritted his teeth. Anger heated his cheeks. His hands clenched.

With no haste the wraith stepped from the cart. She didn't flinch as her bandaged feet touched the ground. Her mouth tightened slightly, but she made no sound of pain.

Irrationally, Bastian's anger became greater. If she'd winced or gasped, if there'd been tears in her eyes, he might have hated her less.

"Endal," he said. His voice was hard.

Yes? The dog sat down beside Liana. He yawned widely.

"You will guard the wraith always. She will never be out of your sight. Do you understand?"

Yes.

"If she tries to leave, bite her. If she becomes unseen, bite her."

The wraith made no sign that she heard his words. There was no expression on her face.

"And if she attempts to harm Liana, you have my permission to kill her."

The wraith met his eyes. She did not appear to be intimidated. She looked almost amused.

Rage flushed hot beneath Bastian's skin. Did she think he mouthed idle threats? He stepped close to her, too close, forcing her to take a step backwards. "I speak with dogs," he told her. "Endal understands *exactly* what I say."

The wraith said nothing. Her gaze was steady on his face.

"And if you harm my sister and Endal fails to kill you, believe that *I* will kill you."

Still the wraith said nothing. Her face was expressionless.

"Do you understand me?"

The wraith made him wait two heartbeats for her answer. "Yes." There was no emotion in her voice.

Bastian turned away before he surrendered to the desire to hit her. "We'll put him downstairs," he said to Liana, as if the house was full of furnished rooms. "If you make up the bed, I'll carry him in."

"Let me see him first," Liana said softly. She walked to the tailboard of the cart, giving the wraith a wide berth. "I'll need to—" For a moment she stood motionless, silent, her lips still shaped for words. Then one hand rose to cover her mouth. Her eyes when she turned to Bastian were wide and distressed.

"He's a wraith too," he told her flatly. "He tried to steal from the salamanders and this was his punishment. He deserves his injuries."

Liana shook her head, her hand still pressed to her mouth. Tears shimmered in her eyes.

"He's just a wraith," Bastian said harshly. "He's not worth sympathy."

He had the impression that the female wraith moved. He glanced at her, but she stood motionless. Her face was as blank as if it was carved out of marble. Dislike glittered in her eyes. "Where is the healer?" Her voice was hard.

He made her wait, as she'd made him wait. Two heartbeats, three. "My sister is the healer."

The wraith's gaze flicked to Liana, then back to him.

Yes, he wanted to say. *The sister you'd let die*. The words would only upset Liana further and so he didn't utter them, but neither did he hide his hatred. He let the wraith see it in his face.

"What is his name?" Liana asked.

Bastian jerked his head around sharply. He didn't want to know the wraith's name, either of their names. "There's no need—"

But Liana looked at him with tears shining in her eyes, and Bastian closed his teeth on the words.

"Hantje," said the wraith.

Liana nodded. "Bring him inside."

CHAPTER SEVEN

THE BEDCHAMBER WAS large and sparsely furnished and smelled as if it had been unoccupied for a long time. It had the same air of decaying grandeur as the house. The walls and high ceiling were panelled with dark, fine-grained wood and the fireplace was deep and wide, but the carpet was threadbare and faded and marked by items of furniture that no longer stood in the room. A tall, arched window let dusky light in, but many of the small, diamond-shaped panes were cracked and the curtains had faded to an ugly shade of pink, streaked and pallid.

The hound lay down on the floor, its pale eyes fixed on her. Melke looked away from that unnerving gaze. She made herself pick up the candles and place them in the branching holders, the task she had taken as her own. Tallow, not beeswax. Peasants' candles.

She struck a spark from a tinderbox that was as tarnished as the candleholders and watched out of the corner of her eye as the man laid Hantje on the bed. He stepped back and wiped his hands on his trousers, a grimace of distaste on his face.

The girl bent over the bed, a pair of scissors in her hand, and began to cut away the charred remains of Hantje's shirt.

"Let me do that," the man said in a tone that brooked no argument. He held out his hand. "You shouldn't be—"

The girl didn't relinquish the scissors. "Go away, Bastian."

Melke struck another spark from the tinderbox. The thin wood shavings began to burn.

"I don't want you to—"

"Go away, Bastian."

She held a twist of paper to the flame. It flared alight.

"I don't want you to see him. It's not decent."

Melke held the twist of paper to the first candle. Her fingers shook with fatigue.

"If I am to heal him, I must see him." The girl continued cutting Hantje's shirt, baring his chest.

Melke lit the second and third candles. The wicks flamed slowly, grudgingly.

The man closed his eyes. His nostrils flared as he inhaled. "Liana—"

"I'll do it," Melke said. She'd swum often enough with Hantje to be undisturbed by his nudity.

"Thank you, but I need to do it." The girl spoke softly, but there was a note of finality in her voice. "We need hot water. Bastian, can you fetch it, please?"

He scowled at her.

Melke looked away. She lit the remaining candles. The man strode out of the bedchamber, taking his black rage with him, and the girl cut the burned shreds of Hantje's left sleeve from wrist to shoulder.

Melke carried the candleholders over to the wide bed, trying not to limp. She placed them on the small table. The brightness illuminated Hantje's face, showing the blistered, black-edged burn clearly. His eyelids were swollen shut, purple with bruising.

She swallowed. Her throat was almost too tight to speak. "How else may I assist?"

The girl glanced up. She was too young, surely, to be a healer. "Can you pull the cloth away as I cut?" She spoke as the man did, in the accent of Bresse. The guttural consonants suited him and his anger, but were incongruous coming from the mouth of so delicate and pretty a girl.

Melke nodded. She moved with clumsy, painful steps to stand alongside her. The hound lifted its head and watched. She thought the black hackles rose slightly along its spine.

She knew her skin was gray with dirt and that her clothes were ripped and filthy and smelled of sweat, yet the girl made no sign that she noticed. "My name is Liana," she said, not looking up from her task. "What is yours?"

The courtesy, so unexpected, brought foolish tears to Melke's eyes. She blinked them back. "Melke," she said roughly.

"And he is your brother?"

"Yes." It was a brusque answer, but her voice was close to breaking. She didn't want to show her grief to this girl. *Never let them see a weakness,*

Mam had said. *Never let them see that you are vulnerable.*

The tears came, though, as Hantje's clothing was cut from his body, despite the battle she fought to hold them back. They leaked from her eyes and slid down her cheeks, silent and warm.

If Liana noticed, she said nothing.

Bruises marked Hantje's skin, huge and livid mottlings, and overlying them were burns. The worst were on his arms and hands, where the skin peeled away, black, as if he'd tried to protect his face from the salamanders' fire. Beneath the burns and bruises were other injuries. Both of his legs were broken. Melke was no healer, yet she knew their shape was wrong. Hantje uttered whimpering, animal-like sounds of pain as Liana felt the bones carefully. Melke's silent tears came faster. Each inhaled breath had a sob in it, exposing her weakness to the girl.

"I can heal this," Liana said softly. She didn't look up from her task.

Grief choked in Melke's throat. "Thank you," she whispered.

There were broken ribs too, Liana said, and broken bones in his wrist. They were less serious.

The girl laid down the scissors and covered Hantje with a much-darned linen sheet. She touched the burn on his cheek lightly and then bent to look at his bruised eyelids. "Do you know when he received the injuries?" she asked, feeling for the pulse at his throat.

"I think today is the fourth day, but I... I don't know."

Liana straightened. She looked at Melke. If she saw the tears on her face, she made no sign.

"There is infection, which is more dangerous than the broken bones. Do you understand?" The clear firmness of her voice, the direct gaze, were at odds with her youth. She was a girl, pretty and soft, but she spoke as a woman, as a healer confident in her craft.

"I understand," Melke said.

Liana bent to the floor and fingered the filthy cloak. She lifted a shred of Hantje's shirt and held it to her nose. "I think..." She glanced up.

Melke knew that the foul substance on Hantje's clothing and his skin, in his hair, wasn't mud. "They defecated on him." The words were harsh and sharp-edged in her mouth.

Liana put down the piece of shirt. "I'm sorry," she said.

The man would have laughed and said it served Hantje right, and she would have been able to lift her chin and stare coldly at him. Liana's sympathy only brought more tears rushing to Melke's eyes.

She averted her face and pressed a hand to her mouth. She wanted to hunch into herself and cry, to let the grief spill from her mouth as it spilled from her eyes.

"I think I can save him. If I do, will you get the necklace back?"

The question was quietly asked.

Melke turned to look at the girl, her hand still pressed to her mouth. Liana watched her. There was no censure on the girl's face, nor any hope. Her fingers were clasped tightly, the knuckles white.

Melke lowered her hand. "Yes."

Liana nodded. "Thank you," she said, turning back to Hantje.

"I'm sorry," Melke's voice was gruff. "I didn't mean to harm you. I wanted only to save him—' Grief cracked the last word, closing her throat and making further apology impossible.

Liana turned her head. For a long moment they looked at each other, and then the girl nodded silently.

The candles flickered, casting shadows over Hantje's damaged face. "I'll see whether the water has boiled," Liana said quietly. "We need to wash him." She walked across the chamber and paused at the door. "Have you eaten?"

Melke nodded. "Yes. Thank you."

The candles flickered again. Melke wiped her face roughly with the back of her hand and limped to the window. It was closed, but cool air leaked in through the cracked glass. She looked out at the deepening dusk. Candlelight and her own filthy face reflected in the windowpanes. The glass distorted her features. She didn't recognize herself. *What have I become?*

The answer was a terrible one: Wraith. Thief.

She drew the curtains closed and turned and looked at Hantje, swaying slightly in her exhaustion. "Why did you do it, Hantje?" she whispered. A draft stirred the heavy, faded fabric at her back. "Why?"

CHAPTER EIGHT

BASTIAN FETCHED WATER from the well and filled the heavy pot Liana used for boiling sheets, grunting as he lifted it onto the cast-iron stove. He thrust a faggot of wood into the flames. Anger and resentment burned in his chest as hotly as the fire that devoured the dry sticks. He didn't want Liana to touch the wraith, and he especially didn't want her to see the filthy, disgusting creature naked. Breath hissed between his clenched teeth and he slammed the stove door shut.

While the water heated, he unhitched and rubbed down the hired horse and led it into Gaudon's paddock. The grass was stubble, no nourishment for the animals. He turned away from fence, tight-lipped. Three generations ago, Vere had bred some of the best horses in the land. Now it was a ruin of a farm.

Gaudon, at least, wouldn't starve. Or the roan while it was here. Every day for a week Gaudon had carried Liana to Arnaul's farm, and every day for a week she had sat at the bedside of Arnaul's infant son and battled the fever that sought to claim him. Arnaul paid his gratitude in hay. Two years ago now but still the hay came, and would until the old horse died.

There wasn't enough for the sheep, though. And he'd never ask. Charity was unendurable.

Bastian hauled more water from the well to fill the horse trough. Each time the bucket fell, he tensed. The day would come when there was no splash of water, when the well was dry. And then Vere would truly be dead.

Soon.

The wraiths' belongings huddled in the cart: two small knapsacks, the leather scarred and thin with age. They'd been hidden at the crossroads, bundled beneath a pile of twigs and leaves. Bastian's lip curled as he hefted the bags in his hand. Pitiful. Then he raised his head and saw the farmhouse in the fading twilight. Pitiful.

His hand clenched around the leather straps. The wraith had stolen more than a necklace; she'd stolen their future.

He strode indoors and threw the wraiths' bags into the bedchamber at the top of the servants' stairs, making no attempt to see that they landed softly on the narrow bed. One of the battered knapsacks burst open as it hit the floor, scattering belongings. In the dim light he saw a comb, a roll of dark fabric, and a red sleeve with flowers embroidered on the cuff.

Bastian kicked the bag, spewing more items onto the floor. Several small stones rattled across the bare wooden floorboards. He crouched and reached for one of them. The stone was red, or perhaps brown. It was difficult to tell. He turned it between his fingers, smooth. It felt good in his hand.

The room became dark as the sun sank behind the hills. Bastian stood and thrust the stone into his pocket. He walked from the room. It wasn't stealing. It was much less than she'd done. She deserved it. He felt no shame.

CHAPTER NINE

THE MAN, BASTIAN, scowled as he brought hot water into the sickroom. "Let her wash him," he said curtly.

Liana made no sign that she heard. "I'll need splints for his legs, Bastian, and bandages to bind them."

His scowl became more ferocious. He turned on his heel and left the bedchamber.

Liana dipped a scrap of cloth in the steaming bowl of water.

"I'll do that." Melke reached to take the dripping rag.

"No." The girl shook her head.

"But your brother said—"

"Seeing the injuries will help me to heal him."

Melke bit her lip, looking at Liana. She was very young. "If you wash his face and... to the waist, I'll do the rest," she offered.

The girl flushed. She glanced up at Melke. Her eyes were shy. "Thank you."

They cleaned away blood and soot and salamander scat. Beneath those things were ugly bruises and weeping burns. Hantje whimpered in his throat as they worked, his skin flinching from their touch.

Liana laid a fresh sheet over him when they were finished. "Bastian can help me set the bones," she said. "It will require strength. Shall I look at your feet?"

For a moment Melke stood speechless. Didn't Liana understand that pain was her punishment? It was what she'd earned, what she deserved. "No, thank you. It's not necessary." The words came with difficulty.

"But, I can—' Liana closed her mouth as Bastian returned.

Melke stepped away from the bed. His hostility tainted the air in the chamber. She tasted it on her tongue, bitter.

She stood silently in the shadows, watching as Bastian and Liana set Hantje's legs. It was clear they were brother and sister, yet the differences were more apparent than the similarities. He was older, much older. His face and throat and forearms were tanned brown by the sun, in contrast to his sister's pale golden skin. The grim set of his jaw, the lines of weariness at mouth and eyes, the coarse stubble, gave his face an intimidating toughness. A mercenary, she'd thought when she'd first seen him. She still thought it. Take away the weariness and stubble and grimness and his face would still be daunting. It was the strength of brow and nose and jaw, the jut of cheekbones. Liana was also blessed with balance and cleanness of feature, but her beauty was appealing; Bastian's was threatening.

His largeness, too, contrasted utterly with Liana. His hands were twice the size of hers. She was soft where he was hard, small where he was large, pale to his dark. Her eyes were a lighter green than his, almost hazel. In the candlelight her hair was silver-white. His was a dark golden-brown, the color of honey, cut uncompromisingly short.

The pain of bone-setting almost roused Hantje from his stupor. He uttered a soft whimper, a sound that made the hairs prick upright on Melke's arms. She stepped forward.

The hound raised its lip at her, showing strong incisors.

Melke halted. She knotted her fingers together and watched as Liana frowned with concentration, her eyes narrowed almost shut. The girl's hands rested lightly on Hantje's leg. "A little more," she said.

Bastian pulled again, slowly.

Hantje made a gasping, sobbing sound. Distress twisted his face. Melke clenched her fingers together more tightly.

"More," the girl said, her eyes squeezing shut. There was an edge of pain in her voice, as if she felt Hantje's agony. "Almost... yes, that's it. There."

In the shadows and light of the candles Melke thought that Hantje's face smoothed momentarily free of pain. She stepped back and leaned against the wall and watched as Bastian and Liana splinted the leg. It was a struggle to stand upright.

When the second leg was set, Bastian stepped away from the bed and turned toward her. "Your room is upstairs from the kitchen," he said flat-voiced, his eyes looking past her shoulder.

Melke raised her chin. She wasn't going to be chased from her brother's sickbed.

When she didn't move, Bastian's gaze shifted to her face. His mouth tightened.

She braced herself for a display of anger, but he turned his back on her and bent his head to speak to Liana. His words were too low to hear. Liana's weren't: "I'll be fine, Bastian. Don't worry."

There was black hatred in his glance as he left the bedchamber. He didn't speak to her.

The candles seemed to burn more brightly with Bastian gone, the shadows to draw back into the corners of the room. Melke pushed away from the wall and walked to the bed, lurching slightly, limping.

Hantje lay silent and still. Clean, his face was swollen and bruised past recognition. Only his hair was familiar, long and black. The length marked him as not of Bresse.

"He has a fever," Liana said.

Melke touched Hantje's brow with cautious fingers. The skin burned. She glanced at the girl.

"The infection."

"Which is more dangerous than the injuries."

"Yes."

"How will you heal him?" She saw no salves or powders, no dried herbs and pastes of crushed plants.

"I have a... a gift."

A gift to heal. Melke had heard of such magic, rare and precious. She suddenly understood the pain in the girl's voice while Hantje's legs had been set. Hope swelled in her chest. Liana's magic would save Hantje more certainly than an apothecary's salves and pastes and powders.

"You need not stay," the girl said. "There is nothing more you can do."

Melke nodded. She opened her mouth and then closed it again. *Never let them see a weakness*, Mam had said, over and over. She swallowed and said hoarsely, "He's afraid of the dark."

"I shall remember."

Melke reached out to lay her hand on Hantje's cheek, but fear of hurting him curled her fingers into her palm. She turned away from the bed without touching him and halted at the sight of the open doorway and the dark corridor beyond. Fear lurched beneath her breastbone. She swallowed. "May I have a candle?"

"Of course." Liana picked up one of the branching candleholders and held it out to her. Their fingers touched, but the girl made no sign of distaste.

Melke clutched the tarnished stem tightly. "You won't need it?"

The girl shook her head. "One is sufficient."

"Thank you."

The hound rose to its feet as she walked across the room.

"Melke."

She paused unsteadily in the doorway. "Yes?"

Liana knelt beside the bed, Hantje's hand clasped in hers. Her face was in shadow and her hair shone whitely in the candlelight. "Take some bandages for your feet."

She nodded stiffly.

"There's hot water in the kitchen, and food, should you want it. And if you need help, Bastian—"

"I need no help," Melke said, and then flushed at her ungraciousness. "Thank you, but I shall require no assistance."

Liana nodded. "Very well. Good night."

"Good night." The words came awkwardly. Her throat was almost too tight to utter them. Liana's kindness hurt more than Bastian's hatred.

The hound followed at her heels as she left the bedchamber. Her progress down the dark corridor was slow. Her body winced with each step that she took and her breath came in shallow grunts. The candles and bandages were almost too heavy to carry.

The kitchen was dimly lit and as empty as it had been two mornings ago, when she'd come to steal the necklace. The door that had stood open to the dusty yard was closed and bolted against the dark.

A staircase led up from beside the scullery, servants' stairs, steep and narrow and uncarpeted. Melke struggled to lift her feet. The hound followed behind her, its claws clicking on the bare wood. At the top, panting and light-headed, she leaned against the cold wall and closed her eyes.

She rested there for seconds, perhaps minutes, her cheek pressed to the wall. The effort of opening her eyes, of moving, was too great. Easier to stay here than to—

Her eyes opened suddenly. The warmth at her calf was the hound's breath, feather-light on her skin where its teeth had ripped through her trousers and drawn blood. She lurched forward, tightening her grip on the candleholder. The hound followed.

There were several closed doors and one ajar. Melke pushed the door open more widely. It was a maid's room, small and plain and unadorned. The narrow bed was bare. Linen and blankets lay on a wooden chair underneath the window. A tiny shelf was fixed beside the bed and three clothes hooks were screwed into the wall. There were no other furnishings: no clothes press, no looking glass, no washstand with basin and ewer, no rug. A chamber pot sat discreetly beneath the bed.

Her bag lay on the floor, its contents spilled out. There was no need to guess who'd been so rough.

Hatred. It was what she'd earned. She had broken the vow she'd made to Mam and Da, had become the thing she'd never wanted to be.

CHAPTER TEN

H E WAS TOO late by several hours. If he'd had Endal with him he would have found the animal alive. As it was...

Bastian closed his eyes. Flies buzzed heavily.

You owe me this sheep's life, wraith.

No. That was unfair. It wasn't the first death this spring. Three other ewes had died in lambing, and he'd been able to do nothing more than watch helplessly. The animals were too weak. Life drained out of them as quickly as water leaking from cupped hands. It had been futile to send Endal running for Liana, futile to hope, but each time he had.

There had been two sheep dead like that in the past fortnight, with Liana coming to stand silently beside him, her hand reaching out to hold his. And the third... Endal hadn't brought Liana back. He'd found the dog after hours of searching, sitting at the foot of a tree, and the death of a sheep had been eclipsed by a far larger disaster.

Catastrophe. Utter catastrophe. *Don't think about it.*

Bastian opened his eyes and looked grimly at the carcass. Four sheep had tried to give birth now, and all had died. No lambs lived. Five ewes remained, their bellies round and awkward.

The odds were not good.

Failure sat heavily on him, slumping his shoulders and pressing him into the cracked, dry ground. It wasn't merely a sheep or a lamb dead, it was the farm one step closer to dying. If Endal had been with him, this sheep would have had a chance. If not for *her*...

Bastian spat into the dust.

The hat, with its broad, battered brim, shaded his face, but still sweat stung at the corners of his eyes and trickled down his cheek. The sound of the ocean was in his ears, a whisper of waves dashing against the shore. This close to the sea, the air should have been moist; it was dry and harsh in his throat.

Bastian wiped the sweat from his face. He unslung the waterskin, pulled the stopper and drank deeply. The water was lukewarm and tasted of dirt.

The walk back to the farmhouse was long; the tiny flock roamed widely these days, trying to find sufficient food to survive. He missed Endal's presence at his side, his pragmatic dog comments, his alertness, his uncomplicated cheerfulness. Bastian's boots scuffed dust from the hard ground and snapped the brittle stems of grass. With each step he took, the farm died slightly. The curse would claim Vere this year.

Which means the psaaron will come. Which means—

For an instant Bastian smelled the dark, sea-rich scent of the creature. Childhood terror surged inside him, closing his throat and making the hairs rise at the nape of his neck. And with the terror, inextricably linked, were grief and despair.

For twelve years he'd been unafraid. He'd *wanted* the psaaron to come. He'd wanted it more fiercely than anything else life could give him. Now, when the creature must surely claim the necklace, he no longer had it. And he or Liana must pay forfeit for that loss.

Fear twisted easily into rage. Bastian bared his teeth. The wraith. He'd see her dead before he allowed the psaaron to touch Liana. Let the wraith be broken; let her bleed. Let her pay the price.

The wraith was fortunate not to be in the yard. He'd have spat at her again.

The walk back to the dead sheep with the shovel, the chipping away at hard dirt to dig a hole, the dust he inhaled and blinked from his eyes, the blisters that formed on his palms and the sweat that dripped off his face—all served to dull his rage.

He pushed the sheep into the hole with the blade of the shovel. It fell with a thud, limp and heavy. The flies that blackened eyes and nose, gums and tongue, rose buzzing and then settled again.

Bastian took off his hat and wiped the sweat from his brow. His mouth tightened as he looked at the sheep's grotesquely swollen belly. If he'd arrived sooner, he might have been able to save the animal. The lamb might have lived. New life at Vere.

He filled the hole, his jaw clenched. Sour hatred fermented inside him.

The remaining ewes had already straggled some distance away, searching for grass. Bastian leaned on the shovel and watched them. They were the same pale gray as the dirt, too thin, with their fleeces hanging in loose folds. It would be a miracle if any of them survived lambing.

He shouldn't have bred them this year, but he'd known that the rain would come, that the river would run again and the grass grow.

Bastian closed his eyes. Vere was a weight on his shoulders. Even if he had the necklace, even if the psaaron took it and lifted the curse, would Vere survive? Grass would spring up again and trees put out leaves, but he had no money to buy new stock. He could scarcely buy food for himself and Liana, and the house was close to derelict.

Bastian opened his eyes and saw dry, sparse grass and dirt and scrawny sheep. He sighed and straightened. Vere was his responsibility.

Back at the farmhouse he watered the two horses. Gaudon was no longer useful on the farm; Vere was too harsh for an old horse. The hired roan... Bastian rubbed his jaw. He'd have to return it. Tomorrow. Market day in Thierry. For an instant his day brightened, the gray weariness lifting. Silvia.

"And you'll come too, Gaudon," he said, smoothing his hand over the horse's warm flank. "Market day."

Gaudon's ears flicked. Did he understand? Bastian ran his fingers through the horse's mane.

The last of the famous sal Vere horses. Too old to work on the farm. Too old to chase wraiths. "Market day," he said again, a promise to himself and the horse. They'd need to leave at dawn; Gaudon's pace was slow, and he wanted time with Silvia. An hour. Perhaps two.

Silvia.

Anticipation was warm in his chest. Bastian whistled under his breath as he hauled another bucket from the well. This one for himself, to wash away sweat and dust. The whistle died when he saw the cloudiness of the water.

Soon there'd be no water on Vere at all.

CHAPTER ELEVEN

MELKE WOKE TO a bright square of sunlight warming her chest. Her eyelids rose drowsily and she saw a bare wall and a small, empty fireplace. Awareness came as sharply as a blow across the face.

There was too much to remember, too many splinters of memory. Stealing and running. Fear. The black hound. Cold river water in her mouth and the necklace's song prickling over her skin. The hot, choking scent of the salamanders. Hantje.

What have I done?

She sat up too quickly. Muscles cried out in silent protest. She hissed an indrawn breath and was answered by a deep growl.

The hound stood at the foot of the bed, even blacker in daylight than he'd been last night.

Melke gasped another breath, and stared at him. He was as large as a wolf, larger, with fierce, pale eyes and snarling teeth.

She dared not move, dared not even blink her eyelids. Long seconds passed, then minutes. The square of sunlight moved on the bare mattress. Her bladder was full and her stomach cramped with hunger. Thirst was a sharp pain in her throat. The water she'd gulped in the cart yesterday hadn't been enough.

Coward.

"Good morning, Endal," she whispered.

She doubted whether the hound heard her; she scarcely heard the words herself. He looked away and yawned. A few more seconds passed, and he sat down heavily on the floor and yawned again, stretching his jaw wide.

Breathing became easier. She could think of things beside fear. *Hantje.* Liana was with him; she healed him.

Hantje didn't need her. She couldn't heal.

Melke rubbed her face, feeling grime there, as gritty as sin on her skin. She'd roughly bathed her feet last night, but sleep had been more important than washing her face and making the bed, more important than picking her belongings off the floor. She swung aching legs over the edge of the bed and reached down for the bowl of water she'd placed there.

It was empty.

Melke rubbed her dirty face again. Her skin crawled with filth. "Were you thirsty?"

The hound made no reply, other than baring his teeth slightly at her.

Melke sighed. "Very well," she said. "Let us fetch more water. I need to wash my face." Perhaps if she talked to the beast, his hatred of her would ease.

She stood and flinched from the raw, hot pain in her feet. With the rush of pain came something else, something much more urgent than the desire to clean her face. Before she negotiated the stairs, she needed to use the chamber pot.

Melke hobbled across the tiny bedchamber and opened the door. "Go. Outside."

A curling lip and sharp white teeth were her answer.

Melke swallowed her fear. "Out," she said firmly, pointing.

The hound's growl was audible this time. Hackles rose along his spine. He didn't move.

Melke stared at him, remembering Bastian's words. *You will guard the wraith always. She will never be out of your sight.* And he'd gone further than that. *If she becomes unseen, bite her.*

She'd not realized until now just what those words meant.

Melke held her head high as she closed the door. She limped back across the room and bent stiffly to pull the chamber pot from beneath the bed. Pride had been another of Mam's lesson. *Stand tall. Hold your head high.*

She'd bathed her feet in the pot last night before wrapping clumsy bandages around them. Bloody water slopped inside, thin and red-tinted, and bile rose in her throat as she saw it. Melke clenched her jaw and inhaled a shallow breath.

Shame was hot in her cheeks as she unfastened her trousers. Tears burned in her eyes. She couldn't look at the hound.

But when she did look at him, afterward, he lay with his head on his paws and his eyes closed.

Melke stood watching him, while the humiliation in her cheeks cooled. "Thank you," she said. The hound slitted his eyes open.

She was stiffer than she'd been yesterday, but some of the heavy weight of exhaustion was gone. It was easier to negotiate the stairs. She was too slow for the hound, though. She was aware of him close behind her, almost pushing at her legs.

It was easy to guess the reason for his haste, and she limped across the kitchen and opened the door into the yard. "Your turn."

The hound didn't appear to mind that he had an audience, so why did she mind if he observed her? *Because he is a hound and I am a person.*

A person? A wraith, something to be kicked and beaten and spat at.

Melke rubbed her brow with hard fingers. She was more than a wraith, and she'd undo the harm she'd caused. If it was possible.

She sighed, and leaned against the doorframe and looked around the yard. The vegetable garden inside its fence, the henhouse and the washing line, everything seemed ordinary. Except... the vegetables struggled to survive. She saw it in the withered leaves and stunted growth. When she'd come to steal she'd not noticed how cracked and bare the ground was, how parched. It was as if there was a drought and no rain had fallen for months.

But it was spring and the river was in flood.

It wasn't spring in this garden, this yard. The soil had seen no water for a long time.

Melke shook her head. The barrenness was more than poverty; something was ill here.

She shivered and rubbed her arms.

The hound came back into the kitchen. Melke closed the door. "Are you thirsty?" she asked him. "I am." He sat on the cool flagstones and watched with pale, suspicious eyes as she opened a cupboard.

Earthenware crockery, much of it chipped, was stacked neatly on the shelves. She took down a bowl.

The only water she could find was in a pot on top of the stove, the same pot she'd taken water from last night to bathe her feet. The stove was cold, as was the water. Melke filled the bowl and placed it on the floor. "Here," she said to the hound.

The hound rose to his feet and walked over to the bowl. He sniffed the water, his eyes on her, and began to drink.

Glasses were in the next cupboard. Melke took one out and turned it between her fingers. The glass was finely blown, thin and tinted blue, chipped. These people had once had money.

She took water back upstairs in the largest bowl she could find. She needed to see Hantje, needed to see the rise and fall of his chest and the pulse beating in his throat, to know that he slept and that he lived and that he was all right. But she also needed to wash. Hantje had Liana, who could heal him, whereas all she could do was stand uselessly and watch.

"I'm going to bathe," she told the hound, shutting the door and looking at him. "I'd prefer it if you didn't watch."

Perhaps the hound understood her. He stretched out on the hard floor and closed his eyes. He appeared to be asleep.

Melke used the last precious sliver of soap, wrapped inside her washcloth at the bottom of her bag. The scents of salamander and sweat were finally gone, overlaid by sandalwood.

Dressing was easy; she had so few clothes left now—two blouses and a skirt, a change of undergarments—all of which lay scattered on the floor. Wrapping fresh bandages around her feet was less easy; her legs refused to bend properly. She concentrated on the strips of cloth and not on her flesh, swollen and bruised and torn, winding the fabric firmly and tying tight knots.

Combing her hair took forever. The braid was a tangled, knotted mess. Her arms ached long before she'd finished and her scalp felt as if it had been stripped raw. "Easier to cut it off," she said to the hound. He didn't bother to open his eyes.

There was no looking glass in the room, but she didn't want to see herself, didn't want to look into the eyes of the creature she'd become.

Hunger knotted painfully in her belly. Her hair could be re-plaited later. The room, her belongings...

The comb and her stones went on the shelf. The second blouse, the belt and its knife, the knapsack with its few remaining items at the bottom—the herbs she used to wash her hair, the spices in twists of paper, her nightshift—hung on the three hooks on the wall. Putting the linen on the bed took a mere minute. "Servants' bedding," she told the hound as she tucked a sheet over the musty mattress and shook the thin pillow into a pillowcase.

The hound opened his eyes, and closed them again.

Another sheet went on top, darned at the hem, and then the thick blanket she'd slept under last night. Melke smoothed it carefully with a grazed palm. The coarse weave caught at the scabs.

"Come," she said. "I must see my brother. But first, food."

The hound's eyes snapped open. His ears pricked. He sat up.

"Yes," she said. "Food."

But there was little food in the kitchen. Melke frowned as she examined the contents of the pantry. The storeroom, too, was nearly bare. The hatred that she felt for herself became stronger. These people were poor, poorer than she and Hantje.

The bread was stale. There was no butter or cheese, but there was honey. It had a strong, almost spicy flavor. Melke chewed doggedly. The hound licked the honey from his slice and then raised his eyes to her. She imagined that the expression in them was almost beseeching. "I'm sorry," she said. "I could find nothing else. You don't have to eat it."

The hound sighed and sniffed the slice of bread again.

Melke examined the kitchen as she chewed. The size of the room, the decorative moldings on the cast-iron stove and the large diamond-paned windows, spoke of wealth, but the whitewash on the ceiling was peeling. Several of the window panes were missing, and the pantry was almost empty.

She forced herself to eat two slices of bread, but the food sat uneasily in her stomach. Her thieving had been wrong; she'd known that before she'd set foot on Bastian's land. But she'd reasoned that one necklace of sea stones wouldn't be missed. That Hantje's life was worth it. That the act of stealing would harm no one but herself.

What had she done?

Melke rinsed her plate and knife and set them to drain. "Come," she said to the hound. He followed as she walked down the corridor.

Last night there had been no chairs in Hantje's bedroom. Today there were two, plain and wooden. Liana sat on one, beside the bed. Melke watched from the doorway. The quiet concentration on the girl's face, Hantje's utter stillness, the handclasp they shared... an artist could paint the scene and call it *Devotion*.

Sunlight shone on the girl's hair. Its whiteness was almost blinding. Moon-white. At home, Liana would have been named Asta. Moon Daughter.

The girl glanced at the doorway. She smiled. "Hello."

"Hello." Melke's answering smile felt awkward on her lips.

"Did you sleep well?"

You need not to be nice to me, she wanted to say. Instead she said, "Yes, thank you," and limped toward the bed. "He looks better," she offered. The burns were less vivid, the bruises paler, the swelling of his eyelids much reduced.

"The injuries. Yes, I've made a start. But the fever..." The girl shook her head. Exhaustion smudged beneath her eyes.

"Have you slept?"

Liana shook her head again, her gaze on Hantje's face.

"What time is it?"

"After noon."

"What?" Melke was appalled. How many hours had she slept and Liana not? "Then you must sleep."

Liana closed her eyes. "Will you watch him?"

"Of course," she said, mortified that the girl felt she needed to ask.

"Thank you." The words were a weary sigh. Liana released Hantje's hand and laid it gently at his side. She stood, her movements slow and stiff. "He must drink." Her voice was husky with exhaustion. "He needs as much as possible." She gestured to a bowl on the small table beside the bed.

Melke nodded. Shame was tight in her throat.

Liana looked almost elderly as she walked to the door. "If you need me—"

"I won't." The words were too abrupt, too rude. Heat rose in Melke's face. "I mean..."

Liana halted in the doorway. She smiled, a tiny lifting of her lips. "I know what you mean."

Melke couldn't trust herself to speak. She nodded.

She stood long after Liana had left, looking down at her brother, almost hating him. It was worse than hating herself. Hantje was all she had, all and everything.

CHAPTER TWELVE

THE KITCHEN WAS empty. No fire burned in the stove. The things that ordinarily welcomed him home, that he looked forward to at the end of a long day, were absent. There was no smell of food, no Liana to greet him with a smile.

Bastian stood in the doorway. Unease prickled over his skin. If he was superstitious, he'd say that death walked here.

Liana wasn't in the sickroom. The wraith was, Endal stretched out asleep on the floor behind her.

She didn't see him. She used a scrap of cloth to trickle water into her brother's mouth. Hair screened her face, falling over cheek and shoulder and down her back, as black as Endal's coat, gleaming. Her blouse was red. The one he'd seen on the floor, with flowers embroidered at the cuffs. Not crimson, but a warmer, gentler color.

She looked womanly, as soft and feminine as Liana.

For a moment, just for the merest second, it felt as if the ground shifted slightly beneath his feet. Bastian touched a hand to the doorframe to steady himself. He bared his teeth at the wraith. It was a sly magic she used, and he'd not fall for it. He knew what she was: a feral, thieving creature. He hissed at her silently. *Scum. Vermin.*

Endal raised his head. His tail thumped on the floor, once. The wraith didn't glance up. All her attention was for her brother.

Are you well? he asked Endal.

The dog yawned. *Bored.*

Where is Liana?

She sleeps.

It explained the empty kitchen, the cold stove. He'd have to cook. Bastian closed his eyes, suddenly weary, aware of the ache in his shoulders and the sting of blisters on his palms.

Perhaps the wraith would cook.

He shuddered, and opened his eyes. He'd rather eat dry grass than food that... that *thing* prepared. He turned away.

Bas. It was a silent whine.

He looked back at Endal.

The dog rose to his feet and wagged his tail. *May I come?*

The wraith, with her long, sleek hair and embroidered blouse, appeared harmless. He knew it was untrue. No, he told Endal, firmly. *You must watch her always.*

Endal's tail drooped.

Bastian sighed. All day he'd missed Endal. It was an ache, an itch, an essential something that was missing. He scowled at the wraith. Everything was her fault. *Are you hungry? I'll bring food.*

Endal's tail wagged again slightly. *Food?*

And water. Guilt flushed hot in his face. He'd ignored the wraith this morning, and ignored Endal too. He'd not thought to feed his dog, to give him water. All he'd wanted was to get away, as far from the wraith as he could. *Have you drunk?* Anger kindled in his chest. Had the wraith let Endal suffer? Had she—

I have a bowl. Endal sat heavily on the thin carpet.

Bastian's anger and guilt flared more hotly. The wraith had done what he'd forgotten. He clenched his hands and turned away before the wraith could become aware of his presence.

Lighting the stove, seeing the dry twigs burn fiercely, improved his mood. Examining the contents of the storeroom darkened it again. A string of onions hung from the ceiling. The potatoes were soft and withered, the sack less than half full. No cheese, no meat, no other vegetables. Bastian squeezed a potato in his hand. The flesh dented beneath his fingers. *The sal Veres die.*

He boiled the potatoes and then fried them with chopped onions in fat Liana had saved in a bowl. There was salt, but he found no peppercorns to grind.

When his mother had died he hadn't known how to cook. This—boiling and frying—had been beyond him. Arnaul's mother had shown him what to do. She'd taught him how to make soups that would last for a week and thick stews, how to knead bread and set it to rise, how to roast a leg of lamb. She'd taught him how to care for a baby, how to wash and feed Liana. How to darn the holes in his clothes and sew on buttons.

Bastian lit candles and sat at the table and chewed his food while the sun set. The kitchen was silent except for the muted crackle of wood burning in the stove. It had been like this when he was a boy: quiet. If he turned his head he'd see Liana, asleep in the woven baby's basket.

He pushed the empty plate away and rubbed his face with a weary hand. He closed his eyes. Arnaul's mother was dead now, but memories of her lessons were still strong: mashing cooked vegetables for Liana and stewing fruit on the wood stove, plucking and gutting a hen, soaking dried beans in water and cooking them until they were soft enough to eat.

Quiet footsteps came down the corridor. Bastian stiffened and opened his eyes. "Liana." He stood.

Liana smiled, so like their mother in the candle-light that his heart skipped a beat in fear. Delicate, too easily broken by the psaaron.

"You cooked."

"Yes." It was impossible not to smile when Liana smiled. "It's not as good as your—"

She shook her head, half-laughing at him. "You taught me to cook, Bastian."

Because our mother was dead. Bastian stopped smiling.

The laughter faded from Liana's face. "What is it?"

He shrugged and turned away. *The wraith. The curse. The psaaron.* He picked up his plate and laid it in the stone sink. "Another ewe died today."

"And the lamb?

"Dead."

Liana sighed. When he turned to look at her, he saw shadows on her face that had nothing to do with night-time and candlelight.

"How does your patient?" he asked.

The shadows on her face darkened. "He's very ill."

"But he'll survive." He knew the strength of Liana's gift. He'd have lost a leg last autumn, perhaps died, if not for the quiet, wondrous magic she possessed. She had knitted flesh and bone and muscle, had staved off infection and saved him.

Liana clasped her hands together. "I don't know."

"What? He might die?" Fear jerked beneath his breastbone. If that creature died, the bargain with the wraith was void. The necklace, the psaaron—

No.

Bastian inhaled a slow, calm breath. He smiled at Liana. "It'll be fine," he said. "Don't worry. Here." He pulled out a chair for her. "Eat. You must be hungry."

Liana shook her head. "I'll take a tray. I should get back to—"

"A few minutes."

Her headshake was firm.

Bastian spooned food onto a plate while Liana fetched a tray from the scullery. "And this bowl's for Endal," he said, filling it high.

"What about Melke?"

Melke. The wraith had a name. He didn't want to know it. "I didn't cook for her."

"Bastian." There was faint reproof in Liana's tone.

He clenched his jaw.

Liana handed him another plate. He took it from her and slapped food on it, with no care for neatness. Let the wraith choke on the meal.

Liana placed the plate on the tray, then she reached up and laid a cool hand against his cheek. "It'll be all right, Bastian."

It was his role to give comfort, to say such words. He flushed, angry with himself, with the wraith. "Go eat," he said brusquely.

Liana smiled and removed her hand. She picked up the tray.

"I'm going to Thierry tomorrow," he said to her back. "The horse and cart must be returned." *And I need to see Silvia, need to forget for a few hours.* "The storeroom... we need food. If there's anything—"

"I'll write a list. Thank you, Bastian."

He nodded and watched her go. Market day. His disgruntled anger faded. He was aware of lightness in his chest, a quicksilver edge of anticipation. He'd be free of Vere for a day, free of responsibility and dust and throat-parching dryness. *Freedom.* With Silvia, he'd be able to lose himself in pleasure and forget the curse.

The anticipation was laced with a familiar guilt. Bastian bolted the door to the yard and picked up the candleholder, while the anticipation congealed inside him and twisted into knots of shame. The secret he kept from Liana, the stolen moments of intense pleasure... He was a man and had a man's need to lie with a woman. It was purely natural—so why did he feel guilt? Why did he hide it from Liana?

Because I escape and she doesn't.

Bastian went to bed, accompanied by a sense of his own selfishness.

CHAPTER THIRTEEN

I T WAS FULLY dark when Liana returned. "How is he?" she asked from the doorway. There was color in her cheeks and the smudges beneath her eyes were gone. She carried a tray.

Melke rose to her feet, catching her breath at the sudden jolt of pain. "His fever grows, I think. I'm no healer."

Liana placed the tray on the little bedside table. She laid her fingers lightly at Hantje's throat, where the skin burned with heat and his pulse throbbed, fast and weak. "The infection..."

"Worse?"

"Yes." Concern furrowed Liana's brow. She sat quickly.

Melke stepped back into the shadows, not wanting to disturb the girl. Candles burned in the holder. She had fetched fresh water and new candles hours earlier, had found the cesspit and emptied her chamber pot into it, had tidied the sickroom and rebandaged her swollen feet, had done everything and anything she could think of— while Hantje's fever rose. There'd been nothing else she could do. She had no gift of healing, no powders to give him, no salves to smooth on his burns. She was helpless, useless.

The tray held two plates and a bowl. "You haven't eaten."

Liana didn't appear to hear. Her attention was on Hantje. She held his hand, her fingers interlocking with his.

"You must eat," Melke said.

The girl glanced up. Her eyes didn't fully focus on Melke. "Oh," she said. "No, it's—"

"You will be no help to Hantje if you become ill."

Liana blinked. "But—"

Melke stepped closer to the bed. "You must eat."

The girl blinked again and then smiled. "You sound like Bastian."

I hope not. "Please, Liana." It was the first time she'd used the girl's name. "Eat."

Liana sat back in the chair. The smile was in her eyes now. "If you insist."

"I do." Melke smiled too, faintly, awkwardly. It felt strange. How long since she'd last smiled?

Given the state of the pantry and storeroom the meal was surprisingly good, but when she thanked Liana, the girl said, "Bastian cooked."

The food suddenly sat uneasily in Melke's stomach. "He what?"

Liana laughed.

Melke placed her plate on the tray. How long since she'd laughed?

"Bastian can cook. He taught me," said Liana. Her smile became crooked. "My mother died when I was a baby."

"Oh." Melke didn't know what to say. "I'm sorry." She stood and walked to where Endal lay. The hound looked at her with pale wolf-eyes and thumped his tail on the carpet. His bowl was licked clean. She bent to pick it up.

"She died because of the curse." The girl's voice was flat.

Melke glanced up, Endal's bowl in her hand. Liana smoothed the darned hem of the sheet with a fingertip. The silver-white hair hid her face.

"Your brother said there was a curse." The words were stiff and clumsy on her tongue. "Forgive me, but... can you tell me?"

Liana turned her head. Tears were bright in her eyes.

"I'm sorry," Melke said. "I didn't mean to distress you. Don't—"

"He didn't tell you? You don't know?"

Melke shook her head.

Liana smiled weakly. The tears still shone in her eyes. "How like Bastian. He..." She shook her head and made a sound that was half laugh, half sigh. "I don't know how to explain it. It's... when I heal, I feel things. I feel who a person *is*. Your brother..."

"What?" Melke asked, her fingers tightening around the bowl.

Liana touched Hantje's brow lightly. "What I feel from your brother is despair."

Melke looked down at the bowl in her hands.

"He has an honorable heart. I feel that too."

Melke closed her eyes.

"Bastian." Liana laughed, a quiet sound. "He does everything with passion. It's under his skin, in his blood. It... it *hisses* inside him. That's why he hates you so much. Why he won't talk to you."

And why shouldn't Bastian hate her? It was no more and no less than she deserved.

"I don't know about you." Liana's voice was cool.

Melke opened her eyes. She placed the bowl on the tray and held her hand out to the girl, palm up. "If you wish..." The injury was nothing, a graze, tender and scabbed over, but it would tell Liana who she was. *I have the same despair as Hantje, but my heart is no longer honorable.*

Liana met her gaze. She made no move to touch her. The expression in her eyes was assessing.

Melke closed her hand and let it fall. "It was never my intention to harm," she said. The words choked in her throat, halting. "I didn't know there was a curse."

"A curse." Liana's mouth twisted. She turned her head away.

A draft ruffled the closed curtains and made the candles flicker. The patterns of light and shadow shifted on the walls. Liana's hair shone, as white as the moon.

"Sit," the girl said, her face still averted. "I will tell you."

Melke sat. There was tension inside her. It stiffened her spine and made arms and legs awkward. Her fingers knotted together, white-knuckled.

Endal yawned widely. He laid his head on his paws and closed his eyes.

"You know what the necklace is." It was a statement, flatly said.

"Sea stones."

Liana looked at her sharply. Her eyebrows drew together. "Sea stones?"

"The salamanders said... sea stones." Pretty, and of little value. "Are they not?" Melke clenched her hands more tightly together and felt a scab split. What had she stolen?

"No," said Liana. "They are psaaron tears."

For a moment Melke couldn't breathe, couldn't speak. She was on her feet, but had no memory of standing. "No," she said. "*No.*"

Liana's face was mostly shadowed. Her eyes glittered as she looked up at Melke. "Yes."

"I didn't know." The words were useless, worthless sounds. She might as well bleat like a sheep for all the value they were. "I didn't *know.*"

Liana's mouth tightened. She looked away, to Hantje.

Psaaron tears. Rare beyond anything, priceless. Melke sat, blindly. "How did you come to have them?"

The girl's laugh was bitter. "We stole them."

CHAPTER FOURTEEN

ELKE OPENED HER mouth, but no words came out.

Liana glanced at her and laughed again, a sound as sharp-edged as glass.

Melke found her voice. "You and Bastian *stole* the psaaron tears?" She shook her head.

"No, not us. The sal Veres. Our family."

"Oh."

Liana held Hantje's hand. "You know what psaaron tears are?"

Melke nodded. "When a psaaron dies, it sheds a tear." How many stones had been on the necklace. Fifty? Sixty? "Each tear is... they say it holds memory or... or *soul*." The necklace had sung to her. Voices had crept over her skin, inside her. Voices of the dead. Tiny hairs rose sharply on her skin. She shivered.

Liana nodded. "A part that never dies." She raised one hand and touched a fingertip to her throat, a gesture that seemed unconscious. "Imagine... your family never dies. You have them with you always."

Melke blinked back tears. *Imagine.* She cleared her throat. "The necklace... it was a family?"

"Many generations of a family, yes."

"And somebody stole it." It took her breath away. She couldn't believe that anyone could be so stupid.

"My grandfather's uncle. Alain sal Vere."

Melke shook her head. "How?" It was impossible, surely, to steal from a psaaron.

"The necklace likes sunlight, did you know?"

Melke shook her head again. There were no psaarons in the oceans of her home. They preferred warmer, southern waters. She knew of them through myth only, and that, very little.

"That's what the psaaron had been doing. Sunning the necklace. On our shore. And Alain—" Liana closed her eyes. Her face contorted.

Melke looked at the floor, at Endal dozing, his black coat swallowing the candlelight. The expression on Liana's face was too personal.

A draft whispered through the curtains. Candlelight flickered.

"Do you know why he stole it?" Melke asked quietly, watching Endal sleep.

"Greed. Arrogance. The sal Veres were a proud family." Liana's voice held a bitter note.

Melke looked at the worn nap of the carpet. *And now they are humble.* "What happened?"

"The psaaron wanted it back, of course." There was a sound. Not laughter, something harsher.

Melke looked up. "Could it not have been returned?"

"He hid it. Alain hid it. In the limestone caves." Liana gestured with her hand, west.

"But surely—"

"He was young and wild. He refused to tell where he'd hidden it. And before the family could make him, he died."

"The curse," Melke guessed.

Liana shook her head. "No. He rode an unbroken stallion and broke his neck." Her mouth tightened. "Arrogant."

"Oh."

"It was less than he deserved. Much less." The girl's expression, the tone of her voice, were almost frightening.

The candles flared slightly in the draft and for a moment it seemed as if the shadows on Liana's face sank into her skin. Her shining innocence, her youth and gentleness, her loveliness, were overlain by a mottled stain of hatred. It disfigured her.

And then the curtains moved again, and the candlelight flickered again, and the shadows on Liana's face were merely shadows, nothing more.

"His brothers drowned," she said. "All three of them. *That* was the curse."

Drowning. It was unsurprising. Psaarons were denizens of water: ocean and lake, river and rain. But all three brothers? Melke shook her head. She didn't understand. "If the necklace was found, why would the psaaron curse—"

"It was found by my father. Too late to save them. Too late to save my mother." Liana tilted her head so that hair hid her face. Melke heard grief in her voice, as clearly as she'd heard the hatred.

"I'm sorry," she said softly. "But I don't understand."

The girl looked up. Tears shimmered in her eyes. "I'm not explaining it well."

Melke shook her head. "No. Not at all. It's a difficult story to tell."

"Yes. Difficult." Liana laughed without humor, a grim sound. She looked down at Hantje and her expression softened. She reached out to touch his face. Her other hand held his in a firm clasp. "It was like this. Alain stole the necklace and he hid it and... he died." Her eyes met Melke's. "Do you understand?"

She nodded. "Yes."

Liana stroked Hantje's cheek with a fingertip. "The psaaron wanted the necklace back. It cursed the sal Veres."

"Water?"

Liana nodded. "The curse has grown with time. It no longer rains here. You've seen the ground?"

"I thought it a drought."

"An unnatural drought." Liana's lips twisted into a bleak smile. "The rivers ceased to flow. The sea... we can't set foot on the beach, daren't fish. Boats sink and swimmers drown."

"The three brothers?"

"Yes. Water is deadly to us. To our family."

"Your mother," Melke said softly. "I'm sorry."

Liana shook her head. "No. That was the other part of the curse."

Something in the girl's voice, a flatness, told Melke that worse was to come. She sat rigidly in her chair. Did she want to hear this?

"The psaaron comes, once in every generation. It waits a day and a night for the necklace to be returned. And at night, while it waits—"

"No." Melke shook her head. Something clenched in her chest. *No. It can't be.*

Liana held her gaze. Her eyes were fierce, shining with tears. "What have you heard?"

She didn't want to speak, didn't want to utter the words. They gagged in her throat. "Psaarons..." She swallowed. "Psaarons are like salamanders, like gryphons and lamia. They like to... to lie with humans."

"Yes." It was a whisper.

Gryphons were the worst. They raped and killed. But they lived in the central wastes and were rarely seen. Salamanders were more numerous, but they didn't use force, paying for sexual favors with gold and jewels and other treasures. The giant serpents, lamia, were always female, and liked to lie with men when in their human form. It was said that men enjoyed their embrace.

And psaarons... Psaarons lay with humans to punish them, to hurt them.

Or so the myths said.

"The first time, it was Alain's sister. She hanged herself afterward. She was as old as I am."

Melke closed her eyes. She didn't want to hear it.

"Her brother, my great grandfather, he wanted to save his children. He threw the sal Vere fortune into the sea, all of it, until there was nothing left. But it made no difference. His son was next. Pascal."

There was silence while the words settled, the weight of them dreadful.

"Pascal didn't kill himself, but he never spoke again. He was mute. He and his father drowned, years later."

Too horrible. Too much. Melke opened her eyes, stretching them wide. The images inside her head remained though, shadowlike, hovering at the edges of her vision.

Liana sat, holding Hantje's hand in a tight grip.

Melke swallowed. She made herself speak. "And next was your mother."

The girl nodded, staring down at Hantje.

"I'm sorry."

A tear slid down Liana's cheek. She brushed at it roughly with the back of her hand.

They sat in silence and candlelight for long minutes. The only sounds in the room were the stirring of the curtains and Endal's soft exhalations. Liana's voice was loud and startling when at last she spoke. "She jumped off the cliff afterward, into the sea. I was only a baby. Bastian was nine."

Poor Bastian, was Melke's instinctive thought. He'd been old enough to understand what had happened to his mother, to know that she'd never come back. She closed her eyes again, briefly.

"I don't really remember my father. After... Bastian says he hardly ever came home. He lived in the caves, searching for the necklace."

Bastian was a tough man with a mercenary's face, but he'd been a nine year-old boy once. All Melke could think was, *poor Bastian.*

"Father found it when I was six," said Liana. She smiled, but it was without happiness. "He gave it to Bastian, and..."

The pause was heavy. It grew in the room, sucking Melke's breath. *And what?*

Liana turned her head. She stared at Melke. Her eyes were hazel, bright and sharp. "He wanted to be with my mother, so he jumped too."

Melke couldn't breathe, couldn't inhale, couldn't—

"Excuse me," she said, standing and pushing the chair aside. Her steps were fast and clumsy as she ran down the corridor and through the kitchen. She slammed back the bolt on the door and rushed outside. She could breathe here, huge gasping breaths.

What had she done?

Melke sat heavily on the ground and hugged herself, her eyes squeezed shut against tears. Endal sat down beside her. He whined.

She cried in the dark and empty yard while Endal lay beside her, pressed against her hip. She felt his warmth, the softness and thickness of his coat, and smelled the hound-scent of him.

The tears stopped. It was impossible to cry forever. She'd learned that as a child. The air was dry and cool against her skin, the ground hard. Endal was a solid warmth.

It was dark.

Self-loathing gave way to fear. *It's dark.*

Blackness, darkness. It was impossible to move, to breathe. Panic rose in her chest. There was a scream inside her. She was alone in the dark and she would die here. They'd hurt her. They'd make her beg. They'd—

Endal shifted against her. He laid his chin on her knee.

Melke shut her eyes. She inhaled a shuddering breath that smelled of dust and dryness and hound.

This was no cell with a stone floor and rough, dank walls that pressed in on her. There were no guards. She was free.

And she had done a terrible wrong.

She stood, stiffly and clumsily. Her heart hammered in her throat. The breaths she inhaled were shallow, panicky. Darkness smothered her. Her eyes were wide and sightless. Endal leaned against her leg.

It took forever to reach the farmhouse, minutes and hours, a thousand endless steps. She walked backwards, facing the darkness. Her fingers groped for the door. She pulled it shut behind her and bolted it, but the kitchen was dark, black. It had walls of stone and *there was no light*—

There was light in the sickroom, though, shining through the doorway. The terror that clutched in Melke's chest eased fractionally. She could breathe, could *see*.

Liana looked up, her hair shining as brightly as snow in sunlight. Her expression altered, became sharper. "Are you all right? You look—"

"I'm fine," Melke said, standing in the doorway, panting, the darkness pressing at her back. *Stand tall*, Mam had said. *Hold your head high. Never let them see your fear.* Her heart thudded in her chest. "I'm sorry. I needed to... to get some fresh air."

Liana's gaze was searching, her brow faintly furrowed.

Melke walked slowly across the room. With the candlelight and the relief came awareness of her feet again. She managed not to lurch or wince. The pain was huge, a raw and swollen burning.

She clutched at the back of her chair and sat. The sharpness of pain faded. Breathing became easier. There was light, and another person. Her heart began to beat more slowly.

Endal lay down on the floor. His flank touched her ankle, warm and strangely comforting.

Liana still watched her.

Perspiration slicked Melke's skin. She felt it beneath her eyes, under her lower lip. She wiped it with a hand that trembled.

"What is it?" Liana asked quietly.

"My feet." She tried to smile. "It's nothing."

"No. That's not what I meant."

"Oh." Shamed heat rose in her cheeks. "I don't like the dark, is all."

Liana looked at her for a long moment, then glanced at Hantje. "You said he doesn't either."

"Yes. It's nothing." She pushed the memories back: the terror, the panic, the aloneness. "I'm sorry. You were telling me about—"

"My parents." Liana's scrutiny was an adult's assessment, not a child's. "It upset you."

"How could it not?"

Liana sighed, a soft sound. "I'm glad it upsets you." There was no malice in her voice, and none in her face. All Melke saw was sadness. "You'll get the necklace back, won't you?"

Melke nodded.

The girl reached out and touched Hantje's cheek lightly.

"How long until it comes?"

Liana stiffened. She glanced up. "The psaaron?"

Melke nodded.

"Spring equinox." The girl's lips twisted into something that couldn't be called a smile. "We've been waiting for twelve years. Bastian says it'll be this year. The well is almost dry. The farm can't last much longer."

"Spring equinox?" Melke's heart was thudding again. "Are you certain?"

"It's always spring equinox," Liana said quietly.

"But that's…"

"Next full moon." The girl's gaze was clear and steady.

Next full moon. So soon. Too soon. Hantje would be unable to help her. How could she hope to succeed alone?

Liana watched her.

She had to succeed, because if she didn't, then either Liana or Bastian must—

Horror shuddered inside her. It roughened her voice and made her hoarse. "I'll need to talk to my brother. I don't know how they caught him."

"He was stealing?" Liana's face creased, at brow and eyes and mouth. "Bastian said he was, but he doesn't feel as if—"

"I can only guess. He was gone in the morning when I woke." Melke's throat tightened in memory. The disbelief, the sick realisation. "Why else would he be in the salamanders' den?"

Liana shook her head. "He doesn't *feel*…"

I thought I could never steal, either. And look what I have done. "He did," Melke said flatly. "He did."

For a long time there was silence. Endal was a warm weight against her ankle. How strange that she wasn't afraid. The ferocious wolf-beast lay touching her, and she was unafraid.

In the silence she was aware of Hantje's breathing, shallow and rapid, and the hectic flush of his cheeks. His pulse beat erratically in the hollow of his throat. "He grows worse," she said.

Liana met her eyes. "Yes."

"I know you heal him, but while you sleep, when it's just me…" Melke tried to articulate the helplessness, the uselessness, she felt. "Please, there must be something I can do."

"I'm sorry," the girl said.

"Are there no salves I can put on the burns, no powders to reduce the fever?"

Liana looked down to where her fingers clasped Hantje's hand. "No."

There was a brief silence, and then the girl stirred slightly and glanced up. "Tomorrow. I'd forgotten. Bastian's going to Thierry to return the horse and cart. I don't know how much money we have left, but perhaps—"

"I have some coins."

"You do?" Liana's face lit with eagerness. "Then there are powders for the fever and—"

"I'll fetch the money." Melke stood. Here at last was something she could do, a way of helping.

The hound opened his eyes and yawned and sat up.

"May I take one of the candles?"

"Of course."

There was no contempt in the girl's voice or face, nothing that hinted at scorn, but blood flushed warmly beneath Melke's skin. She prised one of the candles from the holder, spilling wax on the little table, and made her slow way from the sickroom. She shielded the flame carefully. To have it blow out in the darkness of the corridor, the kitchen, would be—

"Stupid," she whispered under her breath. It was foolish to be so weak, so hindered by fear of the dark. She knew it was ridiculous—*knew it*—and yet her heart beat fast and she was tense with terror that the candle might blow out.

She climbed the stairs, slowly, wincingly, with Endal at her heels, and stepped into the darkness of her bedroom. It was so like a cell that something clenched in her chest. *Stupid.* She lit the candles in the candleholder on the shelf beside the bed. Light swelled in the bedchamber. Tension and fear dissolved. It was no cell, merely a maid's room that had seen better days.

Endal lay down stiffly on the wooden floor. Melke looked at him. His irises were icy pale. Wolf eyes. But he didn't snarl at her, didn't show her his fearsome teeth.

"You need a rug to lie on."

The hound laid his head on his paws and closed his eyes.

Melke lifted her knapsack from the hook on the wall and tipped the contents out on the bed. Underclothes, one of her stones, the black one with the white veins of marble running through it, spices in their twists of paper, her purse...

The coins were tied together, threaded on a loop of string. Mostly copper, but silver too. Melke held them in her hand and felt the meager weight. Their savings, hers and Hantje's. Six years of hard work, of long hours and sweat, and she held the results in the palm of her hand.

She undid the string clumsily. The thin scabs on her palms threatened to split open with each movement of her fingers. A silver coin for Hantje's medicine:

salves and powders she could give him while Liana slept. For the food, another silver coin. Extravagant perhaps, but the debt she owed couldn't be repaid, not with mere coins.

The disks were small and thin, stamped with Bresse's crown. She laid them on the tiny shelf and retied the string awkwardly. The remaining coins clinked dully as she tightened the knot.

The underclothes and spices and purse went back into the knapsack. She held the black stone for a moment, smoothing it between thumb and finger, feeling a sense of home before placing it alongside the others on the shelf.

One. Two. Three. Only three. Where was the red stone?

Anxiety tightened her chest. She couldn't have lost it. Not that one, not any of them.

Where was it?

Endal raised his head. His pale eyes steadied her. She hadn't lost the stone, couldn't have. It was in the knapsack or on the floor. She'd find it tomorrow.

Melke exhaled a slow breath. She picked up the coins and the candleholder. "Come, Endal."

He padded silently behind her, down the stairs, across the kitchen, along the corridor. In the sickroom, Melke held the two coins out to Liana. "Here."

The silver glinted in the candlelight. Liana's eyes widened.

"For the salves and the powders. And for food. Maybe a round of cheese, or some ham. And vegetables. And some more candles. And... whatever you think."

"Silver?"

"Yes."

Liana made no move to take the money. "Thank you, but—"

"It's not stolen, if that's what you think." Melke said the words stiffly. "I've never stolen anything." Sudden heat scorched her face. "I mean... other than the necklace."

I'm a thief. That's what I am now. A thief.

Liana met her eyes. "I don't think you stole it," she said. "But... silver. It's too much money."

"Please."

Liana held her gaze for a long second. Then she nodded. "Very well. I'll give it to Bastian."

"Thank you." The coins clinked thinly as she passed them to the girl.

An awkward silence grew in the room. The curtains stirred. Melke had been awake less than half a day, but already her body was heavy with tiredness. Muscle and bone ached. Her feet burned. Her eyes... She closed them briefly.

"There's no need for you to stay," Liana said. "I'll wake you when I need to sleep."

Melke opened her eyes. She couldn't blame the girl for wanting to be rid of her. Bastian would have been less tactful. At least Liana didn't say the words *filthy wraith* out loud.

She got to her feet and managed not to wince.

Endal raised his head. She thought he sighed as he slowly stood.

"Good night."

"Good night." The girl didn't look up. Her attention was on Hantje. His torn lips were parted. Each breath he took was shallow and ragged. The skin stretched tightly over his bones, flushed and beaded with perspiration.

Melke hesitated. Hantje struggled to live. She saw it quite clearly. He fought for each beat of his heart, each breath.

"Liana."

The girl glanced up.

"Will he...?" Melke couldn't speak the words, couldn't say out loud what she feared.

Liana's grip tightened on his hand. "He will live the night. I promise." Something in her voice, quiet and strong, made Melke believe her.

"Very well." It came out as a whisper. She reached out and touched her brother's face lightly, feeling heat and dampness. "Good night."

Grief ached behind her eyes and in her throat. *Live, Hantje. You are all and everything. Without you, I die.*

CHAPTER FIFTEEN

BASTIAN ROSE BEFORE dawn. He went downstairs quietly.

Liana sat with the male wraith, leaning forward, her head bent so that her hair fell almost to touch him. She held one of his hands in both of hers.

He spared the wraith a quick glance. The bruises were fading, the burns less vivid. The scum would live.

"Liana."

She looked up. For a moment it was as if her eyes looked through him. Then she blinked. "Bastian." Her smile was weary.

He frowned. The dark shadows beneath her eyes had nothing to do with the candlelight. Her skin was almost as pale as parchment. "Go to bed," he said. "You need to sleep."

"Hantje needs me."

"Nonsense. That cursed creature will be fine."

Liana shook her head. "He almost died in the night."

"What?" Bastian looked at the figure in the bed again and felt a flicker of alarm. The wraith's breathing was weak, his face flushed. Sweat glistened on his skin. "Fever?"

"Yes."

"But he'll live." It was a statement, not a question. The wraith *had* to live.

"The infection grows worse." Liana reached for a piece of paper on the bedside table. "Can you buy some things for me? I've made a list."

"Of course." He took the list, frowning to read it in the dim candlelight. "Willowbark tea?"

"To reduce the fever."

There had been no healers in the sal Vere line for more than a century. Liana's gift was precious, a gift to be treasured and used sparingly, one they were both still learning to understand, but... "Do you need this? I thought—"

"I can't be with Hantje always." Her fingers tightened their clasp on the wraith's hand. "These will help. Melke can use them while I sleep."

Bastian read further. There were a lot of items on Liana's list. Not merely medicines, but food and candles and other supplies. He shook his head. "Liana, we can't afford—"

"Here." Liana picked something up from the table and held it out to him.

He opened his hand automatically. Metal clinked and he felt the coldness of coins in his palm. "What? Silver?" His eyes narrowed. "She gave them to you, didn't she?"

Liana nodded.

Anger flared in his chest. "We don't need her filthy money!"

"It's not stolen," Liana said mildly.

"Of course it is!" He wanted to slam upstairs and throw the coins in the wraith's face, to—

"Bastian." There was a note in his sister's voice that surprised him, firm and adult. "We need the money."

"No, we do not!" Charity, that's what it was, *charity*. From a stinking, thieving piece of scum.

The man in the bed stirred. His breath was sharp, gasping. Liana bent swiftly over him. One hand cupped his cheek, the other held his limp fingers. "Take the money," she said, her voice low. "Unless you want him to die."

Bastian clenched the coins in his hand. They burned into his palm. Stolen money. He wanted to throw them away.

"Very well," he said stiffly. "I'll be back at dusk."

He left the roan and Gaudon with the stableman and walked around to the inn entrance to redeem his signet ring. The wooden sign with *Ronsard* carved into it swung above his head in the breeze, creaking slightly.

Bastian pushed open the door. The room was dark after the bright sunlight and he paused to let his eyes adjust. This close to noon, customers crowded the taproom. The air was thick with the smells of sweat and chewing tobacco and beef stew. A fire burned in the wide grate. Years of wood smoke had blackened the low ceiling. Male voices rose loudly, and beneath them was the sound of cutlery scraping against plates. A shout of laughter rose to his left as he crossed the room.

Ronsard's son leaned against the long wooden counter, a hint of swagger in his posture, while a serving girl poured a tankard of ale for a stout farmer.

Bastian felt in his pocket. The wraith's silver burned there, filthy. "For the horse and cart," he said, pushing several thick copper coins toward the youth.

Julien straightened and smiled his father's smile, wide and insincere. "I'll get your ring."

Bastian nodded.

"Ale?" The serving girl had a plain and friendly face. When she smiled she became almost pretty. In contrast to Julien, the smile reached her eyes.

Bastian nodded again, shortly, and watched as she poured. "Thank you." The ale was warm and hoppy on his tongue. He swallowed deeply.

"Your ring," Julien said behind him.

Bastian turned.

The signet ring lay on the youth's palm. Even though light was dull in the room, the silver gleamed coolly.

Bastian put down his tankard. He reached for the ring. The black surliness that had edged his morning eased as he slid it onto his finger. The ring's smoothness was comfortable and familiar. It weighed more than silver. It weighed of family, of his father and grandfather, of generations of sal Veres.

The ring warmed swiftly on his finger, until he no longer felt its coolness. He found that he was standing less tensely than he'd been half a minute ago, as if his body recognized the signet ring and relaxed. Bastian picked up the tankard again and decided that he'd eat lunch here. He leaned an elbow on the counter. The thick slab of wood was dark with age and worn smooth by the hands of countless customers.

"Women," Julien said, straightening one of his cuffs. The shirt was finer than anything Bastian owned, the linen thick and dyed a deep and expensive green.

Bastian grunted and turned slightly away. The youth's assumption that he wanted to listen to him, the way he laid his forearm along the counter as if he owned it and not his father, irritated him. *Cocksure.*

"Stupid bints don't understand the word *No.* You ever noticed that? Nothing up here." Julien tapped his forehead. "Dumb."

The ale soured in Bastian's mouth. He put the tankard down.

"Girls from down by the docks are the worst." Julien's tone was self-important, almost boastful. "Take my advice and stay away from them."

Bastian straightened away from the counter. *You think I'd take your advice?* He didn't waste his breath uttering the words. Instead, he felt in his pocket for a coin. His hand itched with the urge to take Julien by the scruff of his neck and drag him outside. He hadn't been able to hit the wraith, but Julien would be easy. *Too easy,* he told himself. The youth was soft beneath the fine clothes and had the uncalloused hands of someone who did no real work. It would be like beating a child. Or a woman.

"Sluts," Julien said expansively. "All of those dockside girls. They're sluts."

Bastian clenched his teeth together. The silver coins were small and heavy in his pocket, dirty. The copper coins were larger. He felt for the thinnest of them and slapped it down on the counter. The serving girl saw the movement and exchanged a last, laughing word with her customer. She came toward Bastian and reached for the coin.

Julien ignored her. "Spread their legs for you, then say they're pregnant and expect you to marry them." His tone was aggrieved.

The serving girl paused with her fingers on the coin. She glanced at Julien. The good humor was gone from her face.

"As if I'd marry a dockside girl." Julien's upper lip curled in disgust. "I'm not a fool."

Bastian curled his hands into fists on the counter, and then flexed them open. A brawl would be satisfying, but he didn't want to come to Silvia with split knuckles and blood on his clothes. "You give a very good impression of one," he said, his voice flat with contempt. "Only a fool would speak as you do."

The serving girl raised her eyes and smiled at him. Her face transformed from plain to pretty. Bastian nodded at her and pushed away from the counter. He didn't want to eat at Ronsard's after all.

BASTIAN'S ILL TEMPER slowly evaporated as he strode through the town. It was impossible to be angry, with the signet ring on his finger again and Silvia two streets away and the bustle of the Thierry market around him. So many scents: hay and freshly slaughtered meat, leather and herbs and peppercorns, cow dung, fish, and sweet toffee apples. The large square was a medley of color and texture. He saw skeins of coarse black wool, the pale yellow and violet of spring flowers, the dull brown of workaday cotton and the vivid red of silk ribbons.

The metal bender had come from Isigny, as he did several times a year. He was doing good business. Housewives queued with dented pots and farmers carried broken scythes and crooked plough blades. Children had gathered to watch the man shape metal between his fingers as easily as if it was butter.

Sounds swamped him: loud bargaining and bleating sheep and the giggling whispers of young girls, the apology of the housewife who brushed so busily past him, the exhortations of the pie-seller who thrust a steaming pasty beneath his nose.

Bastian inhaled deeply, tasting the market on his tongue. This place was alive, as Vere wasn't. It lived.

He was aware of the dogs, aware of images and impressions and a faint babble of sound nudging inside his head. Nothing was clear, not like with Endal. But Endal's voice had always been strong, even as a pup.

Usually he blocked the confusing blurs of sound and image from the other dogs, the yammers of excitement, but he missed Endal. Bastian's anger smouldered back to life. Endal should be at his heels, should be with him and not guarding that verminous wraith. His face twisted into a scowl. A young lad, a farmer's son by his garb, shied away from him.

But anger was impossible to maintain when Silvia's bakery was around the next corner. His hands unclenched. Three more steps, and then down the cobbled alley that led to the back. The buildings were made of gray stone, rough to touch, with steep slate roofs. Silvia's back door was open, the stone step scoured white. The open door and the shutters at the windows were painted blue, the color of the sky on a hot summer's day.

Bastian leaned against the doorframe and inhaled the scents of sugar and baking bread and stewing fruit. One of Silvia's shopgirls kneaded dough, the sleeves of her blouse rolled up and her hair tied back in a scarf. Voices came from the front of the shop, a woman's laughter.

The girl glanced up. Her face was freckled and alert. "Mistress Silvia," she called, not pausing in her kneading.

Bastian watched the girl's strong hands pull and twist the dough. Sweet dough, white and soft, to be filled with cinnamon and fruit and sprinkled with sugar crystals when it came out of the oven.

"Bastian."

Silvia stood in the arch that led through to the shop. Her apron was smudged with flour, her long hair hidden beneath a lavender blue scarf.

Bastian straightened away from the doorframe. She was beautiful, and he was hungry for her. Hungry for the warmth and softness of woman, for uncomplicated physical pleasure, for the ecstasy-pain of release.

Her mouth curved slightly. She wanted him too. He saw it in her eyes, in the tiny smile, in the way her hand rested lightly on the wall.

"Come upstairs," she said. "Elsa, you're in charge."

The kneading girl nodded. Her gaze flicked from Silvia to Bastian and he thought he caught something in her eyes. Not contempt or disdain, not condemnation, nothing like that. He crossed the kitchen and glanced back at the girl, puzzled. She was watching them, watching him.

Silvia's hand was on his arm, warm. "Come, Bastian," she said, her voice low.

Color rose in the girl's cheeks and she looked down at the dough.

He caught a glimpse of the shop—polished counter, a stout townsman handing coins to another of Silvia's employees in an apron and headscarf—as she pulled him into the corridor and toward the staircase. She was laughing softly.

"What?"

"My girls like you."

Bastian realized what he'd seen so fleetingly in the shopgirl's eyes: envy. Blood rose in his face.

Silvia laughed again. She paused on the second step, her eyes level with his. "That handsome face," she said. "Those eyelashes." She touched a light fingertip to the corner of his eye.

He followed her up the stairs to her bedroom, hot with embarrassment, hot with desire.

They undressed swiftly, pulling at clothes and discarding them on the floor. Silvia's mouth was as hungry as his was, kissing deeply. She was so soft and ripe and willing, sprawled on the bed, the lush, pale curves of her body so tempting that he couldn't take it slowly. "I'm sorry," he said, his voice harsh with need. "I can't—' And then he was inside the heat and softness of her. He shuddered and groaned and thrust deeply, and anger and fear were swallowed by passion, raw and urgent, and the pleasure built until he was bursting with it, and then it came, that high, sharp moment of release when nothing else mattered and everything was all right.

"I'm sorry," he said again, afterward, with his face pressed into her hair and his arm around her waist. The sheets were creased beneath him and his skin was hot and damp with sweat. A square of sunlight warmed his back.

"For what?"

"Too rough. Too fast."

"I liked it," Silvia said.

Bastian turned his head and opened his eyes. "You did?"

"It made me feel young again." She touched a finger lightly to the bridge of his nose. "You have such long eyelashes."

Young. Silvia was pretty, one of the prettiest women he'd seen, but there were lines at her mouth and eyes and gray strands in the curling blonde hair. He'd never asked how much older than him she was. Ten years, he guessed, but would never say so aloud.

"And besides, I know we're not finished yet." Her hand was on his shoulder now, sliding down his ribs, at his waist. She curved her fingers around one of his buttocks. "Are we?"

"No." Desire stirred inside him again.

This time Bastian took care to give as much pleasure as he received. He caressed her generous curves, the plumpness of her breasts and belly and hips. He stroked inside her with his fingers, making her tremble and arch her body and close her eyes in pleasure. A slow and laughing hour passed in the rumpled, sunlit bed. And at the end, there was another long moment of exquisite release.

They lay drowsily afterward. Bastian closed his eyes, enjoying the soft warmth of Silvia's body alongside him and the scent of sex, of male and female musk, of sweat.

He knew she had other men. She was a widow and pretty and lived alone; of course she had other lovers. The knowledge didn't bother him. He didn't care, as long as he could have moments like this, moments of contentment and utter relaxation.

Silvia sighed and sat up. "I must get back to work."

Bastian opened his eyes. He saw whitewashed walls and a low ceiling with rough beams. Bright sunlight came in through the window.

"Will you stay to lunch?" Silvia brushed her fingers through his hair.

Bastian thought of the long list Liana had given him, and of the wraith's tainted silver coins. His contentment evaporated. "No. I can't." The signet ring was suddenly heavy on his finger, reminding him of responsibility and Vere and the curse.

"Ah, well." She stroked his cheek lightly, then bent to place a kiss low on his abdomen. "You'll visit again."

"Of course." *Always.*

CHAPTER SIXTEEN

ASTIAN CHEWED THE last of the bun Silvia had given him. His feet had brought him to the watch house without him being truly aware of it. This was his usual routine in Thierry: an hour or two with Silvia, and then an ale with Michaud. While Liana stayed at home, with bone-dry dirt and sheep that slowly starved to death.

The bun became as tasteless as dust in his mouth. He swallowed and scowled at the watch house. It was built of gray stone and had a steep slate roof like the other buildings in Thierry, but the windows had thick iron bars as well as shutters. *Watch House* was carved into the stone above the door. *To protect and to serve justice*. And for those who couldn't read, the crown of Bresse and two crossed watch staves.

The heavy door stood open. Bastian took the shallow steps in two strides and stepped inside. He didn't have to call for Michaud. The watch captain stood in the middle of the room, tall and burly, his hands on his hips, frowning. At his feet was a brindle pup. The little creature cowered on the straw-covered floor. Every one of its ribs was visible.

Apart from man and dog, the large room was empty. No officers lounged at the long table in their hobnailed boots and thick leather jerkins, no drunks slept off a night's carousing in the four sparsely-furnished cells.

Michaud looked up. "Bastian." The frown on his bearded face became less fierce. He gestured at the pup. "Here, take this thing. I don't know what to do with it."

Bastian crouched. "I don't need another dog," he said, while his hands reached for the animal. *Hello, little one.*

The thin, trembling body squirmed in his grip and a wet tongue licked under his chin. He heard no words in his head, just a jumbled puppy-babble of fear and hunger and a desperate desire to please.

"Well, what do I do with it then?" Michaud said, exasperation in his voice. "I don't want it, Bastian. It pisses all over the floor and—"

Bastian stood. The pup shivered in his grip, warm and bony, anxious. *Don't be afraid, little one*, he told the animal. *No one will hurt you.* "He doesn't know any better," he said, walking across to the table and pulling out a chair. Both table and chairs were sturdy, the wood scarred and stained with use. "He'll learn not to. Although that straw is so dirty you'd scarcely notice if—"

"The straw was changed yesterday," Michaud said stiffly.

Bastian grinned, and stroked the pup. "So what will you name him?"

Michaud exhaled sharply through his nose. He folded his arms across his broad chest. "I'm not keeping it."

"Nonsense," said Bastian, as the pup's heart beat swiftly beneath his hand and jumbled eager-hopefulness pressed into his mind. "If you saved him, he's yours."

"I'd look ridiculous with a puppy trotting at my heels. I'm a watch captain, not a—"

Bastian laughed. The sound made the pup flinch. *Hush*, he soothed. "He'll be a big dog, maybe as big as Endal. Look at the size of his paws."

Michaud grunted sourly. "Where is that black beast of yours?"

"At Vere." Bastian lost his good humor. He stopped teasing Michaud. "Find a home for him. Someone must want a dog."

The watch captain grunted again. He walked across to the table and sat. The chain mail shirt under his leather jerkin clinked and the chair creaked beneath his weight. "Here, give it to me." The annoyance in his tone lacked conviction.

"He's hungry." Bastian watched as Michaud settled the pup against his chest, stroking the little creature with large, blunt-fingered hands. The brindle tail wagged tentatively. "Do you have any food?"

Michaud avoided his gaze. "I sent Vaspard out for a bowl of stew."

Bastian grinned at his friend. The watch captain grew the curling brown beard because it made him look fiercer, but underneath the leather jerkin and the chain mail beat a kind heart. "Been busy?" he asked.

Michaud shook his head. "Couple of tavern fights. Pickpocket at the market." He caught Bastian's glance at the empty cells, two on either side of the room. "Not today. Last week. A dockside kid. We kept him overnight." He yawned, showing strong white teeth. "Don't think he'll do it again. We scared the crap out of him."

Bastian nodded.

"And one of Widow Juneau's pigs is missing." Michaud jerked his head at the barrel in the corner of the room. "Have some ale."

The long list Liana had given him was folded in Bastian's pocket. The stiff, folded edges reproached him through his shirt. "I can't stay long."

"Half a mug of ale. Bring me one too."

Bastian grunted a laugh and pushed himself up from the chair. Straw scuffed beneath his boots as he walked around the table. Mugs and bowls and plates were stacked on a shelf. Used by prisoners and watchmen alike, they were scratched and dented and chipped.

He lifted the lid of the barrel and dipped two mugs inside. The ale was thick and dark, opaque, smelling of hops and malt. "A missing pig?" he said as he carried the mugs back, dripping.

"It'll be in someone's stewpot. We'll never find it."

Bastian jerked his head at the pup. "That's why you need a dog. Got good noses, dogs."

Endal had chased the wraith, unable to see her, through an afternoon and a night. Bastian clenched his jaw. "Your health," he said brusquely. He raised the mug and swallowed deeply.

Michaud grunted into his ale.

For a moment there was silence. The pup huddled against Michaud's chest, his nose pressed into the watch captain's armpit. Dust motes danced in the sunlight that slanted through the high, barred windows.

Michaud laughed into his mug, a choking sound. "Oh, and someone broke all the mayor's windows."

Bastian lowered his mug. "Was it you?" he asked. The question was only in jest.

"No." The watch captain shook his head, a frown settling on his face. He patted the pup absentmindedly. "Curse it, Bastian. We need to patrol in pairs at night! Particularly down by the docks. Fool of a man's going to get someone killed."

Bastian grunted his agreement.

Michaud rubbed the pup's ears. The thin tail wagged against his scarred leather jerkin. His scowl eased slightly.

Bastian drained the mug and set it on the table.

"And you?" Michaud asked. "Everything well at Vere?"

Bastian looked at his friend's face, square beneath the beard, determined. If he told Michaud the necklace was gone, that a wraith had stolen it, the watch captain would do his job. He glanced across at the cells and imagined the female wraith manacled there, with iron bands around her wrists and ankles. She wouldn't huddle in the corner, peering through her hair. She'd hold her head high and stare back at him, bold and feral, unrepentant. She would be marched to the capital, looking down her nose at the curious crowds, and be tried and exiled. The male wraith, her brother, would die from his injuries, probably on the straw-covered floor of the cell. He'd not last the journey to Desmaures.

They were filthy, lying thieves. Cells and manacles and exile was what they deserved, but the necklace would never be recovered and the psaaron's curse would grind to its inevitable conclusion. Bastian couldn't let that happen. Just as Michaud couldn't knock on the door of the salamanders' den and demand the necklace back. Magical creatures walked their own paths. The laws of men couldn't touch them. To do so would risk upsetting the balance of things.

"Everything's fine," he said.

Boots thudded on the steps outside. A figure momentarily blocked the door. "The stew, sir." It was Vaspard, the youngest of the watch recruits, his ginger hair shaved short.

Michaud put down his mug. He glanced at Bastian, his expression sheepish, and put the pup on the floor.

"Don't let him eat too much," said Bastian. "He'll be sick." Although that was what the straw was for, to soak up the blood and vomit and spittle of the drunks who were brought in.

"Another bowl," said Michaud. He snapped his fingers at Vaspard, who hurried to do his bidding.

Bastian bent to stroke the pup's soft ears. *You will be safe here*, he said. *They'll look after you.*

The pup looked up, his brown eyes trusting. He licked Bastian's hand and wagged his tail.

While Vaspard scooped a few spoonfuls of stew into an empty bowl, Bastian explained to the pup why relieving himself in the watch house was unacceptable. Yes, the straw was more comfortable, but the gutter outside were where he should do it. He wasn't sure the pup fully understood. "I'll try again next time," he told Michaud. "He's very young."

Michaud nodded, watching as the pup wolfed down the stew, the scrawny tail wagging furiously. His face was stern beneath the beard, as if he tried hard not to smile.

Bastian stood. "Good bye."

The watch captain nodded, his attention on the pup.

Bastian walked to the door, and paused. "What will you call him?"

There was a moment of silence. "Lubon," said Michaud gruffly.

CHAPTER SEVENTEEN

MELKE WIPED HANTJE'S face again with a cool cloth. The bruises showed as faint, gray blotches. His skin was red and shiny where the blistered burns had been. Liana had a strong gift to heal such injuries so quickly. The fever, though, was rising again.

She trickled water into his mouth. The torn lips were only slightly swollen. If he woke, he might even be able to open his eyes.

He wouldn't wake, though. Not today. She was no healer, but she knew that Hantje was deeply unconscious. He slept as if drugged, heavy and limp.

Melke put aside the cloth. "Well," she said to Endal. "Let us have another look."

Walking was less painful than it had been yesterday. Her feet healed, even without Liana's touch.

She climbed the stairs to her bedroom slowly, with Endal following behind.

Three of her stones lay on the little shelf. She picked them up and held them in her palm. Even the roughest stone was smooth to touch. She'd handled them so often, every day for years. *Home.* When she held them she smelled the flowers in the garden and the scent of baking bread in the kitchen, the leather and soap smell of Da and the warm, lavender scent of Mam's hair. She heard their voices, heard the wind in the fir trees behind the house. She was swooping through the air, laughing, Da's hands at her waist. She was standing at the stove with Mam, stirring spices into a stew. There was a cat rubbing against her leg, and Hantje was flying a kite in the meadow with Da, and she was *home.*

But the red stone was missing, the stone that meant standing on top of the hill with Da, that meant making gingerbread with Mam. The stone that was Hantje shrieking with laughter as he ran through the long grass and the scent of autumn bonfires and the sound of Tass barking at blowing drifts of leaves.

Melke put the stones back on the shelf. There was a knot of anxiety in her chest. She lifted her knapsack from its hook and emptied it on the bed, as she'd already done once this morning. Perhaps this time...

No.

She stripped the bed, shaking out the sheets and turning the pillowcase inside out, pulling the mattress off the bed and turning it over. Nothing. She searched the floor next, crawling on hands and knees, feeling in the shadows with her fingers.

Endal watched with his head cocked slightly to one side. Her heart was beating faster. She had to find it. Had to.

Hantje's knapsack then, although Moon only knew how the stone could be in there. No. Where else? Where could it be? It wasn't in the clothes she was wearing, wasn't anywhere in this room.

She lit a candle and searched the shadowy landing on hands and knees. Then the staircase, step by step. Endal followed. *What are you doing?* his pale eyes seemed to ask.

Melke blew out the candle and sat on the lowest step. The hound lay down at her feet. Her chest was tight and she was panting slightly. She wiped perspiration from her face, roughly, with the back of her hand. She couldn't have lost the stone. It was here somewhere. It had to be. *Had to be.*

The kitchen floor was next, every inch of the cool flagstones, the scullery, the pantry, the storeroom. Sweat trickled down her face and stuck the blouse to her skin. Her hands were dirty, her skirt streaked with dust. She rose stiffly to her feet and opened the door to the yard. The cart had stood there. Bastian had taken her knapsack, had carried it indoors and up the stairs and thrown it on the floor. The stone must be out here. There was nowhere else.

The yard was a bare expanse of hard-packed dirt. There were so many places a small stone could lie, covered in dust. *Impossible*, said a voice in her head.

Melke closed her eyes, and then opened them and stepped out into the yard.

The ground was rock-hard, dry and cracked and dusty. It was easiest to crawl on hands and knees, to feel with her fingers for something small and smooth. The sun beat down on her and sweat dripped from her face. *Please, Moon, I beg you. Let me find it.*

Endal sat in the shade of the doorway and watched, whining once when she caught his eye.

She could see where the cart had stood. There were marks in the dust. She searched, blurring those marks with her fingers, brushing her hands over the rough ground until the scabs cracked and her palms began to bleed.

The stone wasn't there. It wasn't anywhere.

Melke sat on the hard ground, her skin sticky with sweat and dust. She bowed her head into her hands.

Endal was a sudden, warm weight against her shoulder. She jerked her head up. His eyes were level with her own, wolf-pale, and she caught her breath in fear. Then he lay down, stirring the dust, and stretched out with his back pressed against her leg.

It was only a stone, the least of all things to lose, and yet she cried. It was home, and it was Mam and Da. It was the memory of happiness, of a time before soldiers and cells and fear, before she'd become a wraith.

Endal's warmth was comforting. "We had a hound," she whispered to him. He'd been the color of gingerbread, with gray hairs at his muzzle. The soldiers had killed him.

"His name was Tass," she told Endal. And she cried.

MELKE SAT WITH her brother while the morning ripened into a hot afternoon. The air in the sick-room became stuffy, despite the open window. Despair slowly filled the space inside her chest. She could hold Hantje's hand and wipe his face and trickle water into his mouth, but other than that she was helpless. His lips began to crack as the day wore on. His skin grew hotter.

"Don't you dare die," she whispered, and the hound pricked his ears. "Do you hear me, Hantje? Don't you dare."

Looming over her, a dark shadow, was the knowledge of what came. Spring equinox was one day closer than it had been yesterday. She counted the days in her head. Fourteen... no, fifteen days.

So soon. Too soon. *I can't do it.* And yet she had to, was going to. It was as inevitable as the next beat of her heart. She would enter the salamanders' den.

Hantje's breathing became more labored, his pulse fainter, as the shadows lengthened on the thin carpet. Melke's sense of helplessness grew until it was almost panic. Her relief was intense when she heard Liana's light footsteps. She turned her head and saw the girl standing in the doorway. "He grows worse," she said, an edge of desperation in her voice.

Liana came swiftly across the faded carpet, her eyes on Hantje. She laid a hand to his flushed cheek. "Yes," she said. "He does." She shook her head. "This fever feels wrong."

Melke released Hantje's hand and stood, giving the girl her seat. "Wrong? How?"

Liana laid her fingers on the weak pulse at the base of his throat. "It feels... how can I explain?" Her brow creased as she searched for words. "It feels as if there's something unnatural about it."

"Unnatural?"

"I think the infection comes from the salamanders. From their..." She gestured awkwardly.

Melke understood what the girl was trying to say. "From their scat."

Liana flushed at the bluntness of the words, and nodded. "Yes. Some part of it must have entered his blood." She took hold of Hantje's hand.

Melke knew there had to be punishment for stealing. To beat and burn a thief, *that* was punishment. To defecate on someone... the obsceneness of it turned her stomach. Such a degradation, so grotesque and abhorrent an act.

But salamanders didn't abide by human conventions; none of the magical creatures did. They walked their own paths, had their own right and wrong. And salamanders were cruel. It was part of their nature, as avarice and lust were. Cruelness shone in their flame-bright eyes and the scent of it rose, sharp and hot, from their skin.

"Will it kill him?"

Liana's hand tightened around Hantje's limp fingers. "I won't allow it."

Melke believed her. If anyone could purge the infection from Hantje's blood, the creeping filth that fuelled the fever, it would be this girl with her shining pale hair and her kindness.

"Thank you," she said.

Liana nodded, not looking up. Her attention was focussed on Hantje.

Melke looked down at her hands. New scabs were forming. There was still dust on her skirt, and she brushed at it. The second chair was empty. She could sit beside Liana and watch and be neither hindrance nor help, or... "Have you eaten?"

The girl shook her head, her eyes on Hantje's face. "No."

"Would you mind if I cooked?" There'd been no one to ask yesterday and she'd not dared to light the stove and make a meal. She was less than a guest in this house. Much less.

"Would you?" Liana glanced up. There was a note of relief in her voice. "Bastian won't be home until dark and he'll be too tired to—"

"Of course." To have a task eased some of the tension inside her. She was not completely useless. "Come, Endal."

The hound opened his eyes. He yawned.

How long until dusk? An hour? Two?

"Come, Endal," Melke said again, more briskly, and turned toward the door. She wanted to be out of the kitchen before Bastian returned. His hatred and the depth of his rage frightened her almost as much as the salamanders did.

CHAPTER EIGHTEEN

THE SUN WAS close to setting when Bastian reached the bridge. He paused and wiped sweat from his face. His legs were weary with walking. Gaudon nudged his shoulder and he put up a hand and rubbed the horse's smooth, warm cheek. "Almost home."

Home, where the grass was dead and the ground was cracked and it never rained. He sighed, and led Gaudon onto the bridge. The horse's saddle was laden with provisions.

Water rushed beneath the wooden planks, high and brown and dangerous. The wraith had swum in it and survived. He dared not; too many sal Veres had died in this river.

He heard the hiss of swift water and, beneath that, a creak of timber. Fear lifted the hair at the nape of his neck. Had the bridge just swayed?

He tightened his grip on Gaudon's reins and walked faster, pulling the horse, almost running. At the other side, with his feet on solid ground, he turned and looked back. The bridge was old, older than the curse. It had no straight lines. Sun and wind and the force of the river had roughened it, softened it.

He'd have to check. If the bridge fell...

It didn't bear thinking about. Bastian turned his back on the river. Tomorrow.

There was no Endal running to meet him, no Liana. The farmhouse might as well have been empty. Unease curled inside him, a shiver of fear. An empty house was somehow more terrible to come home to than a pile of rubble with Liana and Endal standing beside it. *I can cope with losing a house, I can't cope with losing...*

He couldn't say the words, couldn't even think them.

The sun sank behind the hills and the grays and purples of dusk thickened. Bastian unstrapped the purchases, removed the saddle, and rubbed Gaudon down, working fast. He drew water from the well. The sheep clustered around the trough, thirsty.

"Here," he said, slitting open the sack of grain he'd bought and cupping his hands full.

The sheep liked the grain. It was more than they would have eaten all day in their grazing. Bastian frowned. One, two... four sheep with round, awkward bellies. There was one missing.

He squeezed his eyes shut. *No. Not another one.*

Bastian opened his eyes and turned toward the meadows, but darkness was descending. Already he couldn't see the line of dead trees that marked the dry stream's course. It was too late to search. That was another task for tomorrow, and he knew what he'd find. He exhaled in frustration. Breath hissed between his teeth and the sheep shied away from him.

His mood was grim as he entered the kitchen, but wood burned in the stove and the smell of food made his stomach growl. The house wasn't empty; he was home.

It took only a few minutes to unpack the provisions he'd bought. The storeroom and pantry, if not full, were at least no longer empty. He hefted the bundle of medicines in his hand and caught the herb scent of them faintly.

Liana was in the sickroom. So were the wraith and Endal. The dog opened his eyes. Bastian made a staying gesture with his hand. *No,* he whispered in his mind. *Don't move.*

Endal whined silently, inside his skull.

Bastian's mouth tightened. If not for the wraith he'd walk into the bedchamber and hug Liana, would let Endal jump in enthusiastic greeting. She had watched once and he hadn't cared, but tonight he didn't want her to see him bare so much of himself.

He stood in the shadows of the doorway, quiet. Candles were lit in the room. Liana's hair shone white, and the wraith's was black and gleaming. For a fraction of a second, the flicker of an eyelid, he saw her as a woman, with rounded breasts beneath her blouse and soft hair and smooth, pale skin.

He shook his head angrily. Liana was a woman, Silvia was a woman, the serving girl at Ronsard's was. The wraith was a... a *creature.*

They looked like friends, Liana and the wraith, sitting so closely together. He didn't like it at all. It was intensely wrong, as if the wraith's evil could somehow infect Liana. His fingers clenched around the parcel in his hand. *Get out of my house, wraith*, he wanted to shout. *Get out!*

Bastian turned on his heel. He stalked back to the kitchen and the mouth-watering smell of food.

The meal consisted of potato and onion only; it was all that had been in the storeroom. But the potatoes were golden and crisp, the onion spicy. He filled his plate a second time, and a third.

He'd taught Liana how to boil potatoes and chop and fry onions, how to grind spices with a mortar and pestle. She had stood alongside him on a stool and watched with serious eyes, and when she was tall enough to reach the stove without standing on the stool, he'd let her cook.

Now she cooked better than he did.

The world was less bleak with food in his belly. The tension in his muscles, the knots of anger and frustration and fear, loosened and relaxed. Memory of Silvia coiled warmly inside him and softened the sharp edges of the day: the creaking bridge, the missing sheep, the wraith.

"Bastian."

He looked up from his plate. "Liana." Wood scraped on stone as he pushed the chair back.

"I was worried. It's dark and I thought you weren't back."

"I'm sorry. I didn't want to disturb you." A small lie only, but it was unsettling how easily it came to his tongue. The wraith's fault.

He hugged Liana. It was always like this when he held her: the awareness of how delicate she was, of how much he loved her and to what lengths he'd go to protect her. He'd rocked her to sleep as a baby, had held her hand while she learned to walk, had picked her up when she'd fallen and wiped away the tears, had watched her grow.

His need to protect her was a primitive thing, instinctive. It went beyond thought and reason. In this he was like Endal, an animal, not a man. *I won't let the psaaron harm you.*

He released her. "How fares your patient?"

The smile on Liana's face died. "Not well."

"I have the medicines." The cloth-wrapped bundle lay on the table.

He sat while Liana untied the string and peeled back the cloth. "This is delicious," he said, scooping food on his fork and raising it to his mouth. "Where did you find the spices? I thought we hadn't any left."

"Melke made it." Liana opened a jar of salve and sniffed it. "Perfect. Just what I—"

Bastian spat out his food and pushed the plate away from him. It fell off the edge of the table. The sound of pottery smashing on stone was loud. His chair tumbled over as he stood and the candles flared sharply in the draft of his movement. "What? She did *what?*"

Liana's eyes were wide with astonishment, the jar of salve still held to her nose.

"I will not have that thing cooking my food!"

Liana put down the salve. "Bastian."

It was one word, spoken as if he was the child and she the adult.

His cheeks flushed hot. "I will *not*—"

"I haven't the time. If you want to eat, you'll let Melke cook."

"*I'll* cook," he said stiffly.

"You haven't the time either."

He pushed aside thought of the dead sheep, the bridge. "I'll make the time."

"Bastian."

Again that tone of voice. He clenched his jaw.

"Melke wants to help. Let her."

"No," Bastian said, stubbornly. He sounded like a child. He heard it.

"You liked her cooking. Don't you think—"

"No." He jutted his chin and narrowed his eyes. He wasn't going to back down on this.

Liana sighed. There were shadows on her face, cast by candlelight. "Bastian, please."

He had lost. The instant he heard the sigh, the plea in her voice, he knew he'd lost.

The tallow candles flickered softly in the dark kitchen. Morsels of food speckled the table where he'd spat them. The chair lay at his feet. "Fine!" Bastian flung up his hands in a sharp gesture. "Fine! If that's what you want!"

Liana's smile was grateful. She stood on tiptoe and kissed his cheek. The rosemary scent of her hair lingered briefly in his nostrils. "Thank you, Bastian."

He couldn't make himself say anything in return.

"I have to get back." She picked up the open bundle of medicines with both hands.

He nodded, and watched her go. The wraith would be cooking his food. He wanted to vomit.

CHAPTER NINETEEN

IT TOOK BASTIAN the best part of the morning to find the dead sheep. The lamb's nose pushed from the ewe. The tongue protruded, swollen and purple. Flies swarmed obscenely over it.

Bastian closed his eyes as bile rose in his throat. He might have been able to save this one, to have eased the lamb back inside and pulled it out by the forelegs. Instead, a nose, a tongue.

And I was bedding Silvia. The fault was his.

There was no Endal to make the moment bearable. It wasn't even possible to tell himself that it would be all right in the end, because deep inside himself he was afraid it wouldn't. No necklace lay coiled in the chest under his bed. He had nothing to give the psaaron when it came.

Everything rested on a sly and deceitful wraith. She'd given her word of honor, but what was that worth?

The curse might never be broken. Never.

Something swift and sinuous darted inside him. A wish. A hope. What if the curse wasn't broken…?

Weight lifted off his shoulders. No farm to rebuild, no responsibility. Freedom.

What if he left? What if he just took Liana and left?

For a moment there was soaring lightness, and then guilt twisted inside him. His parents had died for Vere. They'd *died*.

Rage at himself, at the wraith, at life, fuelled Bastian as he dug into the iron-hard dirt, jarring wrists and shoulders and neck, tearing open the blisters on his palms.

The sweat and pain didn't erase the guilt. Nothing could. He was sick with himself, at himself. When the sheep was buried he threw the shovel aside and wiped his face with a gritty forearm. There was a trembling inside him. Not tears. Never tears.

His father had cried—

Bastian shut his eyes. "No," he said out loud. He wouldn't remember, *refused* to remember.

The bridge was easier to deal with than the sheep. It was inanimate, had never lived. Bastian walked slowly, testing each board with his feet, not putting his full weight on the planks until he was certain they'd bear him. Some creaked, some didn't. He didn't test the railings. If they gave way he'd not survive the water.

He stood in the center, with his feet apart and his eyes half-closed. Yes, there was movement. The bridge swayed slightly to the tug of the river.

Bastian closed his eyes fully and pinched the bridge of his nose. *Not this. Not now.*

On the far side, the side where the soil was moist and the plants grew lush and green, he slid down the bank and looked at the bridge from underneath. The structure was simple: one wooden pile, with the river parting in a foamy wake around it.

It seemed to him that the pile yielded to the push of water. He saw the strain of the wood. It looked ready to snap and be swept away.

He shook his head. *No*. But the truth was there to see.

How long until the river ripped the pile free? How long before the bridge buckled and fell?

Soon.

There was a ford four miles downstream that he dared not use. The water would swallow him. Arnaul's bridge was the only safe way across the river. Eight miles upstream. Eight long miles.

If the wraith kept her word, if he had the necklace to give to the psaaron, if the curse was lifted... There'd still be no money to rebuild the bridge. It was utterly beyond his means.

Bastian turned his back to the river. The weight of Vere pressed down on him. He'd never be free of it. It would bury him.

Something lay hidden in the ferns. He saw a gray that was neither stone nor timber. Bastian frowned. He crouched, pushing the curling green fronds aside and felt the weave of fabric beneath his fingertips. A cloak, woollen, folded neatly. Beneath that was a small sack with something inside.

Bastian pulled the sack free of its hiding place, undid the drawstring, and tipped it upside down. Half a loaf of bread, dark and heavy and speckled with mold, fell out. A bladder of water, its belly soft and bulging. A folded piece of parchment.

He opened the parchment and spread it on the ground. It was a map. The two closest towns were marked, the crossroads, the salamanders' den, the river, Vere.

Rage blurred his vision.

CHAPTER TWENTY

I N A SMALL earthenware pot stamped with an apothecary's mark was a salve to reduce the swelling and the bruising. It was the color of pale sand, fawny, and smelled of herbs. Melke replaced the lid.

For the burns Liana had prepared a bowl of liquid, the juice of fresh ginger root. It would ease the inflammation if applied to Hantje's skin, she said. The scent was strong in the room.

"And this tea will help bring the fever down. He must drink as much as you can give him."

The teapot was warm. Melke lifted the lid and sniffed. "Peppermint?"

"And elderflower and yarrow flower."

Melke nodded.

"And this will help the bones knit. Comfrey. He should drink this too."

She nodded a second time.

"If you need me..."

"I'll wake you."

Liana smiled wearily.

"Sleep well," Melke said.

But Liana seemed reluctant to leave, despite the dark smudges of fatigue beneath her eyes. She bent and cupped her hand to Hantje's cheek.

Despair, and an honorable heart. Melke knew that was what the girl felt when she touched Hantje. An honorable heart. How could that be? He'd crept into the salamanders' den, had tried to steal. And because of that creeping, that attempt at thievery, this girl exhausted herself healing him and the curse might never be lifted. Someone would be hurt dreadfully, Liana or Bastian, and the farm would die, and the psaaron would lose its family's tears forever.

How could you, Hantje? We promised we'd never be wraiths.

There was a knot of anger inside her. Had he learned nothing from the years of imprisonment? Didn't he remember Mam dying? The splintering *thwack* of the crossbow bolt in her back, the sound that came from her mouth and the way her body fell. Didn't he remember the promise he'd made?

Folded into the anger was grief, and guilt, because she knew why he'd done it. A man would do anything if his despair was great enough. *I failed you, Hantje. I didn't see what lay behind your smile and your jokes.*

She would make it right for Hantje and for this girl. She'd undo the harm. If it was possible.

Liana straightened from the bed.

Melke managed a smile. "Sleep well," she said again.

The girl nodded. Her eyes were already half-closed, half-asleep. She turned toward the door.

Melke reached for the bowl of pungent juice. It was a relief to be able to do something for Hantje. The salve, the ginger root, the teas. She felt less useless, more hopeful, as if the small things she did gave him greater chance of recovery.

Morning became afternoon, and she opened the window wide. Heat shimmered from the parched dirt outside. The grass was colorless, so dry it should burst into flame in the sunlight.

Rain would never fall here if she didn't steal back the necklace.

Eyes of flame. The heavy scent of musk. Darkness. Heat.

Melke shivered and turned away from the window. "Come, Endal. Time to cook dinner."

Endal rose to his feet and shook himself. His pale eyes were alert. Her limping walk wasn't fast enough for him. She sensed him behind her, almost pressing into her skirt. He wanted to stretch his legs, to be outside.

Poor creature. He was caged, guarding her. She should tell Bastian that the hound's presence was unnecessary, that she wouldn't run.

But Bastian would laugh at her and disbelieve. And why not? She was a wraith, after all. Untrustworthy, dishonest. All the tales said so.

"I didn't ask for it," she said to the hound. "I didn't want to be a wraith."

Endal looked at her, his ears pricked, alert.

Melke sighed and unlatched the storeroom door. The room was fragrant with smoked ham and strong cheese and fresh herbs. Hunger stirred in her stomach. She looked at the items on the shelves, in the sacks, and made her decision. Potatoes again, and ham, and... there was a bunch of rosemary, tied with twine, but no chives. Were there some in the garden?

Endal bounced on his paws and shook himself as they stepped outside. He had the look of a puppy about him. He wanted to run and play. "Here," she said, walking to the woodpile on throbbing feet. "Chase this."

She threw a stick and watched it curve in the air and fall. Dust puffed up from the ground. "Go on," she said, pointing. "It's yours."

Endal's playfulness was gone. He stood stiff-legged and motionless, watching her through narrow wolf-eyes. His black coat shimmered in the sunlight. His hackles weren't raised, his teeth not bared, but it was close, very close. Melke almost heard a growl.

She felt no fear, only disappointment. Her hand fell to her side. "Fine," she said, and turned her back on him. Her jaw was tight. The bare dirt burned through the grubby bandages on her feet.

No hens roosted in the henhouse. Its emptiness looked old, as if it had been years since birds had last laid eggs there. The plants in the garden withered. It was spring and there should be unfurling shoots and vigorous growth, greenness. Instead, brown-edged leaves curled in on themselves. She could see at a glance that the peas would never grow plump, nor the beans.

Melke touched fingertips to her forehead and closed her eyes. Someone had tried here. The soil was tilled, the plants carefully spaced.

She could water the garden.

Melke opened her eyes and stepped toward the well, and stumbled to a halt. Endal stood in front of her. The piece of wood lay between them. He wagged his tail.

For a moment she couldn't move, couldn't do anything more than blink. Something eased slightly in her chest.

"So you want to play."

Endal shifted his weight, impatient. His eyes were on her. He whined. She needed no gift to know that he was telling her to hurry up.

Melke experienced the urge to laugh, an unfamiliar emotion. She bent and picked up the stick. "Ready?"

He was running before she threw it, muscles moving smoothly and strongly beneath his black coat, his tail flying high.

She watered the garden while Endal chased the stick with enthusiasm, bringing it back to her repeatedly, panting, his tongue hanging from his mouth.

There were chives, but they were thin and pallid. Melke poured water on them carefully and took none. This garden barely survived. She'd use peppercorns and other spices to flavor the meal.

Endal lay in the open doorway and chewed the stick while she peeled potatoes. There was a song in her head. She hummed it under her breath as she grated the potatoes and mixed them with spices, as she formed thin, round fritters and fried them in hot fat. It was one of Mam's songs. *If I turn my head I'll see her. She'll be standing beside me, singing.*

Mam had loved to cook, and when she cooked, she sang. Even in the fort, when their rooms had been a prison and the door was barred and guarded, she had cooked and sung. The argument with the guards had been loud, but Mam had won. No meals from the fort kitchen, but a skillet and stewing pot and fresh provisions. And Mam had knelt at the hearth and cooked, and sung.

I miss you, Mam. I wish you were here.

She heard hard footsteps outside and the crunch of dry dirt beneath a man's boots. Bastian. The hummed song died in her throat. For a moment breathing was impossible. She stood stiff, frozen, the spatula clasped in rigid fingers.

Hold your head high, Mam had said. *Never let them see how much you fear them.*

She saw him out of the corner of her eye. He filled the doorway, the top of his head almost brushing the lintel. Endal was on his feet, pressing close to Bastian, wagging his tail and making eager noises in his throat. The stick lay forgotten on the floor.

Melke stood as tall as she could. She placed another fritter in the cast-iron skillet, not flinching as the hot fat hissed and spat.

"I found something of yours." Bastian's voice was flat.

Tension loosened in her chest. The red stone. A smile gathered inside her. She turned her head and looked at him fully.

The sun was bright behind Bastian and for a moment all she saw of his face were shadows. Then his features became clear, the jut of jaw and cheekbones and nose, the hardness of mouth and eyes. The rage.

He was furious. She could almost taste the bitterness of his anger on her tongue, could almost feel the heat of it on her skin.

Melke's heart gave a loud, frightened beat. Hairs pricked upright at the back of her neck, on her arms. The smile inside her evaporated as swiftly as a drop of water on a red-hot skillet. In its place was fear, knotting beneath her breastbone.

Charcoal gray fabric was clenched in one hand, a sack in the other.

She understood Bastian's anger. She didn't need to be told.

Don't cower. Stand tall. Never let them see your fear. Melke raised her chin. "Yes," she said. "Those are mine." There was no quaver in her voice, despite the trembling inside her. Cool and polite. Mam's voice, when the guards bullied and blustered.

She was holding herself so tightly still that she didn't flinch when he threw the items on the floor. The sack hit the flagstones with a soft smacking sound, spilling its contents. The bread tumbled out, rolling almost to her feet.

Melke met his eyes. She couldn't see their color with the sun behind him. He deserved an apology, but there was nothing in his face that made it possible. Too much anger, too much hatred. A mercenary's face, implacable and without compassion. The face of a man capable of hurting, of killing. He wanted more than words of apology. He wanted things she couldn't—*wouldn't*—give him: blood, tears, abasement.

"Thank you," she said politely.

She'd said the wrong thing. She knew before she heard the indrawn hiss of his breath and saw the rage bloom more fiercely on his face. He moved slightly in the doorway, fisting his hands, leaning forward, a threat so silent and strong that she almost put up a hand to ward it off.

Hackles raised along Endal's spine. His wolf-eyes pinned her. He growled low in his throat.

Melke's heart beat faster. "You mistake my words," she said, clutching the spatula tightly. "I had no intention of mocking."

She saw the astonished flicker of Bastian's eyelids. His air of menace wavered slightly, a tiny moment of uncertainty, of surprise. The fat crackled and spat in the pan, and the smell—

"Excuse me." She turned hastily back to the stove, to the fritter and the hot fat.

Awareness of Bastian prickled over her skin as she laid down the spatula and reached for the tongs, as she turned the fritter and placed another one beside it in the pan. There was no song in her head, no soft, almost-heard voice. Mam had gone. She was alone.

Bastian didn't move. She was aware of him at the edge of her vision, aware of menace and rage and bafflement. Perspiration beaded on her skin. The hairs were still upright on her arms and at the nape of her neck. Her breathing was shallow, her heartbeat fast. She kept her movements calm and deliberate, unafraid.

When she put down the tongs and turned her head, Bastian still stood in the doorway. His arms were crossed over his chest and his face was closed, hard. Endal sat. His coat lay smoothly over his shoulders and down his spine. His attention was on the bread.

"Are there any other items that I should expect to find?" Sarcasm was ugly in Bastian's voice.

Fear stopped Melke from blushing. It was impossible for blood to rise in her face when she was so afraid.

The stone, whispered a voice in her head. *Ask him.*

She dared not.

Mam would have asked.

Melke gathered her courage. She lifted her chin. "Actually, yes."

Bastian's face tightened and his eyes narrowed. He uncrossed his arms. His hands were clenched.

"A stone," she said, holding on to her courage. "A red one, quite small." She showed him with forefinger and thumb. "Did you see it in the cart?"

His laugh was hard and loud. "A stone?"

She'd not meant to mock him earlier, but he was clearly mocking her now. Heat mounted in her cheeks. It seemed she was less afraid of him than she thought; she could blush when the insult was great enough.

Melke turned back to the stove and the pan of fat. "Yes," she said. Pride made her voice cold, however hot her cheeks were. "A stone."

"It has value." The words were flat.

She picked up the spatula, keeping her back to him. "No. It has no value. But I have lost it. Have you seen it?"

Bastian laughed again, a loud, harsh sound of disbelief. "A stone? No, I have not seen it. But I shall take care to look for it." The contempt in his voice was so sharp that it almost cut into her skin.

Melke stood with her back tall and straight. *Fool. Why did you ask?*

Because of Mam and Da, because of Tass. Because of home.

"Thank you," she said, her tone polite, her cheeks hot. If he chose to think she was mocking him for his rudeness this time, he was correct.

She heard the indrawn hiss of his breath again and felt the menace of his anger brush over her. There was silence, while fear crawled up her spine, and then she heard the crunch of his footsteps outside in the dry yard.

Melke was able to close her eyes then, and to bow her head.

When she opened her eyes the fritters were burned and Endal was chewing the loaf of bread.

CHAPTER TWENTY-ONE

DESPITE THE MINTY tea, Hantje's temperature rose. He lay corpse-like, his face flushed with fever, his pulse and breathing faint. Liana entered the room as the dark shadows of evening fell. Her smile faded when she saw Hantje, and faded further when she bent over him and touched her fingers to his throat.

Melke rose from the chair, anxiety making her arms and legs stiff. "He's no worse than he's been, surely?"

"No worse," the girl said, sitting swiftly. "But no better either." She glanced up. "It will kill him if it continues like this. He wastes away. He can't drink enough, can't eat—"

"I gave him the tea."

"I know," Liana said. "But it's not enough. A natural fever can be healed. This…" She shook her head and picked up Hantje's limp hand. "I must try harder." Tiredness marked her face. She was paler than she'd been three days ago, thinner. She looked fragile, breakable.

What was Hantje's life worth? When did the cost become too great?

"Liana." Melke waited until the girl looked fully at her. "Don't give too much of yourself. Please. Don't harm yourself." *We're only wraiths. We're not worth your life.* "I'll try to recover the necklace, whatever happens."

Liana's grip on Hantje's hand tightened. "I know you will. But I have to try."

"He wouldn't want you to give your life for him."

"I know," the girl said softly, her voice little more than a whisper. Her gaze slid to Hantje's face. "I know."

"Please—"

Liana glanced up and met her eyes. "I'll be careful."

There was nothing more Melke could say. She nodded. "Have you eaten?"

Liana shook her head.

"I'll bring some food." Melke reached for a candle. She'd pile the plate high and make sure the girl ate every mouthful. She'd—

"Oh! Wait."

She halted.

"This is for you." Liana held something out. She flushed slightly. "I forgot this morning. I'm sorry."

Melke took the object automatically. A tiny earthenware pot. She opened it. "Salve?"

"For your feet. I'm sorry. I meant to—"

"For me?" Those two words were all she was capable of uttering. Sudden tears choked in her chest and throat and stung her eyes. *For me?*

"They'll heal more quickly. And it will help with the pain."

Melke nodded dumbly, the little pot clutched in her hand. The girl's kindness overwhelmed her. *I don't deserve this. I am a thief.* "Thank you," she managed to say. Her throat was tight, her voice rough.

It occurred to her, as she limped down the corridor, that Liana's motive wasn't kindness. If her feet didn't heal, she wouldn't be able to steal back the necklace before the psaaron came.

CHAPTER TWENTY-TWO

BASTIAN ATE DINNER in his bedchamber. If he saw that wraith again today he'd—

Rage and hunger grumbled in his belly. She'd been as proud as a queen, looking down her nose at him, mocking him. He snarled silently in memory and speared ham on his fork.

He had sworn not to eat her food, those cursed potato things she'd been cooking, but the smell of them... One. He'd taken one.

Bastian cut a piece and lifted it to his mouth, sneering at it. He'd spit it out if he didn't like it. He'd take it outside and grind it into the dirt with his heel.

The scent of it, the crispness, the delicate spices on his tongue...

Bastian closed his eyes. He hated the wraith, *hated* her.

He went downstairs and helped himself to more fritters. Anger churned inside him. Anger at her, at himself. Curse her for cooking so well.

Four. No, five fritters.

CHAPTER TWENTY-THREE

PERHAPS IT WAS the salve, perhaps not, but Melke's feet hurt less in the morning. She went downstairs without limping. The sick-room was dark. Her heart constricted. "Liana?"

There was silence.

Melke crossed the room with outstretched hands. Panic spurted inside her as she fumbled for the curtains and drew them hurriedly back. "Liana?" she said again, turning toward the bed.

The girl sat slumped and motionless, her head resting on Hantje's shoulder.

Melke's heart thudded fast in her chest. She shook the girl's arm. "Liana!"

Liana sighed, a soft and drowsy sound. She didn't move.

Melke knelt on the worn carpet and felt for the girl's pulse. Endal pressed close, whining. He sniffed Liana and licked her cheek.

A pulse, yes, strong and regular.

Melke sat back on her heels. The girl's face was smooth of care. She was no paler than she'd been last night. "Liana," she said again, without the edge of panic in her voice.

Hantje muttered.

Melke stood hastily and looked at him. There was a difference in how he lay, how he breathed. The deep and unnatural stillness was gone. He was close to waking.

Weight sloughed off her shoulders. Hantje was going to be all right.

"Liana." She bent and shook the girl gently.

Liana smiled faintly and sighed again. Her breathing was calm. It was a sleep of exhaustion, nothing to worry about.

Melke rubbed her face, looking down at the girl. She couldn't carry Liana upstairs. She hadn't the strength.

"Where is your master?" she asked the hound.

He looked at her uncomprehendingly.

Melke went back to the kitchen and out into the yard. It helped that she could walk without limping. There'd be no weakness for Bastian to see, no vulnerability.

She narrowed her eyes against the pale glare of morning sunshine and looked around. An old horse stood in a barren paddock, flicking its tail, shaded by a dead tree. There was no other movement. Bastian was nowhere in sight.

Melke took a deep breath and set her jaw. *Stand tall. Show no fear.* "Find Bastian," she said to Endal.

The hound's ears pricked and his tail lifted slightly. He understood those words.

She followed him out of the yard. His pace was brisk, the angle of tail and ears jaunty. He was eager to see his master.

The thin strips of cloth that bound her feet were no substitute for leather. Stones pressed through the bandages, sharp. Melke walked slowly. Her shoes had vanished in the river. She'd need new ones if she was to enter the salamanders' den.

If? When. There was no doubt. It was something she was going to do.

Musk and flaming eyes and heat.

The hairs at the nape of her neck rose and she shivered. *Fool*, she told herself. There were no salamanders here. Nothing to fear.

Endal wanted to run, to bound ahead and stretch his legs. He waited for her, telling her to hurry up with the angle of his ears and tail, with his edgy, restless stance.

"How much further?" she asked, glancing back over her shoulder. They were almost quarter of a mile from the farmhouse. The sun beat down and the dirt was hot beneath her feet. Perspiration pricked on her skin.

The ground rose slightly. She heard the sound of an axe. *Thock. Thock.* Sharp noises, the thud-split of wood being chopped. Bastian.

A week ago she would barely have noticed this gentle rise. Her steps would have been fast and striding; now she climbed slowly, fighting the urge to wince, to limp. The bandages were beginning to fray.

Endal waited at the top, impatient. Melke paused and wiped her face with a sleeve. In front of her the ground dipped again. Wisps of brittle grass straggled from the dry dirt. At the foot of the short slope a tree lay fallen, shorn of branches. The wood was the same pale gray as the soil, dead.

Bastian had discarded his shirt. A sheen of sweat glistened on his sun-browned skin. He had a fighter's body, hard and strongly muscled. He'd be able to wield sword and mace and lance easily, to kill. A mercenary's face, and a body to match.

The hairs pricked at the nape of Melke's neck again. She squared her shoulders and stood tall.

Bastian didn't look up. He raised the axe. Sunlight glinted off the blade. She heard it whistle through the air and flinched at the sound it made—*thock*—and the sharp splitting of the wood.

Melke opened her mouth and found that Bastian's name was impossible to utter. What lay between them was too hostile.

She swallowed. "Excuse me," she said, but the axe went *thock* again and he didn't hear her.

Endal trotted down the slope.

Bastian turned before the hound reached him. Endal had made no sound, but somehow the man knew he was there. There was a moment of silence, while hound and man looked at each other, and then Bastian's eyes lifted to her.

His grip on the axe handle tightened. She saw his knuckles whiten. The expression on his face was ferocious. "What's wrong with Liana? Endal says she won't wake up."

Melke fought the urge to step backwards. "She's exhausted." Her voice didn't betray her. There was no hint of fear.

Bastian flung the axe aside and reached for his shirt. He came fast up the slope. Dirt and grass crunched beneath his boots.

Never let them see your fear.

Melke stood her ground. "There's no cause for alarm. She's deeply asleep, is all."

He was level with her now. She felt the heat of his body, of his rage, of his fear for Liana. He leaned toward her. His lips drew back from his teeth in a snarl. "She's *my* sister. *I'll* decide whether there is cause for alarm. Not *you*."

Melke saw the green of his eyes, narrowed in hatred, and smelled the fresh sweat on his skin. He could kill her. She had no doubt of that. It would be easy for him to clench his fingers around her throat and choke the life out of her, to snap her neck.

Never let them see.

"As you wish." She trembled inside herself, but her voice came out coolly, politely.

Anger darkened his face and he made a sound that was part snarl, part growl. The animal savagery of it made her flinch slightly from him.

Triumph flared in Bastian's eyes. His laugh was hard. He turned sharply away from her and strode toward the farmhouse, shrugging into his shirt.

For a long moment Melke couldn't move, couldn't breathe. She stood, hugging her arms tightly, holding herself, and watched him walk away. Tears pricked her eyes. She had flinched. She had let Bastian see that she feared him.

Melke forced herself to follow him. She didn't want to. She wanted to turn her back on the farmhouse and leave, to flee. The trembling inside her was stronger. She shook deeply, within her chest.

There was agitation, and something more than agitation, something that was close to hysteria.

She had let him see her fear.

Endal trotted to keep pace with his master. They were a hundred yards ahead of her when they reached the farmhouse. The man didn't look back, but the hound stopped and waited. He wanted to be with Bastian; she saw it in the way he shifted his weight. His coat gleamed in the sunlight, intensely black.

Endal didn't follow her into the kitchen; he pushed ahead and led the way down the corridor to the sickroom.

Melke made herself enter, made herself stand closer to Bastian than she wanted to and not show her fear again.

Bastian ignored her. She heard him say the girl's name softly, "Liana." He stroked her hair, her cheek. His touch was gentle.

It was a different man, this, to the one who'd just growled at her, who'd shaken her and spat at her outside the salamanders' den. There was no savagery and rage, only tenderness. He loved Liana. She'd seen it in the way he'd greeted her three days ago, lifting her off her feet and holding her tightly, as if she was precious, his face pressed into her hair.

Melke watched as Bastian carefully gathered his sister in his arms. When he turned toward her, he no longer had a mercenary's face. It was a strong face, but not the face of a killer.

Melke raised her chin and met his eyes. She stood as tall as she could.

His jaw tightened, but his glare was soft. Having Liana in his arms muted his rage.

Endal followed him to the door and whined as he left. She knew what he said to Bastian: *Take me with you.*

The sound of Bastian's footsteps faded. Endal's tail drooped. He sat down heavily on the floor.

Melke crossed to the bed. The sunlight was brighter in the room now that Bastian was gone, the air easier to breathe. She laid a hand on her brother's cheek, a touch as gentle as Bastian's had been. She said his name softly, "Hantje."

Her brother stirred. She thought his eyelids flickered. He was close to waking. Close to being able to tell her what had happened in the salamanders' den.

HANTJE CONTINUED TO improve as the day slid into afternoon. He no longer lay still and silent. He shifted in the bed, turning his head, muttering. Emotions twisted across his face. He quieted when Melke held his hand and spoke to him. She told him stories, the ones Mam had read when they were children, struggling to recall the words.

The morning's tension slowly faded. She no longer shook inside herself. Hantje would live. That was all that mattered.

She roasted the potatoes this time, with cracked peppercorns and salt and sprigs of rosemary. She didn't have to be in the kitchen so much, didn't have to risk encountering Bastian. *Coward*, she told herself. Mam would have been disappointed.

CHAPTER TWENTY-FOUR

E NDAL LEANED AGAINST his leg, warm. His tail beat softly in the dust. Bastian frowned, and rubbed the dog's ears. There was a song. It had been nudging inside his head, half-remembered, while he watched the wraith unpeg washing from the line. Something about ebony and ivory. The minstrels sang it at the summer fairs. How did it go?

Ivory-white is her skin, and ebony-black her hair,
And her lips, oh, her lips,
As red as rubies, as sweet as honey.
And when she kisses me, oh, when she kisses me...

Bastian stopped rubbing Endal's ears. He spat into the dirt and glowered at the wraith. She was a

woman. He saw that clearly now: the soft round-
ness of breasts beneath her blouse, the smooth
skin, the long, shining hair.

A woman. A wraith.

He snarled at her silently, and she turned and
caught him with his lips peeled back from his
teeth.

She didn't recoil, as she'd done when he startled
her yesterday. Her chin lifted slightly. There was no
trace of fear in her face, in the way that she stood.

That was the line he'd forgotten. *My love has
eyes as brilliant as the sky, as deep as the ocean.*

The wraith didn't have blue eyes. Hers were
gray. The color of smoke and stone and ashes.

He almost spat into the dirt again.

"Yes?" Her voice was haughty.

He wasn't going to tell her that he'd needed to
feel Endal's warmth, had needed to pat the dog and
rub his ears. "Nothing," he said, and his voice
matched hers in coldness.

He saw disdain on her face as she walked past
him, the basket of dry laundry in her arms, and his
fingers tightened in Endal's coat.

Endal whined slightly.

Bastian released his grip. *Forgive me. I didn't
mean to hurt you.* And then he said it aloud, for
she was out of earshot. "Forgive me, Endal."

Endal licked his hand.

The wraith entered the kitchen. Endal stood and
shook himself. *Must I still guard her?* His tone was
hopeful.

"Yes," Bastian said firmly.

Endal sighed, and trotted across the yard. He
paused at the door and glanced back.

I know, Bastian told him silently. *I wish you could be with me too.*

Endal sighed again, inside Bastian's head, and followed the wraith into the kitchen.

DUSK WAS CREEPING over the hills by the time the last of the firewood was stacked beside the henhouse. Bastian tipped his head back and stood for a long moment with his eyes closed. His arms ached from chopping, from carrying. His skin was sticky with sweat and gritty with dust. Thirst hurt in his throat.

He opened his eyes and stared up at the darkening sky. Blue shaded into lavender. The palms of his hands stung. He looked down at them. The blisters were bloody. Too many graves dug, and the chopping on top. He always gripped the axe handle hard now, too hard, but memory of last year's accident was still vivid: the handle slipping in his grasp, the blade biting into his leg. There'd been no pain at first. The shock had been too great.

Bastian shuddered. But for Liana...

He closed his hands and felt the sharp, raw pain of the blisters. There was more wood to be chopped, but perhaps no more graves. While he had grain the sheep would be penned here, close to the farmhouse. And maybe the next lamb wouldn't die.

He turned to the well and hauled water for Gaudon and the ewes and for himself. It was a primitive way to wash, rinsing the sweat and dust from his skin with handfuls of water, upending the bucket over his head.

Bastian used his shirt to dry his face and chest and arms. The first time he'd held the necklace in his hands, years ago, hope had soared inside him. He'd dreamed of large flocks of sheep, of stallions and new-born foals, of unbroken windows and a roof with no holes. He had dreamed that the bathhouse would be used again. Hot and cold water, steam. He knew now that Vere would never prosper. The curse had made them too poor. Extravagances like restoring the bathhouse, with its cracked tiles and broken pipes, would always be beyond them.

Water dripped from his hair and trickled down his neck. Bastian clenched the damp shirt in his hand and looked at the farmhouse. Candlelight glowed from the kitchen window and through the open door. He smelled woodsmoke.

Endal met him at the step. He nudged his head into Bastian's hand and wagged his tail.

Bastian stood in the doorway, reluctant to step into the kitchen. The wraith was at the stove, her back to him. Her presence made him want to turn on his heel and walk away, to not enter his own home.

I hate that woman, he told Endal. And there it was again, that word, *woman*. When had he started to see her as not merely a wraith?

It was the clothes. The blouse with flowers embroidered at the cuff, the skirt, the way the fabric outlined the curve of hip and waist and breast, making her look soft and feminine. It was the way she hung the washing and cooked the food, as his mother had done, as Liana did.

A wraith in the kitchen soured milk and spoiled eggs, or so the tales said. And yet this one could cook.

Her hair gleamed in the candlelight. The song whispered in his head again. *Ivory-white is her skin, and ebony-black her hair, and her lips, oh, her lips...*

Bastian shook his head angrily. Her hair was as black as pitch and tar and soot. There was nothing beautiful about it. He stepped into the kitchen.

The wraith saw the movement. She turned her head and looked at him.

Vermin, he said silently, so that only Endal could hear. She mocked him when she stood like that, proclaiming herself better than him, standing tall and haughty and unafraid.

He wasn't going to scurry from his own kitchen because of a supercilious wraith. Bastian leaned against the doorframe and ignored her. He scratched behind Endal's ears. The dog closed his eyes and sighed with pleasure.

"Do you have any books?" The wraith's voice was cool and polite.

Bastian glanced at her. "No." *None that you may borrow.*

Her eyebrows arched slightly. She looked down her nose at him. "No books?"

Her disdain brought heat to Bastian's face. He felt belittled, a grubby schoolboy, ignorant and unable to read.

His fingers tightened around the shirt. He stopped scratching Endal's ears and straightened. He wished he'd put the shirt on, wet or not, wished he'd taken the time to dry his hair properly, so that water didn't trickle down his face and the back of his neck.

Vermin. He almost said it out loud, almost spat the word in her face. *Don't sneer at me.*

Endal yawned and leaned against his leg. *She fears you.*

The comment was so startling, so absurd, that Bastian blinked and stopped looking at the wraith. *What?* He stared down at Endal. *Nonsense. She doesn't fear anything.*

Endal yawned again. *She's afraid of you.*

You're mistaken.

I can see it, said Endal. *I can smell it.*

Bastian glanced back at the wraith. He saw no fear. The set of her shoulders and chin, the expression on her face, were proud. *You smell it?*

Yes.

He almost shook his head. All he could smell was food.

The wraith turned away from him. She stirred a pot on the stove. Bastian stared at her back. *Are you certain?* he asked Endal.

Yes.

He smiled as he walked across the kitchen, as he climbed the stairs to his bedchamber. The wraith feared him. Satisfaction was smug and warm in his chest. He wanted to laugh out loud. In the privacy of his room, he did.

SHOW ME, HE said to Endal the next morning, as he stood in the shadows of the sickroom doorway. *I want to see her fear.*

Endal stretched and rolled over on the floor. *Watch,* he said.

The wraith used a wet cloth to wipe her brother's face. The room smelled strongly of ginger root.

Watch for what? Bastian asked.

The wraith looked up. He saw her stiffen, saw her sit taller in the chair, saw her chin rise.

Do you see?

That's fear? It looked like pride to him, haughtiness, disdain.

Yes.

"What is it?" The wraith's voice was cool.

Are you certain?

Endal stopped rolling on the floor and sat up. His tone was exasperated: *Yes.*

"What is it?" asked the wraith again.

Bastian grinned. "Nothing."

He left her staring at him, a frown pinched between her eyebrows. There was laughter in his chest. He whistled as he walked down the corridor, as he crossed the kitchen and stepped outside. The sky was high and arching, pale blue. Sunlight warmed his skin.

The ewes clustered in the pen, wanting grain. The whistle died on his lips. "No," he said, laughter shrivelling inside him.

Another one was dead.

CHAPTER TWENTY-FIVE

THERE WAS A book. Liana had fetched it for her. Melke put it aside while she bathed Hantje's burns in ginger juice and spread salve thinly on the fading bruises, while he drank as much of the herbal teas as she could make him. His sleep was restless. He tossed and turned and clawed at the sheets. His eyelids flickered. He spoke, muttering, the words ill-shaped in his mouth, too distorted to be understood.

"Hush," Melke said softly, and laid her hand on his cheek.

Hantje grew still at the sound of her voice. His head turned toward her.

"I have a book, Hantje. You'll recognize the stories."

The tome lay on the floor. It took two hands to lift. The pages were thick parchment and the binding was leather, darkened and worn thin by the touch of many hands. Melke smoothed her fingers over the cover, tracing the curling letters. *Tales of Magic and Magical Beasts*. The deserts and mountains and lakes of a continent separated her from where she was born, but this book was familiar. It was *home*.

She opened it carefully, smoothing the pages. The print was different, finer and more elaborate, and the pictures were tinted with color, but the stories were the same. She turned the pages with care, looking for her brother's favorite.

"Here it is, Hantje. Listen." She read the title aloud, "The Stonecutter and the Gryphon."

She glanced at her brother, and it seemed that he waited, wanting to hear the story as much as she did.

Melke sat back more comfortably in the chair. "'It is a well-known fact that gryphons are partial to the sweet flesh of virgins and that their high, rocky eyries are littered with the bones of unfortunate young women. Girls who live in the towns and villages that border the Wasteland often stop and scan the sky with anxious eyes, and no virgin dares step outside when the sun is at its highest and the gryphons hunt.

"'Now, it so happened that the stonecutter's sweetheart was outdoors at noon, the most dangerous hour of the day. Her brother had tumbled from the barn roof and lay groaning with one of his legs twisted beneath him. 'Don't go!' he cried, but the stonecutter's sweetheart (whose name was Irina) picked up her skirts and ran to fetch the bonesetter. She looked over her shoulder as she hurried down the stony track, but even so she didn't see the gryphon until its great wings blotted out the sun.

"'Irina was a simple girl, the daughter of a poor farmer, but although she could neither read nor write she was wise enough not to faint when the gryphon seized her with its lion-claws and carried her up into the hot, blue sky, and she was wise enough not to weep and cower when it released her on the wide ledge outside its eyrie. She wanted to marry the stonecutter, not die in a high, windy cave, so instead of huddling on the sun-hot rock and begging for her life, Irina ran into the dark eyrie and hid.

"'When the stonecutter saw the gryphon carrying his sweetheart high into the sky, he ran as fast as he could to the house of the wisest woman in the village. 'Mother Nonni!' he cried. 'Mother Nonni! You must help me!'

"'Mother Nonni, being wise, knew that the stonecutter had very little hope of rescuing his sweetheart. And, being wise, she also knew that there was nothing she could give him except courage. 'Take this,' she said, handing him a spear. 'It belonged to Yuri the Slayer. With it you cannot miss your mark.'

"'The stonecutter (whose name was Ivan) slung the spear over his shoulder and hurried into the Wasteland, and if his sweetheart had not been a resourceful girl, he would have been far too late. But gryphons' eyries are untidy places, full of rock and bones and shadows and places to hide. The gryphon hunted for the stonecutter's sweetheart, tearing at the rubble with its claws and snapping its vicious beak into the crooks and crannies, but Irina was well-hidden. At last the gryphon threw back its fearsome eagle's head and uttered a shriek so blood-curdling that shards of stone fell from the roof. It backed out of the eyrie and spread its wings in a thunderclap of sound and sprang into the sky, snapping its beak in fury.

"'The spear that Mother Nonni had given the stonecutter was as good as a spear could be, which is to say that it was very little use against a gryphon. It hadn't, of course, belonged to Yuri the Slayer, for that spear must long since have disintegrated into dust, but the stonecutter didn't think about such facts. All he knew was that Yuri had killed two gryphons with the spear, and he was going to kill a third. He ran across the Wasteland for hours, while the sun's heat made the rocks twist and shimmer. Then he climbed the high crag to the gryphon's eyrie, where the hot wind tried to pluck him from the cliff face, until at last he stood on the wide stone ledge.

"'Now, as everyone knows, gryphons are difficult to slay, being part lion and part eagle, but a well-placed spear can kill even the most dangerous of creatures. And so the stonecutter stood in front of the eyrie and gripped the shaft of the spear tightly with both hands and shouted: 'Gryphon!'

"'It was no gryphon that came from the dark cave, but his sweetheart, and the stonecutter was so overjoyed that he laid down the spear and picked her up in his arms. He almost didn't see the gryphon's shadow as it passed over them. 'Get back!' he cried to Irina, pushing her toward the cave. He snatched up the spear and turned to face the gryphon. But Irina didn't leave him. She stood at his back and braced him as the gryphon swooped low. And because the stonecutter believed it was Yuri the Slayer's spear and knew that he couldn't miss, the spearhead pierced the gryphon's breast and slid deep into its heart.

"'The weight of the gryphon snapped the shaft of the spear. It tumbled the stonecutter and his sweetheart to the ground and very nearly swept them off the rocky ledge. The gryphon shrieked as it fell down the cliff, a sound as sharp and fierce as a battleaxe slicing through armor, and its claws scored long grooves in the granite. By the time it hit the stony ground, it was dead.

"'The sharp lion-claws had cut open the stonecutter's face, but his sweetheart didn't panic. She took out the needle and thread that were tucked into her bodice and calmly sewed up his cheek. And then they climbed down the cliff together and skirted the gryphon's great broken-winged body and walked home across the Wasteland.

"'I broke the spear, Mother Nonni,' said the stonecutter, when they reached the village. 'Please forgive me.' But Mother Nonni laughed and told him that it didn't matter at all.

"'The stonecutter was known as Ivan the Slayer thereafter. He had been a plain lad before, and with the broad scar across his face was even plainer, but Irina certainly didn't care, and nor did anybody else.

"'The stonecutter married his sweetheart and they lived very happily. When Mother Nonni passed away, Irina became the wisest woman in the village, although she could neither read nor write, and people came from far across the Wasteland to seek her advice. In the corner of their little stone house, there always stood a spear. Sometimes the shaft was made of ash, sometimes maple, but it was always strong and sturdy. And from time to time Irina gave the spear to folk who had desperate need of courage. 'This is Ivan the Slayer's spear,' she would say. 'With it you cannot miss your mark.' And they never did.'"

HANTJE'S WORDS BECAME clearer as the day progressed. "Dark," he said, distress twisting his face. He gripped Melke's hand tightly.

"It's not dark." She stroked strands of black hair away from his face. "If you open your eyes you'll see sunlight. I promise you, Hantje, it's not dark."

His head turned blindly toward her.

"It's not dark, Hantje. The sun is shining."

The deep lines of distress smoothed from his face. His eyelids flickered.

"Open your eyes, Hantje," she said softly. "Open them and see for yourself." She held her breath.

Long seconds passed.

Her exhalation was a sigh of disappointment. "Please, Hantje," she whispered. "Look at me."

Her brother opened his eyes.

"Hantje!" She leaned close.

He blinked and didn't seem to see her. His hand was limp in her clasp.

"It's all right, Hantje. See, it's not dark. The sun is shining." She reached out with her free hand to touch his cheek.

Her brother flinched from her.

Melke froze with her hand outstretched. There was pain beneath her breastbone, as if a knife blade was buried there. Hantje was afraid of her.

Her fingers curled into her palm. She lowered her hand. "It's me," she said, a tremor in her voice. "It's Melke. It's *me*."

His gray eyes focused slowly. He blinked with heavy eyelids. "Mel...?"

"Yes. It's me." She still held his hand, and his fingers moved weakly, as if to clutch at her. "You're safe, Hantje. See? The sun is shining. It's light."

She reached out to touch him again, slowly, and this time he didn't flinch from her. She stroked his cheek and smoothed back his hair. "It's all right, Hantje."

His face twisted. She saw his distress. "Hush," she said. "Hush. It's all right."

"No." His fingers fisted around her hand. Tears filled his eyes.

How much did he remember of his crime, of his punishment? Melke eased her hand free of his clenched fingers. "Hush," she whispered as she gently gathered him close. "Hush. It's all right."

She held her brother while he wept, too thin, too weak, too warm still with fever. His words were choked. *Sorry*, she heard him say. *I'm sorry, sorry.*

HANTJE SLEPT AFTER that, rousing only when she made him drink, opening his eyes and staring at her. He seemed to recognize her. He didn't flinch again or draw away in fear, but he said nothing, made no answer to her words of comfort. He closed his eyes and slept again.

"The fever," said Liana, when she came at dusk. "He's not fully lucid. It will take several days." She bent over Hantje.

Melke lit the candles and drew the curtains closed. The bedchamber became full of shadows. She stood back and watched as Liana placed her hand lightly on Hantje's brow. "Is there another candleholder? I think we need more light."

Hantje's eyes opened. His breath was sharply indrawn.

Melke stepped hastily toward the bed. "There are candles, Hantje. See, it's not dark."

Hantje didn't hear her. He sat up, clawing at the sheets in frantic panic, fighting Liana's grasp. "Dark!" He almost screamed the word.

Endal leaped to his feet. He barked, loud. The sound terrified Hantje into stillness.

"There are candles," Melke said.

Hantje's gaze fixed on her. Breath sobbed in his throat. His eyes were wide and staring.

"Candles. You can see me, Hantje. It's not dark."

He sat hunched in the sheets, panting, trembling, his gaze clinging to her face. He didn't appear to notice that Liana touched him gently, that she stroked his hair and smoothed her palm down his cheek.

The girl soothed him with her hands, a frown of concentration on her face. Hantje's ragged, gasping breaths became slower and more steady. The tension that corded beneath his skin eased. He didn't flinch when Liana sat on the bed beside him, didn't pull away as she continued to touch him.

"It's all right," Melke said, and Hantje seemed to understand. He stared at her, his eyes wide, as if by keeping her in his sight everything *would* be all right. He didn't resist as Liana put an arm gently around him.

The girl's embrace seemed to melt the last of Hantje's terror and panic. His eyelids drooped slightly. He leaned into her, passive.

"I won't let it be dark," Melke said. "I promise, Hantje."

His eyes squeezed shut. He turned his head and pressed his face against Liana's shoulder. His hair was as black as midnight against the silver-white of hers. Tears glistened as they slid down his pale cheek.

It hurt to see Hantje's terror, his panic, those silent, despairing tears. Distress choked in Melke's throat. She wanted to push the girl aside and hold him herself. But Liana helped Hantje more than she could, her touch soothed and healed.

Her hands curled into helpless fists.

Liana met her eyes. "You're right. Another candleholder. There's one in my bedchamber."

Speech was impossible. Melke nodded.

The extra candles pushed the shadows back. Hantje's silent weeping stopped. He slid into a calm sleep.

"Go to bed," the girl said softly, wiping the tears from his thin cheeks. "He'll be all right now."

Melke turned away without speaking. It was Liana her brother needed, not her.

Sleep was a long time coming. She lay on the hard, narrow bed and watched the candles burn, tightness in her chest and throat, behind her eyes. Hours passed, while she listened to Endal's breathing as he slept on the blanket she'd given him, and heard her brother weep and cry out in terror, over and over again. *Dark.*

CHAPTER TWENTY-SIX

BASTIAN SLICED HIMSELF another piece of ham and sat at the kitchen table, chewing slowly. It was wrong to be so alone in his own house. Liana ought to be here, sharing lunch with him, and Endal should be lying on the cool flagstones.

Bastian pushed the plate away. He rose to his feet and stood listening. The silence and emptiness made him uneasy. He wanted to go upstairs and quietly open Liana's door and hear her breathe while she slept, to reassure himself that he wasn't alone. He wanted to talk to Endal.

He walked soundlessly down the corridor. A voice came from the sickroom, a soft murmur. It was the wrong voice. The wraith's, not Liana's. Her pitch was lower.

"'There is a little magic in this world. It runs in certain bloodlines.'"

Bastian frowned. He recognized those sentences. He strode to the door, quietness forgotten. Breath hissed between his teeth. The wraith had the book. *His* book. The one he'd read aloud to Liana when she was a child. The one his mother had read to him.

Endal opened his eyes.

Where did she get that book? Bastian demanded.

Liana gave it to her.

Liana. Bastian's hands knotted. How could his sister have done such a thing?

Why are you angry? Endal asked. His mouth stretched in a wide yawn.

Because I don't want her touching it, Bastian told him. That book was precious. It shouldn't be pawed over by a filthy wraith.

Endal's shrug was silent. *The sick one likes it. He rests more easily.*

I don't care!

He heard, clearly, how petty his rage was, how selfish. He glared at Endal, daring him to say anything.

"'Here is the tale of a girl who could run as fast as the wind.'"

The wraith spoke with the accent of an easterner, the soft *s* and purring *r*, the long vowels. The cadence was almost musical.

Bastian stopped glaring at Endal. He raised his eyes and watched the wraith as she read aloud. "'Her name was Ennia, and she lived high in the mountains of Gaillac, where the gales blew strong and wild.'"

Not feral, not if she read so well. She had been educated somewhere. Where? Who'd taught her to read? Who'd taught her to cook?

"'Ennia's eyes were the color of storm clouds in the sky and her skin was as pale as the winter snow. She rarely spoke, for she was listening to the wind.'"

Where was the wraith from, and how had she come to be in Bresse? Why was she here?

"'*Come run with us*, the winds cried, as they howled through the sharp mountain peaks, tugging slates lose from the roofs and making doors slam. But only Ennia heard their invitation. She raised her face to the sky and whispered: *I can't.*'"

Bastian turned away from the door, frowning. The wraith had been at Vere a week, and he'd not thought to ask those questions. He had a creature in his house he knew nothing about. Nothing.

CHOPPING ANOTHER FALLEN tree into firewood didn't ease Bastian's disquiet; it merely made him tired and irritable. He ate his dinner in the empty kitchen.

He was chewing the last of his meal when he heard footsteps. He put down his fork, ready to snarl at the wraith, but it was Liana. The kitchen was suddenly warmer, cosier.

She bent and kissed his cheek. "How are you?"

He grunted.

"Grumpy." She touched his cheek lightly with her fingers, where she'd kissed. "Another sheep?"

Bastian pushed his plate away. "How could you give her the book?"

Liana's eyebrows rose. "What?"

"It's *our* book. I don't want her touching it."

"Bastian." Her tone was quiet and disappointed. It made him feel like a small child.

He clenched his jaw. "She's not to have it."

"I know you don't like her, Bastian, but you go too far in your hatred."

"No, I don't."

"Bastian." Just his name, quietly, and disappointment in her eyes.

When had Liana become an adult? He kept thinking of her as a girl, young and in need of his guidance, but she was eighteen. Old enough to be married, old enough for motherhood. An adult.

"All right!" Bastian lifted his hands in a gesture of defeat. "All right. Let her read the book."

Liana smiled and touched his cheek again lightly with her fingertips. She turned toward the stove. "Something smells delicious."

"It's..." *Edible*, he'd been about to say, but the word stuck on his tongue. Too petty, too churlish. Too childish. "It is delicious. Have some."

"I'll eat in a little while," she said. "With Melke."

Melke. The wraith's name. An eastern name, to match her accent. "Liana, has she told you anything? Where she comes from? Why she's in Bresse?"

Liana tilted her head to one side. Her brow creased. "No. She hasn't."

"Nothing?"

Liana thought for a moment, and then shook her head. "No."

Bastian's mouth twisted. Anger kindled in his chest. It was his fault. He should have asked, should have insisted that the wraith tell him everything before he let her set foot in the house. He pushed back his chair. "I'll ask her now."

Liana stopped him with a hand on his arm. "Tomorrow," she said. "You're too grumpy."

"I am not—' he started to say, crossly, and then realized how ridiculous he sounded.

Liana met his glare without flinching. Her mouth tilted in a small smile. She rose on tiptoe and kissed his cheek. "Go to bed, Bastian."

When had she stopped being a child?

He went to bed.

CHAPTER TWENTY-SEVEN

BASTIAN HAD NO doubt that the discussion with the wraith would be an argument, loud and ugly. She would try to lie, to hide her sordid past. He waited until she came into the kitchen; he didn't need Liana to tell him that raised voices in the sickroom would distress the patient.

The patient. Another wraith. He almost spat in the dirt. What did he care about a thieving wraith? Nothing. But he waited with the sun warm on his face, sitting on the kitchen step, until Endal pushed his nose against the back of his neck and he heard the woman's footsteps on the flagstones.

Morning, Endal, he said silently, as he stood.

He rested his hand on the dog's head and let his eyes adjust to the relative dimness of the kitchen. The wraith was measuring tea into a pot. He recognized the packet. He'd bought it at the apothecary.

She stood tall and straight-backed, with a haughty tilt to her chin. Two days ago it would have made him angry; now it told him she was afraid.

He stepped into the kitchen.

The wraith paid him no attention. Her hand was steady as she sprinkled dried herbs into the teapot.

Bastian leaned his shoulders against the wall. Stone pressed hard and cold through his shirt. He folded his arms across his chest and watched the wraith, letting the silence grow.

She closed the packet of tea. Her chin was higher than it had been before. Not disdain, but fear. Bastian smiled. He was going to win this argument.

"You've not told us where you and your brother are from, or what you are doing in Bresse." The accusation was mildly spoken. There was no need to raise his voice yet.

The wraith glanced at him. "You haven't asked." Her tone was coolly polite.

"I'm asking now."

The wraith lifted the lid of a pot on the stove, the one they used to boil water. Faint steam rose from it. She replaced the lid and turned toward him.

Bastian straightened away from the wall, ready for bluster and evasion.

"What would you like to know?"

He narrowed his eyes. Lies, then, not bluster. "Where are you from? Precisely."

"Precisely?" Her eyebrows rose and he'd have thought she mocked him, except that he knew she was afraid of him. "We are from Stenrik. From a village in the south, called Granna."

Did she tell the truth? He had no way of knowing.

She speaks the truth, Endal said.

Bastian frowned down at the dog. *How do you know?*

I can see when humans lie, Endal told him.

Bastian stared at the dog, astonished. *You can?*

Yes. Endal lay down on the flagstones. He yawned and closed his eyes.

"Is there anything else you wish to know?"

The wraith's tone, polite and cool, failed to grate. Bastian glanced at her, and then back at Endal. *Will you tell me if she lies?*

The dog opened his eyes. *Yes.*

"Yes," he said firmly, raising his gaze to the wraith's haughty face. "I have other questions."

"Very well."

"Why are you here in Bresse? Why did you leave Stenrik?"

The wraith looked at him for several seconds, expressionlessly, and then turned back to the stove and lifted the lid of the pot. The water boiled. "It is a complicated tale," she said. "It will take time to tell."

He recognized evasion when he saw it. Anger sparked faintly in his chest. "I have time."

She paused, lifting the pot from the stove. Silence, and then, "Very well." There was more silence as she poured water into the teapot. She put the pot back on the stove and reached for the lid.

His anger kindled into flame. She was preparing lies. "Now," he said, the word a short, peremptory command.

She glanced at him. "Let me set this to steep."

"Now."

The wraith placed the lid on the teapot and turned to face him. She crossed her arms over her chest, mirroring him. "Stenrik has a king," she said, in her cool voice. "His name is Jonnas. You may have heard of him."

Bastian shook his head. He knew of Stenrik from the minstrels and the storytellers, from *Tales of Magic and Magical Beasts*. Lamia nested in those cold, stony soils. But rulers? Why would he know their names? Stenrik was almost at the edge of the world.

"His reign has been... very bloody. He is the reason we left. We came to Bresse to find a new home."

Silence. He waited, but she appeared to have nothing more to say. "That's it?"

"Yes."

He narrowed his eyes at her. "And your leaving had nothing to do with the fact that you are wraiths?"

"No."

She lies.

"Liar," Bastian said loudly, uncrossing his arms and taking a step toward her.

"I beg your pardon?"

"Endal knows when you lie."

Her eyes flicked to the dog. She said nothing, standing stiff and tall with her back to the stove.

"I'll ask my question again." Bastian's tone was hard, with an edge of anger. "Why did you leave Stenrik?"

"To find a new home."

"No." He shook his head, a sharp and angry movement. He took another step toward her, his hands clenched. "The *other* reason. Wraith."

The wraith met his eyes. She didn't speak. Silence grew loud in the kitchen.

He had thought that intimidating her into truthfulness would be easy, that it would be a simple matter to stand over her and raise his fist and shout. It wasn't. However straight-backed she stood, she was still a woman. He was taller than her, stronger. He should be able to threaten her easily and yet... he couldn't. Not when she had a woman's soft lips and skin, not when her hair hung so long down her back and the skirt and blouse showed the female shape of her. He felt like a bully, standing before her. He *was* a bully. And that made him even angrier.

"Very well." The wraith's voice was cool and toneless. "If you insist."

Bastian's relief was intense. He took a step back, away from her. Another step. "I do."

The wraith looked past him, to a point on the wall he couldn't see. "Being a wraith is a magic that runs in certain families. It runs in ours. My father called it the family curse." Her gaze shifted. She held his eyes. "We didn't want it."

Fine words. Bastian leaned back against the wall and crossed his arms.

"Da said... My father said that our family always kept apart from ordinary folk, so no one could learn our secret. In Stenrik they burn wraiths."

Bastian blinked. Burn?

"My father was a wraith. My mother wasn't, but she was his cousin and she had the blood in her. They wanted... My parents wanted to be ordinary people in an ordinary town. They moved south and for fourteen years they managed." The wraith looked out the doorway. She was silent, her gaze on the cracked, brown-gray dirt outside.

"Until someone made a mistake," Bastian prompted.

Her gaze flicked to him for a brief second. "Not us. Da made us promise that we'd never, *ever* become unseen. Once Hantje..." She shook her head slightly. "He wanted to see if it was true that if you throw salt at a wraith it becomes seen. Da was furious. I've never seen anyone so angry."

A pause, and then she glanced at him again. She didn't need to speak. He knew what she was thinking. *Until you.*

His jaw tightened in memory.

The wraith's gaze slid from his face. She looked at the wall again. "We don't know what happened," she said, her voice flat. "A mistake was made, but not by us. One of our family in the north. A child perhaps, or..." She shrugged and shook her head.

"Or what?"

She hesitated. "Mam said that sometimes, in childbirth—"

"The baby?" Bastian asked, startled.

She shook her head again. "Not the baby. The ability to become unseen doesn't come until later. No, the mother." She met his eyes. "To become unseen feels like turning yourself inside out, like *pushing* yourself inside out."

He thought he understood. "And sometimes in labor..."

"Inadvertently. Yes. And if a midwife is present, then..." Her shoulders lifted in a shrug again.

Then the family secret is a secret no more. Bastian nodded to show he understood.

"Soldiers came." She turned her head and looked out the door again. "They knew about Da. We were taken to the fort, all of us."

Her father had been burned alive. Horror clenched in Bastian's chest.

"Wraiths are useful, you understand. They can be spies or assassins." She met his eyes again. "The king forced my father to work for him."

Forced. An ugly word, as ugly as him standing over this woman and making her tell him her story. Bastian cleared his throat. "How?"

"Us. He used us. Hantje and me and Mam."

"Hostages."

"In a fashion." Her face became even more expressionless. She could have been carved of marble.

"How?"

The wraith's arms tightened across her chest. She turned her head again, showing him her profile. "We were put in cells," she said, staring out at the dusty yard. "Under the ground."

"In the dark?"

"Yes."

A shiver crept over his skin. "For how long?"

"Da said it was three weeks."

Bastian opened his mouth, and then shut it again. Three weeks. In the dark. "Cells? You weren't together?"

"No." She glanced at him, and perhaps she saw the horror on his face, for she said, "It was worst for Hantje. He was younger."

Bastian shook his head. They were wraiths, yes, but even so. "How old were you?"

She looked away again. "Hantje was ten. I was thirteen."

Inhuman. Wraith or not, she'd been a child. Huddled in a cell. Alone. For three pitch-black weeks.

The wraith continued in a toneless voice, "When Da agreed to work for the king we were moved to one of the towers. We lived there for five years."

Imprisoned in a tower. It was a storyteller's tale. Bastian closed his eyes. He shook his head again. He should never have asked. He should have kept on hating her.

"My father came sometimes, for a few days. He never said what he did for the king. Mam told us not to ask."

Bastian opened his eyes. "But you escaped."

"Yes."

The silence lengthened. He knew before the wraith took a long breath, before she opened her mouth again, that he didn't want to hear the tale.

"Da died. We don't know what happened. He never came back." He saw her knuckles whiten, saw her fingers dig into her arms. "They came for me and Hantje. They didn't know we were wraiths, but they... wanted to make us tell. We'd always known they would, one day. We had a plan. We knew what to do."

She fell silent. Her lips were pressed tightly together.

Bastian cleared his throat. "What was the plan?"

"To become unseen. To escape."

"Obviously it worked."

The wraith made no reply. Her mouth tightened further.

Bastian waited.

The wraith looked at him. Her eyes were as hard as chips of granite. "Mam died. We escaped. We came here. Do you have any other questions?"

"How did she die?" he asked. His voice was quiet.

"Crossbow."

Silence. Bastian cleared his throat again. "How did you get here?"

"We walked. It took six years."

More silence. He heard Endal's breathing, the soft inhalation and exhalation of air.

"Why here?"

"We wanted to be by the sea. We wanted somewhere safe."

Where they exiled wraiths instead of burning them.

"You stole." But her crime, her terrible misdeed, had shrunk in the past few minutes.

"No!" Anger flashed across her face. "We earned our money."

He'd forgotten the silver coins. *A lie?* he asked Endal.

No.

So the coins had been untainted.

"I meant the necklace," he said, flat-voiced.

Faint color flushed the wraith's cheeks. Her chin rose. "To save Hantje. Yes."

Is she afraid?

No, was Endal's reply.

Not fear then. Defiance. Pride.

Bastian narrowed his eyes. "Tell me."

The wraith's jaw tightened.

He waited, leaning against the wall, the stone hard at his back.

"I don't know why he did it." Her voice was almost bitter. "He didn't tell me. But... there's a farm down the coast, past Thierry." She stopped and bit her lip.

He shifted his shoulders against the stone. "A farm?"

"We couldn't afford it." She looked out the door again. "Even small farms cost more than a few silver coins."

Bastian pushed himself away from the wall. "So you decided to steal from the salamanders." Contempt was sharp in his voice.

"No," she said, turning her head. Her glare was fierce. "We did *not* decide that."

Does she lie?

No.

The wraith looked away again. "Hantje was gone the next morning. I don't know why he did it."

Bastian knew. "He wanted the farm."

"He wanted a home. We both did."

I have a home. It hasn't brought me any joy. But Bastian understood her brother's motive. He understood the need to have a place to belong, a place to be safe, to have a family.

The wraith met his eyes. She stood slightly taller. "I didn't know what the necklace was. The salamanders didn't tell me."

Does she lie? he asked again.

No.

Even so, he curled his lip at her. "Psaaron tears are unmistakable."

"We have no psaarons in our oceans. It's too cold."

Was he meant to forgive her now? "Congratulations." His tone was cutting. "Your first theft."

Color rose in her cheeks. Bastian waited for an apology from her, but she said nothing.

There was silence in the kitchen. He heard the hiss of water boiling in the pot, felt the hiss of anger low in his belly.

"Do you have any more questions?" The wraith's voice was cold.

"No." He turned on his heel and walked out the door.

CHAPTER TWENTY-EIGHT

BASTIAN SPENT THE rest of the morning sitting on the dunes, watching as the sea ate into Vere. The sheep were safe in the pen, with food and water, and the bridge would fall no matter what he did. There was enough firewood.

Hatred and pity. They were incompatible. One or the other, but not both. He hated her. He pitied her.

It was barbaric that they burned wraiths in Stenrik. It was barbaric that children were put in dark cells underground and that the king could keep a family locked in a tower.

Isn't that what I'm doing? I keep her brother hostage so that she'll do my bidding. I force her to act against her will.

No. This was undoing a crime. What he did was *right*. She had stolen the necklace. Her theft, any theft, was unforgivable.

But if she hadn't known, if her brother's life was at stake…

Bastian frowned at the foaming surf. Waves clawed at the beach and cast themselves on the rocks and beat against the distant cliffs. There had been a pier once. The sea had swallowed it. If he set foot on the beach, the sea would swallow him too. The waves would snatch him off his feet. They'd pound and drown him.

A breeze tugged at his hair and shirt. The salt-tang of the ocean was in his nostrils, fresh and dangerous. Despite the hot sunlight on his skin, Bastian shivered. He had another question to ask the wraith. He should have asked it in the kitchen: *Will you get the necklace back?*

Endal would tell him whether she intended to keep her promise. And if she didn't…

There was no way to physically force the wraith to become unseen, no way to make her to enter the salamanders' den. He could threaten violence, but that was all it would be, a threat.

Bastian pushed to his feet. He needed to find out now, while there was still a week left. While he and Liana still had time to flee.

HE HAD SAT too long by the sea, with the salty wind blowing through him. One of the ewes was in labor. Bastian's frantic haste was too late. The ground jarred his knees as he knelt. A breath, a heartbeat, a flicker of life, and then nothing. The sheep was dead.

"No," he said. "No!"

But the loudness of his voice couldn't make the animal breathe again or make its heart beat.

Bastian pulled the knife from his belt and cut swiftly. Blood spilled over his hand, hot. The scent was rich and thick, and the lamb... it was too limp. He tried to make it live, tried to breathe life into it, while its mother's blood soaked into the dry ground. It was a futile effort; there was no milk for the lamb if it lived.

Too late. Always too late.

He knelt with the lamb in his hands and the scent of blood choking in his throat. Sunlight burned through his closed eyelids.

This death, these deaths, were his fault. He had intended to check every hour, but instead he'd sat on the dunes and stared at the sea. The blood on his hands was his punishment.

Bastian opened his eyes. Already the first fly buzzed around the sheep. "Get away," he snarled at it.

The sheep filled his afternoon. Draining the blood, butchering it, burying the lamb. He was filthy, sticky with blood and sweat and dust. His clothes and skin stank.

He stood in the dusk with his trousers and shirt stiff with blood. His skin was tight where it had dried on him.

He wanted to scrub himself clean. He wanted the bathhouse. Or failing that, the public baths in Thierry. He didn't want a bucket of cold water from the well.

Candlelight glowed in the kitchen. *Please let it be Liana.*

It was the wraith. She turned her head and her face lost its customary cool blankness.

They stared at each other for long seconds.

"Are you all right?" she asked, finally, and he heard faint shock in her voice.

Endal was at his feet, whining, pressing close.

Don't touch me.

"I'm fine," he said. His voice was grim. "Will you haul water from the well for me?"

She didn't move. "The blood...?"

"A sheep died."

She said nothing more, but wiped her hands on a cloth and walked to the door. He stood aside for her to pass.

He stripped off his shirt while she lowered the bucket. "Pour it over my hands."

The sun sank behind the hills while she did so. He rubbed his hands together, scrubbing with his fingers, letting the water wash his skin clean. Blood and sweat and dust were gone. When the bucket was empty he didn't look at her. "I need no more assistance," he said stiffly. "Thank you."

Darkness lapped at them. The wraith put the bucket down, and then she surprised him. "You're welcome," she said.

He watched as she walked across the yard. "There's meat in the cool-cellar," he said curtly.

She turned her head. In the encroaching darkness she was monochrome, white face, black hair.

"Liana will show you. Use it."

The wraith didn't speak, merely nodded. She entered the kitchen without looking back. Endal lingered in the doorway. *I'm fine,* he assured the dog silently. *Don't worry.*

And then he pulled off his trousers and washed his body. Two buckets. Three. It seemed he'd never feel clean.

It was fully dark when Liana came. "Bastian?"

He turned from her. "Go away."

"I have fresh clothes for you. Melke told me."

Bastian closed his eyes. He stood with his toes buried in mud. How many buckets? Too many. They hadn't water for him to waste like this. "Thank you."

"Another sheep?"

"Yes."

"I'll put the clothes here. And here's a towel. And Bastian, there's food in the kitchen."

Bastian bowed his head. "Thank you," he said again.

"Are you all right?" Her voice was soft, tentative.

He scared her, standing outside in the dark, washing himself until his skin rubbed raw. "Fine," he said. "I'm fine."

CHAPTER TWENTY-NINE

HANTJE WAS MORE alert in the morning, closer to wakefulness, to talking. The burns were faint blotches on his skin, pink and almost unseen. His mouth was healed, his eyelids no longer swollen. He muttered, turning his head on the pillow and clutching at the sheets.

"Hush," Melke said, smoothing back his hair. "Rest easy, Hantje."

His face twisted. The words became more distinct. "Sorry," he said. "Sorry."

"Hush," she whispered again.

His breath came in sobbing gasps, as if he wept. Distress furrowed his face.

"Don't cry." She leaned close and pressed a kiss to his brow, smelling his despair. "It's all right, Hantje. It's all right."

His body turned toward her. He burrowed his face blindly against her shoulder.

Melke put her arms around him and held him close. "Shh," she whispered into his hair. "Hush. It's all right."

He was a child in her arms, thin and warm and shivering, crying. She heard his sobbing breaths and felt the trembling of his body. There was no question of withholding forgiveness. She loved him too much for that. Whatever he'd done—wraith, thief—she forgave him. She closed her eyes and rocked him gently. "Shhh."

The sound of his breathing, those soft, choked gasps, the sobs... this was how he'd sounded when Mam died. His grief had been audible beneath the yells of soldiers and the thud of booted feet running on stone. She'd not seen him, but she'd heard him, heard *this*. She had reached toward the sound and fisted her hand in his shirt and pulled at him, made him run. And while they ran, he'd sounded like this. *This*.

Hantje's breathing slowly steadied. The trembling stopped. "Hush," Melke whispered, rocking him, loving him. "Sleep."

When she laid him down, distress no longer twisted his face. He slept calmly. She stroked the hair back from his brow, so black against the white of the pillowcase. "It's all right, Hantje. Everything's all right."

The words were a lie. It wasn't all right. But she wanted Hantje to heal, to not cry. To not scream that it was dark.

The memories were close to the surface. Too close. She'd buried them for years, had tried not to remember, but yesterday Bastian had asked and it was close again, the darkness, the rough, damp walls and the moldy straw. The hunger. The terror. Da's face. The sound Mam made as she died. Hantje sobbing.

Dark, he'd screamed.

What had happened to him in the salamanders' den?

Melke went to check on her broth. The scent... it was Mam. Lifting the lid, stirring the broth: Mam. But Mam's scent was also blood, and the sound of her was also a crossbow.

Melke pressed fingers to her mouth. There was an ache in her throat. *No*, she told herself. *I will not cry.*

But the tears were there and she couldn't choke them back. There were too many tears, too many reasons to cry.

She climbed the stairs blindly, closed the door to her bedchamber, and sat with her back to it. Mam. Da. Hantje sobbing, unseen. His scream: *Dark*.

She wept, hugging her knees. It was too much. Too much. Far too much.

Endal pushed his head under her arm. He whined.

She couldn't stop crying. The gulping sobs were endless.

The hound was half in her lap, heavy and warm, leaning against her. She hugged him, and cried, pressing her face into his black coat. Mam and Da. Hantje.

Endal stayed where he was, even when the tears had stopped. The hound-scent of him was warm and comforting. He smelled like Tass.

"You're meant to bite me," she whispered.

CHAPTER THIRTY

S OMEONE HAD WASHED his bloodied clothes and hung them out to dry. Bastian sat on the henhouse step and watched as the wraith unpegged them. Her hair was sleek and very black in the sunlight. She wore a different blouse. This one was blue-gray, the color of the sea during winter storms. Her skirt was the same, though. She'd worn it every day. Liana would know what to call the color. He didn't. He'd seen plums that shade sold at the market, dark, neither black nor blue nor purple.

The wraith's face was expressionless. She looked like an animated statue, living but lifeless, carved of marble, bloodless. *She has no emotion*, he said to Endal, rubbing a hand over the dog's head, pulling gently at his ears. She'd never throw back her head and laugh deeply, from her belly, never love with passion, never weep as if her heart had broken.

She cries.

Bastian's hand was startled into stillness. *Nonsense*, he said. And then he remembered the traces of tears he'd seen on her face at the salamanders' den. *For her brother.* He'd grant her that; she felt emotion for her brother.

Not only for her brother.

He looked down at Endal. What would the dog know?

She searched for something, Endal said. *In her room, on the stairs, in the kitchen. Out here in the yard. When she couldn't find it, she cried.*

Bastian glanced at the wraith. He couldn't imagine her searching, crying. *Nonsense*, but his tone was uncertain.

I do not lie, Endal said firmly. *Scratch me.* He nudged Bastian's hand.

He rubbed his fingers over the dog's head, watching as the wraith reached up and unpegged his trousers and folded them neatly.

Do you know what she looked for? But even as he asked the question, Bastian remembered. Guilt twisted in his chest. It was an unfamiliar emotion.

No. I could not help her. Endal's tone was regretful. *But if you ask her, maybe I can find it for her.*

Guilt was forgotten. Bastian was surprised into stillness again. Did Endal like the wraith?

The wraith turned, his folded clothes in her hand. She hesitated. Her chin rose slightly.

Endal nudged his hand again. *Ask her.*

There is no need. I know what she was looking for. Guilt twisted again inside him.

"These are yours." The wraith held the clothes out to him, as haughty as a queen giving alms. Flowers were stitched on the cuffs of her blouse.

Bastian took them wordlessly, making no move to stand. The fabric was warm. The wraith turned to go.

"Wait." It was a command.

He saw her stiffen, saw her chin rise a fraction higher. She turned back to face him. She met his gaze unflinchingly.

Bastian put the folded shirt and trousers on the step beside him. *Endal, tell me if she lies.*

The wraith looked down her nose at him. "Yes?"

"You gave your word, at the salamanders' den. Do you intend to keep it?"

She wasn't as emotionless as he'd thought. He saw a tiny flare of anger in her eyes, a tightening of her mouth. "Yes."

Endal was silent. She told the truth.

Tension eased inside him. Bastian began to rub the dog's head again. "It must be soon," he said. "The psaaron will come when—"

"When the moon is full. I know." The wraith's voice was brusque, edged with hostility. She turned to go.

"No." His hand stilled. Tension returned, tight in his gut. "When the tides are high. The moon need not be full."

The wraith halted and turned her head toward him. Her dark, arching eyebrows were drawn together in a frown. "Liana said spring equinox. That's full moon, is it not?"

"A psaaron reckons by the tides."

The wraith shook her head slightly. He saw that she didn't understand.

"It's equinox when the tides are high. Not merely when the moon is full, but several days either side."

Her frown deepened. "But—"

"A psaaron's measurement of equinox is not as narrow as ours."

"So... sooner."

"Five days."

Her expression was proud and cold, her posture very straight-backed. Endal stirred slightly.

What? Bastian asked.

She's afraid.

"Very well," the wraith said, her voice as haughty as her face. "Thank you for telling me." She began walking toward the kitchen door.

"The necklace," Bastian said to her back. "Do you believe you can steal it?"

The wraith halted again. This time she turned around fully. She made him wait several seconds before answering. "Will I succeed? I don't know."

It wasn't the reply he'd wanted. Honest, but he'd hoped for confidence, for certainty.

"I don't know how they caught Hantjë. It may be something I can avoid. It may not."

There was dryness in his throat, in his mouth. If he and Liana packed their belongings and left now, today, would they be far enough away when the psaaron came? Nowhere near water. Inland.

"I will need shoes. I have none."

The words jerked his attention to her feet. He saw no bandages beneath the hem of her skirt. Bastian frowned. "Are those—"

"Liana lent them to me. But they're unsuitable for travel."

He recognized the slippers. Soft leather, thin-soled, with a pattern of beads stitched on the toe. Unsuitable for travel.

The slippers were his mother's.

Yesterday he would have been furious. Today he didn't hate her enough.

"I can buy shoes in Thierry," he said. "Tomorrow. If you give me your size, and some money."

Her nod was that of a fine lady to a servant, but even that failed to make him angry. The proud tilt of her chin hid fear, and some part of him respected her for that. He'd rather have haughtiness than cringing.

Bastian rubbed Endal's ears. The dog leaned against his leg. His weight, the warmth of his body, were comfortable and familiar. He was aware of Endal's contentment. It hummed in his mind, like the purring of a cat. "If..." He hesitated. Was he a fool to ask such a question? Or a fool not to? *Endal, tell me whether she lies.* "If I take Endal with me to Thierry, will you be here when I return?"

Something flashed in the wraith's eyes again. She looked down her nose at him. "Of course." Two words only, but they were ice-cold and contemptuous.

She turned on her heel and walked away.

Bastian ignored her scorn. *Did she speak the truth?* he asked the dog.

Yes.

He experienced an odd skip of lightness in his chest. Thierry tomorrow, with Endal.

And he'd visit Silvia.

He watched the wraith enter the kitchen. The fabric of her skirt moved softly.

Bastian frowned and looked away abruptly. It was thought of Silvia that made him think of warm cotton moving against skin, of womanly curves. He didn't desire the wraith. The woman he desired was Silvia.

Endal rose and stretched. *We'll go to Thierry tomorrow*, Bastian told him. *You and me.*

The dog froze in mid-stretch. *We will?*

"Yes," Bastian said, aloud, and then laughed as Endal pranced like a pup, shaking himself, bounding up to lick his chin.

The dog followed the wraith into the kitchen, his step jaunty and his tail wagging. Bastian sat on the henhouse step and watched him go. Was he doing this for himself, or for Endal?

Both, he decided, closing his eyes and rubbing his face. He needed this as much as the dog did.

Endal liked the wraith.

Bastian opened his eyes. He stared down at the hard dirt.

The wraith had searched for something and cried when she'd not found it.

Guilt twisted inside him.

Bastian stood and felt in his pocket. The pebble was there, small and round and smooth.

He took it from his pocket and held it in his hand, his fingers clenched, hiding it. Why had he taken it? What had possessed him to steal?

She'd said it had no value. Then why had she cried?

Bastian uncurled his fingers reluctantly, not wanting to see the stone. It was red, flecked with black, small and unremarkable. And because of it he was a thief.

To return it would be a confession.

He swung his arm and cast the stone from him, throwing high and far. It landed amid the stubble of Gaudon's paddock. Gone.

But the guilt wasn't gone. He was still a thief.

CHAPTER THIRTY-ONE

MELKE TRACED THE outline of her feet on
the back of the map. The innkeeper's fin-
gerprints were on the paper, smudged. He
had thought her request odd, but for a copper coin
he'd taken pen and parchment and done as she asked.

She folded the paper so that Liana couldn't see the
map. *Thierry. Vere. Salamanders.* Her guilt, sketched
in black ink on parchment. "Here." She gave the girl
two coins, copper, thick and heavy.

Liana took the paper and the coins and placed them
beside her on the little table. "I'll give them to
Bastian."

Melke nodded. She clasped her hands together.
"Will Hantje be able to talk tomorrow?"

"Perhaps," Liana said, looking down at Hantje. He
slept quietly. A dozen candles burned in the room and
the mutton-scent of tallow was strong. "Or perhaps

the day after. For clearness of thought he needs to be stronger. It will take time."

"I'll make more broth."

"Broth, yes. And rest. It can't be hurried." The girl reached out to stroke Hantje's cheek. "He called me Asta. What does that mean?"

"Asta? It means Moon Daughter."

Liana removed her hand from Hantje's cheek.

"It's a compliment."

"The moon?" The girl's voice was stiff.

"Where we come from, the moon isn't feared. To you, she's evil; to us she's... she's gentle and kind and pure."

"Pure?"

"Yes." Melke nodded. She could almost smell the cold, woodsmoke-scented night air, almost feel the coarse woollen weave of her cloak, almost hear Mam's soft voice as she pointed at the moon. "She guides the innocent and protects their souls and she forgives." Mam's words, as they'd stood on the hillside above their house.

Liana touched Hantje's cheek lightly again, with her fingertips. "Really?"

Melke nodded.

"Your view of the moon is very different from ours."

"Yes."

"I like yours better."

"So do I." Melke followed the girl's gaze. Hantje slept peacefully. "He called you Asta because your hair is the color of the moon. It's a mark of beauty among our people."

"Beauty?" Liana flushed. Her upwards glance was shy.

"Yes."

"Oh." The girl's blush deepened.

Beauty without vanity, kindness and gentleness and silver hair. Hantje was right to name her Asta.

Silence grew in the room. There was nothing more to say. "Good night."

Melke shielded the flame of her candle as she walked down the dark corridor. Her slippers slapped softly on the flagstones in the empty kitchen. Shadows scurried across the floor and hid in corners, shrinking from the candlelight.

She climbed the stairs slowly to her bedchamber. Endal's claws clicked behind her. It was wonderful to walk without bandages, to feel no pain from her feet, but she needed to do more than walk. She needed to be able to run.

There were no curtains in the little room, no way of hiding from the sun or the moon. Melke stood at the window and looked out. Blackness. Stars. A waxing crescent.

Five days, not nine.

It was sooner than she'd thought, this thing she had to do.

CHAPTER THIRTY-TWO

T HIS TIME SILVIA was in the kitchen. She looked up as he stepped into the doorway, blocking light. "Bastian!"

"Good morning." He stayed on the doorstep. Silvia had never turned him away, not once in eight years, but he didn't want to walk into her house without invitation.

Silvia put aside the wooden spoon and wiped her hands on a cloth.

"If you're busy—"

"No." She put up a hand to stop his words. "Now is fine. Very fine."

The smile on her mouth and in her eyes, the tone of her voice, brought heat to his skin. "If it pleases you."

Silvia laughed. "Always, Bastian. Always." She undid her apron.

Stay here, Endal, he said, aware of the dog stretching out in the sunlight behind him. He stepped into the kitchen, inhaling the scents of baking bread and cinnamon and sugar, almost closing his eyes in pleasure.

Silvia's fingers slid around his wrist. "Come," she said, smiling. In the corridor she called: "Elsa, you're in charge," and he caught sight of the counter and the freckled face of the shop girl as she glanced back.

The fury and frustration were gone today. Bastian undressed Silvia leisurely, the headscarf first so that her hair fell over her shoulders and down her back. He ran his fingers through it. Soft and curling, blonde.

Silvia's hands were at his throat. She pushed aside the collar of his shirt. Smoky heat rose inside him as he felt her tongue on his skin.

He moved slightly faster, undoing the hooks on her gown. She tugged the shirt free of his trousers and he shrugged it off. He released her breasts from their binding. So ripe, so generous. He made a sound in his throat as he reached for them, a low animal noise, and Silvia laughed.

He bit lightly, teased, and then pushed her back on the bed and stripped the gown from her hips, baring her. Such lush, delicious curves.

Bastian touched her slowly and leisurely, without hurry. He knew her thoroughly, knew the texture and taste and scent of her, knew how to make her laugh and how to make her gasp, how to bring her to release, shuddering, with her fingers clenched in the sheets.

A tiny guttural sound slipped from her mouth when the pleasure peaked in her.

Bastian lay back on the bed. There was heat in every part of him. And there was smugness.

Silvia lay panting and flushed, her eyes tightly closed. "Get your trousers off. *Now*." Her voice was hoarse.

Bastian laughed and did as she demanded, and it was his turn while sunlight warmed the sheets. His awareness of the world narrowed to the light touch of fingertips and the nip of teeth, the softness of lips. The tickle of long hair on his skin. Heat grew inside him until he almost burst with it. And then came the clenching, the swift, soaring ecstasy, the long, slow float back down.

It was always twice. Eight years of always twice. And the second time he was inside her and it was even better. They lay together afterward, skin to skin. Bastian closed his eyes. He heard her light breathing and smelled the scent of their sweat, their pleasure. Her heart beat slowly beneath his fingertips.

He wanted this more than a few times a month. Not just the physical pleasure, but the togetherness, the being with someone. When the curse was lifted and rain fell again on Vere, when there was green grass and birdsong and water flowing in the dry riverbed, he'd find himself a bride and bring her home.

"Did you hear?" Silvia asked drowsily. "A girl was killed down by the docks."

Bastian opened his eyes. He saw sunlight and rumpled sheets and blonde hair. "Killed?"

"Strangled," Silvia said, turning her head to look at him.

Drunken brawls were common by the docks, where the poorer folk lived and the whores plied their trade, but deliberate murder was a rare occurrence. "When?"

"The night before last."

Bastian rubbed a hand over his face. It would be easy to close his eyes again and fall asleep. "One of the whores?"

Silvia shook her head. "No. A respectable girl. Although they say she was pregnant." Her mouth twisted, a tiny movement of regret, gone almost before he'd seen it. *I'm barren*, Silvia had told him the first time they'd lain together. *You needn't worry*. And he'd been relieved, hadn't heard bitterness or sorrow in her voice. Now he wondered if he'd been mistaken. Did she grieve that she'd never have a child?

Bastian lowered his hand. His sleepiness was gone. "Do they know who?"

"The killer?" Silvia asked. "Or the father of her child?"

"Either. Both."

"No." She shook her head. "Although Ronsard's son was questioned."

"Ronsard's son?" Bastian propped himself up on an elbow. "Julien?"

"It wasn't him." Silvia yawned, and stretched on the warm, cotton sheets. "He was working with his father that night."

Bastian grunted and lost interest. He reached out and smoothed his palm lightly over the curve of her hip. Silvia was a beautiful woman. The only woman he'd ever lain with. What would it be like to have someone else in his bed?

A fleeting dream-image came, pale skin and a slim body, breasts much smaller in his hands, black hair wrapping around him.

Bastian lifted his palm from Silvia's hip as if he'd been stung. The wraith had no place in his head. Especially not here, in this room, with this woman.

Silvia reached out to touch his cheek. Her smile was slow and contented. He managed to smile back at her.

"The pastries won't make themselves." She yawned again and sat up, pushing the hair back from her face.

Bastian sat up too. Thought of the wraith had extinguished his sense of well-being, like a candle being snuffed.

Silvia stretched, a movement that ordinarily would have drawn his attention. Bastian looked away. He stood and reached for his underbreeches.

Silvia rose from the bed. She hummed softly as she untangled her clothes and shook the creases from her dress. She didn't seem to notice that his mood had soured.

Bastian fastened his trousers and shrugged into his shirt. He was dressed before Silvia. He helped with the hooks of her gown, and afterward she placed her hands on his chest and kissed him. "Thank you."

His mood lightened. He pulled her closer. "My pleasure."

She kissed him again in the empty kitchen, surrounded by the scents of sugar and rising dough. It was smaller than the kitchen at Vere, but the windowpanes were uncracked and the whitewash didn't peel from the walls. Copper pots hung from hooks beside the cast-iron stove, gleaming. Earthenware mixing bowls were stacked on the dresser and wooden spoons and birch twig whisks stood in a wide-mouthed stone jar. A rolling pin as thick as his arm lay on the table.

He heard the tiny sound of a bell as the door to the shop opened and closed. Voices murmured. Silvia stepped back from him. "You'll come again?"

"Of course. Do you doubt it?"

Silvia shook her head. She tied an apron around her waist, businesslike, and then shivered and rubbed her arms. "A wraith just walked past."

The smile stiffened on his face.

Silvia's eyebrows rose. She stopped rubbing her arms.

Bastian forced a laugh. "Quick, throw some salt."

"Silvia?"

The girl with the freckled face stood in the doorway. Her gaze flicked to Bastian, and then away. "Mistress Solande wishes to order a cake. She'd like to discuss the decoration with you."

"Of course." Silvia was already halfway to the door. She glanced back at him over her shoulder. "Good bye, Bastian."

"Good bye."

But he didn't leave immediately. He reached for the saltpig and took a few grains between his fingertips. Salt. To cast on a wraith.

Bastian let the grains fall from his fingers. Was it true that salt made wraiths seen? That milk turned sour in a wraith's presence? That eggs spoiled in their shells?

He scowled as he stepped out into the alley. There'd been no wraith in the kitchen, but that black-haired creature had been in his head, upstairs in the sunny bedchamber. For an instant, the merest second, he'd imagined lying with her.

Endal was outside, basking in sunlight.

Come, Endal, Bastian said, and spat into the gutter.

CHAPTER THIRTY-THREE

BASTIAN STRODE INTO the tavern stable yard, Endal trotting at his heels. "My horse," he said, tossing the stableman a copper coin. Afternoon shadows lay across the cobblestones and unease itched between his shoulder blades. There was no time to visit Michaud. He'd spent too long haggling over shoes with the cobbler. Liana was alone, without Endal's protection, and he should have left Thierry hours ago. "Fool," he muttered under his breath. It had been self-indulgent to visit Silvia, self-indulgent to bring Endal to Thierry with him. What if the wraith changed her sly mind and fled?

"Come to stare at me, have you?"

Bastian turned his head.

Julien strolled across the stable yard. "I didn't do it, if that's what you think." His walk was swaggering, his tone defiant. "Someone else killed the stupid bint."

Bastian turned away. "I have no interest in what you do."

"Plenty of men had her," Julien insisted. "She was a slut."

Unease and impatience twisted easily into anger. It would be satisfying to grab Julien by the scruff of the neck and douse his head in the nearest horse trough. Satisfying, and foolish. More foolish than bedding Silvia had been.

Don't be a fool twice over, Bastian told himself, folding his arms over his chest. He frowned across the cobbled yard, to where the stableman untied Gaudon. Movement caught his eye. He turned his head slightly. Ronsard hurried toward them, a wide smile on his face. "Bastian," he said.

"Ronsard." Bastian gave the man a curt nod.

"I hope my son hasn't been boring you with—"

"No." Bastian shifted his weight, impatient, and watched as the stableman led Gaudon toward them.

"Go inside, son," the innkeeper said. "Bastian sal Vere has no interest in our little problems."

"But—"

"That's enough, son. Go inside." Ronsard's voice was smooth and jovial.

Endal stirred at Bastian's side.

What? he asked the dog.

I don't like these people.

Neither do I, he said, reaching for Gaudon's reins.

Julien turned away, the set of his mouth sulky. It wasn't until the youth had entered the kitchen that Bastian thought to ask the dog: *Why don't you like them?*

Because they lie.

Bastian looked down at Endal. *They do?*

Yes.

Bastian began to buckle his purchases onto Gaudon's saddle. His fingers moved slowly.

"I apologize for my son," Ronsard said, affable and smiling. "The last few days have been difficult for him."

"So I understand."

Ronsard laughed, a hearty sound. "As if anyone could suspect my son of harming someone! It's absurd!"

Bastian tightened the last strap and turned and looked at the man. "Is it?"

He had asked the question mildly, but outrage swelled Ronsard's chest and flushed his face. "Of course it is! My son didn't kill that whore."

Does he tell the truth?

No.

Bastian smiled at the innkeeper. "Then you have nothing to worry about." He inclined his head in farewell. "Good day."

CHAPTER THIRTY-FOUR

LIANA WAS AT the farm with two wraiths, alone and unprotected. All he wanted was to get home as fast as possible. It would take Gaudon hours on the stony track; the sun would be close to setting before he reached Vere. And yet...

A girl had died.

Bastian headed toward the main square of Thierry and the watch house, although his feet wanted to turn in the opposite direction. Curse it. He didn't have time for this.

Where are we going? Endal asked.

To see Michaud. I have to talk to him.

Endal's ears pricked. He liked the big watch captain.

They walked through Thierry's cobbled streets as swiftly as Gaudon's pace allowed. The dog said nothing more. He trotted alongside Bastian, his nostrils flaring as he caught interesting scents. In the square, Bastian tied Gaudon to a hitching post and strode fast up the steps to the watch house, Endal at his heels.

He halted just inside the door. The main room was as busy as Ronsard's inn on a market-day afternoon.

Three of the cells were occupied. A man sang tunelessly in one, swaying as he held onto the bars. His face was unshaven and his laborer's clothes were stained and dirty. In the cell alongside him sat a sullen man in the burn-scarred leather apron of a blacksmith. A watchman stood in front of the cell, his arms folded over his chest, listening with an impassive face to a young woman. She held a baby in her arms. A toddler clutched at her long skirt. "My husband had a right!" she insisted. "Claupry hadn't paid."

Across the room, the occupant of the third cell sat with his head in his hands. A bucket stood on the straw at his feet. Another drunk, Bastian realized, as the man opened his mouth and began to vomit.

Several watchmen sat at the long table, empty plates in front of them. Their faces were weary. They didn't talk among themselves.

Michaud stood with his back to Bastian. "We're doing our best."

The woman he spoke to was older than the blacksmith's wife, the cloth of her gown coarse, her hair gray. "But you've found nothing yet." Tears choked in her voice.

The drunk began to sing more loudly, drowning Michaud's reply.

"You can't arrest my husband!" the blacksmith's wife protested shrilly. The toddler raised her head and began to wail.

The woman talking to Michaud clutched at his arm. Distress twisted her face. Michaud didn't brush her hand away. He bent his head low and spoke quietly.

Endal whined.

I don't like this either, Bastian told him.

The gray-haired woman released Michaud's arm. Bastian stood aside as she walked toward the door. Her eyes stared through him, blind with grief. She didn't appear to notice the noise or the smell of vomit. She paused on the threshold for a moment, gripping the doorframe. Then she stepped outside.

"Michaud," Bastian said loudly.

Michaud didn't hear him. He jerked his head at the singing prisoner and gestured sharply. The ginger-haired recruit, Vaspard, pushed back his chair and stood. He nodded a greeting to Bastian as he exited the watch house, an empty bucket in his hand.

The brindle pup, Lubon, came out from beneath the long table.

Endal put his ears forward, interested.

This is Lubon, Bastian told him. The pup approached, wagging his tail tentatively. Ribs still showed beneath the brindle coat, but there was no hunger in the eager jumble of Lubon's thoughts.

Endal sniffed the pup.

Bastian stepped further into the room. "Michaud."

The watch captain turned his head and saw him. "What?" His tone was harassed.

"I need to talk to you."

"Now?" Michaud turned his head, scanning the room. His gaze rested briefly on the man singing, on the blacksmith's wife and crying child, and on the drunk now groaning on the wooden bench in his cell.

"Fenin." He snapped his fingers. "Clean him up."

Another watchman pushed back his chair and stood. His face was tired and unshaven.

"Yes," said Bastian. "Now. It's important."

Vaspard came panting up the steps, a dripping bucket in his hands. He crossed the room and raised the bucket and threw its contents.

The loud, drunken singing stopped. "You," said Vaspard. "Quiet!"

The toddler stopped crying. She stared at the sodden prisoner, open-mouthed. In the silence, the sound of dripping water was loud.

"Finally," Michaud muttered under his breath. He turned his attention to Bastian again. "What?" The word was short, impatient.

"I need to talk to you privately."

"Bastian, I don't have time." Michaud gestured at the cells. "There's—"

"It's about the girl. The one who was killed."

Michaud closed his mouth. He looked at Bastian and then nodded, a sharp movement of his head. "Upstairs." He caught the eye of the watchman standing in front of the blacksmith's cell. "Stay where you are."

The man nodded.

The blacksmith's wife shifted her attention to Michaud. "You can't arrest him!" she cried, clutching her baby. Brown hair straggled from her bun. "He's done nothing wrong!"

"Madam, he nearly killed a man," Michaud said.

"He had a right," she insisted, her face plain and fierce. "Claupry wouldn't pay."

"Then your husband should have spoken to his alderman," Michaud told her.

The baby began to cry, a thin, hiccupping sound. The toddler joined in, clinging to her mother's skirt. The blacksmith paid no attention to his family. He spat into the straw at his feet.

Michaud jerked his head toward the door at the back of the room. Bastian nodded. *Come, Endal. We're going upstairs.*

The drunk raised his voice in querulous complaint: "I can sing if I wan' to."

"Not in my watch house," Michaud said curtly, as he crossed the room. He held open the door for Bastian. "As many buckets as it takes, Vaspard."

The door was thick and solid and bound with iron. With it shut, there was silence. Bastian heard the *click* of claws on stone as Endal climbed the stairs, the pup scrambling to keep up.

Upstairs was another square room, with bunks instead of cells. The windows were unbarred and the floor not strewn with straw, but the table and chairs were as scarred and stained as those downstairs. Half a dozen staves leaned in one corner, sturdy, their grips bound with leather. Two watchmen slept fully clothed. One lay with his face to the wall. The other slept on his back, snoring softly.

"Tell me," Michaud said, picking up a chair and carrying it over to the window. "And it had better be good, Bastian. I don't have time for—"

"Neither do I," said Bastian. He didn't sit. Urgency kept him on his feet. Liana had been alone with the wraiths for too long. He needed to know that she was safe.

Michaud grunted. "So?"

"Ronsard and Julien are lying. The lad killed her."

"Her?"

"The girl. The dockside girl."

"Her name was Helene," Michaud said, stretching out his legs. Hobnails studded the thick soles of his boots. "You saw her mother downstairs."

Bastian remembered the shine of tears in the woman's eyes, the way her fingers had groped for the doorframe. He felt swift shame that he'd begrudged the time to come to the watch house.

Michaud watched him, his eyes assessing, his face weary. "Tell me why you think Julien killed the girl."

"I don't think it, I know it."

"Really? How?"

Something in his friend's voice made Bastian stiffen. "Endal told me."

"Really," Michaud said again, flatly. He stood. "Bastian, I don't have time for—"

"Wait." His voice was equally flat. He grabbed hold of Michaud's arm. "Listen to me."

The watch captain shrugged off his hand. He exhaled sharply through his nose. Bastian didn't need Endal to tell him that Michaud hovered on the brink of anger.

"You know I can speak with dogs." He held the watch captain's eyes until he nodded, a short, stiff movement of his head. "Endal can see when people lie."

Michaud exhaled through his nose again, a frustrated sound. "Bastian, I can't—"

"Let me show you."

Michaud hesitated for a long moment. Behind them, one of the sleeping watchmen snored, a whistling, snuffling sound.

"Fine." The watch captain sat. He folded his arms across his chest. Leather creaked and chain mail clinked. "Show me." His expression was closed.

He didn't want to believe. Bastian looked away, disappointment sharp in his chest. *Endal, come here please.* Not everyone was comfortable with magic, but he'd never thought the watch captain fell into that category. He always seemed to enjoy hearing Endal's comments relayed.

The dog rose from where he'd been lying in a patch of sunlight, Lubon nipping at his ears. *Yes? Tell me if Michaud lies.*

Endal cocked his head to one side. Bastian sensed his confusion. Friends didn't lie to each other. *It's a game*, he told the dog.

Endal understood the concept of games. He wagged his tail and sat, his gaze fixed on Michaud.

"The day we met. Do you remember the brawl?" Bastian had watched the fight erupt, several farmers' sons rounding on a youth in the crowded marketplace.

The watch captain lifted his chin in a nod. Even then, ten years ago, his arms had been thickly muscled. Bastian had seen him land some solid punches before going down on the cobblestones.

"Three against one."

Michaud grunted.

It hadn't been the unevenness of the odds that had made Bastian come to his aid. He'd wanted to fight, to hit someone with all his weight behind him. And he'd enjoyed it, had enjoyed the solid, painful thud of his fist on a bony jaw and the breathlessness of being punched in the stomach. He'd enjoyed grazing his knuckles on someone's teeth and wrestling on the cobblestones, knocking into stalls and scattering apples and baskets of nuts. He'd even enjoyed the taste of blood in his mouth from a split lip. For a few minutes he'd been able to forget about Vere and the curse and his responsibilities and concentrate on shoving his knee into a fleshy stomach and bouncing his fist off the broad, freckled face of a farmer's son.

"They said you'd goosed a girl, one of their sweethearts."

Michaud grunted again.

It wasn't until they'd been hauled into the watch house, all five of them, that Bastian learned what the fight had been about, and Michaud's name.

"Did you?"

"No."

It was what Michaud had said ten years ago, emphasising his point by spitting on the straw-covered floor downstairs.

Endal?

He tells the truth.

"I always thought you'd done it."

Michaud glanced at Endal. "He says I don't lie?"

Bastian nodded.

"No point goosing a girl who doesn't have a bonny figure." Michaud made as if to stand. "Bastian, I need more than—"

Bastian held up his hand. "Just wait."

The watch captain settled impatiently back in the chair.

"When you trained in Desmaures, was there a girl?"

"No." Michaud pushed up out of the chair. "I've had enough of this, Bastian."

Endal?

He lies.

The watch captain headed for the door. "I'm too busy for this nonsense—"

"You had a girl."

"What?" Michaud swung around to look at him.

"Endal says you're lying. You had a girl in Desmaures."

Michaud's cheeks reddened above his beard. "Lower your voice," he said, coming back across the room.

Bastian leaned against the window sill. "What does it matter? So you had a girl. All the recruits do."

"I was courting Geneve."

"Courting, yes. Betrothed, no." Michaud had waited until he'd come home with his watchman's leather jerkin and wooden stave before he'd asked his sweetheart to marry him.

"I shouldn't have done it," Michaud said, his face and voice stubborn.

Bastian shrugged. He glanced down at Endal. The dog sat patiently while Lubon chewed on his tail. "Convinced?" he asked.

"No. I'm sorry, Bastian. Ronsard's an alderman. I need good cause to question his word."

Bastian's head swung up. "Curse it, Michaud! Endal was right twice!"

One of the sleeping men stirred.

"Lucky guesses."

Anger flared in his chest. He wanted to grab Michaud by his burly neck and knock some sense into him. *Don't be a fool*, he told himself, gritting his teeth, curling his fingers into the palms of his hands. Words, not punches, would make Michaud see reason. "Fine," he said tightly, unclenching his hands and reaching down to pick up Lubon. "What about the pig?"

"What pig?"

"The one that was tied up in the square last year. Dressed like the mayor." Lubon squirmed in his grip and tried to lick his face.

"What about it?"

"Do you know who put it there?"

Michaud folded his arms across his chest. "No."

The truth?

No.

"Endal says you're lying."

Michaud glanced down at Endal. His mouth tightened.

"Was it you?" Bastian asked.

The words jerked Michaud's head up. "I am not going to answer that question."

"Was it you?" Bastian asked again, while Lubon wriggled in his arms. The pup's tail beat against his chest.

Michaud cast a quick glance behind him at the sleeping men. "No," he said. "No, it wasn't me."

The truth?

No.

"Liar," said Bastian.

The watch captain's eyes narrowed. He leaned close, his bearded face fierce. "Don't you dare tell anyone!" The words were low and hissed. "I'll lose my job!"

Endal whined, anxious. *Bas?*

It's all right, Bastian told him. *Don't worry*. And then he said the words aloud to Michaud, "Don't worry. You know I won't tell."

The seconds stretched, while Michaud scowled at him and the pup wriggled in his arms. One of the sleeping men muttered.

Michaud released his breath in a sharp exhalation of sound. He shook his head, the anger falling from his face. "Looked like him, didn't it?" His teeth flashed as he grinned. "The pig."

"I didn't see it," Bastian said, patting Lubon. It had been the morning of spring equinox. He'd been waiting for the psaaron.

Michaud grunted. He rubbed his face. "All right. I'll talk to Ronsard and Julien again."

Bastian pushed away from the window sill. "The lad killed her," he said, setting the pup on the floor.

"I can't just arrest him. You know that. I need proof, or a confession."

"I know," Bastian said, following the watch captain across the room.

They walked down the stairs in silence, Lubon scrambling ahead with clumsy eagerness. "She was only fifteen," Michaud said at the bottom, while the pup scratched at the door.

"The girl?"

Michaud nodded.

Bastian thought of Julien, cocksure and arrogant, lying. "You'll get him?"

Michaud nodded. His face was hard. "Yes. I'll get him." He opened the heavy door. The smell of vomit and unwashed bodies enveloped them. The blacksmith's children were still crying. The drunk sang, loud and tunelessly.

Michaud's expression became even grimmer.

"Give Endal my thanks," he said.

Bastian nodded. *Stay here*, he told Lubon, as the pup tried to follow them outside. On the doorstep he met Vaspard, puffing, another bucket of water slopping in his grip.

CHAPTER THIRTY-FIVE

BASTIAN RETURNED WHILE Melke was in the kitchen. Broth simmered on the stove and mutton roasted in the oven. She stiffened when she heard his footsteps and her fingers tightened on the spoon she held. She turned her head.

Endal trotted across the kitchen, his tail wagging, and touched his nose to her leg. *Hello*, the gesture seemed to say.

Bastian didn't greet her as he came in out of the dusk. "Shoes," he said, placing a string-tied bundle on the table. His voice was flat. "And your change." The small copper coin clinked thinly as he put it down.

She nodded. A cool nod. Mam's nod to the guards.

"And this." He set a small basket on the table and pushed it toward her.

Melke put down the spoon. "What is it?"

He made no answer, merely opened his hand in a gesture she understood. *See for yourself.*

Melke stepped toward the table. Straw and... "Eggs." An insult. She reached into the basket and took one in her hand, brown and smooth, and flexed her fingers around it. "They won't spoil, if that's what you think. It's a fishwives' tale."

Bastian shrugged, a slight movement of one shoulder. His face was expressionless.

"Did you bring milk, too?" Her voice was sharp. "That won't spoil either."

He crossed his arms over his chest and leaned back against the wall, still watching her. "No milk."

Anger made her reckless. She placed the egg back in the basket before it shattered in her hand. "Tell me, do you become a hound when the moon is full?"

Bastian's eyebrows lowered. He pushed away from the wall and uncrossed his arms. "Of course not."

She smiled at him, tightly. "And I don't sour milk or curdle eggs or become seen when salt is cast at me. Or chase all the spiders from a house. Ask Endal whether I lie."

"I have asked him." Bastian's smile was as tight as her own, mocking. "He says you tell the truth." He snapped his fingers. "Endal."

The hound transferred his attention to Bastian, his head slightly cocked.

"Don't let her out of your sight," Bastian said. The words, the flat hostility in his voice, were insulting. He'd left her unguarded all day and now he set his hound on her again. "Bite her if she becomes unseen."

Melke crossed her arms and raised her chin, to show him that she didn't care.

"The equinox starts in four days."

He was gone before Melke found her voice. "I know," she whispered. "I know."

SHE WORE THE new shoes in the morning. They fitted well. Hantje wasn't able to answer her questions, though. He said her name when he woke, and smiled at her, but she couldn't get him to speak beyond that. His gaze was slightly unfocused. She'd seen it before, in the eyes of the desert nomads who smoked poppy resin. The world was still unreal to him.

Hantje drank both tea and broth willingly, and allowed her to wash his face and comb his hair. He smiled again when she offered to read a tale to him, and was asleep before she'd finished the second page.

Melke laid the book on the floor and touched her fingers lightly to his cheek. He looked well. His breathing was even, his pulse strong and steady. Fever didn't heat him or twist his dreams into nightmares. It was impossible to tell where the burns had been, and Liana said the bones had knitted. But he hadn't the strength to think clearly.

"Sleep, Hantje," she whispered. "Grow strong." *And hurry. Time is short.*

She stood. "Come, Endal. I need to wear in my shoes."

The house told her what the sal Veres had been, and how much they'd lost. Melancholy settled on her as she walked through room after empty room, high-ceilinged and with large windows and wide stone fireplaces. She could see where pictures had hung on the panelled walls. The furniture was gone, the carpets, even the curtains.

She opened doors to a formal parlor, a study, a library with tall shelves and no books, and a large room with bay windows and a fireplace that dwarfed all the others. Melke touched the dusty mantelpiece. Clusters of leaves were carved into the stone. She looked around her. Was this where the family had gathered in the evenings?

Alongside the kitchen was a dining room, empty but for a single chair. Fabric was roughly bundled on the wooden seat and half a dozen buttons lay scattered on the floor.

Melke's footsteps echoed as she crossed the room. The chair stood beside a window. The view was of bare meadows and the dusty track that led away from the farmhouse. She picked up the bundle and carefully shook it out. A blouse, with long sleeves and a plain collar. It lacked only buttons.

Had Liana sat here waiting for Bastian to return with the necklace?

Melke fingered the fabric. The cotton was coarse and undyed. It didn't match the room; the elegantly panelled ceiling and the ornate cornices demanded something finer.

She smoothed the creases and laid the blouse on the chair and bent to pick up the buttons, while Endal sniffed the fireplace. The buttons were made of bone, as simple and plain as the blouse. She turned one over in her fingers. Had Bastian made them?

Melke opened cupboards until she found where Liana kept the buttons. The deep shelves must once have held porcelain and silver; now they were almost bare. A few needles and a handful of pins lay on one shelf, a wooden spool of thread, scissors and a thimble. Buttons. Pieces of fabric were neatly piled on a lower shelf: the undyed cotton of Liana's blouses and Bastian's shirts, the sturdier dull brown cotton that his trousers and her skirts were made from, scraps of old bed linen.

She looked down at the embroidery on her cuffs. Flowers and leaves, intertwined. Stitched in thread a few shades darker than the blue-grey of her blouse.

Melke pressed her lips together and closed the cupboard. Liana should wear coloured fabrics: apple greens and soft pinks, forget-me-not blue.

"Come, Endal."

She climbed the wide staircase and halted at the top. She'd stood here twelve days ago, unseen, her heart knocking against her breastbone. A door had stood open, part way down the corridor. She'd heard the creak of a floorboard, a woman singing. The words had been too low to hear, the phrases broken by long pauses and the sound of a bed being stripped of its linen.

Today there was only silence.

The door to Bastian's bedchamber was closed, as it had been that morning. *The firsst door on the right*. Melke walked over to it and laid her hand on the cool wood.

She had stood in this precise spot, afraid and determined, her ears alert to the singing down the corridor, her heart banging against her ribs. *Do it. Do it. Do it.*

Bastian's door had opened silently, showing her a large room with high windows and green curtains, empty. There'd been no creak of stiff hinges, nothing to give her away. She had stepped quickly inside and closed the door and stood with her back to it, her breathing shallow, her heartbeat fast. She'd seen wealth, not poverty, had noticed the expensive panelling and the commanding size of the bed, not the bareness of the room.

It isss in a chessst. Beneath the bed.

She had committed her crime swiftly, crossing the room and kneeling on the hard floorboards, reaching beneath the bed to pull out the chest.

"Forgive me," she'd whispered, to Mam and Da, to the occupant of the room.

The chest was old and plain, the wood dark with age. A handful of items lay inside: a crocheted baby's blanket, a battered wooden rattle, a thin and knotted skipping rope, a wooden spinning top with the paint worn off. The necklace was wrapped in a piece of linen. The cloth was embroidered in a child's crooked stitches.

She had felt relief, kneeling on the floor. The necklace wasn't valuable; the ordinariness of the other items told her that, rattle and skipping rope and spinning top. These things were mementos. The salamanders had told the truth. *Not jewelsss. Sssea ssstonesss.*

Why do you want the necklace? she'd asked, when the salamanders had stated the price of Hantje's freedom. The answer had been a sinuous shrug. *We like pretty thingsss.*

Pretty. Priceless. But the creatures wouldn't have cared whether the necklace was strung with psaaron tears or diamonds and rubies. It was merely another treasure to add to their pile.

The shimmering stones had become unseen once the necklace was around her throat. She'd folded the cloth and put it on top of the baby's blanket and pushed the chest back under the bed. *Forgive me* she'd whispered again, to the person who'd kept the necklace so carefully wrapped. To Bastian.

She had stood, a thief, and opened the door and crept back down the stairs, a thief, hearing Liana's soft singing and the sound of a broom sweeping and the rapid beating of her own heart.

Guilt had been heavy in her belly, but stronger than guilt had been determination. *I'm doing the right thing*, she told herself as she stepped out into the yard, as she followed the rutted track at the half-jog, back toward the river. *I'm doing the right thing.*

Melke lowered her hand from Bastian's door. "It wasn't the right thing," she told the hound, her voice flat.

Endal pricked his ears.

The wrong thing. The worst thing. And now she must be a wraith again, a thief. It was the only way. Laws of nature couldn't be broken; the psaaron would never ask the salamanders for the necklace, any more than the salamanders would give it back. The magical creatures chose paths that never crossed, and it was well for mankind that they did: their battles would make the mountains bleed and oceans boil dry.

She turned away from Bastian's door. The corridor was silent apart from the *clack* of Endal's claws on the wooden floor as he walked beside her. Two rooms down was Liana's bedchamber, the door now shut as the girl slept.

She knew without having to ask that the blanket was Liana's as a baby, that the toys in the chest had been the girl's, and the cloth with the crooked stitches.

If the psaaron chose Liana, Bastian would be broken more surely than if the creature chose him.

Whatever choice the psaaron made, brother or sister, the result would be the same: pain beyond bearing for one, unendurable grief for the other.

Melke blew out a breath. "I will get it back," she told the hound. "I *will*."

Endal wagged his tail.

Beyond Liana's room were other bedchambers, and around the corner a nursery. Melke opened the doors, peering inside. The rooms were empty of furnishings, bare. Dressing rooms and wardrobes opened off them, but no clothes hung inside.

Upstairs from the kitchen were four rooms for servants. Only hers had a bed. There had been no malice in Bastian to give her a servant's bedchamber; there was nowhere else she could have slept.

Melke stood on the tiny, dark landing. There should be noise, footsteps and voices, children's laughter, bustle in the kitchen. Instead, the house was empty around her, quiet.

The psaaron had destroyed a family. Did it know that?

She touched the wall. The stone was cold and rough beneath her fingers. There were no expensive wood panels here, where the servants had slept.

Vengeance. A family for a family. The necklace of psaaron tears for the flesh and blood of the sal Veres.

HANTJE WOKE AGAIN, drank tea and broth, listened to two more pages of story, and fell asleep again.

"Outside, this time," Melke said to Endal. The house was too silent, too empty.

But the yard was also silent. The henhouse had no hens. One horse stood in a bare paddock, eating hay beneath the shade of a dead tree. Two sheep, heavy with lamb, watched her from a lean-to pen. A lizard sunned itself by the well.

The garden had once been much bigger, three times the size it was now. The rows of dry, turned dirt looked like long graves. At the end, a small cesspit had been dug into the abandoned land. Another lizard watched the flies with heavy-lidded eyes.

The barn was empty except for a few implements: hoe and spade and rake, a rusted scythe. There was no cart, no plough. She saw a small dairy with a churn and a stone cheese weight, but no cows. More pens and paddocks, fenced and empty. A cobbled stable yard. Melke's eyes widened slightly as she counted the stalls.

She walked slowly, opening doors. She found an empty tackroom, living quarters for grooms, and a bare and dusty feed room. With each step she took, each door that she unlatched, her horror grew. It was a tumor in her chest, swelling. Vere was far larger than she'd thought. What the sal Veres had lost was immense.

Her steps become slower. She didn't want to see, didn't want to know how vast the fall had been. She was scarcely moving now. Decay surrounded her, peeling whitewash and cracked panes of glass and missing slates on the roofs. Everything was so empty, so silent.

Melke halted. "Let's go back, Endal." But the hound wanted to continue. He waited for her at the end of the long building.

And around that corner were the ruins of a pleasure garden, with paths and fountains and ponds. The fruit trees were dead, as were the shrubs and low hedges. No flowers bloomed in the neatly laid-out beds.

Melke shivered. The skeletons of the plants were worse than the empty rooms in the house, worse than the stables and the bare paddocks. This was something she could reach out and touch. This was death.

She walked briskly through the garden, back toward the house. Endal trotted beside her with his tongue hanging out. He didn't appear to mind the barren garden. She did. Her skin was cold despite the sun's heat. She didn't want to linger here, didn't want to imagine what the flower beds might have looked like years ago.

At the end of the garden, alongside the house, was a bathhouse.

Melke stepped inside, cautious and curious. Lizards darted to hide. Endal pricked his ears at their rustlings, alert.

She stood and turned her head. She saw lapping waves and round-eyed fish. An octopus. A spouting whale. Beaked turtles. The tiles were laid out in patterns, greens and blues, white, and the pink of seashells. She reached out with a fingertip and felt smoothness, coolness.

Melke explored, her mouth slightly open in wonder. There had been hot water and cold. A changing room, a room to bathe in, a room for steam with benches around the walls, and... she almost laughed. Latrines, three of them, stone with wooden seats and a channel below where water used to flow. And basins for washing hands. Just like a public privy.

It was extraordinary. It was marvellous.

A short path paved with white and gray pebbles led back to the house and a side door. The door was locked.

Melke sat down on the step and clasped her hands around her knees. Endal sat beside her. She looked at the bathhouse. Someone had enjoyed designing it. There was a sense of whimsy in the patterns on the tiled floor and walls. A gayness, a lightness of heart.

She smoothed the skirt over her knees. "Lunch time."

Endal's ears pricked.

"Yes. Lunch." Melke stood, and touched her fingers lightly to his head. "Eggs for me, and a bone for you."

He knew the word *bone*. He pranced alongside her as she walked around to the front of the farmhouse. Beneath the empty, curtainless windows of the largest room was a small courtyard, prettily paved and with a sundial at its center.

Melke paused and looked at the shadow it cast. An hour past noon.

The tiny tiles were laid in an ornate pattern. She moved her feet to see the design. The four elements, the four magical creatures. They stood opposite one another, as divided in the mosaic as they were in reality.

Fear crawled over her skin, a pricking of hairs standing upright. This courtyard was perilously close to veneration. Representations less detailed than these had started town riots in Stenrik; statuary had been smashed, paintings torched.

But this was Bresse, where people believed that no harm came from making images of the magical creatures.

Melke bent to wipe the dust away. Her hand cringed from the task. She forced herself to brush aside the grains of dirt, to touch the tiles. Everything she'd been taught as a child told her it was dangerous.

Endal nosed at the tiles. *What?* he seemed to ask.

"Superstition," she whispered. That's all it was. She'd seen the statue in the square in Desmaures. It had stood for centuries, and no furious gryphon had come to punish those who dared fix its likeness in stone. Superstition, only superstition.

Even so, she shivered as she uncovered the first image.

Where she'd stood, was Earth: a lamia beneath the arch of a cavern roof. She was half-changed, a woman from the waist up, lush. A forked snake-tongue flickered from her mouth. Below the waist she was a serpent, the coils thick and sinuous.

And here was Water. Melke's hand faltered as she wiped away the dust. A psaaron. The tiler had been skilled. She could almost see the webbing between the creature's fingers and toes, the ridged scales that served for its skin. The psaaron stood tall, its head turned sideways so that the spiny crest was visible. Waves curled at its feet. It was neuter, neither male nor female.

Melke laid a fingertip on the creature's chest. "You will have your necklace back," she whispered, and then shivered.

Endal sat down and began to scratch himself.

She stepped around the hound, bent, and brushed away more dust. Air. The word was spelled out in cursive script. Beneath those letters a gryphon screamed with outspread wings and open beak.

And lastly...

It was difficult to breathe, almost impossible to wipe away the last of the dust. She smelled musk, strong and spicy. Fire, read the curling letters. A salamander stood in a circle of flames, lithe and female. Her irises seemed to burn.

Melke stepped back and averted her eyes from the salamander. She looked at the sundial, casting a spike of shade, and at the clawed feet and thick serpent's tail that ringed the pedestal.

The differences between lamia and gryphon, psaaron and salamander, were as vast and deep as the ocean, unbridgeable. No magical creature would enter another's territory, let alone stand like this, with only a few inches separating them. Their closeness was... it was *wrong.* The creatures' dealings were with humans, never each other.

Dealings. She hugged her arms, cold in the sunlight. The word was too neutral for what they did: gryphons snatching away virgins and lamiae seducing the unwary, salamanders bargaining for treasures with those desperate enough to meet their price. And psaarons punishing.

Endal stretched out on the warm tiles, unconcerned by the images.

"If this was my house," she told the hound, "I would take up the tiles and lay others in their place."

Endal wagged his tail, stirring dust. His coat gleamed black in the sunlight.

She was glad to turn her back on the courtyard and walk with Endal around to the kitchen. The images were dangerous. They diminished the magical creatures, making them decorations instead of something to fear.

THAT EVENING SHE took Hantje's knapsack down from the hook in her room. The note he'd left for her was folded at the top. Her fingers shrank from touching it. This was the start of it all, this scrap of paper. *I've gone to the salamanders' den. I'll be back by dusk.*

But he hadn't returned. And at dawn the next day she had followed him, and learned the price for his freedom.

His better trousers were near the bottom of the knapsack. Melke held them up to her waist. She had burned the clothes she'd worn to steal the necklace; they'd been ripped and blood-stained, no use even as rags. Hantje's trousers were too large, but with her belt pulled tight and the legs cut shorter... yes, they would do.

She laid the items on the stiff-backed wooden chair: Hantje's trousers, her other blouse. The gray cloak Bastian had found beneath the bridge. Her belt and knife. And the new shoes, placed neatly side by side on the floor. There. She was ready. Now, she just needed her brother to talk.

In the morning, he did.

Melke heard voices before she reached the sick-room.

She halted in the doorway. Sunlight streamed in through the window, bright and warm. Hantje sat up in the bed. Liana leaned toward him, the white-blonde hair falling forward over her shoulder. Her voice was quick and light. Hantje's was slower, but firm and steady, the sentences long. His face was alive. He glanced at the door and saw her, and his smile—

"Mel!"

Melke crossed the room without feeling the floor beneath her feet, scarcely noticing as Liana stood and moved aside. Her arms were around Hantje, her face pressed into his hair. He gripped her tightly back. He was too thin beneath the nightshirt, but alive in a way he'd not been yester-day, strong. She was aware of his health, his vitality.

She hugged him, while happiness leaked from her eyes as tears and her heart felt that it would burst with joy. Then she held his face in her hands and simply looked at him. The burns, the bruises, the torn lips and swollen eyelids, the flushed cheeks and the sweat of fever... they were gone. A dream, forgotten.

"You look well."

Hantje took her hands, held them in his own. "I am well."

This was her brother, the person she loved most in the world, this man with clear eyes and a laugh-ing mouth.

And the despair that he kept hidden from her.

"Sit," he said. "Liana was explaining, but I don't understand. How did I come to be here?"

CHAPTER THIRTY-SIX

THE MALE WRAITH was speaking. Not loudly enough for Bastian to hear, but definitely sentences, full sentences. He sat up in the bed, thin-faced, his hair as long as a girl's, raven black.

He had an eastern voice, lower in tone than the sister's, Melke's, but with the same accent: soft *s* and purring *r*. And eastern hair, too, hanging so long down his back. He had his sister's features, the same line of cheek and jaw, the same blackness of hair and paleness of skin. He should look like a woman with that ridiculous hair, but somehow he didn't.

Bastian watched from the shadows of the doorway. *Hurry up*, he wanted to shout. The tides would soon rise for the equinox and there was no time for this... this *chat*. He took a step into the room.

His boots made no sound on the thin carpet, but the movement caught Liana's eye. She looked up

and shook her head. Her mouth moved silently:
Out.

Endal thumped his tail on the floor. He wanted
Bastian to stay.

Bastian folded his arms across his chest.

Liana's eyebrows drew together. *Out,* she
mouthed again, her expression almost fierce.

Bastian exhaled with a hiss, a sound that made
Endal prick his ears. He turned on his heel and
stalked from the room.

"WHEN?" HANTJE ASKED.

"The equinox starts in two days."

The laughter was utterly gone from his face.
There was no color in his cheeks. His lips were
pressed together, bloodless.

"I'll do it," he said, and in his voice Melke heard
all the horror and shame that she saw in his eyes.

"No," Liana said. "You can't walk."

He held his head slightly averted, not looking at
the girl. "You said I could walk." The words were
stiff, as if shame choked his throat.

"A few steps, nothing more. Not yet."

"But—"

"No." Liana's voice was firm. It brooked no
argument.

Hantje turned his head and met the girl's eyes.
"It's my fault," he said fiercely. "*My fault!* And I
will undo the harm I have caused!"

"If you wish to undo it, then tell me how to enter
the den," Melke said. "Tell me how to succeed."

His glare swung to her. "No."

"Hantje, there's no time. It must be now. It must
be me."

"No! I won't let you!"

Melke recognized the expression on his face, the set of chin and tightness of mouth, the pinching together of his eyebrows. She'd seen it when he was a child trying to hold back tears. She reached out and took his hand. It was a heavy burden he bore: guilt and shame, helplessness. "I'm sorry," she said. "There's no other way it can be. It must be me."

His mouth twisted. He shook his head.

She glanced at Liana. The girl stood. "I'll make some more tea," she said, reaching for the teapot.

With Liana gone from the room, Hantje closed his eyes. "What have I done?" It was a whisper.

"The harm can be undone, Hantje. Just tell me how."

He shook his head, his eyes still closed. "No," he said. "It can't be undone."

Melke tightened her grip on his hand. "Yes, it can."

His eyelids lifted. He looked at her. She saw his despair, dark and hopeless. "I tried to steal," he whispered. Tears shone in his eyes.

"I know," she said quietly. "But it will be all right, Hantje."

He shook his head again. A tear slid down his cheek.

Melke reached out and wiped it away. "It'll be all right," she repeated, even though she wasn't sure it would be. The necklace could be stolen back, the curse broken, but she didn't know whether Hantje would ever forgive himself for what he'd done.

Grief was tight in her throat. "Hantje, tell me how they caught you."

He wiped his face roughly with the back of his hand. "I don't know."

There was a loud heartbeat in her chest and silence, utter silence, in the room.

"What do you mean?" Melke's mouth was dry. The words came out hoarsely.

"They knew I was there. They just *knew*."

"The salamanders saw you?" She remembered the swift terror at the river bank when she'd thought Bastian had seen her.

"No, no. Not that." Hantje shook his head. "They... I don't know. They just..." His face twisted in frustration. "*I don't know!*"

Melke rubbed her fingers over his clenched knuckles. "It's all right." Tension was tight inside her, but her voice was calm. "We'll figure it out. Just tell me what happened. From the beginning."

CHAPTER THIRTY-SEVEN

BASTIAN COULDN'T SIT, couldn't stand still. Time was too short. He paced the floor, restless and edgy, impatient. His head jerked around as he heard footsteps. "Liana!" He crossed the kitchen in three strides.

She had a frown on her face and a teapot in her hand.

"What did he say? Is she ready to go?"

Liana's frown disappeared. She put down the teapot. "Good morning, Bastian."

"What has he said?"

Liana laughed faintly. She rose on tiptoe and pressed a kiss to his cheek. "Always so single-minded, Bastian."

"Yes," he said impatiently, not really hearing her words. "*What did he say?*"

Her face sobered. "Nothing yet."

"What? Nothing?" Bastian turned toward the door. "I'm going to—"

"No." Liana stopped him with a hand on his arm, firmly. "Having you in there won't help."

"But—"

"No, Bastian. It must be slowly. He hasn't the strength for you to shout at him."

"I won't shout," he said stiffly.

Liana's eyebrows rose a fraction of an inch. She said nothing.

Heat flushed his cheeks. "Curse it, Liana, we don't have time for—"

"Patience, Bastian."

He bit back a snarled retort and watched as she prepared another pot of tea. Something bubbled inside him, as water bubbled in the pot on the stove. It wasn't patience. "Liana." Frustration and urgency were sharp in his voice. "The psaaron may come as early as—"

She picked up the teapot. "I know, Bastian. I know. Just give us a few hours. Please."

He shut his eyes. If anything happened to Liana...

"Please, Bastian."

He opened his eyes. "Very well."

"Thank you." Her hand lightly brushed his cheek.

He watched her leave the kitchen. Patience. He wasn't good at patience.

Work helped, though. He doled out grain for the sheep. They were survivors these two, thin and with their fleece as gray as the hard-packed dirt.

Hay next, for Gaudon. The horse would come with them, Bastian decided, as he smoothed his hand over Gaudon's warm flank. If they had to leave Vere. The ewes could go to Arnaul. Eight miles, but still closer than the town. They would probably survive the walk.

He hauled water from the well for the sheep and Gaudon, and then cupped his hands and drank some himself. He almost spat it out. It tasted like mud. He scooped another handful from the bucket and looked at it. Cloudy. Dirty.

Bastian let the water trickle back into the bucket. By the time the moon was full, there'd be no water left on Vere.

Bas?

His head swung around. Endal stood on the doorstep. Which meant that the wraith was in the kitchen.

Bastian strode across the yard. He laid a quick hand on Endal's head as he pushed through the doorway. "Well?" he demanded.

"Well what?" The wraith's voice was cool.

His eyes adjusted to the dimness. The wraith ladled something into a bowl. "What's that?"

"Soup." She indicated a pot on the stove. Her voice was polite, mocking. "Would you like some?"

Bastian brushed the offer aside with his hand. "What has your brother said? What has he told you?"

Her expression didn't change, but something altered in her face. There was a closing, a drawing in, as if she pulled her skin closer to herself.

"Well? What?"

"I know how to enter the salamanders' den without them knowing." Each word in the sentence was precise, without inflection.

Relief swelled in Bastian's chest. "You can steal the necklace."

She looked away, at the steaming pot of soup. "No. I don't know how to do that yet."

The words left him breathless for several seconds. "What?"

"My brother can't remember everything," the wraith said. "It will take time."

"Time?" His hands clenched, in fear, not anger. "We don't have *time*."

"The psaaron won't come today, will it?" the wraith asked, meeting his eyes. "Or tomorrow. Or the day after."

"It might come then." His voice grated like stone in his throat.

"But it's not until night that it requires someone to punish."

The remembered scent of the psaaron, deep and wet, took Bastian's breath away. The terror in the house. His father's anguished face.

"Is it?"

Bastian swallowed. "Not until night."

The wraith nodded. "You will have the necklace by then." She turned back to the stove.

"Will I?" His voice sounded hollow in his ears. He saw her shoulders straighten, saw her chin lift. "You have my word."

"But you don't know how—"

"I will know."

"Will you?" The words were flat and bitter.

The wraith turned her head and looked at him, the ladle held in one hand. "Yes," she said.

BASTIAN TOOK HIMSELF to the bridge next, although the two mile walk did nothing to ease the prickling sense of urgency. He strode, his boots stirring dust. *Someone to punish*. Fear choked in his throat and clenched beneath his breastbone. He could do it, if the choice was between himself and Liana—however much it terrified him. He *had* to.

But the choice was the psaaron's. What if it chose Liana?

They wouldn't be here. They'd be gone. *Gone*.

There was more fear at the bridge. The river was higher than it had been two days ago. The bridge bowed in the current, swaying to the push of water. Its timbers creaked.

Bastian stood and looked, while the weight of Vere pressed down on him and urgency screamed in his chest.

Fear. So much fear.

He raised his face to the sky. The blue was so thin that it was almost white, high and pale, bright. He was a fool to let fear ride him like this. It pushed him close to panic.

Patience, Liana had said. And the wraith: *You will have the necklace*.

Patience.

Bastian stood for a long time at the bridge, his hands in his pockets, his eyes following the river's swift flow. The sound was odd in his ears, unfamiliar, a soft and muted hiss. Cool air rose and breathed against his skin. He inhaled the scent of water, of moist earth and green plants.

His skin drank the dampness of the river. If only Vere could have this water. Cool and wet and alive.

He wanted to touch it, to scramble down the bank and plunge his hands under the water. To bury his face in it and open his mouth and gulp deeply.

He dared not. This was a hungry river. It ate sal Veres.

When the sun reached its zenith in the sky, Bastian turned away from the bridge. The wraith had given her word. It was foolish perhaps, as foolish as panic, but he would trust her.

WHEN HE CAME into the yard the wraith was sitting on the kitchen doorstep with her chin in her hand. Endal lay at her feet.

She gave you a bone?

Yes. Endal's voice was smug.

She looked almost human sitting like that, in her blue-gray blouse and dark skirt. Not haughty or cold or disdainful, just... worried.

Foreboding stirred beneath Bastian's breastbone. "What? What's wrong?"

The wraith glanced up and took her hand away from her chin. "Hantje doesn't remember everything."

He looked down at her, seated on the step with her black hair and pale skin and a tiny frown between her eyebrows. The sense of foreboding grew like a thunderhead gathering in the sky. "What specifically can't he remember?"

"Specifically?" The repetition wasn't mocking. Her voice lacked the cool, overly polite tone he was familiar with. "He can't remember how the salamanders knew he was there."

There was silence. Endal gnawed on the bone.

Bastian cleared his throat. "They felt him walk past," he suggested. The thunderhead inside him swelled, gray and black, piling higher. "They shivered."

Even sitting on the doorstep the wraith managed to look down her nose at him. "A fishwives' tale."

His teeth clamped shut. He clenched his jaw briefly. "They're salamanders, not men."

She shook her head. "No. They were at a distance from him. He remembers that."

The foreboding pushed out through his pores and crawled across his skin. "You can't get the necklace back."

The wraith's chin lifted. "I didn't say that."

"But if your brother doesn't remember—"

"There is an answer," she interrupted, leaning forward. "I know there is. I just haven't asked the right question yet."

Bastian shook his head, his mouth tight.

"Yes."

"No," he said flatly. "Tell Liana to pack. We're leaving." He turned away from her. Gaudon could carry the—

"No! Give me this afternoon."

The fierceness of her voice halted him. He turned his head.

The wraith stood on the step. "Give me this afternoon," she said again. "What can it matter? The psaaron won't come tomorrow, will it?"

She was no marble statue now, but a passionate woman. The transformation was startling. There was color in her cheeks. Her eyes were as fierce as her voice. He read determination in her face, in the set of her mouth.

Endal had abandoned the bone. He stood with his muzzle raised, watching the wraith.

Bastian turned around fully. He folded his arms and looked her. She was as tall as he was, standing on the step. She didn't flinch from his gaze.

The silence stretched, while heat shimmered up from the bare dirt and harsh sunlight glinted on Endal's black coat, on the wraith's hair.

She was right. The psaaron wouldn't come tomorrow. And it probably wouldn't come the day after that, when the tides began to swell, and probably not even the day after that.

Probably.

But it might.

It had never come so early before.

Bastian swallowed. He uncrossed his arms. "Very well."

A flicker of something crossed the wraith's face, too swift to recognize. The tension eased in her shoulders. "Thank you," she said, cool and polite. A statue again.

Bastian said nothing. Was he a fool to hope so much?

CHAPTER THIRTY-EIGHT

THE SICKROOM GREW stuffy, despite the wide-open window. A thin breeze stirred the faded curtains. The touch of it was hot and dry on Melke's skin. Endal lay in front of the empty hearth, asleep.

"Let's try again," she said. Tension knotted in her chest and belly, but her voice was calm and her fingers, holding Hantje's hand, were loose and relaxed. "Close your eyes."

"But—"

"Please, Hantje."

He hesitated, and then shut his eyes.

"Think back, carefully. You're standing at the edge of the chamber. The salamanders don't know you're there. You watch them."

Hantje's grip was tight.

"What are they doing?"

"Eating."

"Now remember carefully, Hantje. What happened? How did they know you were there?"

"They stopped eating," he said flatly. "They turned their heads. They knew." His eyes opened.

"No." Melke kept her voice calm. "More slowly, Hantje. How did they stop eating? All at once? Gradually?"

"There's no point."

"Please, Hantje."

He shook his head. There were lines on his face that shouldn't be there, etched into his skin. Bitterness. Despair.

"How did they stop talking? Please, Hantje."

"I don't know." She saw self-hatred in his eyes, in the twist of his mouth.

"Yes," she said quietly. "You do know. Think. Gradually or—"

"I *don't* know. They..." His voice faltered. "Not all at once. First one, then the others."

Melke's heart beat slightly faster. She leaned closer. "And did they turn their heads immediately or were they listening? Did they seem to shiver, or—"

Hantje's eyes stared at her, but his gaze was focussed inward. "They lifted their heads." He raised his own chin slightly, tilted his head to one side. "Not listening, not listening, but..."

Melke held her breath.

"Smelling!" Hantje's fingers tightened triumphantly on her hand. He straightened from the pillow, his face eager. "Smelling! They *smelled* me."

There was a sudden, swift lifting in her chest. "Are you certain?"

"Yes! Yes! Look. Listening is like this." He showed her. "Smelling is this. It's different. See?"

She did see. It was in the angle of head and chin, ears, nose. A difference. Endal, as he sat cocking his head at the sound of their voices, he listened.

"You're certain? You're absolutely certain?"

"Yes!" Elation shone in Hantje's eyes.

Melke laughed. "Remember what Da said?"

"Yes!" Hantje laughed too.

"It can be done."

"Yes!" But as she watched, his face changed. The excitement dimmed, as candlelight dimmed at dawn. The exultation faded.

Her heartbeat faltered slightly. "What?"

"It should be me."

She looked at him and saw in his eyes, his face, the words that he couldn't utter. Some part of her agreed. It should be him. He needed to undo what he'd done. He needed the absolution of it so that he could hold his head high, so he could laugh again, from his heart, and meet his own eyes in the mirror.

It was an absolution she needed too.

"I'm sorry," she said. "I wish you could come with me, but Liana's right. You can't."

Hantje released her hand. "I can walk."

Melke shook her head. "Your legs were broken. Even with her gift, it's too soon."

He averted his face. "I want to come."

She heard in his voice, so quiet, how much he needed to come. She saw it in his profile, in the closed eyes and tightly shut mouth, in the bowed angle of his head.

Melke touched her hand to his cheek. "I'm sorry," she said.

CHAPTER THIRTY-NINE

WHEN HANTJE SLEPT again, Melke went to find Bastian. There was no need to ask for Endal's help; he was at the well. She stood on the step and watched as he hauled the rope, hand over hand, as easily as if the bucket was empty. His shirt was unbuttoned at the throat, the sleeves rolled high up his arms. Sweat stuck the rough cotton to his skin. Dark skin, brown from the sun, with the strong flex of muscles underneath. His hair was honey-brown, honey-gold.

He cared about this land, the parched gray soil and the dry grass and the dead trees. And, far more than he cared about Vere, he cared about Liana. She saw it in his eyes, in the way his face softened when he looked at his sister, heard it in his voice when he spoke to her. Liana was the most important thing in his life.

Melke stepped into the yard. Endal trotted ahead of her, his tail waving. She understood why the hound adored Bastian, and why Liana did. He had a strength that had nothing to do with muscle. Integrity. Honesty. He'd never lie, never steal. And he wasn't always so bleak-faced and stern; there were laughter lines at his mouth and eyes. He was smiling now as he greeted Endal, rubbing the hound's flank with rough affection.

He was a good man. One who protected those he loved.

"Yes?" The face he turned to her was unsmiling. He stood with his hand on Endal's head. Something in the stillness of his body spoke of tension.

"My brother has remembered. I know how to avoid being caught."

He didn't move, didn't speak, but she thought the stiffness of shoulder and arm and hand, the stiffness of the fingers resting on Endal's head, eased slightly. He inhaled a long, slow breath that expanded his chest.

"I'll leave tomorrow, at dawn."

Bastian nodded, not speaking. His eyes seemed darker, the green more intense. They glistened strangely. She saw the muscles in his throat move, saw him swallow.

She couldn't wait forever for him to speak. The shadows were long on the ground and she'd made no start with dinner. Melke lifted her chin slightly, to show that his silence didn't daunt her, and turned away.

"Thank you," he said, and she heard roughness in his voice, faint, as if something grated in his throat.

Melke halted. She looked down at the ground, at the hard, cracked dirt and the dusty hem of her skirt. *No.* She turned and met his eyes and crossed her arms tightly over her chest. "Don't thank me."

Endal's ears pricked forward at the sharpness of her tone. Bastian made no movement. His face was utterly expressionless, as blank as an outcrop of rock. She saw no flicker of surprise, no tiny flaring of anger.

The moment stretched, full of silence and hot sunlight, and then Bastian dipped his head slightly in acknowledgement and turned back to the well.

Melke couldn't hold her head high as she walked across the yard. Shame burned in her cheeks. She didn't deserve gratitude. She deserved what he'd given her at the salamanders' den, to be sworn at, spat at, hated.

But he didn't seem to hate her any more. Dislike, yes, but not hate. He hadn't worn his mercenary's face for several days, ugly and brutal, hadn't bared his teeth at her. Not since she'd told him about Mam and Da.

There was tightness high in her chest, beneath her breastbone. Did he pity her?

Coolness settled on her skin as she entered the kitchen. Endal was at her heels, pressing against her skirt. She reached down and touched him. His warmth was comforting, the roughness and softness of his coat, the way he pushed his head against her hand, the wag of his tail.

Not pity. Never pity.

Melke cooked with fierce attention. It was easier to concentrate on the frying potatoes and worry about the proportion of the spices than to think about tomorrow. The salamanders. Their swiftness and agility, their cleverness. Her mind flinched from what she must do: not the stealing, but the stepping inside, the daring to enter. And it was easier to cook than to remember what had happened in the yard. Bastian thanking her, pitying her.

Liana came as darkness fell. She stood in the doorway and smiled. Shadows spilled around her, almost hiding the pinch of anxiety at her eyes and mouth. "Has Hantje remembered how they caught him? Has he remembered why?"

"Yes." Melke nodded. "The remedy is simple."

The shadows fell away from Liana as she stepped into the kitchen. Hope was tremulous in her voice. "Simple?"

"Yes. I'll go tomorrow, at dawn."

The girl seemed to stand straighter, as if a weight she'd carried on her shoulders was gone. "Will you tell me how?"

"Of course."

Liana pulled out a chair at the table and sat. Her face was eager, her eyes bright. In the candlelight her hair shone like spun silver.

Melke set the pan of fat aside to cool. "The salamanders caught Hantje because they smelled him."

"What?" The word was loud. It snapped in the air.

Melke jerked her head around. Bastian stood in the doorway to the yard. His hair and face were wet.

He'd startled her, and her heart beat fast. Her voice, though, was calm. "They smelled him. Just as Endal smelled me."

Bastian's brow lowered. "Then how do you propose—"

"It's quite simple. I'll distract them with scented oil. Aniseed, or something strong. Peppermint."

"But—"

"They won't be able to smell me, or anything else."

Bastian's frown became fiercer. "They'll know you're there."

"Yes," Melke said, and her throat tightened as she uttered the word. "But they won't know where I am. They won't be able to see or smell me. And I'll take care to make no noise."

Bastian closed his eyes briefly. "Simple," he said, and then his eyes opened and she almost stepped back from the anger in them. "Are you insane? They're salamanders, not sheep! They won't run around aimlessly. They'll *hunt* you."

"I only need a few minutes," she said calmly.

"You won't have a few minutes! They're *clever*."

Melke lifted her chin. "I'm aware of that."

Bastian's mouth tightened. "You can find it, just like that." He made a sharp gesture with his hand. "So quickly that they won't be able to catch you." The words themselves were mocking, but she heard no mockery in his voice, just anger.

Melke crossed her arms. "It won't take me long to find the necklace."

"You know where it is?" There was mockery now, in his voice.

Pride stopped her cheeks from flushing. "I know approximately."

"Approximately!" Water trickled from his hair, down his cheek. He brushed it away impatiently with his hand. "Are you such a fool!"

Yes. I am such a fool. But she didn't utter the words aloud. She kept her mouth shut and met his eyes. Hard eyes. Angry eyes. In the candlelight and shadows they looked almost black.

"Bastian..." There was soft rebuke in Liana's voice.

Bastian made no sign that he'd heard his sister. "You're going to do this?"

"Yes." She had to. For Liana and for Bastian, for Hantje. For herself.

His eyes narrowed. "And you're not afraid?"

Afraid? The word was too mild for the cramping in her belly. Not fear; terror. If she thought about it she'd—

Best to ignore it. Best to push it aside and meet his glare.

Bastian laughed when she didn't answer, a short, harsh sound. His mouth twisted, and the anger was abruptly gone from his face. He stepped into the kitchen and bolted the door behind him. "I forbid you to go." His voice was flat. "Liana? Pack your belongings. We're leaving."

"No!" Melke overrode his command. "You can't forbid me."

Bastian turned his head and met her eyes. "Can't I?"

"No."

There was a moment of silence, while he looked narrowly at her. "Then I shall lock you in your room."

Melke's heart beat in alarm, once, loudly, and then a second time in treacherous relief—*to not go*—before she realized his error. "That's something you cannot do."

His eyes were mere slits. "Why? Because wraiths can walk through doors?"

"Of course not. That's just a fish—"

"A fishwives' tale." He made a sharp, dismissive gesture with his hand. "I know. So enlighten me. Why can't I lock you in your room?" His voice was low, the threat in his question unmistakable.

"Because there is no lock."

Bastian didn't move, didn't make a sound. Melke thought she felt his anger brush over her skin, a scorching heat, thought she heard it roar in her ears, thought she inhaled it, sharp and bitter. He wanted to yell. She saw the muscles move in his throat, in his jaw. His fingers flexed. He wanted to grab her by the scruff of her neck and shake her.

His breath hissed as he inhaled. He raised a hand.

"Bastian." Liana stood hastily. Her face was pale. Melke doubted he heard the girl. "If I have to nail shut your door, I will," he said. Rage vibrated in his voice. His hand clenched, the knuckles whitening, and then he jabbed a stiff finger at her. "You are *not* going to the den. Do you understand me?"

"Yes," she said, as calm as he was furious. "I understand you."

"Liana!" His words were for the girl, but his eyes were still on Melke, fierce. "Start packing. Now."

He took his rage with him when he left, but some part of it lingered in the kitchen, acrid. Endal pressed against her skirt. He whined.

"Don't worry." Melke crouched and put her arms around the hound's neck. "Everything's fine." There was pain in her chest, a sharp ache. She closed her eyes.

"I'm sorry."

Melke opened her eyes. Liana stood in the doorway, twisting her hands. The candlelight cast anxious shadows over her face. "Bastian's not usually so... so—"

"It's all right." Melke rose to her feet.

Liana shook her head. Distress creased her brow. "Bastian would never *hurt*—"

"I know." Melke smiled at the girl.

"He was angry because—"

"Because he's trying to protect me." Something inside her clenched as she spoke the words. "Don't worry, Liana. He didn't frighten me."

The girl bit her lip. She spoke hesitantly, "Are you... certain?"

Melke nodded. If Bastian had worn his mercenary's face, she'd have been afraid, but he hadn't. This anger had been different from his rage at the salamanders' den. Worse. "Go pack," she said gently.

Liana looked at her for a long moment, through the shadows and the candlelight, then she nodded and turned away.

Melke sighed. She laid her hand on Endal's head. "Your master is a good man," she whispered.

She understood Bastian's anger tonight. He was the oldest child. He tried to protect, to make things right. She saw it in him, recognized it. But he overreached himself. Liana was his responsibility, and Endal, the sheep in the pen, the old horse, Vere. She wasn't. She was just a wraith.

"Come, Endal."

Melke climbed the stairs slowly, a candle in her hand. She closed the door of her bedchamber and lit the candles in the tarnished holder. Light flared in the room.

"Everything's all right," she told the hound. She took her knapsack down from its hook and felt for her purse. The coins clinked as she counted them. Coins for the oils, for the horse she'd hire in Thierry. Because she was going. This was something she had to do.

A crime couldn't undo another crime, but it could go part way toward doing so. She had to get the necklace, *had to*. Terror was unimportant. She had to do it for Liana and Bastian, for Vere. For Hantje. And she had to do it for herself. She could never go back to the person she had been before she'd stolen, but perhaps she might reclaim a little of her honor.

Melke laid the coins on the chair, beside the neatly folded clothes. Cloak, trousers, blouse. Belt and knife. The shoes she wore. And Endal.

"I hadn't planned for you to come." She sat on the bed and gently rubbed the hound's ears. "I thought your master would be more reasonable. I thought... he wouldn't care."

Don't let her out of your sight, Bastian had ordered. She dared not ask him to release Endal from that task, not now. He'd likely command the hound to bite her if she left her room.

"He makes a mistake, Endal. He should hate me."

Endal liked the movement of her fingers. He leaned against her leg, heavy, warm, and closed his eyes.

"He's a fool." It was a low whisper. "He forgets I am a wraith. His compassion is misplaced."

Endal didn't understand her words. His tail thumped on the floor.

She must leave tonight. Bastian's unexpected rage, his forbidding her to go, made travel at dawn impossible. Food, and a little rest, and when the moon was high... Melke shivered. Darkness. Night.

She'd done it once before, for Hantje. She could do it again. She wouldn't be alone. "I confess, Endal, I shall be glad of your company."

CHAPTER FORTY

H E KNEW IT was a dream, but he couldn't wake up. He hung over the sea. The water was deep and green, terrifying. *Wake up*, he told himself, trying to drag his body higher, away from the hungry waves.

But his dream-self didn't obey him. One moment he was hovering, hanging in the air, the next he was falling. Bastian screamed in pure terror as the sea rushed up at him. He tried to claw at the air with his hands. *Wake up!* he yelled at himself. *Wake up!*

He squeezed his eyes shut just before the moment of impact. For long seconds there was darkness and the frantic pounding of his heart, a sense of speed, and then he opened his eyes again.

He flinched back from what he saw, a wail of terror building in his throat. He was flying, skimming above the waves, fast. Spray flicked up into his face. He tasted salt on his tongue.

It was then, while his heart galloped with fear in his chest, that he realized he was a bird. A seagull.

Tall limestone cliffs stood to the west. Ahead was a curving strip of white sand.

Bastian recognized the beach, even as his wings took him in an upward swoop, high, higher, so high that his stomach threatened to rebel. And then he was hanging in the air again, hovering, looking down on Vere.

But this was a green Vere. The fields were lush with grass and the trees thickly-leaved. Clear water ran in the streams. Fat sheep grazed alongside sleek cattle.

He wanted to see more, but he had no control over where he was going. *Wait!* he cried, as he swooped westward. *No! I want to see!* But all that came from his mouth was a seagull's shrill cry.

The long stretch of beach was below him. A horse and rider cantered on the white sand. He didn't recognize the young man, or the horse he rode. The cliffs came closer, and Bastian began to feel uneasy. *Wake up*, he told himself, trying to twist out of the dream. He didn't want to see where his mother and father had died.

His dream-self halted before reaching the high cliffs. Bastian hung in the air, relieved, not understanding. He saw movement in the water, a dark shape swimming beneath the surface.

Scales. A bristling crest of spines.

A whimper of fear rose in his throat. He began to pant, to struggle more fiercely to wake.

A psaaron stepped from the sea. Bastian watched with a sense of rising panic as the creature strode up the beach. He knew it would look up and see him.

The psaaron unwound a necklace from around its neck and laid it carefully, reverently, on the warm sand.

Bastian's heart stopped beating. He understood what he was seeing. Fear fled, replaced by an urgent desperation. *No!* he cried. *Don't leave it! Not here!* But the psaaron paid no attention to his seagull's voice. He wheeled and swooped, trying to attract the creature's attention, screaming, but the psaaron turned. It waded into the sea and slid beneath waves.

Bastian circled the necklace frantically. *No!* he shrieked. *No! No! No!* But the horse and rider didn't see him any more than the psaaron had done. He yelled until his throat was raw and all he could utter were harsh croaks, until he tasted blood in his mouth. It made no difference.

He watched helplessly as the rider dismounted and knelt to examine the necklace, as he touched it with fingertips that were first cautious, then greedy. *No*, he croaked as the youth stuffed the psaaron tears in his pocket and leapt onto the horse's back.

His dream-self made him stay, circling wretchedly, until the psaaron came again, stepping out of the water. The creature stood for endless seconds, staring down at the bare sand, the booted footprints, the hoof marks. Then it raised its head and howled at the sky.

It was a sound that made Bastian sweat in terror.

His dream-self was inexorable. It dragged him limply back to the farmhouse. Glass sparkled in the windows, the brightness almost blinding him. The fruit trees were in blossom. Their petals trembled in the breeze.

He watched miserably as the psaaron strode into the stable yard, making horses rear with terror in their stalls. *Father*, he croaked, as a man came to stand in front of the creature, tall and proud. A woman clutched the man's arm, her face pale with fear. Tears of recognition filled his eyes as he saw her white-blonde hair. *Mother*.

Time moved dizzily and the sun swung around in the sky, morning, noon, afternoon. A young man rode into the stable yard.

Bastian looked for his mother, but she was gone. His father was there, his mouth grim, his arms folded across his chest.

The rider dismounted and handed the reins to a stableman.

Bastian didn't hear the argument. He saw his father's mouth move, saw the young man answer, but heard nothing. It was as if the psaaron's roar had deafened him. The horses in stalls heard. They moved restlessly, their ears back. The sparrows heard. They stopped pecking for grain and flew up to the safety of the roof. Lizards scuttled for cover. Stablemen listened, sweeping busily, their eyes averted.

Fury suffused his father's face. He yelled, jabbing the air with his finger, incensed. The young man tossed his head, defiant. He turned and walked away across the stable yard.

His father yelled more loudly. Bastian heard the words faintly, thin squawks at the edge of his hearing. *Come back here, Alain! Don't you dare walk away from me!*

Bastian knew the sequence of events. *No!* he croaked, trying to flap his wings, to fly, to stop what was about to happen, but his dream-self held him anchored above the stable yard.

He watched, panting and sweating, straining to move, as Alain swung his leg over a fence, as he stalked across a schooling paddock to where a groom stood with a young stallion, as he snatched the leading rope from the man's hands. Whatever he said made the groom's face tighten with dislike.

No! cried his father. *Don't you dare!*

Alain flung himself up on the stallion. He sat, triumphant, scornful, while the horse stood motionless, quivering in shock at the weight of a rider.

No, Bastian croaked again, and watched with a sick sense of inevitability as the stallion's nostrils flared. Muscles tensed beneath the gleaming black coat.

He saw it slowly, as if his seagull's eyes stretched each brief instant into long seconds. The horse erupted into motion, his frenzied rear tossing Alain high. The young man's mouth opened in a cry. His hands clutched at the air. Bastian saw the solidness with which his head struck the ground, the way his body jerked and then lay still.

His dream-self took him in a long swoop to where Alain lay. The young man's head lolled at an unnatural angle on his neck. Slow blood trickled from his mouth.

His father was suddenly there, below him, kneeling, reaching out with shaking hands to touch Alain's face.

My son, he heard his father say, in a voice choked with grief. *No, not my son.*

The dream swung Bastian away then, so swiftly and dizzily that he began to retch. It became dark, while his stomach heaved and bile rose in his throat. The moon was full and the tide high. And then he saw the psaaron, and nausea clenched into fear.

The creature knelt on the sand, weeping. Tears gathered in its cupped hands. *A curse.* The words swelled in his ears, as fierce and relentless as the ocean tides. *A curse on the family of sal Vere. On their children and their children's children. On their land. On their livestock and their crops, their rivers and their wells.*

The psaaron opened its hands. Shining tears spilled out and soaked into the sand.

For a moment everything was still, the breeze in the tussock, the moonlight, the lapping waves, and then time started again. *No!* Bastian screamed, but he was plummeting, hurtling downward. The sea surged up at him, hungry. The psaaron threw back its head and *howled*—

He jerked awake, gasping for breath, a yell in his throat. Beneath him, the sheets were twisted and damp with sweat. His heart beat loudly in his chest and the psaaron's howl echoed in his ears.

Bastian sat up and dragged air into his lungs. The muscles in his jaw ached and his throat felt raw, as if he'd been screaming. He tasted bile on his tongue. His hands trembled as he wiped the sweat from his face.

A dream. Just a dream.

He fumbled for the tinderbox. The candlelight pushed away the dream. It became tattered in his mind, wispy and insubstantial.

Bastian shoved back the bedclothes and stood. The bare floorboards were cold beneath his feet. There were several hours yet until dawn, but sleep wouldn't come again. He'd never been awake in quite this way before, with such anxiety and dread, such urgency.

He surveyed the bedchamber. His clothes were packed, what few he had. All that remained was to strip the bed. Mattress and bedstead, the wooden chair, the tall mirror... all were too bulky to take with them. But they could take the bed linen and perhaps sell it for a few copper coins.

He dragged fingers roughly through his hair and rubbed a hand over his face. Sweat was clammy on his skin. Today was the end, the last day that sal Veres would be at Vere.

He dressed swiftly. On his way downstairs he opened Liana's door. She slept, her breathing soft. The male wraith slept too, his face pale and troubled in the dim light of the burned-down candles beside his bed. Bastian watched him for a moment. A boy, really. Only a few years older than Liana. Needing candles beside him while he slept, because he was afraid of the dark.

It was impossible to hate him.

Bastian sighed and turned away from the sick-room.

The kitchen table was piled high with bundles. Linen and clothing, pots and pans, food. He sighed again and closed his eyes and pinched the bridge of his nose with his fingers. He'd not believed this day would come.

Embers glowed in the stove. They flared eagerly to life as he pushed in fresh kindling. Tea first, then breakfast, and then everything else that must be done today.

A pot sat on the stove, half-filled with water, still faintly warm. A thick layer of silt hid the bottom. The tea leaves couldn't disguise the taste of mud; it would be there, as it had been for days.

Mud. Water. They were becoming the same thing.

Bastian walked slowly around the table while the pot heated. He touched folded sheets with his fingers, the rim of a drinking glass, fork tines, the blunt edge of an earthenware bowl. So few things they could take with them. Most of it would have to be sold. Some things, though... He laid his hand on a large, rectangular bundle. Some things would never be sold.

Liana had wrapped the book in a bed sheet. He unwrapped it carefully. *Tales of Magic and Magical Beasts*. He traced the letters lightly with a fingertip. This was for his children. He would teach them to read from it, as he'd taught Liana.

But as he turned the pages, brushing his fingers over the tinted illustrations, he knew he'd never have children. Not with the curse unbroken.

Bastian closed the book.

Where would they live? Not by the sea. Inland. Away from rivers. Away from lakes, too. In the north, where it was cold, where the psaaron would be less likely to follow them.

A town without rivers. Did such a place exist?

* * *

"Good morning." Liana's voice was quiet.

Bastian turned away from the sheep pen and looked at her. The smile on her mouth went ill with the sorrow in her eyes.

It was stupid, smiling at each other on such a morning.

He put his arms around Liana and hugged her close. *All will be well*, he wanted to say, but the words stuck in his throat. He knew they weren't true.

It was still cool outside, this early in the day. The warmth of the sun was mild on his skin and the light soft. The burning heat would come later, the harsh glare. It would hurry them on their way and make it easier to leave.

Liana sighed against his shirt. "What is left to do?"

"Can you wake her? The wraith. I need Endal to help me with the sheep."

Liana pulled away from his embrace. "She has a name, Bastian."

He closed his eyes, too tired to argue. "Please, Liana, just wake her."

She didn't speak for several seconds. He heard her scuff the dirt with her shoe. Finally she said, "Very well."

"Thank you." Bastian opened his eyes and turned back to the pen. The ewes watched him, edgy. They sensed the tension beneath his weariness.

He picked up a length of rope. "A new home," he said soothingly, stepping over the fence. "Where it rains and the grass is green. You'll like it."

The two sheep sidled away from him.

"Bastian!"

He turned his head.

Liana ran across the bare yard, a piece of paper clutched in her hand. "She's gone!"

"Give me that." He snatched the paper from her. The wraith couldn't be such a fool, *couldn't*—

A smudged map on one side, the outline of feet on the other—and words.

Yes. She was such a fool.

Bastian crumpled the paper in his hand. "Where's Endal? What's she done with him?" Why hadn't the dog barked?

"He's gone too."

He stood with his mouth open. The wraith had taken Endal. She hadn't shut him in her room, she'd *taken* him.

"Bastian... I think we should do as she asks. I think we should wait."

He clenched his hand more tightly. "No."

"One day, Bastian! She might—"

"She won't. This—' he opened his fingers and let the crumpled note fall to the dirt, "—this tells us she's dead."

"No."

"Yes!"

He'd thought the wraith smarter than this, had thought that she'd understood last night.

Liana folded her arms across her chest. "I want to stay. One day, Bastian. One day."

"No!" Fear made his voice savage. "Go inside and finish packing! Once I've caught the sheep, we're leaving."

Liana's chin jutted. "No." Her face was stubborn, determined.

There was silence, while the sunlight warmed his skin. The yell inside him drained away. "Liana..." He reached out and touched her cheek lightly with his fingers. "I beg you. Please. You haven't seen this creature. You haven't seen what it can do."

Her gaze fell.

"Please," he whispered.

Liana bit her lip. She gave a tiny nod.

"Thank you." Bastian cupped his hand behind her head and bent to kiss her soft, shining hair. "Thank you."

He watched until she had stepped inside the farmhouse. She didn't understand. The psaaron would break her as easily as it snapped a twig.

The remembered scent was thick in his nostrils, wet and seaweedy. He turned, a swift jerk of movement, fearful even though he knew the tides weren't yet rising.

No psaaron stood behind him. Not yet.

Bastian looked at the sheep. He rubbed a hand over his face. He needed Endal for this.

The dog had more sense than to enter the salamanders' den. He'd come back. They'd meet him on the road.

Bastian rubbed his face again, more roughly, and turned his attention to the sheep. The animals didn't like him trying to catch them. If he had grain in his hand... but he'd used the final handfuls last night, before he'd heard the wraith's foolish plan.

The salamanders would kill her.

He was less swift than he normally was, distracted, clumsy. The ewe that he finally caught was unaccustomed to the halter around her neck. She kicked and struggled despite her hugely swollen belly.

Bastian tied the rope to a fence post. He wiped sweat from his face. Now all he had to do was strap the bundles on Gaudon's saddle. They'd go the long way, via Arnaul's farm. It was a safer bridge, and Arnaul would take the sheep and feed them. Perhaps one of the lambs might even live.

Bastian squinted at the sun as he walked across the yard. They'd be gone by noon.

At the kitchen doorstep he paused and looked back at the sheep pen. The ewe was on her knees, the rope pulling her head up. She was in labor. "No!" He began to run.

Seconds turned into minutes as Bastian knelt beside the sheep, and then hours. He looked up. The sun was high and fierce in the sky. The lamb was coming out wrongly.

Bastian rolled up his shirtsleeves. "Steady," he told the sheep. "Steady."

He closed his eyes as his fingers slid inside the ewe, his wrist, his forearm. There was wetness and tightness, warmth. He groped carefully, twisted slightly, pulled.

The lamb came out readily enough. It was dead.

Bastian knelt in the dust. Birth fluids dripped down his arm. He closed his eyes and tipped his head up to the sky. *No*, he wanted to yell.

When he opened his eyes he saw it was past noon. He stood, unsteady, stiff from kneeling so long beside the sheep.

He washed his arm in the trough, then cupped water in his hands for the ewe to drink. She didn't seem able to stand. "Not today," he said, while she lay gasping on the ground. "Please, not today."

But the words made no difference.

Bastian looked up at the sky again, closed his eyes in despair, then opened them and turned toward the farmhouse. "Liana!" he shouted, as he entered the kitchen. "Liana!"

She was in the sickroom, the male wraith's hand clutched in hers. Her eyes stared at him, wide in her white face. "The psaaron's here?"

The wraith pushed back the bedclothes.

"No," Bastian said, panting. "Sorry, I didn't mean to scare you. It's one of the sheep. I need your help."

It wasn't until the color flowed back into her cheeks that he realized how deep her terror had been. She released the wraith's hand and pushed at his chest. "No, Hantje, don't get out of bed. It's all right."

The wraith didn't yield to the pressure of her hand. His fingers were clenched in the sheet. "Are you certain?" He spoke to Liana, but his eyes sought Bastian's.

"Yes."

He had a thin face, too thin. The black hair made his skin seem as white as his nightshirt.

Bastian didn't need to be told that the wraith was too weak to walk to Thierry. Or even to Arnaul's. "It's in the pen," he told Liana as she stood.

He didn't follow her from the room. Instead he stayed, looking down at the wraith. "Do you wish to come with us?" But how? Gaudon couldn't carry this lad as well as their belongings. *And why do I care? He's a wraith.*

He cared because the wraith was thin and pale and still in need of Liana's care. Because he was young and alone. Because his sister was dead.

The wraith shook his head firmly. "I'll wait for Melke. She'll be back." His chin rose, silent emphasis to the confidence in his voice.

How like his sister with that uptilted chin, almost as alike as twins. The raven-black hair, the pride.

She's dead, you fool. But Bastian didn't say the words aloud. Instead, he said, "As you wish," and turned on his heel before the arguments spilled from his mouth. Let the wraith hold on to his hope.

Liana knelt in the dirt beside the ewe, her hand on the animal's flank. He saw how it struggled to breathe. "Can you heal her?"

She looked up and shook her head. "Not quickly. It will take several days."

"Then I'd best kill her." He reached for his knife.

"No!"

"We don't have several days, Liana. We have *now*."

"But she might recover." Liana clutched at his arm. "Please. There's a chance."

"Leave her?"

She nodded.

"Think, Liana. She'll die of thirst."

Liana's chin became stubborn. "Melke will bring the necklace back. It will rain again."

"No!" The fierceness of his voice startled the last ewe, standing behind him. "No, she won't. She's dead, Liana. *Dead*." And something in his chest clenched as he said the words. Not grief, it couldn't possibly be.

She shook her head. "No," she said, her lower lip jutting. "I won't believe that."

Bastian looked down at Liana. Tears glistened in her hazel eyes. He slid the knife back into its sheath.

"You have an hour to do what you can for the sheep. Then we're leaving."

Her fingers tightened on his arm. "You won't kill her?"

He shook his head.

It took longer than an hour to bury the lamb, strap their belongings on Gaudon, and eat a hasty meal. Bastian's tension grew, building inside him, little knots that tied tighter with each second that passed. He didn't attempt to catch the last sheep. There was no longer any point; it was too late to go via Arnaul's. If they were to reach Thierry tonight they'd have to travel quickly, directly across their own bridge.

He filled the trough with muddy water and left the gate open to the pen so the last sheep could forage. He opened the gate to the garden too. It offered better food than the parched fields.

Liana left the ailing ewe and washed her hands.

Bastian looked up at the sun with narrow eyes. It was lower in the sky than when he'd last looked. The knots of tension tied themselves tighter. He gathered Gaudon's reins in his hand. "Come, Liana."

"I have to say goodbye to Hantje."

"There's no time." Urgency was brusque in his voice. "We must leave. Now." He held out his hand to her.

"No."

"Liana!" But she was already running back across the yard, stirring dust, the white-blonde hair whipping over her shoulders.

His urgency and alarm, his fear for her, twisted into anger. Bastian crossed the yard fast and bellowed her name as he entered the kitchen. His footsteps were loud as he strode down the corridor. They echoed, flat, as if the floorboards flinched from his feet.

Liana was in the sickroom, bent over the bed, talking to the male wraith in a low voice.

"Now," Bastian said. It was a tone he'd never used with her before, harsh with anger.

Liana's glance was startled. "But—"

"*Now.*"

There was a long second of silence, and then Liana straightened. "Very well." Her voice was quiet, calm. She touched her fingertips to the wraith's hand briefly, where it lay clenched on the sheet, and turned away from the bed.

Bastian couldn't meet the wraith's eyes, couldn't look at his face. He should force the youth to come with them, instead of abandoning him. "Goodbye," he said roughly, and walked out of his home for the last time, treading on floorboards, flagstones, the doorstep.

He pulled the door shut and allowed his fingers to linger for a moment. The handle was fashioned of metal, dark with age and smooth from use. *Goodbye.*

Liana stood in the yard. She said nothing as he took hold of Gaudon's reins.

Tension was rigid inside him, and guilt clenched hard-knuckled at the base of his throat. He couldn't swallow the guilt away, couldn't cough it out. The lad would be all right. There was food left, and water in the well. He'd be fine. The psaaron wouldn't touch him. And by the time he lost hope, he'd be well enough to walk to Thierry.

But the guilt refused to be dislodged. It choked in his throat. And with the guilt, was grief at leaving Vere, sitting on his skin, a cloak as light as cobwebs.

Liana walked beside him, her head slightly bowed. The cobweb cloak of grief rested on her skin, too.

"Liana." His voice was quiet, rough. "I'm sorry I yelled at you."

"It's all right." She raised her eyes.

"No. It was wrong of me. I didn't mean to—"

Her hand slipped into his, small and warm. "It's all right."

Some of the tension in Bastian's chest eased, unravelling slowly like a row of knitting, and he found it easier to draw breath. The guilt remained, though, a thick lump at the base of his throat.

He gripped Liana's hand. The late afternoon sun beat down, scorching through his shirt and glaring into his eyes. The air was hot and dry in his throat, the ground hard and dusty. Dead land. Land his family had loved, land they'd given their lives for. The curse would never be lifted. It would be with him forever, like the signet ring on his finger. He'd never be without it.

Shame twisted snake-like beneath the guilt and grief, the fear. He lost his honor by fleeing, and he risked upsetting the balance of things. The crime hadn't been his, all those years ago, but it was his duty to accept the punishment, to let the psaaron choose himself or Liana.

Liana.

No. It was better to have no honor, better to take the risk.

The psaaron would chase behind them until they died, but if he was careful and cautious, if he used his wits, they'd be safe. He would learn to live with fear cold in his belly and crawling up his spine, with shame twisting in his guts. He'd learn to look over his shoulder and to sniff the air.

He would learn, and they would live.

The wraith... There was tightness beneath his breastbone when he thought of her, regret. He should have nailed shut her door.

Her name was Melke, and if she wasn't already dead she would be by the end of the day. And her brother waited for her.

The sun was hot and glaring, so hot and glaring that his eyes watered, and the ground was so hard that his bones ached with each step. But Liana held his hand and said it was all right. She lived. She breathed. She was unharmed. And for now, that was enough.

CHAPTER FORTY-ONE

S O MANY DIFFERENT kinds of fear. The confused, panicked terror when soldiers burst through the bedroom door. The smothering fear in the cell, when time became so vast that she couldn't count it and minutes had become months, when she'd tried desperately to hold on to who she was. The fear with grief so tightly interwoven that they were one and the same thing—fear and grief, grief and fear—when the crossbow bolt had speared Mam and she'd not been able to stay, had grabbed Hantje and run. The prickling fear of stealing into the farmhouse, reluctant, determined. The sharper fear, edged with desperation, of being up the tree.

She wasn't afraid of Endal now, and this fear was a new one. It made her retch. Her hand trembled as she raised the waterskin for a final drink. She sweated, even though it was cool beneath the trees. Her heart was a hammer in her chest, beating against her ribs, trying to batter its way out.

Melke retied the neck of the waterskin. She looked around, checking. Splashes of sunlight sneaked through the leaves. She smelled damp moss and sulphur. The horse she'd hired cropped grass beside the tiny creek, young and strong-legged and swift enough to carry her from the valley ahead of the salamanders. It was loosely hobbled, with a knot she could fumble undone in seconds.

Nothing was left on the ground. Her shoes were firmly fastened, the trousers belted at her waist. The knife was in its sheath, her hair in a plait out of the way.

She tied the waterskin to the horse's saddle, alongside the rolled bundle of her cloak, and checked the satchel of oils again. The phials were rough, stoppered with blunt corks and wrapped with rags so they'd not clink against each other. She checked that each cork was loose, easy to remove, that the phials were tightly-packed together and wouldn't spill. Twice she checked them, and the leather strap across her shoulder and chest.

There was nothing more to check. Her heart thudded in her chest. Endal pressed against her legs, whining.

Melke touched his head. "I need you to be flexible, Endal. I don't wish to tie you. I'd like you to be free to go if something should happen to me."

His ears pricked. The pale wolf-eyes were anxious.

"You must run, Endal, if they catch me. You'll be safe outside the valley. Salamanders don't pursue beyond their territory."

Endal didn't understand. He whined again and pressed closer to her.

Melke blew out a shallow breath. She couldn't put this off any longer. "Very well. Let us try."

She kept her hand on Endal's head while she did it, the concentration, the turning inside out of herself, the swift prickling of it. Her fingers were pale against his black fur, and then... nothing. She wasn't there.

Exultation jolted through her, sharp. There was a sense of freedom in letting go and being purely a wraith. The shadowless thief, the unseen assassin. She was at once stronger and bolder; there was excitement and calmness. *I am a wraith*.

Endal pulled away from her touch. He uttered a short bark.

"Hush," Melke said. "Hush."

The hound's lips were pulled back from his teeth. Hackles stood along his spine, stiff and black. A thin growl came from his throat.

"I know," Melke said softly, soothingly. Exhilaration tingled under her skin. "He said to bite me if I became unseen. But I don't think you will. Will you?"

She reached out to him slowly, holding her palm to his nose.

Endal flinched from her. His ears were flat against his head. The growl came more strongly.

"Hush," she whispered. "It's just me." She moved her hand again, so that his breath was moist against her palm. "If you must bite me, do it, but I beg you not to."

Endal didn't jerk his head back this time. She saw him inhale the scent of her skin.

Melke crouched and slowly placed her hand on his neck. She stroked him carefully. "See? It's just me. No need to bite. I know Bastian said to, but you're smarter than that, aren't you?"

It seemed that he was. The fearsome teeth were no longer bared and the stiff hackles lay closer to his spine.

"Good hound," she whispered encouragingly, running her hand over his thick, warm fur. His tail moved a fraction, the tiniest wag.

Sweat was cold on her skin and bile bitter in her throat, and the illicit, shameful wraith-tingle was in her blood. The sun sank toward the hills and late afternoon. She couldn't put this off any longer. Salamanders hunted at night, and she must be far from here before the sun set. "It's time, Endal. You may come as far as the den, if you wish."

The hound followed as Melke stepped from the trees. Long grass brushed against her legs. She heard the hum of insects in the sweet-smelling meadow flowers and the high notes of birdsong. The den squatted in front of her. Two hundred yards, as close as she'd been able to hide the horse.

She walked, her breath coming jerkily from her mouth. Grass clutched at her trousers, pulling, slowing. *Not so fast.* It wrapped itself around her legs. *Slower.*

She was close enough to see the coarse texture of the walls, close enough to taste sulphur on her tongue. Close enough to touch.

There was cramping in her belly and the need to retch again. She could only take small, shallow breaths. Her heart hammered against her ribs. And yet, beneath the fear was a flicker of something.

Not excitement or anticipation, not anything she could name, just a tiny flicker of... something.

The rough mass of rock and red, hard-baked clay towered above her, irregular and misshapen, as if it had pushed itself out of the ground. The scent of the salamanders filled her nose and throat. Melke clutched the satchel to her chest, feeling the weight of the oils.

Endal pressed against her leg. His whine was almost inaudible. The sound stopped when she touched his head lightly with her fingers.

He followed closely as she walked the circumference of the den. The few small fissures in the walls were too narrow to climb through, letting fresh air in and the spicy, pungent odour of salamander out.

At the back of the den was the midden. Her entrance, so Hantje said.

The stench was foul, a carnivore smell, thick and heavy; charred bones and old meat, the remains of beasts the salamanders had eaten, and the familiar, noisome stink of their scat. A midden and dungheap.

A low wall enclosed the spill of waste. Melke laid her hand on it and felt roughness and warmth beneath her palm. Her heart seemed to be pushing its way up her throat. "You can't come any further, Endal. You must wait here."

She swung her leg over the crude wall and stepped carefully into the midden, first one foot, and then the other. Once there, she couldn't move. She stood frozen, her eyes flinching from the grotesqueness of it all. A goat's ribcage, the bones splayed wide. The eviscerated carcass of a deer. A leg, with hoof and hide and strands of goat hair, burned. Sinew and bone and skulls with gaping eye sockets. Teeth and hooves and horns and scorched hides. And scat, stinking piles of scat.

Flies rose buzzing. They swarmed everywhere, feasting, black and torpid. White maggots writhed.

If she hadn't been retching all day she would vomit now, but there was nothing left in her stomach. Her skin crawled, as if the flies were on her hands and face, her throat, her scalp. She couldn't inhale, couldn't suck the air into her mouth; it was too rank, too revolting, too thick with decay.

She gagged.

Endal uttered a short bark.

"Hush." Melke choked out the word, turning to him. His front paws were up on the wall.

He barked again.

"Hush!" And she could breathe again, because she had to. She reached out and circled Endal's muzzle with her fingers, firmly. "Shhh. You must be quiet."

Endal whined. She felt the vibration of it through her hand.

"Quiet," Melke said, reinforcing the command with a gentle flex of her fingers, and: "Wait," pushing his head back slightly. "You must wait."

His ears were flat against his head. The sound he uttered was neither bark nor groan nor whine, but a combination of all three, distressed. "Shhh," she whispered, and she released his muzzle and put her arms around his neck and pressed her face into his thick black fur. "You can't come, Endal. You must *wait*."

Beneath the suffocating stench of the midden, she smelled his hound-scent, clean. "Wait," she said against his throat, while behind her the flies buzzed and swarmed and crawled.

Endal let her push him back, so that all four paws were on the ground again. Melke gave the command one last time, soft and fierce, afraid he'd follow. "*Wait.*"

She turned her back on him, clenched her teeth together, and forced herself to take one step. Another step. A third. Flies rose, sluggish, as her shoes sank into the decaying refuse, sliding and squelching. They buzzed around her, becoming unseen as they landed on trousers and blouse, on skin. She brushed them off, batting with her hands, holding her breath and gagging at the same time, choking on the foulness of it all.

Where the debris was at its thickest was an opening into the den. It was a slit at waist height, wide and low, dark.

Melke glanced back at Endal. He had done as she asked, stayed and waited.

There was nothing graceful or elegant about her entry into the salamanders' den. It was an awkward, stealthy scramble. The precious satchel of oils swung and scraped against the filth-encrusted lip of the opening, a tiny sound that almost caused her heart to stop beating.

Melke landed on her knees. She stayed crouching, her palms pressed to the rough, warm floor.

It was hot. It was dark. The rich musk of the salamanders pushed into her nose and mouth. She groped with one hand for a phial of oil. Her heart beat frantically, thumping so loudly that she heard nothing else. She was deaf and she was blind and the scent of the salamanders was thick and choking and—

The blackness became gray. Her heart beat slightly less loudly in her chest. There were no salamanders here.

Melke straightened cautiously, the phial clenched in her hand. She was in a small space, as black as pitch when she'd scrambled in, but easily seen now that her eyes had adjusted to the gloom. A rough-walled passage curved out of sight.

She inhaled a breath, and another one. Hantje had been here. He'd stood where she was standing now. He had done it, and so could she.

Had he felt it, too? That emotion beneath the fear? There was no word for it: a treacherous flicker of pleasure in her wraithness, a tingle of exhilaration, a sense of invincibility.

It was wrong, she knew, wrong and shameful, and yet inside herself, in some dark part of herself, she revelled in being a wraith.

Guide me, Moon, she whispered soundlessly. *Don't let me stumble from myself. Don't let me become what I don't wish to be.*

The red clay of the walls was coarse-textured and warm to touch. Melke pressed close. She walked slowly, breathed slowly, gripping the phial in her right hand with her thumb against the cork, ready to open it and throw the scented oil. The ceiling was lost in darkness. As the passage curved, shadows slid down the walls and crept toward her across the uneven floor. And when darkness seemed about to swallow her, light came again, the glow of living flame. A torch, thrust into a bracket, fierce and hot, smoking. And beyond the torch...

This was the chamber Hantje had described, a vast cavern with a pit of fire burning in the center.

Half a dozen narrow fissures in the walls let in thin slivers of daylight. Shadows pooled on the floor and cringed away from the torches and gathered as black as storm clouds beneath the high, arching ceiling. There were only two openings: the one in which she stood and another, like a gaping mouth, which must lead to the entrance with its iron door.

Heat smothered her. Perspiration beaded on her skin and trickled down her cheek. The scent of musk was thick. She tasted it on her tongue, just as she tasted the smoke. Her eyes stung with it.

And in the glare of flame and the darkness of shadow, jewels glittered. Amethyst brooches and sapphire and ruby rings, necklaces of emeralds and diamonds. The gleam of gold and glint of silver, chalices and bowls, beautifully crafted, lying tumbled on the floor. And more gold, a deep spill of coins across the red clay floor, thin and round, thick and oblong, some smooth-edged, others serrated, all stamped with the crests of ruling houses and the faces of kings and queens, living and long-dead.

And as brilliant as any jewel or precious metal, as vivid as flame, were the salamanders.

They slept, sprawled on the thickly-piled golden coins. Five of them. Four kits and their mother.

Melke's throat was too tight to breathe. She couldn't inhale, couldn't exhale, could only stand with the phial clutched in her hand and stare. The mother... she was a beautiful creature, blood-red, with a cruel crest of spines. Larger than her kits, taller and stronger, more dangerous.

One of the kits opened its eyes. Its head lifted, alert, seeking. She'd seen that movement before. Hantje had mimed it.

Terror held Melke still while her heart beat loudly beneath her breastbone, once, and then the cork was gone and she threw the oil as far as she could. Aniseed. The scent came to her strongly, overriding smoke and musk. A second phial, while the salamanders came to their feet in swift, lithe movements. Peppermint. A third phial, over herself and the floor, while she moved away from the passage, sidling sideways. Peppermint again. A fourth phial, a fifth, casting them wide.

Hair rose sharply on her skin as one of the kits uttered a high, hissing shriek. Time blurred in a rush of heat and fear as the salamanders erupted into movement, sleek-skinned and agile and terrifyingly fast.

Melke made for the pit of fire in the center of the chamber, low to the floor, a spider scurrying. Her heart jerked fast in her chest as the salamanders shredded the shadows where she'd stood. *Careful. Make no noise.* A kit darted so close that she felt the brush of air. It was gone before her heart had a chance to falter. The razor-sharp claws passed over her head. It didn't smell her, didn't hear her.

It was hotter here, close to the flames. The sweat evaporated from her skin. Melke crouched and searched frantically with her eyes. The rough floor was hot under her palms, through the soles of her shoes. She saw gold coins, round and thick, emerald rings and a necklace of rubies and diamonds, an upturned silver bowl, studded with garnets. And there—*there*—where the mother had been lying, the gray-green-blue of the psaaron tears.

Melke snatched at the necklace. Smooth stones, cool, the color of the sea, deep and shadowy, precious. Once in her hand, the necklace became unseen. She wrapped it swiftly around her wrist and turned back to the passageway.

But Bastian had been right. These were no sheep to run at random, caught in a mindless panic.

Her escape was blocked. Two kits barred the passage to the midden, two more the passage to the iron door. And between her and them was the mother, fierce and clever and furious.

She was trapped.

Melke experienced a moment of blank terror, when thought and reason were impossible, when her heart failed to beat and she was incapable of breathing. It was a moment of flaring torches and leaping flames and fierce, fire-bright eyes, of utter terror. And then clarity of thought returned. She couldn't fail. For Liana and for Bastian, for Hantje, she had to succeed. *She had to.*

The heat was stifling but Melke was cold, as cold as ice, clearheaded. She backed away from the adult salamander, slowly, placing her feet with caution while she lifted the flap of the satchel and felt inside. This time she threw the phials—two, three, four—so that they hit the walls and rolled across the floor, spilling oil.

The salamander jerked her head swiftly, following the sounds and movements. Her slitted nostrils flared. Peppermint and aniseed mixed with musk and smoke in a nauseating blend of smells.

A dozen quick steps and Melke was pressed against the wall, alongside one of the thin cracks that let in air and daylight. The four corks were clenched in her hand. One of the phials she'd thrown lay at her feet, empty. The scent of peppermint was sharp.

There was heat from the fire-warmed air and from the clay at her back, as hard and uneven as rock, and coolness around her wrist from the necklace of tears. And coolness inside her head, where each thought was as clear and hard as ice.

"You can't run, little wraith. You can't hide. There isss no essscape." The hiss and crackle of flames was in the salamander's voice. Her crested head turned as she sniffed the thick air and listened. "No one can sssteal from usss."

Melke inched sideways until she felt the featherlight touch of a fresh breeze at the nape of her neck and knew that she stood in front of the crack.

"We will find you, little wraith. And when we do, you will wisssh you were dead." Flame curled from the salamander's lipless mouth as she laughed.

Melke ignored the words. Her head was clearer than it had ever been, her vision sharper. She saw the glinting edge of a gold coin, the reflection of firelight in the curved side of a silver chalice, the pulse beating in the salamander's throat, fast, beneath scales as finely grained as skin.

Now. It had to be now.

Melke took one of the corks between thumb and finger. She held her breath, focussed, and threw with careful precision. The cork landed on the sprawling pile of gold coins with a soft, wary *chink*.

The salamander's head snapped around, her sharp crest becoming more erect. The colors of flame and blood pulsed brightly on her skin.

Melke turned her back on the creature and crouched and peered into the crack. It was too narrow for escape, perhaps too narrow for what she had in mind, perhaps too deep. Fresh air touched her face, a caress as light as a butterfly's wing. It was sweet in her nostrils, clean and cool.

Please, Moon, she begged silently as she reached her arm into the fissure. Rough clay scraped at her sleeve, snagging the cotton, and then... air, cool on her fingertips. Relief swelled in her chest. She glanced back, over her shoulder.

"Imposssible to sssteal from usss, foolisssh little wraith," the salamander hissed. She moved lithely, in a circling, sidling movement that brought her closer to the thick spill of gold coins. Her head tilted as she scented, as she listened. The snake-like tail was taut, the slender tip arching upward.

No. Not impossible. Not if Endal's ears are sharp enough. Melke scratched her fingernails against the outside of the wall, *scritch, scritch, scritch*. The sound didn't penetrate the den.

"Do you know how we punisssh thievesss, little wraith?"

Melke paid no attention to the question. She watched the salamander, and scratched, dragging her fingernails across the hard clay. Seconds were as long as hours. *Come on, Endal.* It was fifty paces, no more, to where she'd left him. Surely he'd hear.

"We have a hole for thievesss, little wraith."

A wet nose pressed against her fingers, so sudden that Melke's heart jerked in her chest.

The salamander laughed again and flames spilled from her mouth. "A grave, little wraith, filled with the bonesss of thievesss."

Melke withdrew her arm from the fissure. Her head was so clear that the chamber seemed as bright as day, the shadows dissolving and the smoke drifting away. Yellow and orange flames leapt in the firepit and sooty torches flared. Golden coins reflected the firelight. She saw the glint of ruby and amethyst and emerald, the iron-red of floor and walls and arching ceiling, the fierce sheen of the salamanders' skins, the fire in their eyes.

"No one stealsss from usss."

She unwound the necklace from her wrist and placed it carefully around her left hand. It hung in two long loops, unseen.

"Essspecially filthy little wraithsss."

Wrong. Melke took another cork and held it in her right hand, lightly, carefully. *I am stealing. Now.* And she threw the cork.

It landed on the coins again, with another soft and wary *chink*.

The mother salamander leapt, a movement so fast that Melke's eyes couldn't follow it. Curved talons slashed through the air, tossing gold coins high. A piercing shriek made the hairs on her scalp stand on end, but the clarity in her head left no space to be afraid of such fury, such speed and agility.

She stretched her left arm into the fissure, while coins spun in the air and struck the floor loudly. Her fingertips touched Endal's wet nose again. She felt the warmth of his muzzle, the prickle of whiskers and the dome of his skull. It was a scrabble to push her fingers over his ears.

The coolness of the necklace was gone. Endal had it now.

The salamander shrieked again and more coins dashed against the floor. Melke withdrew her arm. She pressed her face into the crack. Clay was hard and gritty against her cheeks and sunlight bright in her eyes, blurring her vision. "Go home," she whispered. "Find Bastian."

The dark shape that was Endal didn't move. If he whined, she didn't hear him.

There was silence behind her as the last of the coins stopped rolling over the floor. "Tricksss," the salamander said, rage burning in her voice. "The little wraith playsss tricksss."

Melke took another cork in her fingers, blindly, still watching Endal. "*Go!*" It was a fierce whisper. She had succeeded, had stolen the necklace and given it to the hound, and clear in her mind was what she had to do next: confuse the salamanders with scents and sounds, draw them away from the—

Movement rustled behind her.

Melke froze. Terror clutched so tightly in her chest that her heart failed to beat.

"Little wraith..." The low hiss of sound drew her head around.

The adult salamander stood behind her, so close that heat brushed against Melke's skin. Her scent was strong, heavy and spicy.

Melke's heart began to beat again, to batter its way out of her chest so loudly that surely the creature heard it. The sound filled her ears, deafening.

The salamander turned her crested head. Slitted nostrils moved delicately as she inhaled.

You cannot smell me. Peppermint, only peppermint.

The creature raised her head, dipped it, scenting. The cruel, lipless mouth opened. Her teeth were sharp barbs.

Peppermint, only peppermint. I am not here.

A plume of flame curled out of the salamander's mouth, bright and hot. Melke felt it lick across her ear, heard the dull hiss of burning hair, smelled her hair burn.

The salamander smelled it too. Fire flared in her eyes.

There was no time to unsheathe her knife, no time to raise her hands and defend herself. No time even to scream.

CHAPTER FORTY-TWO

THE BRIDGE SAGGED. The creak of timber was
audible above the swift rush of water.

"No." Liana shook her head. Bastian saw
terror in the paleness of her face. "No."

"Yes," he said calmly. "We have to, Liana."

"No."

"We'll be quickly across." Bastian ignored the knot
of fear in his belly. "A few seconds and—"

"No!" There was a note of panic in her voice.
"You can't make me, Bastian. I won't!"

He understood her terror. He struggled with it himself. So much water, so swift and deep, so deadly.
"Liana, we have to."

She shook her head again.

"The pile is still standing. It's perfectly safe. Look,
I'll take Gaudon across first." He tightened his grip
on the reins and stepped firmly onto the bridge. Two

313

steps, three steps. The planks creaked and the bridge swayed. Water hissed and rushed. Sweat was cold on his skin. "Come, Gaudon." He tugged at the reins.

But Gaudon utterly refused to step onto the bridge. He wouldn't be coaxed and he wouldn't be pulled. White showed at his eyes and his bay coat was dark with sweat when Bastian finally conceded defeated. Relief leapt beneath his breastbone, and panic too. The sun was sinking toward dusk.

"Arnaul's." He held out his hand to Liana. "Come on."

She shook her head. "It'll be dark soon."

"We can sleep there. Arnaul won't mind."

Liana shook her head again. "No."

"We don't have time to argue—"

"Bastian, please, let's go home."

She was exhausted. He heard it in her voice and saw it in the dark smudges beneath her eyes. How many hours had she slept last night? He'd bullied her to bed late, past midnight, and she'd risen just after sunrise. She needed sleep. "No," he said. "We can't. The psaaron—"

"Arnaul is closer to the sea. If the psaaron comes tomorrow, do you want to bring it there?"

He opened his mouth to tell her that the psaaron wouldn't come tomorrow, that it had never come before the tides were full, but the image she'd conjured in his mind was vivid and horrifying. It dried the words in his mouth. The psaaron standing in Arnaul's yard, its scent sending the horses mad with terror in their stalls.

Psaarons were as ruthless and unpredictable as the sea. If Arnaul sheltered them, who was to say that the creature wouldn't curse him too?

Liana was right. They dared not sleep at Arnaul's. It was best to return home and be gone at daybreak, to cross Arnaul's bridge and avoid his house entirely.

BASTIAN SADDLED GAUDON in the chill gray of predawn, the time when night slid into morning and everything held its breath. The ailing ewe had died while the sun was down, but Bastian ignored the limp huddle of her body. There was no time to dig graves and bury sheep. Endal wasn't back yet, but there was no time even to be anxious about him. They'd find him. They'd meet him on the road. He wasn't lost.

He didn't believe that the psaaron would come today. It was the first day of the equinox and the tides had barely begun to swell. The creature had never come so early before, but fear still rode him, pushed him. *What if—*

"Liana!" He strode across the yard.

Her voice came faintly from inside.

Bastian halted on the doorstep. He turned and looked over his shoulder. Color flushed the sky, pink, a hint of gold, the pale and blushing glow of dawn. Fear prickled over his skin, raising the hairs.

"Liana! Hurry!"

A scent teased at the edges of his memory, dark and sea-rich. It stroked over his skin, moist. He inhaled it as he breathed.

Childhood terror surged inside him. He jerked around. Nothing. A bare and empty yard. Gaudon standing saddled. No psaaron.

"Liana!" It was a bellow, afraid.

"Coming."

And there it was again, the scent, filling his mouth and nose. The smell of wet things, of dark caverns beneath the ocean, of salt spray and sleek fish and rotting seaweed, of rain and flood-swollen rivers, a smell that was rich and deep and monstrous.

The scent was familiar. It had lived in his nightmares for eighteen years. The emotion it elicited was familiar too.

Bastian jerked his head around again.

The yard was no longer empty. Gaudon pulled back on the rope that tied him to the fence, frenzied, trying to free himself. His whinny was shrill.

Sea-man, mer-man, fish-man. Arms and legs, like a man, but with serrated scales, not skin. A ridge of rough spines cresting a domed skull and long, dripping spurs hanging like wattles from the chin. Webbed toes, and webbing between the long, clawed fingers. Eyes as deep as the ocean, blue and green and gray, with flecks of gold.

Moisture rolled off the creature like mist rolling off the sea, cool and damp, leaving tiny droplets of water on Bastian's skin. The dusty ground was wet where it had walked.

The fish-mouth opened, showing carnivore's teeth. "Do you have my family's tears?"

Bastian heard the sound of water in that voice, of waves on rocks and rain falling, of something as deep and inexorable as the ocean tides. Vengeance.

Terror clenched in his chest.

The psaaron stepped closer. It towered over him. The thick scales were the color of seaweed, green and brown, blending into each other. "My family's tears."

This time he heard an undercurrent of grief in the deep voice, but he was nine years old again and terror had made him mute. He could only shake his head while coolness breathed over him and beads of water gathered on his skin.

He heard footsteps behind him, tentative, on the flagstones. "Bastian...?"

He blocked the doorway. Liana couldn't possibly see the psaaron, but her voice told him that she knew, so faint, trembling with fear.

Bastian turned his head.

Candles burned on the long, scrubbed table, casting cheerful light. Liana's face was bloodless, as pale as ivory. She clutched the back of a chair with white-knuckled fingers.

And behind her, shouldering his way through the doorway, came the male wraith. Determination was fierce on his thin face. He limped across the floor on bare feet and stood in front of Liana, too weak to protect her, needing protection himself, but as full of foolish bravery as his sister had been.

"Where are the tears?"

The psaaron's voice was in his ear, so close that he heard the sound of shells tumbling over one another in the surf. Cool water slid down his cheek. The scent of salt spray and seaweed smothered him, choking.

Bastian took a stumbling step into the kitchen, a second, a third. He was a child again, panic-stricken, terrified. Fear shrieked in his chest: *Don't touch me!*

The psaaron followed him, ducking its spiny head as it stepped through the doorway. The wraith didn't move, except to lift his chin higher.

It was like a slap across Bastian's face, that raised chin, so calm and unafraid, as if the wraith took him by the scruff of the neck and shook him. *Stand tall, be a man.*

Bastian swallowed. He tried to hold his head up, as the male wraith did. His heart beat so fast that it would surely burst. He couldn't seem to drag any air into his lungs.

"Where are—"

Bastian found his voice, hoarse, the words rasping together. "It was stolen. We had the necklace, but it was stolen."

"Lies!" The word was the roar of waves surging against sharp rocks.

"No," said the male wraith, his voice cool and unfaltering. "He tells the truth. He had the necklace, but my sister took it. She has gone to recover it. She'll be back soon."

There was a taut moment of silence, while Bastian's heart labored in his chest. The wraith's stance was bold, as proud and unafraid as if the psaaron was a fish flopping on the floor. Bastian didn't need Endal to tell him that the youth's haughty expression hid fear. Liana stood behind the wraith, her head bowed so that her forehead pressed against his shoulderblade. She clutched his upper arm with tight fingers.

"If you come back tomorrow my sister will—"

The sound of foaming water filled the kitchen, the sound of waterfalls and fierce rapids. Laughter, anger. "While you flee? I see the horse outside. You plan to run."

The wraith appeared undaunted. "Wait with us, by all means." He gestured grandly to one of the chairs. "My sister will be back by nightfall."

She's dead, you fool. Dead. She won't be back.

And tonight the psaaron would punish them. Now it was neuter, but when the sun sank behind the hills it would choose, male or female, him or Liana.

Liana, tonight.

No.

Bastian cleared his throat. The lie came awkwardly from his mouth: "Your sister may need some assistance. Liana, perhaps you should go to help her."

The wraith's gaze shifted sharply. Bastian met his gray eyes, and saw that he understood. "Yes. My sister isn't the best horsewoman. Liana, why don't you—"

"Bastian should go."

Liana had lifted her head. She stared at him over the wraith's shoulder, fiercely.

"No." Bastian tried to speak calmly, as if the psaaron didn't stand beside him, but desperation edged his voice. "Liana—"

"Melke *will* be back. She will! If she needs help, then it's best that you go, Bastian."

He shook his head. It was only a tale, an excuse for her to escape. "No. Liana—"

"Let the man go." The weight of the oceans was in the psaaron's voice.

Bastian shook his head again. Panic tightened his chest.

"Go, Bastian. Go!" Color rose in Liana's cheeks. Her eyes shone with a brightness he recognized as hope. She truly believed that Melke would return.

"No." He wouldn't leave her here, couldn't. Not to flee, and not to rush off on a futile chase. Liana hoped, he didn't; Melke was dead.

"You'll be back by nightfall with my sister." That was the male wraith, as calmly as if he spoke of the likelihood of rain tomorrow or asked what time lunch would be served.

Bastian shook his head again. The risk was too enormous. If anything delayed him, if he failed to be back in time... he shuddered. The psaaron wasn't human. It would have no compunction in punishing Liana for a crime she hadn't committed, no compunction hurting her, breaking her. "No."

"Please, Bastian, *go.*" It was as if a fever glowed in Liana's cheeks. Her eyes were bright and full of hope.

"No."

He flinched as the creature moved past him. A sensation crawled over his skin, as if sea foam licked him, cool and salt-stinging.

"Go," said the psaaron, as it sat. The chair creaked beneath its weight. There were wet footprints on the flagstones where it had walked. Eyes the color of the ocean stared at him. Beautiful eyes. Ruthless eyes. The eyes of a creature that could weep its soul as tears, a creature that could change gender with its mood, as the tides changed. A creature that could inflict brutal punishments.

"No," Bastian said. The word came out as a croak, scarcely audible. When the psaaron took someone tonight, it would be him. Not Liana. Never Liana. Him. *Him.*

"Don't be a fool." Liana spoke sharply. "You're faster than I am. Go and help her!"

No, he started to say again, but the fierce hope in her face made his protest die. Liana had hope. She *hoped.*

"Go." The wraith's voice and his eyes were calm and steady.

What if...

There was no *what if*. Melke was dead, but Liana had hope and he couldn't extinguish that. And what if...

No. She was dead.

But Liana still hoped, and there was a whole day until sunset, a whole day before the psaaron took a bed partner and committed foul rape, a whole day when Liana could hope instead of fear. And perhaps...

If there was a chance, however slight.

Bastian met the male wraith's eyes. He pointed a finger at him, fierce, terrified. "You protect her."

The wraith nodded. "I will. You have my word." Bastian believed him. The young man meant what he said.

He turned and ran.

IT WAS TWO miles to their bridge and another twenty to the salamanders' den. He couldn't run that twice, not by nightfall. But the miles between here and Arnaul's, those he could run, and Arnaul would loan him a horse.

The baked dirt, as hard as stone, jarred beneath Bastian's boots. Dust lifted and brittle grass disintegrated. Sweat dripped off his skin and there was fire in his lungs, in his throat. *For Liana.* The words echoed in his head, in time to the pounding of his feet and the whistling gasps of air. For Liana he'd run, he'd try, and tonight... tonight he'd lie with the psaaron. Him, only him. He'd not let the creature choose her.

There was sweat in his eyes, stinging, and rawness in his throat and dust rising from the ground. *For Liana.*

Such a sweet baby she'd been, smiling, trusting him, grasping his fingers as she learned to walk, planting wet kisses on his cheek, shrieking with laughter as he swung her in the air. Such an eager-eyed young girl, finding beauty everywhere, delighted by ants' nests and yellow autumn leaves and lizard tracks in the dust, listening open-mouthed to the tales he read. Such a gifted woman now, too young in her womanhood, too gentle and precious, to be harmed.

He ran on rocks now, steeply rising and tufted with dry grass. Limestone, carved into fluted shapes by rain that no longer fell. Bastian ignored the twisting path. He climbed the slope fast, grabbing at rocks, hauling himself up, slipping, snatching at rough stone, tearing his palms, leaning forward—*faster*. At the top was a line where green grass met brown. Arnaul's land.

His descent was scrambling and urgent. The ground no longer jarred beneath his feet. Fat sheep and cattle grazed in green paddocks. The air wasn't dry in his throat. He ran more easily.

Arnaul's farmhouse was smaller than Vere, but glass sparkled in the windows, uncracked, and the garden was bright with flowers. A large tan-colored dog came barking from the open door, stiff-tailed and showing his teeth.

Bruno, he greeted.

The dog bounded forward, making puppy noises of pleasure.

Bastian swayed, panting. He laid his hand on the shaggy head. *Where is your master?*

Bruno didn't speak as clearly as Endal. The words and images flickered and blurred. It took Bastian a moment to understand. *Shoeing a horse?*

Yes, said Bruno.

The dog followed as he ran, stumbling now, around to the cobbled stable yard. Bastian inhaled the scent of straw and horse manure. "Arnaul!"

Bruno added his voice, barking.

He saw swift movement in one of the stalls and a startled face. "Bastian? What...? Is everything all right?"

Bastian shook his head, panting. "Need to borrow a horse. Please."

Arnaul's hair was as shaggy as his dog's. It bristled on his head, brown, and tufted at his eyebrows. "What's wrong?"

Bastian shook his head again, beyond words. He dragged air into his lungs. His throat was raw with running, raw with thirst.

"Your hands are bleeding."

Bastian looked down. There was blood on his palms. He didn't care. "Please, a horse."

"Of course."

Bastian walked over to the trough, lurching slightly. He cupped his hands and drank. The water tasted of blood and sweat and dust. He gulped it down, aware of Arnaul working hastily behind him.

I am a fool to do this.

But hope had been bright in Liana's eyes. He had to try.

"Here."

Bastian wiped the water from his face. He looked at the colt, leggy and strong. "Isn't this—?"

"My fastest horse."

And the most valuable. "Arnaul, I can't."

"Yes, you can."

It was too much, the horse too valuable. Bastian pulled the signet ring clumsily from his finger, but Arnaul stopped the gesture, closing his hand over Bastian's. "No."

There was silence while they looked at each other. Arnaul was his neighbour, a year older than him and an inch shorter. He was a man who had everything: rain and green grass, healthy livestock, a wife and children. But this horse, this refusal of payment... He saw in Arnaul's eyes that it wasn't charity. It was friendship.

"Thank you."

Arnaul nodded. He released his grip on Bastian's hand and gave him the reins. "Go."

CHAPTER FORTY-THREE

I T WAS PAST noon when he reached the salamanders' valley. Both he and the horse were
muddy and sweating, exhausted. Bastian slid
from the saddle, holding the colt's mane to keep
his balance. He took a lurching step out from
under the shade of the trees. "Endal!" His voice
was a dry croak.

There was silence, except for bees humming
and the call of birds.

He pursed his lips and whistled, loud and
shrill.

The valley stretched ahead of him, green and
bright with flowers and butterflies. The den
looked like a crouching red beast in the distance.

Bastian whistled again. *Endal!* he shouted in
his mind, although the distance was too great.

He saw movement, a black shape pushing through the long grass.

Bastian didn't remember kneeling, but he was on his knees. His arms went around Endal's neck and he hugged the dog fiercely to him. Images of Endal's distress boiled in his mind, smells and emotions. The dog trembled and whined.

"Hush," Bastian said aloud. "It's all right. It's all right." And he buried his face in Endal's warm fur.

Something cold and smooth pressed against his cheek, and when he drew his head back...

Bastian was frozen for a moment, on his knees. *Endal? The necklace?*

Endal whimpered. *Take it off. I don't like it.*

He lifted the necklace carefully from around the dog's throat, speechless with disbelief. It was impossible. It couldn't be.

It was. The necklace of psaaron tears lay in his hands, cool. He *had* it.

His joy was so fierce that it brought tears to his eyes. Liana was safe.

"Where's Melke?" he asked, clenching the necklace in his hands. *Where is she?*

Endal whimpered again. The explanation came swiftly, spilling into Bastian's mind; sight and sound, a twist of emotions. Traveling at night with the sharp scent of Melke's fear, the bustle of Thierry, the nap in the woods, his disobedience in not biting Melke when she was unseen, in not following her into the den.

Endal whined, pressing against his chest. "Hush," Bastian said, smoothing a hand down the dog's flank. *You did the right thing.*

She was burning. I smelled her burning.

Bastian's hand halted. He closed his eyes. *They caught her?*

Endal whimpered. The dog's memories nudged into his mind: a choking stench, waiting, furtive sounds, *scratch scratch scratch*, Melke's hand reaching from the wall. The necklace being pushed over his head, whispered commands, the scent of burning hair, burning flesh.

You waited all night?

Endal whined again, pressing closer. *Yes.*

Bastian had known she was dead, so why the clenching in his chest to hear it? Grief. Gratitude.

She had saved them.

Bastian hugged the dog close. *It's all right.* But it wasn't. It wasn't.

Moisture blurred in his eyes as he stood. *Come*, he said. *We must hurry.*

But Endal was whining, his ears flat against his head.

What? Bastian asked.

Endal was too distressed to speak clearly.

We have to leave. Bastian turned to the horse. *She's dead.*

Endal's bark was short and sharp. *No.*

What? Bastian's head snapped around. He stared at the dog. *She's alive?*

But Endal didn't know. He twisted his body and whined, full of uncertainty.

Bastian stood rooted to the ground, the necklace clutched in his hand. The horse in front of him or the den behind him. Liana or the wraith.

Liana or Melke?

Why did he hesitate? There was only one choice he could make.

Liana. It had to be Liana.

There was bile in his throat as he heaved himself into the saddle, as he yelled at Endal to come, *now*.

ONCE HE WAS out of the valley, some of the stomach-knotting tension eased. A psaaron's territory was as wide as the ocean and as long as the longest river; a salamander's was its hearth, close. He was beyond the reach of the creatures. They'd not step out of their valley to pursue him.

It began to rain. The muddy track became a mire and the tired horse slowed to a walk. Still, he had the necklace. He'd be home by dusk. Liana was safe; he was safe. The wraith…

Perhaps Melke was alive.

He couldn't think about her, couldn't, *could not*.

Thunder rumbled behind them, frightening the horse and making Endal press closer. The necklace began to sing, whispers of sound that crawled over his skin, half-heard voices.

Bastian fumbled with it, touching the living stones as if they scorched his fingers. He transferred the necklace from shirt pocket to saddle pommel, but the colt began to sidle and buck as if he heard the voices too, as if the soft, crooning song of dead psaarons shivered over his hide.

The necklace went into his pocket again, so that the voices burrowed inside him and whispered at the edge of his hearing. For Liana, he'd do it. For Melke.

The sky grew darker. Rain came down more heavily. The road was a river and the horse struggled, fighting for each step.

Bastian gripped the reins and ignored the singing in his ears. Rain blinded him. It filled his mouth and ears. The hours dissolved. His world narrowed to himself and the necklace, the horse, Endal, the rain and the mud, and Liana waiting at Vere. Nothing else was important. Nothing else mattered.

The female wraith.

He shouldered thought of her aside, as he shouldered aside mud and rain and exhaustion. He shouted at the horse, shouted at Endal. *Come on, hurry!*

They reached the bridge as darkness began to gather.

The central pile was gone.

A hole gaped in the bridge, huge. Water roared and foamed, tearing at the splintered timber. There was no way across.

For a moment it was too much. Bastian couldn't think, couldn't breathe. His heart failed to beat.

Liana.

Arnaul's bridge was eight miles upstream, and there was too little daylight left.

"*No!*" It was a scream.

RIDING WAS THE only thing Bastian could do. The rain was a torrent, choking him, blinding him. Voices rippled over his skin and sang in his head while dusk darkened toward night.

A white flash of lightning braided across the sky. Thunder boomed. The colt shied, rearing. Hard ground came up to meet Bastian, knocking the breath from his body. Pain jolted in his head.

He lay, dazed, drowning in half-heard voices and drenching rain.

Bas? Endal was a black shape above him. *Get up!*

Dizziness, and water in his eyes and mouth.

Endal nipped his arm. *Get up!*

It was easier to stay where he was, with the cold rain and the cold mud and the voices crawling over his skin and singing in his ears.

And then he remembered why he had to get up.

Panic pumped inside him.

Liana.

CHAPTER FORTY-FOUR

THE SUN SANK behind the hills. As daylight faded from the sky, the last of Liana's hope disintegrated, became dust inside her, became nothing.

She was hollow.

Liana drew the curtains closed. "I must go," she said.

"No! I won't let you—"

Hantje's voice faded in her ears. His mouth moved, but she heard no words. His face faded too. She no longer saw him.

The corridor was wider than it had ever been, longer, darker. It swelled and stretched as she walked, her feet not quite treading on the floor. She was light and floating, hollow.

The psaaron waited for her in the kitchen, more monstrous in candlelight than it had been in daylight.

The sharp spines of its crest almost brushed the ceiling. She couldn't smell it. The scent of psaaron, of seaweed and salt, of rain and wet plants, had soaked into the house, into her skin.

Behind the psaaron was an empty, open doorway and an empty, darkening yard.

Bastian, where are you?

Liana stepped into the kitchen, walking but not walking, too light for her feet to touch the flagstones.

"You come to pay your family's debt." Water swirled in those words, it rushed over creek stones and foamed on sandy beaches.

"Yes."

The psaaron tilted its head to survey her, stripping her naked with its eyes, peeling off her clothes and leaving her bare.

The hollowness inside her became greater. There was grayness at the edges of her vision, a leaching of color. She was feather-light, a skin only. The psaaron couldn't hurt her because she wasn't here. No blood, no bones, nothing. Empty.

"No!"

Hantje pushed through the door behind her. Color snapped back into the kitchen. Her feet were on the floor again. Blood and terror rushed inside her.

Hantje gripped her roughly, his fingers tight around her upper arm. He shoved her behind him and she stumbled, almost falling. "You shall take me!"

The psaaron threw back its head and laughed. The sound filled the kitchen: mirth, delight, waves crashing on rocks. The long tendrils that hung from its chin trembled. Fat drops of water fell to the flagstones.

Liana clutched at Hantje's nightshirt. *No*, she tried to say. *Go back to bed. Don't try to save me.* But her mouth wouldn't utter the words. They stuck in her throat, unspoken.

Abruptly there was silence.

She couldn't look at the psaaron, couldn't raise her eyes to look at Hantje. Cowardice twisted in her chest, shame.

"If you must punish someone, punish me." Hantje spoke loudly. "I'm a wraith. And a thief."

Don't do this, Hantje. But she couldn't unclench her fingers from his nightshirt and push him aside. She was unable to open her mouth to offer herself to the psaaron instead.

Something stirred in the kitchen, as if the creature drew breath. "A wraith." It stepped close. Cool moisture washed over Liana's skin.

"I had this one's mother," the psaaron said. "The experience was quite delicious."

Liana felt a touch in her hair. She closed her eyes tightly. Terror whimpered in her throat.

"Quite, quite delicious," said the creature as its fingers brushed over her cheek, wet and rough-scaled. Terror rose higher in her throat. She couldn't breathe. The stink of seaweed filled her mouth and nose.

"But a wraith..."

The touch was gone.

"A wraith would be even more delicious."

Liana opened her eyes.

Dampness swirled across her face as the psaaron reached to clench its hand in Hantje's hair, pulling his head around, forcing his chin up.

Liana saw the pulse jerk below his jaw as he met the psaaron's gaze.

The fish-mouth opened in a smile, showing sharp, serrated teeth. "I like to punish thieves," the psaaron said. Its voice was as harsh as a winter storm, dark and ice-cold.

Hantje didn't flinch. "Then take me."

"I shall." The scaled hand tightened cruelly, and then the psaaron released Hantje's hair.

Relief leapt sickeningly in Liana's chest, followed almost instantly by horror. Not Hantje. *No.*

Hantje twisted his nightshirt from her grip. "Go to your room, Liana," he said, not meeting her eyes. "Lock the door." He turned away from her.

Liana shook her head, unable to speak. This wasn't how it should be. Not Hantje, not anyone.

She stood frozen and watched as Hantje walked to the kitchen door, a faint limp in his step. The psaaron followed him, a creature of scales and sharp spines, wanting to hurt.

They were gone.

No.

"Hantje." At last she could speak, could move. She ran down the corridor. "Hantje!"

He paused in the doorway of the sickroom and turned his head to look at her. She saw his determination, his fear. He said nothing. Another limping step, and he was gone.

The psaaron followed.

"No!" Liana cried. "He's not a sal Vere!" But her courage was too late, too little.

The door to the bedchamber closed. The key turned in the lock.

HANTJE'S HANDS WERE steady as he undid the buttons, as he shrugged the nightshirt over his head and folded it neatly. His fingers didn't fumble as he untied the drawstring of his underbreeches. He stepped out of them, folded them, laid them on the chair, and turned to face the psaaron.

His heart flinched in his chest. The psaaron was no longer sexless. It had chosen to be male for tonight.

Hantje stared into the psaaron's eyes. Terror was tight on his skin. He deserved this. He deserved pain and blood and degradation. He deserved anything this creature did to him. There was no punishment great enough for what he'd done. No way to wash the stain from his soul. No way to bring Melke back.

Grief was pure and sharp in his breast, and his guilt so intense that he almost vomited from it. *Melke*.

His fault. It was his fault. All and everything, his fault.

He couldn't save his sister, but he could save Liana. Hantje swallowed. "Well?"

"Come closer."

There was a scream in his throat and cold sweat on his skin. He took a step toward the psaaron.

"Are you ready, wraith?"

A new smell mingled with the deep, dark scent of the ocean: something sharp and rank and male.

Terror beat in Hantje's chest. *I deserve this.* "Yes."

And then his punishment began.

CHAPTER FORTY-FIVE

THE DARKNESS WAS absolute. Bastian ran, staggering beneath the weight of rain and voices and exhaustion. Endal was at his side. The colt kept pace, lame.

Too slow. Too slow.

Endal, he shouted silently, groping in his pocket for the necklace.

The dog pressed against his leg.

I need you to take this to Liana. You must hurry. How fast could the dog run those miles?

He lurched to his knees and fumbled to place the necklace around Endal's throat. Voices stroked over his skin and sang in his veins and twisted inside him.

Endal jerked away. He uttered a sound, frantic and high-pitched, almost a shriek. His panic bubbled in Bastian's mind, incoherent, screaming. *Off off off off.*

Bastian grabbed him. "It's all right! It's all right!"

Endal howled, struggling in his grip, tearing at the necklace with teeth and claws, frenzied, desperate.

Bastian yanked off the necklace and threw it on the ground. *I'm sorry*, he said, hugging the dog to him while rain streamed over them. *I'm sorry*.

Endal shook, every muscle trembling. His whimper was audible.

I'm sorry. Bastian pressed his face into the dog's wet fur. *Forgive me, Endal. I didn't know*.

Endal whined. He tried to lick his cheek.

Bastian hugged the dog a moment longer, and then released him. No hope remained. He couldn't run fast enough to save Liana from the psaaron, and Endal couldn't do it for him. Soon she would be screaming as Endal had screamed.

WATER ROARED BENEATH Arnaul's bridge. Rain sluiced over Bastian's skin and voices filled his head. It was eight miles to Vere, and the night was as black as pitch. Endal ran in front and the colt followed, pressing close.

How many hours had he been running? What was the psaaron doing to Liana?

It was hopeless and yet still he ran, staggering, sliding in the mud, falling, dragging himself up. His breath came in sobs. He couldn't save Liana, couldn't stop the creature from breaking her, but he'd run until his heart burst in his chest if it meant an hour less agony for her.

The land began to rise. The downpour eased slightly. Bastian stumbled on rock, on lumps of limestone. The rain became gentle, a drizzle, a mist, nothing. Thick clouds hid the moon and dead grass crunched beneath his boots. The air was dry. Vere.

Bastian pushed ahead of Endal and went down the slope fast. He was sightless in the dark, reckless with desperation, stumbling and falling, hauling himself up. *Faster.*

A rock caught his boot. He fell, clutching at air.

BASTIAN SWAM SLOWLY out of blankness.

A warm tongue licked his cheek. *Bas?*

He opened his eyes. He was lying in bed. No, not in bed. Where? Darkness. Night time. The scent of dust and blood. Pain in his head and a nudging of urgency.

Endal?

Get up, Bas. Get up!

He didn't want to get up, couldn't think of any reason to. He wanted to lie here and wait for the sun to rise.

Liana.

Bastian scrambled frantically to sit. Dead grass crunched beneath his hands, rough limestone, dirt.

He groped for Endal. The dog's fur was almost dry.

There was a scream in his chest: *Liana!*

Bastian fell when he tried to stand. His left leg crumpled. He was on his knees and there was a blank instant of agony.

Endal whined. He felt the dog's breath against his cheek.

His head spun dizzily. He gritted his teeth against pain and nausea and explored with clumsy fingers. Blood soaked his trousers and trickled warm down his leg. He found a gash at his knee, deep and gaping.

Bastian clenched his fingers into the torn, blood-soaked fabric. *Endal, I'm sorry. You must take the necklace for me.*

He heard a soft whimper.

Please, Endal. He reached out and touched the dog's fur. *You're almost dry now. The voices won't be so bad.*

Endal quivered beneath his hand, taut and fearful.

Please, Bastian begged, clenching his fingers in the dog's fur.

Endal's acquiescence was silent, a dipping of his head. He trembled.

Bastian hugged the dog roughly. *Thank you.* He felt in his pocket. It was empty.

Utter panic leapt inside him. There was another scream in his chest. He couldn't have lost it, *couldn't—*

Here, Bas. Endal scratched at the ground.

Bastian's heart beat loud and fast as his fingers scrabbled in the brittle grass. Dirt, chips of limestone—and psaaron tears, smooth and coated in dust.

He held them in his hand, almost sobbing.

The stones were cool and dry. No voices whispered in his ears or over his skin.

Stay with Liana, he said as he placed the necklace carefully around the dog's neck. *Keep her safe.*

I will.

He held Endal close for a moment. He heard no voices, only the thump of Endal's heart. *Is it all right?*

Yes.

Bastian released the dog. *Then run, Endal. Run.*

He felt no hope as he listened to the dog's swift paws. The necklace wouldn't save Liana. She was broken.

Bastian closed his eyes. He'd made too many mistakes.

He wanted to bury himself in the dirt, to stay here in the dark forever, to never open his eyes again. But if Liana survived this night, she would need him.

He had to walk, *had to*. And if that was impossible, he'd crawl.

CHAPTER FORTY-SIX

DAWN. HANTJE LAY on the floor, his cheek pressed to the fraying carpet. His breath came in gasps and broken sobs. *Get up. Get up, before Liana comes.*

He pushed himself away from the floor and staggered to his feet. Pain was unimportant. Just let him hide his injuries before Liana—

Someone knocked softly on the door.

Hantje snatched a sheet off the bed. His hands shook as he wrapped it around himself. He turned his back to the door.

"Hantje?"

"I'm fine." His voice was hoarse. There was blood in his mouth from where he'd bitten through his lower lip. "Go away."

But he heard the sound of the door opening wider, of hesitant footsteps inside the room.

"No," Liana said. "Hantje, let me see. Let me help."

"Get out!"

"No."

Her hand was on his arm. The shaking inside him wouldn't stop. He couldn't hide it from her.

"Let me see."

He turned his head away and squeezed his eyes tightly shut. "Please, Liana, just go away."

But she didn't. He felt her fingertips on his chin where blood caked the skin, thick and sticky.

He pulled away from her touch, stumbling, trembling, his eyes still tightly closed. "Please go away. I need to wash." The words came thickly from his torn lip.

"I'll help you."

"No."

"Yes!" The word was fierce.

He opened his eyes.

She was Asta, beautiful and sweet. And she was more than that. Beauty and sweetness, and also ferocity. He saw tears in her eyes and beneath the tears determination, strong and unyielding.

Tears. She cried for him.

"Liana." He reached out a hand to her but she was already gone, running across the room.

She brought back warm water and soft cloths.

Hantje clutched the sheet more tightly to him. "I can do it myself." Speech brought fresh blood to his mouth. The shuddering of his body wouldn't stop.

Liana ignored the words. "Your mouth first. I'll stop the bleeding. Can you sit on the bed or is it easier to stand?"

Hantje swallowed. "Easier to stand," he whispered. He'd let her clean his mouth, just his mouth, so that he didn't taste blood on his tongue, didn't swallow it, didn't want to vomit quite so much.

"Bend your head."

He closed his eyes while she washed the blood from his chin. He couldn't look at her face, so close, so lovely. He couldn't look at her hair as white as starlight.

He felt a cloth, wiping, wet, and then gentle fingertips where he'd bitten through his lip. Coolness flowed from her touch, a faint lessening of pain.

"There," a soft whisper. "That will stop the bleeding for now."

He opened his eyes. "What?"

"Shhh." Liana laid a finger over his mouth. "Don't talk."

She reached up and pulled the hair away from his face. Hantje hadn't the strength to stay standing and to argue. One or the other, but not both, and so he closed his eyes again and let her knot his hair at the back of his head, let her clean his face with warm water and a soft cloth and exquisite gentleness.

"Let me see your shoulders. There's blood."

Hantje tightened his grip on the sheet. "No." He opened his eyes.

"You think I haven't seen you before? I have!"

He shook his head. "This is different."

"Curse you, Hantje!" There was anger in Liana's voice and tears in her eyes. "Don't be such a fool!"

Tears again. He was helpless when he saw them. He loosened his grip and let the sheet fall slightly.

Breath hissed between Liana's teeth when she saw what the psaaron had done to his shoulders. Her cheeks paled.

Hantje lifted the sheet again with clumsy haste. He turned away from her, stumbling on shaking legs.

"No!" She caught his arm, halting him, and pulled the fabric back from his shoulders. "Oh, Hantje..."

He stood, trembling, and let her clean the wounds.

She didn't ask what had happened and he didn't tell her. It was too bestial; the psaaron biting as it mounted him, sinking its teeth into his flesh, enjoying the sounds of pain that he tried to choke back.

Something in her touch, a quiet magic, calmed the deep shuddering inside him. The touch was so gentle and soothing that his eyelids closed. Memory of the psaaron retreated and became hazy. It hurt a little less in his mind, in his body.

Liana had the sheet down to his waist, briskly, before he was aware of her intent. He opened his eyes, opened his mouth, but her glare stopped his protest. "Don't," she said, sweet and fierce.

Hantje held the sheet tightly at his hips and submitted, ashamed to be standing in front of her with the marks of his punishment on him. She cleaned his chest and arms, his back. Blood trickled from countless rips and ragged cuts. Liana traced a tiny wound with her fingertip. "What did this?"

"Scales."

She healed him, then. Where her fingers touched his skin, the pain and heat and rawness faded and became cool.

At last she lowered her hands and stepped back. "Hantje—"

He met her eyes. "No."

"But—"

"No!"

She bit her lip and turned away. "I'll get some salve. If you wish to clean yourself while I'm gone..."

He did, quickly, washing blood from his legs, wiping away the creature's touch with trembling hands. He had his underbreeches on when Liana returned, although his shaking fingers couldn't tie the drawstring.

"I'll put this on your shoulders," she said, showing him the pot of salve.

"I can do it."

"I will. Lie down, Hantje. I'll help you to sleep."

"I don't need—"

"Please, Hantje." Liana moved closer to him as she spoke. He was aware of the warmth of her body, the soft touch of her breath on his skin. The quiet plea in her voice made him close his eyes briefly.

He deserved pain and punishment, not what she was giving him: care and tears, healing. But he couldn't find the words to tell her or the strength to argue.

It hurt inside him, deep and jagged, as he sat. The pain caught his breath in his throat and almost made him cry out. He choked the sound back and lay down, his limbs clumsy. He couldn't look at Liana's face. His shame was too intense.

The mattress sank as she sat beside him. Her fingers touched his skin. He felt the coolness of salve and smelled the clean scent of herbs. "Sleep," she whispered.

But it was impossible to sleep. There was so much tightness in his chest, so much grief. Melke.

"Hush," Liana whispered, as if he wept. "Sleep."

Hantje closed his eyes, squeezing back the tears. Such shuddering inside him, such aching grief.

"Shhh."

Her fingers and voice soothed him toward sleep. But how could he sleep when Melke... The pain faded, there was no shaking inside him. There was only warmth and darkness. But Melke... *Shhh, sleep.* There was coolness between his buttocks, where he was torn in two, where the psaaron had hurt him most. *No,* he struggled to say the word aloud, to push her hand away. *Shhh, sleep.* Someone was singing softly, a familiar song. "Mel?"

"Not yet. She'll be back."

But she'd never be back. He'd killed his sister.

"Hush. Sleep."

The tears came, wrenching and choking. Someone held him, cradled him. *Shhh, sleep...* kisses in his hair, as light as butterflies' wings... *hush, don't cry...* and he wasn't the only one weeping, he heard someone else's tears... *shhh, sleep...* and he cried for Melke while someone held him and rocked him to sleep.

CHAPTER FORTY-SEVEN

IT WAS ALMOST noon when Bastian staggered into the yard, leaning heavily on the lame colt. Emptiness and silence greeted him.

"Come on, boy." He urged the horse gently with his voice, softly, as he'd done all morning, when all he wanted to do was scream, to howl as Endal had howled. *Liana*.

He reached the door finally, clutching at the frame and hauling himself inside. The colt needed water, needed some of Gaudon's hay, but first...

"Liana." His voice cracked and broke. Something in his chest did too.

He heard light footsteps in the corridor, running, and Liana was standing in the doorway, *standing*, and then she was in his arms and he was crying. He who never cried, cried.

It was a dream. It couldn't be real.

Bastian held her tightly, his injured leg forgotten. "You're all right. You're all right."

Liana said nothing. She clutched him, trembling and alive and uninjured.

Everything was all right. Nothing mattered, nothing except Liana, and she was all right. Bastian stroked her hair. "The psaaron didn't... it didn't..."

Liana pulled away. She looked up at him. Distress twisted her face. "It took Hantje."

"What?"

"Hantje made it punish him instead. He said he was a thief and he's *not*, he's never stolen anything!" She was crying, as fiercely as she'd cried when she was a child, gulping and choking. Bastian gathered her in his arms again. "It hurt him. He was bleeding so much."

He held her tightly and pressed his face into her hair. *Thank you, Hantje.*

He'd underestimated the wraith, both the wraiths, had underestimated their courage and their honor.

Bastian closed his eyes. *I make too many mistakes.*

Endal was at his side, yelping in pleasure at his return, pressing against his thigh, telling him that he'd run as fast as he could but the sea monster had gone, that he'd stayed with Liana as he'd asked and kept her safe.

Bastian opened his eyes. The necklace lay on the kitchen table, a coil of blue-green stones, abandoned. He experienced a moment of blankness, a moment when disbelief stopped the beating of his heart.

The curse was unbroken.

There'd been no point. The running, the mud and the rain, the blood. He hadn't saved Liana, hadn't saved Vere. And Melke was gone.

Hantje hadn't left Liana. He'd saved her.

"Will he live?" His voice was rough.

She didn't answer, just wept.

Bastian held her from him and shook her. "Liana, tell me. Will he live?"

He'd never seen such brightness in her eyes before, such grief. "Where's Melke?" she asked.

Bastian closed his eyes in shame. "The salamanders have her."

"Is she dead?"

Probably. "I don't know."

She pulled away from him.

He opened his eyes and reached for her. "Liana."

But she was walking across the kitchen, down the corridor.

Bastian followed, staggering, limping, leaning against the wall. "Liana."

She stood in the doorway to the sickroom, her back to him.

"Liana."

He saw what she saw: the wraith, Hantje, lying in the bed asleep. A sheet was pulled up to his chin. There were bloodstains on the white linen and blood at his mouth, where his lower lip was bitten through. His thin face was slack with exhaustion, pale and tear-stained.

"He's alive," Liana whispered. "But if Melke dies, he'll... He'll do what father did."

Bastian understood what she saying. The guilt would be too much, the grief. Hantje would kill himself.

"I'll go for her," he said roughly. "If she's alive, I'll bring her back."

Liana turned her head to him. Her eyes were bright with tears. "Now?"

He gestured to his knee, bound with strips of cloth torn from his shirt. The trouser leg was stiff with dried blood. "First you must heal me. And the horse."

Liana uttered a choked cry. "Bastian, I didn't see!"

"No matter."

Hantje mattered. And Melke. He'd made the wrong decision at the salamanders' den. He had to correct it.

IT WAS NEARLY dusk when Bastian left the farm. Endal stay behind, guarding Liana, guarding the necklace.

He let the colt set the pace. He wouldn't make the mistake of rushing again, of injuring himself or the horse.

Too many mistakes.

None of this would have happened if he'd found his courage earlier, if he'd accepted the salamanders' offer and bartered his body for the necklace.

He rode across Arnaul's bridge, above roaring dark water, and turned east, toward Thierry, toward the salamanders' den. There was no rain, just mud, and no clouds to conceal the stars. The moon was his friend tonight, cold and bright. It illuminated the way, showing each dip in the road, each hollow and puddle and rut. He didn't pull his collar high at his throat or avert his eyes.

Moon shadows and moonlight, moon time, time for wraiths. But wraiths had more courage than he did and they had honor, deep honor.

The night blurred into long miles and weariness and mud. Then came dawn, gray through the trees. He saw the salamanders' valley in the pale light of the newly-risen sun.

Bastian slid from the saddle. He lurched and almost fell, grabbing hold of the colt's mane. His body trembled with fatigue and his mind flinched from thought of what came next. Salamanders couldn't change their gender at will, like a psaaron. The adult was female, would never be male, could never rape. Even so, he couldn't think directly of what he had to do, of what it would entail. He shrank from it, feared it.

Water first. And he must find where Melke had hidden the horse she'd hired. "Come, boy." He clicked his tongue and the colt came willingly, flecked with mud and sweat.

Water to drink, then he'd wash the dirt from his body and do what he had to do. Hantje had shown him how, just as he'd shown him what courage was.

CHAPTER FORTY-EIGHT

LIANA WOKE WITH a start, slumped in the chair. Hantje was sobbing in his sleep.

"Hush," she said, blinking back dark dreams. She leaned forward to touch his cheek, "Hush. It's all right." It was a lie, but the words quieted him. The soft sobbing stopped.

Dawn was faint behind the curtains. The candles had burned down to mere stubs, refusing to go out, stubborn. The bloodstained sheet had slipped from Hantje's shoulders, baring torn flesh. Liana laid her fingers lightly on the wounds and felt the heat, the swelling.

She had slept too long.

She didn't need the salve to heal him, but Hantje protested less if she used it. He didn't struggle up from sleep and try to push her hand away. It was as if the scent of herbs made it all right for her hands to be on his body.

Liana healed his lower lip first, gently, smoothing in the ointment, taking the pain away and easing the swelling, knitting his flesh. She healed his shoulders next, coaxing the savage puncture wounds closed and shooing away infection. She willed him well, wishing for smooth, cool skin beneath her fingers, for flesh unswollen and untorn.

She felt his pain, a stinging prickle beneath her skin, and she felt more than that, she felt *him*, a sense of who he was that swelled inside her. Hantje.

The tiny rips where the psaaron's scales had torn his skin were closed, half-healed. They needed only the lightest touch, but where the psaaron had raped him...

Hantje whimpered in pain and tried to twist away from her fingers. Distress contorted his face and his eyelids almost opened. "Shhh," Liana whispered. "Sleep." She pressed her lips to his cheek and said it in her mind, *Shhh, sleep.*

Where he'd been raped the healing was the hardest. Blood still trickled sluggishly. She touched him lightly, taking his pain, willing him to heal. *Let flesh knit and become whole. Let blood stop oozing. Let infection become nothing. Let him be well.*

The magic that was rooted deep inside her flowed from her fingertips. It soaked into Hantje as rain soaked into soil and he healed, as slowly as the blossoming of a flower.

When she had nothing left to give, Liana drew the sheet over Hantje and sat back in the chair, clutching at the seat. The room was dark, lit only by sunlight swelling behind the closed curtains.

She stumbled as she stood, almost tipping the chair over. Her hands shook as she washed them in the basin, as she drew open the sun-warmed curtains. Light fell into the room, sudden and bright.

Liana stood, swaying. She wanted to lie down on the floor and sleep, here, where the carpet was so thin she could see the floorboards beneath.

Blood stained the carpet, splashes that looked like red petals scattered on the floor.

Hantje's blood.

He lay in the bed facing her, curled up on his side, deeply asleep. His eyelashes were dark shadows against his cheeks and his lower lip was swollen, red.

She knew who he was, knew him as well as he knew himself, knew his regrets and his deepest fears, knew his most precious dreams.

She should climb the stairs to her bedroom and lie in her own bed, but that would mean leaving Hantje.

He stirred as the mattress sank beneath her weight, muttered as she crawled to lie behind him, clumsy with fatigue, above the sheet, not touching him. It was all right to lie like this and not touch, to sleep.

Liana closed her eyes. Exhaustion pressed her into the mattress. Her limbs were heavy, leaden.

Soft sobs tugged her back from the edge of sleep.

"Shhh." She struggled to open her eyes.

Hantje wept, dreaming.

She laid her hand on his arm, but still he sobbed.

"Hush," Liana whispered. "Sleep." She moved closer to his warmth, making the mattress dip and creak, and put an arm around Hantje, holding him. "Shhh."

Her hand lay over his heart. She felt his heartbeat through the sheet and she felt him, Hantje, his honesty and his courage, the gentleness that he hid inside himself. She knew him. Knew that he shied away from anger and that he liked to laugh, knew the streak of mischief that twisted inside him, and knew that he was drowning in despair and that he didn't want to wake up, ever.

She felt his emotions for her, sweet and deep and confused, and she felt his fear of the dark, sharp, and his fear of being alone. She held his heartbeat in the palm of her hand and knew him, knew that he was a man who didn't like to shout, a man who hid his fears behind jokes and smiles, who was proud but not vain, not arrogant. Honorable. Despairing. A man who hated himself.

Hantje slept. His heart beat slowly and steadily beneath her hand. She no longer heard his sobs but she knew that in his dreams he wept.

"Don't cry," Liana whispered. "Hush." She pressed a kiss to the nape of his neck. There was tangled hair beneath her lips, and warm skin, and in her nostrils the smell of herbs and blood and the lingering stink of the psaaron. And beneath those, faintly, Hantje's scent, male and subtle.

Liana closed her eyes. "Sleep, Hantje. Sleep."

CHAPTER FORTY-NINE

BASTIAN BEAT HIS fist on the thick door. The metal rang dully.

A minute passed, full of long seconds. Something was wrong with his heartbeat: too fast, too loud, too jerky.

Heat and peppery musk billowed out at him as the heavy door opened. Bastian stepped back and caught himself, made himself stand still. Primitive terror twisted beneath his breastbone. He swayed with the need to turn and run.

He saw ember-bright eyes in the shadows. "Yesss?"

Bastian swallowed, forcing his fear down. "I've come for the wraith."

There was a flash of sharp teeth as the salamander kit uttered a gleeful, hissing laugh.

Sweat gathered on his skin. He swallowed again. "If the wraith is alive, I want her."

"For what prissse, human?"

Smoke and sulphur choked in his throat and acrid musk stung his eyes. Terror was tight in his chest. "For me. For pleasure."

He heard a soft, sibilant inhalation of breath and a rustle of movement. Another pair of bright eyes looked at him. "Wait." The door shut with a grating clang.

Bastian waited, battling his fear. His breath came too shallow, too fast. He still sweated, despite the closed door and the coolness of morning. His hand shook when he wiped the perspiration from his face. The sound of his heartbeat drowned all other sounds. If there was birdsong, he didn't hear it.

The door opened again. Four kits crowded outside, where the sunlight fell on them. Bastian held himself still, his hands clenched, as they surrounded him. They were lithe and sleek, with skin as red as fire.

The salamanders inspected him as if he was livestock. Agile fingers unbuttoned his shirt and bared his chest, pulled the sleeves down his arms and dropped the shirt on the dirt. Hot hands touched his skin, prodding and poking, squeezing muscle, stroking.

"Yesss," said one. "Yesss, a good bargain."

And then those deft fingers were at his waist. Bastian squeezed his eyes shut, trembling, and cringed inside himself as trousers and under-breeches fell to the ground. He felt a light, scorching touch on his thigh, heard a hissing murmur of delight. "Yesss, yesss. A very good bargain."

The salamanders stepped back. They made no sound, but there was suddenly less heat. He swallowed and opened his eyes.

The kits stood in the doorway again, all four of them, as red as the heart of a fire. "You may enter," one of them said.

Bastian pulled up the underbreeches and trousers while they watched, sweating with shame and fear. His hands shook too much to button the shirt. "The wraith?" he asked, when his nudity was hidden. "She's alive?"

A crested head dipped in answer. "Ssshe livesss."

The shame of his nakedness, those watching eyes and bold hands, was suddenly nothing. Melke was alive, and the fear evaporated like sweat on his skin. Stepping into the choking heat and smoke and peppery musk was almost easy.

A torch burned sullenly inside, pushing back the thick shadows. "Let me see her."

"No."

"Then we have no bargain."

He heard a hiss of annoyance. "Very well."

Bastian followed the salamanders, as clumsy as an ox beside their litheness. The rough space of the vestibule narrowed into a passage. It curved and curved again, and widened into a cell-like chamber, small and low-ceilinged.

"Here."

Torches flared smokily in brackets, casting shadows on the coarse red walls.

"Where?"

One of the salamanders pointed to the floor with a sharp-clawed finger. "There."

"No." The word choked in Bastian's throat. He was on his knees, scrabbling to lift the metal trap-door, appalled. The iron was heavy, black and pitted. He couldn't get his fingertips under the edge.

He heard a loud hiss in his ear, exasperated, and a salamander kit pushed him aside. Muscles flexed beneath supple red skin and the trapdoor lifted with a grating sound.

A hole gaped, black and bottomless. The stench of salamander scat and death curled out of it. He could see nothing.

Bastian turned to the kit beside him, too appalled to be afraid. "She's not alive!"

"Yesss."

He shook his head, speechless with horror. Nothing in that pit could be alive.

One of the salamanders thrust a torch into the opening. Shadows lunged back. That was the only movement.

The floor of the pit was fifteen, twenty feet below him. He saw bones, human ribcages and skulls, scraps of cloth, and Melke lying still, a rag doll figure with crooked limbs.

"We keep all our thievesss here." The creature's voice was rich with satisfaction.

Something choked painfully in Bastian's throat. "She's dead." She'd died in the dark, in a stinking pit.

The salamander uttered a sharp sound of denial. "Ssshe livesss."

"I want her out! Get her out! Now!" Bastian was on his feet, gulping air as if he'd just run a race. Melke was afraid of the dark. Liana had told him. Endal had told him.

"Afterwardsss."

"Now! Or there's no bargain!"

The answer was a sinuous shrug.

The salamanders hauled her out using a chain. The kit that went down into the pit was displeased. Tiny flames licked around its mouth.

Bastian watched, clenching and unclenching his hands. He didn't recognize Melke when she lay at his feet. He knelt, hesitant to touch her. Black hair, yes, in a long plait, and the red blouse with flower-stitched cuffs, singed and torn. But it wasn't Melke's face, fine-boned and elegant. This was a stranger's face, black with soot, burned and bruised and swollen. A gaping wound slashed down one cheek. He saw the white gleam of bone.

His fingers curled into his palm. He had no gift for healing. He was useless, helpless, afraid. "Melke?" he whispered.

It seemed to him that she didn't breathe. There was no movement of her lips or chest. She lay as if dead. No defiance, no haughtiness, just death.

"Melke?" Bastian whispered again. He forced himself to touch cautious fingers to her throat.

He felt a pulse, faint and irregular.

"Come." He heard impatience in the salamander's voice, a crackle of fire.

Bastian didn't look away from Melke. "But—"

"Come now or our bargain isss void."

He looked up. The spines that crested the salamander's skull cast long, spiky shadows on the wall. "But she's dying."

"We cannot promissse that ssshe will live beyond today. That wasss not our bargain."

The bargain.

There was a bargain and he had to fulfil it, or else Melke would die on this floor.

Bastian scrambled to his feet. He followed the sala-manders, fast, urgent, almost stepping on their heels. *Hurry, hurry*. The passage opened into a cavernous hall but he paid no attention to the vastness of it, to the heat and the heaped coins and the leaping pit of flames. He pushed ahead of the salamander kits and strode across the floor to their mother.

"We have a bargain," he said roughly, stripping off his shirt.

"Sssss..." It was a sound of pleasure, ripe and sibi-lant.

His heart clenched to a halt. There was fire in those wide eyes, flames licking in the iris.

She stood, graceful and sleek. Her skin was as dark as heart's blood, as bright as the burning core of a bonfire. There was no hair on her body, just that sharp crest. Her face was broader than the kits, but still... a lizard's face, wide-mouthed and lipless, sharp-toothed.

The kits were immature, genderless, but this crea-ture had a woman's breasts, ripe and full. The dip of her waist and the swell of her hips, her musk... She was female.

Bastian's revulsion was strong and instinctive. Bile rose in his throat.

The salamander stepped close to him, as tall as he was, lithe and lush. Her crest fanned over her skull, the spines as fine and sharp as needles. Heat radiated from her skin.

Bastian struggled not to recoil. His heartbeat was staccato in his ears. He couldn't inhale, couldn't exhale. Breathing was impossible.

The salamander touched one razor-sharp claw to his breast. "Pleasssure," she said, and small flames curled from her mouth.

Bastian trembled, the shirt clenched in his fist. Terror beat inside him. *Courage.* For Hantje, bleeding, and for Melke, lying near-dead, he had to do this. *Courage.* He forced himself to breathe, to inhale the salamander's scent, to speak. "Yes."

She showed her teeth in a smile. "Then begin."

His fingers opened stiffly. The shirt fell to the floor. "The wraith needs water."

She gestured with her hand, feminine and graceful, terrifying, and one of the kits ran to do her bidding.

"I don't wish to be watched."

The salamander's smile grew wider, showing pointed teeth. Flames glinted in her eyes. "They will watch."

There was a moment when he couldn't go further, a single, precise, shining moment when he simply *could not*. The moment passed and he undid his trousers with fumbling fingers.

CHAPTER FIFTY

S ILVIA HAD TAUGHT him well. Never mind
that the heat of the salamander's skin
scalded his fingertips and singed his hair,
never mind that his mouth and tongue blistered
as he kissed her breasts, that her strong scent
made him want to vomit. Bastian had promised
pleasure and he gave it. He closed his eyes and
pretended that she was Silvia, that it was skin
beneath his mouth instead of fine scales, that her
smell was sensual, not choking.

They lay on coins in firelight. It was a barbaric
couch, decadent and hard-edged, a king's fortune
in gold. Bastian drowned in musk and heat. The
salamander's hands were on him, caressing him
as he caressed her. His skin was slippery with
sweat, prickling with pain.

He jerked as her tail curled snake-like around his calf, jerked again and almost yelped as hot fingers touched his groin, as she explored his maleness. Her hand was bold and greedy, forcing a response from him. He inhaled sharply. Pain and pleasure twisted together.

Now. Do it now. He mounted the salamander, burying himself in her body, whimpering in his throat at the heat, the pain. The salamander arched to meet him. Flames licked from her mouth.

Bastian squeezed his eyelids shut. There was pain as he thrust, pleasure. Pain. Pleasure. It was a nightmare; a hideous combination of pain and terror, pleasure and scalding heat and intense shame.

The salamander's body clenched around him. Bastian opened his eyes and saw her head bow back, saw the muscles cord in her throat, saw fire erupt from her mouth and then—*shame, shame*—his own release came, so excruciating that he nearly screamed.

Bastian wept inside himself as he rolled off the salamander. Something howled in his chest. *No.*

The salamander stretched beside him, sinuous and fiery, sated. Flames were banked low in her voice, "Very pleassssant."

Bastian closed his eyes. Sobs choked in his throat. The horror inside him was deep and absolute. *What have I done?*

"Would you like another bargain? Gold, perhapsss?"

"No!" Bastian's eyelids jerked open. He pushed himself upright and staggered to stand. "No! Just the wraith."

The salamander's eyes narrowed. Flame curled from her mouth. "I wasss mossst angry with her. But with you, I am mossst pleasssed." More flames slid from her mouth.

Bastian turned his head away. "I just want the wraith. Just Melke. Please."

The adult salamander came to stand behind him as he dressed. Bastian smelled her musk, felt her heat. He pulled on his underbreeches and trousers, his shirt. The buttons wouldn't go into the button-holes. Hot breath licked his ear. A scalding lizard-hand slid around his waist and cupped his groin.

"No!" The word was hoarse, choked.

The hand was removed.

Bastian dragged on his boots. He straightened, lurching upright, and turned to face the salamander. She smiled at him, a creature of sharpness and fire. "A bonusss payment," she said, holding a thick gold coin out to him.

Bastian recoiled from her, stumbling, almost falling. "No!" He hadn't sold his body. It had been an exchange, clean, untainted by payment. He wasn't a whore.

The salamander threw back her head and laughed. Rich flames billowed from her mouth. "Humansss," she said. "Ssso amusssing."

MELKE WAS LIMP and heavy in his arms, awkward. Bastian held her close to his chest and blinked as sunlight streamed in through the open door. His eyes watered at the brightness.

He stepped outside and turned to face the sala-mander kits. They no longer terrified him.

Compared to their mother they were mild and unformed. Harmless.

They stared back at him, clustered in the doorway.

Bastian blinked again. No, not harmless. Swift and fiery and cruel. He cleared his throat. "How did you know about the necklace? How did you know where to find it?"

Eyelids closed lazily, then raised to show firebright eyes. "The lizardsss told usss."

Lizards. Bastian shut his eyes briefly.

"They're not sea stones," he said, as the door began to close. "Did you know?"

A careless shrug was his answer. "The colorsss were pretty."

The heavy iron door swung shut.

He made it to the horses before he vomited. The taste of bile was better than the taste of the salamander. Time passed, the sun moved in the sky. He had no memory of wrapping Melke in her cloak, of lifting her onto the horse she'd hired. He'd always held her, had always sat on this horse, and the colt had always walked behind them.

He couldn't smell Melke, couldn't smell anything except the female salamander. Her musk smothered the scents of blood and burnt flesh and scat. It had sunk into his skin and was ingrained there.

His mind was blank. Utterly blank. What had happened in the den... best to let his thoughts veer away from it, best not to remember. Best to be... blank.

Afternoon, dusk, night. Stars and the moon. Melke, heavy and limp in his arms. Endal, barking. Liana in the candlelit kitchen doorway.

"I brought her back," Bastian said, sliding from the saddle. Endal frisked around his legs. "She's alive." And then he vomited again.

CHAPTER FIFTY-ONE

THE BLISTERING ON his fingertips and palms, on his lips and tongue, at his groin, was mild. He used the salves, not Liana's gift. He didn't want her to see his shame, to understand the details of what he'd done. He hid it.

Bastian found it difficult to be in the farmhouse. It wasn't that it smelled of death, but there was something, a heaviness in the air, a tense silence.

Melke's life hung in the balance. The salamanders' fury was burned into her skin and cut into her flesh, broken into her bones. Her infection was more serious than her brother's had been.

Bastian cooked. That, he could do. Healing Melke, sitting at her bedside and holding her hand... Liana and Hantje did that.

He carried the necklace with him always, but hours melted into days and the psaaron didn't return. Next spring equinox, or the one after. And until then the curse would continue.

He'd made too many mistakes. Melke's injuries and her brother's ordeal need not have happened.

He had lacked for courage, and Bastian tasted the bitterness of shame every day. He seasoned the meals that he cooked with peppercorns and salt, with spices, but the food was always bitter when he ate it.

On the third day, the last ewe died giving birth. Bastian cut the lamb from her body. It was dead.

He squeezed his eyes shut. It was too much. Too much.

But the blood on his hands was better than the salamander's musk. He felt almost clean.

The well became dry on the fourth day.

Empty? asked Endal, when the bucket came up with no water in it.

Yes.

He felt the dog's anxiety.

It's all right. He rubbed Endal's ears. *We'll go to the river.*

He took the colt and the horse that Melke had hired, loading them with every waterskin and bucket he could find. Absurdly, his spirits lightened as he trudged the two miles to the bridge. The ground was dusty, the grass dead, and the glare of the sun merciless, but the air was fresh and dry in his throat and he didn't inhale Hantje's anguish with every breath he took.

The river still ran high. It had eaten most of the bridge. A dozen planks remained on this side, dipping into the water.

Bastian stood on the bank. The scent that rose from the river reminded him of the psaaron. Hairs rose on his skin. He shivered. Seven sal Veres had died in this river since the curse was laid. He didn't want to be the eighth.

The task would have been simple if he'd dared to clamber down the steep slope and dip his buckets in the water, but if he did that the river would rise up and swallow him. Instead, he stood on the bank and used the bucket from the well. The river tugged and pulled at it, trying to jerk the rope from his hands and drag him from his footing. Sweat stuck the shirt to his skin long before he'd finished. His hands were raw and bloody.

Worry weighed on Bastian as he walked back to the farmhouse. Even with every bucket and water-skin filled, he hadn't enough for three horses and a dog, and four people. "I'll take you back this afternoon," he told the colt. Maybe Arnaul would look after the hired horse. Just until...

Until Melke lived or died.

The horses' pace was slow. Dust rose in sluggish spurts from beneath their hooves and precious water splashed from the buckets, slopping to the parched ground. Endal walked beside him, closer than he usually did, his shoulder brushing Bastian's leg. His tail hung low.

Bastian rubbed the dog's head lightly with his knuckles. *It will be all right.*

She smells of death.

He stopped rubbing. *You like her, don't you?*

Yes.

Bastian sighed. It had been easier when Melke was a wraith and he could simply hate her.

He walked in silence, his fingers resting on Endal's head. His world had shrunk to heat and dust and sweat, to dryness in his throat and water splashing down to fall on dead grass, to waiting and hoping, wishing. If he could only go back to that day, if he could just change what he'd done.

Impossible.

I'm going to Arnaul's this afternoon, he told the dog. *You may stay behind if you prefer.*

Endal didn't speak for several minutes. Dust settled on Bastian's skin. Sunlight glared in his eyes and sweat stuck his shirt to his back. The farmhouse came into view before he heard the dog's voice in his head. *I'll stay.*

Very well.

You don't mind? Endal glanced up at him, his eyes icy pale in contrast to the blackness of his coat.

Of course not. He scratched behind the dog's ears. *You stay here. With Melke.*

IT WAS DUSK when Bastian returned, weary. He washed his face in a handful of water and walked upstairs to his bedchamber.

Melke lay in the wide bed, as still as death.

"How is she?" he asked.

Hantje looked up. He shook his head. "The same."

Bastian stepped closer to the bed. Endal lifted his chin from Hantje's feet and wagged his tail.

The injuries were still visible on her face: the shadows of bruises, the pinkness of healing burns, the thick red lines of slashing cuts. Fever flared in her cheeks. She didn't appear to be breathing. He saw no pulse at her throat.

Bastian's lips compressed. He bent to pat Endal. The dog's warmth and aliveness, the familiar soft roughness of his coat, steadied him. He cleared his throat. "She will recover."

Hantje made no answer. His despair was silent.

"I'll be in the kitchen if you need anything."

The young man nodded, gripping Melke's hand, his eyes on her face.

You wish to come? he asked Endal.

He prefers it if I stay.

Bastian nodded.

He walked slowly down the stairs. His whole life he'd slept in that room, in that bed. Twenty-seven years. If Melke died, he would close the door and never use the bedchamber again.

The kitchen stove had gone out. Bastian kindled a new fire and climbed the staircase to the little room that was now his.

Melke had slept in this chamber for more than two weeks. All her belongings were here. He looked around, trying to gain a sense of who she was, but there was little of her in the room. It looked as it always had, except for the blanket lying on the floor where Endal slept and the bowl filled with water.

Bastian looked at the items, blanket and bowl, and realized that Melke was fond of Endal. She'd provided those comforts, unprompted.

The dog liked her. Liana liked her.

Bastian rubbed the back of his neck. Why had it taken him so long to see that she was more than a wraith?

Other than the blanket and bowl, only the spare candles beside the candleholder hinted that Melke had slept here. The candles told him nothing new. He knew she was afraid of the dark, and he knew why.

Alongside the candles was something he'd not noticed before. Bastian frowned and stepped closer. Stones?

He reached out to pick them up, puzzled, and memory flashed behind his eyes. Throwing the knapsacks on the floor, the contents spilling out, stones rolling. He'd held one of these pebbles before, small and smooth. He'd put it in his pocket. And later he'd thrown it away.

Endal said she'd cried when she had searched for it.

Bastian clenched the stones in his hand. They ground into his raw palm, painful.

He took the stairs two at a time, down the dark and narrow servants' staircase and then up the wider one to the family bedrooms. "Hantje," he said, from the doorway. "Do you know what these are?"

The young man turned his head. "They're Melke's stones."

"What do they mean?" Bastian stepped into the room.

"They're... I guess you could say they're home. Those stones are—' Hantje's brow creased. "Your hand is bleeding."

"It's nothing." Bastian brushed the words aside. "These stones are what?"

Hantje glanced up at him. His eyes were dark in the candlelight. "Melke keeps them because they're from home. She says"—his laugh was choked—"she says they help her remember what it was like before everything happened."

Bastian closed his hand around the stones, aghast. He'd thrown away a piece of Melke's home. More than that, he'd thrown away her memories, some of the happiness of her childhood.

No wonder she'd cried.

He was sick with himself.

"There should be four," Hantje said. "There's a red one, too."

"I know," said Bastian. "I know where it is."

CHAPTER FIFTY-TWO

I T TOOK BASTIAN half the morning on his hands and knees searching in the brittle stubble of Gaudon's paddock to find the tiny stone. The horse was curious, coming close to watch. In the end it was Endal who found the pebble, covered in dust.

Is this it? I smell you on it. And Melke.

Bastian rubbed the stone clean, kneeling in the dirt. It was small and smooth, red. He closed his eyes briefly. *Yes. Thank you, Endal.*

The dog cocked his head. *That is what she cried for? Why?*

Because it reminds her of home. Bastian held the stone tightly.

The dog considered this answer for a moment. *Why did you throw it away?*

Bastian opened his hand and looked at the stone, a milder red than the salamanders, flecked with black. *Because I am not a nice person.*

Endal disagreed. He tried to climb into his lap.

Bastian hugged the dog to him. *I make too many mistakes, Endal,* he said, and he rested his cheek against warm, black hair.

You don't make any mistakes, Endal said with such pride in his voice that Bastian managed to laugh.

He put the stone carefully beside the other three on the little shelf where the candleholder stood, and took Gaudon to fetch water. The river tugged more fiercely today, breaking the rope and carrying away the bucket when he still had three waterskins left to fill.

Bastian took a stronger rope the next morning and tied it to his stoutest bucket. The river snapped at the bucket as if it had jaws, ripping and tearing hungrily. He fought the water, panting, straining with every muscle in his body. The river stilled for an instant, and then the water gave a huge gulp and swallowed the bucket. Bastian skidded on dry dirt, slipping, falling—

Only Endal's teeth, buried in his arm, stopped Bastian from tumbling into the river.

It was a frantic scramble up the bank, clutching at dry grass and crumbling dirt while the water snatched at his feet. Endal didn't let go until Bastian lay gasping on solid ground. His heart thundered in his chest. Sweat poured off his skin and blood trickled down his arm.

The river wanted him dead.

If he died, Liana would be alone with a crumbling house and a dead farm and a curse.

Bastian groped in his pocket for the necklace. Relief dripped off his skin, mingling with the perspiration and the blood. He hadn't lost it.

He sat up slowly while his heart hammered in his chest. *Thank you, Endal.*

The dog whined and pressed close to him, trembling. *I hurt you.*

I'm glad you did. He hugged Endal roughly.

His hands were bleeding, his arm was bleeding, and he'd filled only two waterskins. When he took one of those waterskins up to the sickroom, he found not Liana, but Hantje. The young man didn't see him. He sat at his sister's bedside and cried, hunched into himself.

Bastian stood in the doorway. He had heard a man cry like that once before, with heart-deep despair. He'd felt the same clenching in his chest as he did now, the same sense of helplessness.

Is she dead? he asked Endal, the waterskin hanging limply from his fingers. Numbness grew beneath his breastbone, spreading swiftly.

Endal raised his muzzle. His nostrils flared. *I don't smell it.*

Bastian clenched his fingers around the waterskin and inhaled a deep breath. Not dead. Not yet.

He wanted to enter the bedchamber and offer comfort, but he didn't know how. He was nine years old again, frightened by the depth of a man's grief, not knowing what to do or say. *I'll get Liana*, he said as Endal trotted into the room.

He walked quickly down the hall, the waterskin still dangling from his hand, and knocked softly on her door. "Liana? Are you still awake?"

He heard a rustle of movement, light footsteps, and then the door opened.

Liana's face was shadowed and exhausted. The covers were pushed back on her bed. She wore her nightgown.

"I woke you."

She shook her head. "I'd only just... Is something wrong? Your arm!"

"No, I'm fine, it's—"

"Melke!" Her eyes were wide and alarmed.

"No. At least, I don't think so. It's Hantje."

Liana pushed past him and ran down the corridor on bare feet, the nightgown swirling around her ankles. She stopped in the doorway to the sick-room.

Bastian's boots were loud on the wooden floor. The waterskin sloshed in his hand. Liana turned her head as he came to stand beside her. He saw tears shine in her eyes.

"I don't know what to do," he said beneath the sound of Hantje's grief, ashamed.

Liana blinked back her tears. "I do." She took a step into the room.

"Is she dying?"

Liana turned her head and looked at him. "She'll be dead by tomorrow morning if the fever doesn't break." She made a helpless gesture with her hand.

There was nothing to say. Bastian watched as Liana crossed the room and touched Hantje's bent head. She put her arms around him. Her voice was a low murmur, soothing.

Something ached in Bastian's chest. He cleared his throat roughly. *Endal, come on.*

I'll stay.

Bastian pressed his lips together and swung away from the door. It hurt that Endal preferred to stay with Hantje. *He's only a scabby wraith*, he wanted to shout at the dog, but shame twisted in his belly that he could even think such a thing. Hantje was more than a wraith, much more, just as Melke was.

She would be dead by morning.

Bastian threw the waterskin on the kitchen table and walked outside. He took the path blindly. The image he saw wasn't bleached grass and gray dirt, it was his bedchamber, with Melke lying as still as death in the bed he'd always slept in and Liana holding Hantje while he wept.

He stood on the highest sand dune and stared at the sea without seeing it, while the wind blew through his hair. It wasn't fair. None of this was fair. They were being punished for a crime that had been committed a hundred years ago and *it wasn't fair*.

Memory of the sickroom shredded in his mind and blew away. He saw the ocean, cruel and greedy, gray-green. It battered against the shore and ate into Vere. He tasted salt in his mouth, smelled seaweed. Rage swelled inside him. Rage at Alain sal Vere, rage at the psaaron, rage at his father for choosing to die, for leaving them. His hand clenched around the necklace in his pocket.

It was a moment of madness, of grief and impotent fury. He screamed at the waves, cursing them, and he threw the necklace away from Vere with all the strength that he had.

The necklace twisted in the sunlight as it fell into the foaming surf. A tiny splash and then... nothing.

The rage evaporated.

Everything came to a halt, blood and breath, the beating of his heart. It was impossible to draw air into his lungs, impossible to move. He stared at the seething water with eyes that didn't blink.

What have I done?

He'd never get the necklace back. The sea had swallowed it.

Bastian's legs gave way. He sat heavily on spiky tussock and sand. *No.*

The curse would never be broken.

CHAPTER FIFTY-THREE

BASTIAN STAYED ON the sand dune while the sun marched across the sky, listening to the grass shrivel and the soil crumble and the sea gnaw steadily at the shore. Death was a shroud over the farm, as gray as ashes, and it would never, ever, go away.

Vere was dead, irrevocably dead. Soon Melke would die too.

He understood now the tears that his father had cried, that Hantje cried. Despair. Hopelessness. The knowledge that it would never be all right again.

There was moisture in his eyes, on his cheeks. He wept silently, hugging his despair to himself.

Awareness came slowly. The sea was quiet and the scent that he smelled was dark and wet, familiar.

Bastian scrambled to his feet, terror choking in his throat.

The psaaron stood before him, massive. Water slid down its dark scales. And around its neck...

Bastian swallowed. "You found it."

"Yes."

"How?"

"I heard it calling to me." Something shone in the creature's eyes, sparkling like sunlight on water. Joy. "You have my gratitude."

Bastian swallowed again. He could only nod. Voices murmured in his ears, faint, as the tears sang to the psaaron.

"I will return what I took, as you have returned my family's tears." Waves lapped in that deep voice, as the sea lapped gently against Vere's shore. "Water is no longer your enemy. Do not fear the sea." The psaaron turned and walked down the dunes and across the white sand of the beach. It slid into the water, as quick and graceful as a fish, and was gone.

Bastian stood for long minutes, looking at the smooth water in the bay. His anger returned. "You can't give back what you took," he shouted after the psaaron. "They're dead. You can't give them back."

His mother was gone, his father, and soon Melke would be gone too.

The anger ebbed, as the tide ebbed on the beach. Bastian sat again. The weight of Vere on his shoulders was too much. It pressed him to the ground.

He had no money to repair the bridge, to re-roof the farmhouse and replace the glass in the windows. No money to buy livestock or furniture or food. The task of rebuilding Vere, penniless, was beyond his abilities. He could only fail.

Bastian watched the sea for long hours. He'd thrown the necklace into boiling surf; now the water was smooth and calm. The psaaron had heard the tears calling. It had *heard*.

Twelve years he'd had the necklace. Could he have thrown it into the sea at any time? Would the psaaron have heard? Could the curse have been lifted before Vere withered and the well ran dry, before stock starved and sheep died in lambing? Before Melke went into the salamanders' den?

Bastian stared at the sea, flat and blue-green, and decided that he didn't want to know. It didn't bear thinking about. In fact, it was best not to think at all. To not think about loss. To not think about his mother and father. About Melke. Best just to watch the sea.

But the sparkle of sunlight on water only served to heighten the darkness inside him, the despair, the utter hopelessness of it all. The soft lapping of the waves was a funeral dirge.

"Don't die," he whispered. "Please don't die."

Something lay on the sand, as small and bright as a fish's scale. The waves tumbled it gently, left it stranded, and then crept up the sand to tumble it again. Bastian watched for a long time, without curiosity. The advance and retreat of the waves, the widening strip of beach, the shining object on the sand.

A second object gleamed now on the white sand. A third, a fourth. All along the beach, glinting and glittering in the sunlight, small and bright.

I will return what I took.

Hope leapt in Bastian's chest, jagged and painful. "No," he said, scrambling to his feet. "No, it can't be."

He slid down the dune. *It can't be, it can't be.* Hope quickened his heartbeat. He half-ran across the beach, his boots sinking into white sand he'd never dared stand on before.

Silver. A silver coin.

Bastian knelt and picked it up with trembling fingers. The sal Vere fortune. Thrown into the sea by a man desperate to save his children.

The coin lay cold and bright on his palm. With it he could begin to rebuild Vere.

But silver couldn't save Melke's life.

Coins glittered on the beach, everywhere. Dozens of them, hundreds, gold as well as silver. Bastian gathered them into piles, but there was no joy in his heart. He understood why his great-grandfather had thrown the money into the sea and why the psaaron had spurned it; wealth could never equate to family, to a person's life.

Bastian took some of the coins back to the farmhouse with him, a fistful in each pocket. Clouds drifted over the sun. A light drizzle began to fall. The first rain on Vere in years.

He thought that the cracked ground inhaled at the gentle touch of moisture, that it gave a sigh of pleasure.

Bastian climbed the stairs to the sickroom. Hantje didn't notice his arrival. He sat watching Melke, his face haggard. Endal opened his eyes. He didn't lift his chin from Hantje's feet.

How is she? Bastian asked, looking at Melke. She lay unmoving. He'd have thought her dead but for the flush of fever in her thin cheeks.

The same.

There was no point in opening his mouth to tell Hantje that the curse was lifted. It was unimportant. What mattered was the battle being fought in this room. Life or death.

Bastian turned away from the door. *It's raining.*

I know. I smelled it.

He nodded, and walked slowly back down the stairs. In the kitchen he lit the stove and the candles, and then sat at the table and laid the coins out and stared at them. How many deaths were too many? When did it simply become too much?

He'd throw the money away, just as his great grandfather had done, if he knew it would save a life. Her life.

Bastian turned a gold coin over in his fingers. If Melke died, it would be too many deaths. He'd walk away from Vere. Let someone else put fresh slates on the roof and new glass in the windows, let someone else restore the house and farm to their former glory.

Too many bad memories, too much death.

Bastian sat looking at the coins while night fell, and then he pushed them away and made dinner and climbed the stairs to the little bedchamber, where he lay on the bed and stared up at the ceiling in the dark.

Too many. Too much.

CHAPTER FIFTY-FOUR

THE INFECTION RAN in Melke's blood, black, streaked with fire-red. In Liana's mind it was alive. It twisted and knotted and dug in with sharp claws, refusing to leave.

Liana placed a hand on Melke's chest, where her heart beat feebly. She closed her eyes. *Leave her. Let her be. Go away.*

Tonight she was stronger than the fever. Perhaps it was the sound of gentle rain falling outside, so miraculous and beautiful. Perhaps not.

Hours passed while rain fell softly outside and the infection struggled against her. The knots unravelled slowly, the claws loosened their grip by tiny, grudging increments. Melke's heart began to beat more strongly, more steadily. The black faded to gray and the fiery streaks dissolved and at last Melke's blood rushed inside vein and artery, warm and rich and clean.

Liana opened heavy eyelids, exhausted and elated. She smoothed strands of black hair away from Melke's brow. "All's well," she told her. "You will live." *And Hantje will smile again.*

Melke sighed in her sleep. The heat of fever was gone from her cheeks.

The candles flickered, casting shadows over Melke's sleeping face and illuminating the pulse that beat steadily at the base of her throat. How like Hantje she was, inside and out. Honor and despair.

Outside, the wondrous rain fell. It was a night for miracles, a night when wishes could come true. "I want you to stay," Liana whispered. "Both of you. I want this to be your home."

She closed her eyes, and woke to find Bastian standing over her and Endal pressed against her leg.

"How is she?" Bastian's voice was rough.

Melke's fingers lay slack in her hand, warm and full of life.

"She'll be fine."

For a moment it seemed that Bastian didn't breathe, and then she heard him inhale, hoarsely. His eyes glistened in the candlelight. "Are you certain?"

"Yes."

One of the candles had guttered. The others wavered feebly. "It's still night. Why aren't you—"

"I couldn't sleep."

Liana nodded, and yawned.

His expression changed, the curious tightness of his face softening. "You're tired."

He carried her to bed, as he'd done when she was a little girl. Liana's eyelids slid shut. She rested her cheek against his shoulder, safe.

She was dimly aware of Bastian laying her down, of the sheet and blanket being pulled up around her chin. She tried to open her eyes, but couldn't. "Melke. Who'll—"

"I'll sit with her." He kissed her brow. "Sleep, little one."

BASTIAN LIT NEW candles and placed them in the holder. His gaze slid away from Melke. Everything was suddenly all right and he was afraid it would evaporate if he looked directly at her.

It was all too sudden, too incredible.

Relief swelled inside him until he thought his chest would burst with it. The curse was broken. Vere would live, Melke would live, and *everything was all right*.

The book of tales lay on the bedside table. Bastian picked it up and touched the leather, worn with age. He would be able to read these stories to his children.

Joy gleamed inside him as bright and hot as candle flames. *I will have children*.

He sat in the wooden chair beside the bed. Endal lay down with his chin on Bastian's feet. He felt the dog's contentment. It hummed beneath his skin.

Everything was all right.

The gardens would flourish again. There'd be flowers and fruit trees and vegetables, sheep and cows grazing and horses in the stable yard, green grass and trees with leaves. But that would take time, years. The house he could do now. Fresh slates and window panes and paint. Furniture. And the bathhouse. It was frivolous and unnecessary, but he wanted the bathhouse.

Bastian wanted to laugh, he wanted to cry. Instead, he opened the book and turned the pages, searching for a tale that expressed the lightness he felt.

There is a little magic left in this world, he read. *It runs in certain bloodlines.*

He looked at Melke fully for the first time since he'd heard she would live. Magic ran in her bloodline, just as it ran in his.

Her magic wasn't evil; it was simply magic, as his own was. For generations sal Veres had spoken with horses or dogs. One of his children would likely have the gift.

With magic often came beauty. He'd heard it said about Bresse's ruling family, who undoubtedly possessed the gift of peace. A gift that spread beyond Bresse's borders with each royal son and daughter married. And the same had been said about his own family, the sal Veres. *A handsome family, gifted, but cursed*, he'd overheard when he was a boy. Handsome and gifted, and cursed.

No longer cursed.

What would it be like to have a gift that others feared? A gift that could be abused by the unscrupulous?

In Stenrik they burn wraiths.

He looked at Melke and remembered how she'd tilted her chin, how she'd refused to show that she was afraid. Bravado and haughtiness, to hide vulnerability, to hide fear.

Wraiths were always ugly in the tales, but Melke wasn't ugly. Bastian stared at her, lying pale and still, her hair raven-black on the pillow. Elegant. That was the word that fitted best. The arch of eyebrows and the straightness of her nose, the angle of jaw and cheekbones, the line of her throat. Elegant. And her earlobes, softly rounded, her slender fingers, the feet she'd drawn for him on the back of the map. Elegant.

This at least wasn't a fishwives' tale: magic and beauty went together.

Bastian jerked his gaze away from her. He looked back down at the page. No, not that story. He turned more pages, searching. The word *Stenrik* caught his eye. He smoothed his hand over the parchment.

"'Stenrik is a land of dark fir forests and tall mountains and icy seas,'" he read aloud. "'And lamiae asleep in deep, cold caves.'"

He glanced at Melke. Did she miss those forests, those cold seas?

Bastian looked down at the page again and cleared his throat. "'As everyone knows, it is wisest to turn one's back on what might be a lamia, however beguiling and beautiful she is, and to hurry as fast as possible in the opposite direction, for serpent-women can be dangerous creatures. But not all men are wise. This is the tale of one man, Janne, who was very unwise.'"

Endal's tail thumped on the floor. He liked the sound of Bastian's voice.

"'Janne was a nobleman, as handsome as any man might hope to be, and vain and proud with it. He was betrothed to a baron's daughter who had hair as dark and glossy as a ripe chestnut and eyes as blue as a summer sky. The baron's daughter (whose name was Britta) was a good-hearted girl, and it was widely said that she was as lovely as she was sweet and kind. Only the most mean-spirited of people noted that pox scars were faintly visible on her pretty face.

"'Janne was well aware of his worth, and knew that he was due a baron's daughter as a bride. He never noticed Britta's sweet temper and kind nature. When he looked at her he saw only her father's wealth and the pock marks on her face. The wealth he knew he deserved. The pock marks annoyed him. So perhaps it is not surprising that when he came across a serpent-woman reclining on a bed of moss in a glade in the dark forest, he didn't turn and leave.

"'The lamia wore a gown that was as fine as gossamer and a necklace of rubies that hung to her waist. She was beautiful, as all lamiae are. She had lips as red as blood and skin as soft and smooth as white rose petals. Her hair was more lustrous than black opals and her teeth gleamed like pearls, and her golden eyes were dark with the sort of knowledge that gladdens a man's heart.

"'Here, finally, was a woman worthy of Janne's interest. And so, heedless of danger and without thought for Britta and their betrothal vows, he entered the sunlit clearing.

"'Time has a way of sliding past when one is in the company of a serpent-woman. It seemed to Janne that he had barely sat down beside the lamia, had scarcely raised her hand to his lips in greeting, had spoken no more than a few words to her, than the sun sank below the horizon.

"'May I see you tomorrow?' Janne asked. The lamia smiled a slight, secret smile and disappeared among the tall fir trees, as light and graceful as thistledown in her gauzy white robe.

"'Janne came at sunrise the next morning and again the time slipped between his fingers as swiftly as water. A wise man knows to turn away from such haunting beauty, and knows to value such simple things as home and hearth and the warmth of a sweetheart's kiss, be she pretty or plain. But Janne wasn't wise, for all his pride, and he had never valued simple things.

"'Sometimes a serpent-woman finds it hard to weave her spell. Sometimes the man she has chosen laughs in her face and her magic shatters, but Janne was greedy for what the lamia offered. He was easily snared. He forgot his bride-to-be, forgot her father's fortune, forgot even his own name.

"'When the lamia asked Janne to come with her on the night before his wedding, he went willingly. He knew that a serpent's heart beat in her breast and that if he asked to see her pretty tongue it would be forked, but he didn't care. He wanted only her.

"'Britta searched the forest for her unfaithful bridegroom. She climbed the dark slopes every day for a month, calling his name. Then she went home and packed her bridal clothes away in a trunk. A year later she married a baron, a plain, honest man who was happy with his lot in life. The baron didn't see the pock marks on her face. He thought his wife was the loveliest woman in Stenrik. Together they had seven children, each as kind and sweet-natured as their mother and as honorable and faithful as their father.

"'Janne was seen in the forest from time to time. He had dank hair and hollow cheeks and skin as pale as a corpse's, and his breath smelled like a dark cavern. But he was as proud and vain as he had ever been, for he slept on a bed of golden coins and his bride was more beautiful than any woman in the world.'"

BASTIAN HAD READ three tales and started on the fourth when lightness behind the curtains signaled daybreak. Rain still fell softly outside. He wondered how soon it would begin leaking through the broken slates. Perhaps it did already.

He found that he didn't care. Leaks could be fixed. There was enough money for whatever needed doing.

Endal heard Hantje before he did. He lifted his chin from Bastian's feet and wagged his tail.

Bastian stopped reading. He turned his head.

The young man stood in the shadows of the doorway. His face was starkly white. There was anguish in his eyes. "Melke?"

Bastian closed the book. "She's fine."

Hantje gripped the doorframe. "You mean..?"

Bastian stood. "I mean that the fever is broken. She will live."

Joy shone as bright as tears in Hantje's eyes. He crossed the room, walking as if he was blind.

Bastian didn't watch as the young man bent over his sister. He opened the curtains and stared out at the damp landscape. Hantje was speaking to Melke, unheard words, too fast and too low for Bastian's ear to catch, but the joy in his voice... Bastian closed his eyes. He swallowed to clear his throat.

"I'll make us some breakfast," he said, turning away from the window.

Hantje straightened from the bed. Bastian scarcely recognized him. His face was no longer pale and drawn, but vivid, flushed with happiness. His smile shone as brightly as his eyes.

"Thank you," the young man said, and Bastian heard that the words came from his heart.

Bastian walked the few paces to the bed and stood looking down at Melke, asleep, alive. "Don't thank me. Thank Liana."

"I will," said Hantje. "I will. But thank you, too. For everything."

Bastian met the young man's eyes, gray, so like Melke's. He nodded, then turned and walked from the room. Endal came too, pushing ahead of him and charging down the stairs happily.

Everything was all right.

BASTIAN READ TO Melke often over the next two days, while Liana slept. Melke never quite woke, but the sound of a voice seemed to ease her dreams. When he wasn't reading to her, he went to the seashore and gathered more of the coins. They soon piled high on the floor of the maid's bedchamber. He didn't know what to do with so much wealth. There was more than enough for the bridge and the house, the bathhouse, livestock, for everything. And that was just the silver.

He sat on the narrow bed and turned a gold coin over in his fingers, while Endal dozed at his feet. It was an absurd amount of wealth. More than he needed, or wanted.

The square of sunlight on the floor lengthened and became a rectangle. Afternoon. Dusk. Finally he knelt and divided the coins into four gleaming piles on the floor. When it was done, he felt better.

Come, Endal. Bastian went downstairs to make dinner, knowing that he'd made the right decision. Melke and Hantje had risked their lives to save them, to save Vere.

But when he heard Melke's voice that evening, weak and halting, he couldn't bring himself to step into the sickroom. The last time they'd spoken, he had shouted at her. She'd listened while he yelled, while he jabbed his finger at her in fury, while he stomped and snarled and tried to intimidate her.

He didn't think she would welcome him in the sickroom.

Endal had no such qualms. He bounded into the room and put his front paws up on the bed, his body wriggling with joy.

Bastian backed away from the door. He walked slowly along the hall and down the staircase. Tomorrow he'd go to Thierry. He would return the hired horse that Arnaul had been stabling for him and make arrangements for the bridge to be rebuilt and the house repaired. At dawn. He'd leave at dawn.

He needed to thank Melke. But not tonight, not tomorrow. He wasn't avoiding her. It was just that he had things that needed to be done.

CHAPTER FIFTY-FIVE

Melke understood Hantje, sitting beside the bed, and she understood Endal licking her hand, but she didn't understand where she was. The room was strangely familiar, a remembered fragment from a dream, large and high-ceilinged, with faded green curtains.

"Where?" she asked, but Hantje's answer confused her. This wasn't Vere. She closed her eyes while Hantje continued to speak, but again his words made no sense. "No." Bastian wouldn't have saved her.

"Yes. He brought you back."

She opened her eyes. Such weary eyelids, so heavy. "The necklace?"

"The psaaron has it now." Hantje's fingers tightened around her hand. "The curse is broken."

Relief washed through her, as warm as sunlight and as sweet as honey. There was a smile inside her, but her mouth was too tired to move. Hantje's face blurred. Where had that scar come from, under his lower lip?

And she still didn't understand. Hantje must have misunderstood. She tried again. "How did I get here?"

"Bastian. He brought you back."

It was too much effort to shake her head. She closed her eyes instead. "No."

"He did. I tell you, Melke, he *did*."

"What payment?"

There was a moment of silence and then, quietly, "Himself."

Her eyelids jerked open. "No."

Hantje nodded.

It was utterly impossible. Hantje was talking about broken bridges and rain falling on Vere, but she didn't hear his words. Impossible.

She was a wraith, a thief, and Bastian would *never*—

Melke closed her eyes to think about it. She opened them again to find Hantje gone and Liana sitting beside the bed. The curtains were open and daylight streamed in. Hadn't they been shut before? Hadn't candles burned to keep the darkness back?

Liana smiled. Her blouse was plain and her hair unadorned, but she was so graceful and pretty that reality blurred with dream. For a moment Melke thought that Asta herself sat by the bed.

Moon daughter.

"Don't try to talk," Liana said.

Melke had done this for her brother while he lay ill. Now she was the one in bed, weak, unable to drink unaided, unable to wash her own face, too tired to speak. She was grateful for Liana's kindness, for her quiet gentleness, but when the girl traced a slow line across her cheek with a fingertip, Melke moved her head away on the pillow. Her skin itched where Liana's finger had touched. "What are you doing?"

"The salamanders cut your face," Liana said.

"You're healing?"

"No." The girl smiled. "The cuts are healed. I'm taking away the scars."

"You can do that?" The words slurred on her tongue.

Liana nodded. Her fingertip traced the same line on Melke's cheek. Blood had gushed there, spilling down her face and throat. She remembered—

Melke blinked back the memory. "Hantje. His mouth."

"I'll do that too."

"But we're wraiths."

"I don't care about that."

"But it's not necess—"

"No. It's not necessary. But I'm going to do it." The girl's chin jutted stubbornly.

"Why?"

"Because I like you."

Melke didn't know what to say. No reply was adequate. Finally she settled on, "Thank you."

She closed her eyes while Liana's finger traced tight, itching lines on her skin. There was memory of pain, of blood. "How did Hantje get that scar?"

"It's a long story. I'll tell you tomorrow. Just rest now."

It was easy to obey that command. Her body was heavy and warm, the bed deliciously soft. "This room?"

"It's Bastian's."

The answer surprised Melke into opening her eyes. Yes, the curtains were familiar, the high ceiling and the oak-panelled walls. She'd tiptoed into this room, had knelt and groped beneath the wide bed, had stolen.

It was no remembered dream, but reality. Bastian's bedchamber.

"Sleep," Liana said firmly.

But there were other questions, questions too important not to be asked. "How did I get here?"

"Bastian brought you back."

The same answer as Hantje's. It still made no sense. "But—"

"Sleep." It was an order. Liana's hand cupped her cheek. Lassitude spread from that point of contact and it was impossible not to close her eyes, impossible not to sleep.

BASTIAN FOUND HIMSELF standing outside the door to Silvia's kitchen. He watched as she kneaded dough on the scrubbed wooden table, an apron around her waist and the sleeves of her blouse rolled up to the elbow. Wisps of blonde hair escaped from her scarf and curled against her cheek.

For the first time in eight years there was no heat inside him at the thought of bedding her. Instead, there was uneasiness. He smelled the salamander's musk and not the scents of yeast and sugar and baking bread. Panic whispered in his chest. *I don't think I can—*

Silvia looked up. Pleasure lit her face. "Bastian!"

His smile was stiff. He stayed on the doorstep, unable to move, his throat too dry for speech.

Silvia wiped her hands on a cloth. She walked toward him, smiling. "Come in," she said, standing on tiptoe and brushing a light kiss over his lips. Her hand slid down his arm, her fingers curled around his.

Heat, yes, a faint stirring, and also dread. But reluctance was overcome by the knowledge that he needed to do this. He *had* to. It was the only way to wipe the salamander from his mind, to erase the scent, to conquer his fear.

"Thank you," Silvia said.

"For what?" he asked, yielding to the pull of her hand and stepping into the kitchen.

"For what you did. You and Endal."

"What?" Bastian asked, baffled.

"Helene."

He shook his head, not understanding.

"The watch captain arrested Julien."

It took him a moment to understand. The dead girl, the conversation with Michaud. Events from a lifetime ago. "Julien confessed?"

Silvia nodded and tugged him further into the kitchen.

"Why are you thanking me? Why Endal?"

"Because you spoke to the watch captain. He questioned Ronsard and Julien again because of you."

Bastian halted. "He did?"

"Endal knew they were lying. You told him." Silvia's brow wrinkled. "Didn't you?"

"Who said that?" Bastian asked slowly.

"The watch captain." Confusion creased her face. "Didn't you? Everyone thinks you did."

"Yes, I did." He pulled his hand from her grasp. "What's wrong?"

It was impossible to explain. He didn't understand it himself. Dismay, embarrassment. "I didn't think he'd tell anyone."

"Well, he did." She pulled his head down and kissed him. "What you did was good, Bastian. Thank you."

He let her take his hand again and lead him across the kitchen. "I'll give Endal a meat pie as a reward," she said. "Later. Afterward." She smiled at him, and he saw in the darkness of her eyes and flush of her cheeks how much she wanted him. "They're still too hot."

Stay, Endal, he said, but the dog already lay on the sun-warmed doorstep with his eyes closed.

Memory of the salamander crowded into his head. It felt wrong as he walked up the stairs, wrong as he closed the bedroom door behind them. Panic prickled over his skin as he shed his clothes. *I can't.*

But he had to. He needed this. A healing of sorts.

Silvia kissed him. His response was automatic, almost clumsy, but it appeared to please her. Her fingers stroked over his chest, his abdomen, lower.

Heat began to rise in Bastian's blood. Yes, he could do this.

His panic faded at the edges. The scent that he smelled was Silvia, the softness and smoothness of skin, Silvia.

It was going to be all right.

Time slowed into a leisurely blur of kisses and caresses and soft murmurs. The mattress dipped as they sank onto the bed. Sunlight was warm on the sheets. This was nothing like it had been with the salamander. Silvia's taste, the texture of her skin, the soft warmth of her body... This was pleasure, not nightmare.

The panic was gone. In its place was arousal, simmering inside him. He could breathe. Silvia's scent was subtle, not peppery and choking. There were no fine-grained scales beneath his hands, almost too hot to touch. No breath singeing his hair. When he eased his fingers inside her the warmth didn't raise blisters on his skin.

Bastian's eyes closed in pleasure as he slid inside her body. The sound that Silvia uttered was purely woman, nothing like the noises the salamander had made, sharp hisses in which flames had licked and crackled.

Pleasure curled over his skin, delicious, exquisite. Heat pulsed inside him. He pressed kisses across her cheek and buried his face in sleek, black hair.

Bastian faltered. He opened his eyes. He saw tousled blonde hair, not black. Curly, not straight.

"Is something wrong?" Silvia's voice was breathless.

"No. Nothing."

Bastian closed his eyes again and concentrated. Silvia's body was lush and soft. She was beautiful. She was everything he'd ever wanted. So why did he imagine that her curves were less ripe, her limbs slender, her hair as black as a raven's wing?

It was Silvia's bed, Silvia's body, yet he was making love to Melke. Her skin was damp and soft beneath his. His face pressed into her hair, silky and black. The gasps that he heard were hers. Her fingernails dug into his arms. He was inside her heat, blind and hungry, panting, his arousal spiralling to a peak. Delight shivered over his skin. He was almost there, almost poised on the sharp knife-edge of release—

She arched against him, clung to him, cried out his name. "Bastian..."

It was the wrong voice.

Bastian opened his eyes. He saw Silvia's face, pretty and flushed, her eyes closed tightly in pleasure.

I'm in bed with the wrong woman.

He pulled away from her abruptly, separating their bodies. Arousal died inside him as instantly and absolutely as a candle being snuffed. Pleasure was gone. Delight and heat were gone.

"Bastian! What—"

He swung his legs over the edge of the bed and sat there, trembling, dragging air into his lungs. He bowed his head and pressed the heels of his hands hard against closed eyelids. No. Not this. *Please not this.*

"Bastian?" The mattress dipped as Silvia moved behind him. "What's wrong?"

Everything.

The sweat of passion was cooling on his skin. A rag rug lay soft and lumpy beneath his feet. The woman he wanted to bed was Melke.

No.

Silvia touched his back, a gentle caress, smoothing her hand from shoulder down to waist. "What's wrong, Bastian?"

He shook his head.

"Are you ill?"

"No." His voice was rough.

"Did I do something? Did I hurt you?"

"No!" He lowered his hands and opened his eyes and stared at the rug, unable to look at her. "No, not that."

There was silence for a moment, while Silvia's hand rested lightly on his shoulder blade. He felt the warmth of her body behind him, close, not touching.

"What, then?"

Bastian shook his head.

"Is there someone else?"

The rug had three shades of pink. The colors of a woman: the paleness of skin, the blush of cheeks, the darkness of lips that had been kissed.

"Bastian? Is there someone else?"

He closed his eyes again.

"Bastian?"

"I don't know," he whispered.

Silvia stopped touching him. His skin was suddenly cold where her hand had been.

"I don't know," he said again, squeezing his eyelids tightly shut. "I think maybe... Yes." Dismay clenched in his chest as he uttered the words. Dismay and disbelief. How could this have happened?

The mattress moved slightly. Silvia's warmth was gone.

"Who is she?" Her voice was quiet.

Who was Melke? A wraith, a woman. Bastian opened his eyes. "She's from the east."

"Is she pretty?"

He stared down at the rug. Pale pink, flushing pink, dark pink. "She's beautiful."

He heard Silvia pull the sheet around her, hiding her own beauty, the fullness of breasts and belly and hips, the lush shape of her. So different from Melke.

"Do you love her?" Her voice was even quieter.

Panic twisted in his belly, confusion, dismay. "I don't know."

Silvia sighed. Her fingertips touched the nape of his neck, stroking lightly. "Is she aware that you—"

His eyes winced shut. "No! No, she hates me."

Silvia laughed. The sound wasn't happy. "No woman could hate you, Bastian."

It was a compliment, and yet the words stung. Did Silvia look no more deeply than the shape of his face and the strength of his body? "No." He pulled away from her touch and stood. "Not my appearance. *Me*." He turned and looked down at her, jabbing a finger at his chest. "She hates *me*."

Silvia sat on the rumpled bed with a sheet clutched around her and one hand outstretched. She closed her fingers and lowered her hand. "I doubt it, Bastian."

He shook his head and turned away from her, reaching for his clothes. He'd been rough with Melke that first day at the salamanders' den, too rough. He'd pulled her to her feet with his fist in her hair. He'd spat at her and called her *filthy scum* and *vermin*. He'd pushed her so that she fell to the ground.

Melke was afraid of him, and that was worse than being hated. She feared him.

He pulled his clothes on quickly, silently, aware of Silvia watching. She said nothing. When he was fully dressed he turned to look at her.

"This is goodbye, isn't it?" Silvia's eyes were steady on his face.

He wanted to deny it. He wanted everything to be how it had always been, unchanged. No wraiths, no confusion or dismay, just sunny hours in Silvia's bed. But everything *had* changed. He hadn't seen it coming, hadn't wanted it, but it had happened. Whatever it was. He should be in the bed with Silvia, relaxed and sated, laughing. Instead he stood, tense and uncertain and afraid of the future.

In his heart he knew the answer to her question. He nodded.

Silvia climbed off the bed, holding the sheet around her. Something tightened in Bastian's chest. Eight years of unashamed nakedness, and now she hid her body beneath a sheet. What had he done?

Silvia knotted the sheet above her breasts and came across the floor on bare feet. "Tell her." She put her arms around him, a quiet and asexual embrace. "I think you'll be surprised."

Bastian shook his head. Sharpness twisted beneath his breastbone. He raised his arms awkwardly to hold her. "Silvia..." The first time he'd stood in this room, shy and nervous, he'd been a virgin. She had been patient with him, had taught him how to give pleasure and how to receive it. In doing so she'd given him a gift beyond value.

Silvia stepped back.

Bastian let his arms fall. He tried to express his gratitude. "Thank you. For everything."

"It was my pleasure." She laughed, and he saw joy and sorrow on her face. "It was very much my pleasure." She raised her hand to lightly touch his cheek. "She's very lucky."

He shook his head.

"Goodbye, Bastian."

He turned away from her and opened the door.

"Bastian."

He paused, his fingers gripping the door handle.

Silvia's lips brushed his cheek. For a fleeting second he smelled her scent, subtle and female, and felt the warmth of her body. Her whisper was faint, almost inaudible: "You were always my favorite."

There were no words he could utter. Nothing.

"I wish you joy."

Bastian nodded, unable to speak his thanks or farewell. He closed the door and walked down the stairs without seeing the steps.

BASTIAN SCARCELY NOTICED Endal waiting for him on the broad doorstep. He walked down the street, unaware of cobblestones and painted doors and the shade cast by high slate roofs. He could have been anywhere in the realm, surrounded by houses of brick or wood or mud. The details were unimportant. What was important was that, in one sunlit moment upstairs in Silvia's bedroom, everything had changed. His life had tipped upside down. Nothing was the same.

This wasn't a problem he could solve with his muscles, with sweat and hard work. He had to *think*. He had to make a decision. A huge one. As huge as striking a bargain with a wraith or a salamander. A decision that would change his life.

He didn't know what to do.

"Sal Vere."

Bastian barely heard his name. *Think*, he told himself. But coherent thought was impossible.

Logic was lost in a mess of confusion and dismay, edged with panic. And underneath that was a flicker of something that twisted between fear and hope.

He didn't know what to do.

"Sal Vere!"

The fury in the man's voice jerked Bastian's head up. He blinked, and saw the street with clarity. Gray cobblestones and gray stone houses, a housewife sweeping her doorstep, and Ronsard standing in his path.

He saw that rage consumed the innkeeper. It swelled his face, feverish. "My son is going to gaol because of you!"

"He killed a girl," Bastian said flatly, and pushed past the man.

"A dockside slut! She was *nothing!*"

Sudden anger flared inside him. He halted. "Her name was Helene," he said, turning back to face Ronsard. "She was fifteen years old." Beside him Endal stood with hackles raised.

The housewife paused in her sweeping.

"It was none of your business!"

He looked at Ronsard and saw instead the careworn face and gray-streaked hair of the girl's mother, the blind grief in her eyes. "It was," he said.

Ronsard's mouth twisted. "High and mighty sal Vere." He spat. The spittle landed on the cobblestones at Bastian's feet. "Thinking you're better than us. Curse you! And curse that filthy dog of yours!"

Bastian clenched his hands, and then released them. He turned his back on Ronsard and began to walk again.

The housewife stood on her doorstep, the broom in her hand, watching. He nodded curtly to her. *Come, Endal.*

Why is he angry? Endal asked, behind him.

Because you told me he was lying.

Oh. Endal sounded puzzled. *But*—He yelped, a high sound. His presence in Bastian's head was abruptly gone.

Bastian swung around.

Endal lay on the cobblestones, a black shape, unmoving. Ronsard stood over the dog, breathing heavily, an iron doorstop in his hands. "Take that, sal Vere!" he said, and spat again.

A thin rivulet of blood slid from beneath Endal's muzzle.

The sound that came from Bastian's throat was inarticulate and animal. He saw fear on Ronsard's face and heard the clang of iron on stone as the innkeeper flung down the doorstop and began to run.

There was no doubt that Bastian would catch the man. The rage that boiled inside him made it impossible not to. Nothing else mattered, no one else existed, but Ronsard. His world narrowed to one thing, one inevitable thing, and satisfaction filled his mouth like blood when it happened. His right hand closed on the collar of the innkeeper's shirt. He swung him around, exulting in the man's choked cry and the terror on his face.

It was a blur after that. Fury rode him. The busy marketplace held only two people, himself and Ronsard. The shouts of townsfolk were as faint as the chirping of sparrows. Wood splintered and cloth tore and produce tumbled around him. It meant nothing. He gripped Ronsard by the throat, beating his head against the cobblestones.

A choking arm around his neck pulled him back from the blindness of rage. "Let him go, Bastian." The voice was familiar. Michaud.

"No," Bastian snarled, digging his fingers deeper into the innkeeper's flesh.

The watch captain shifted his grip. Bastian's vision grayed. "Let him go."

"No," he croaked. "He killed Endal. And I am going to *kill*—"

"Endal's alive," Michaud growled in his ear. "Look, you fool."

Bastian blinked, shifting his gaze from Ronsard's bloodied face. He saw crushed baskets and unravelling skeins of wool lying on the cobblestones. And Endal, standing lopsided and dazed.

He felt the dog's pain, the sharp ache in his head, his bewilderment, his anxiety. He released Ronsard abruptly.

Endal. He shrugged Michaud's weight off him and stood. People moved hastily out of his way. *Are you all right?* He went down on one knee.

Endal whined. His head hung low. Blood dripped from his jaw, splashing to the ground.

Bastian touched the dog gently, soothing him with unspoken words. *You'll be all right, Endal. Liana will make you better*.

Endal sagged against him. The dog's dizziness pressed into Bastian's mind, and he blinked to clear his vision.

"You'll have to come to the watch house, Bastian."

He glanced up at Michaud. His friend's face was grim.

"I'll pay for the damage," he said, gathering Endal in his arms and standing. He tried to be careful, but still Endal whimpered. The dog's weight almost made him stagger. "But I'm not coming to the watch house. I need to take Endal home."

"Don't make me arrest you," Michaud said.

"Arrest me? For that?" He jerked his head at Ronsard, lying groaning amid the wrecked stalls. "He deserved it."

"The watch house," Michaud said, his voice implacable. "Now, Bastian."

"I SAW IT all," the housewife said calmly. "It was a fair fight."

She still held her broom.

"The innkeeper provoked him?" Michaud asked, not looking at Bastian.

The housewife nodded. "He cursed him, and then he attacked the dog." She sat neatly in her starched white apron. Her manner was an unhurried as her voice. "Sal Vere had a right. Any man would have fought."

She had a sturdy, imperturbable face. A woman who'd be undaunted by wailing babies and bloody brawls. Being in the watch house hadn't ruffled her composure. She'd glanced at the straw on the floor, the scarred and stained table, the bare cells, and had sat without fuss and recounted her tale precisely.

"Thank you, madam," Michaud said.

"You're most welcome." The housewife rose to her feet.

Bastian stood, too. "Thank you," he said.

The housewife nodded and walked to the door, the broom in her hand and her brown hair tucked tidily beneath a plain scarf.

"You're lucky she saw it," Michaud said, watching her go.

"I know." Bastian sat and rubbed a hand over his face, suddenly weary. Endal slept on the straw at his feet with the pup, Lubon, sprawled alongside.

"I need an ale," Michaud said. "And so do you."

Bastian was too tired to argue.

The cells were empty, the other watchmen still at the marketplace cleaning up the mess he'd made. The watch house was quiet and peaceful. Michaud placed a full tankard in front of him. "I arrested Julien."

"I heard." He raised the tankard and swallowed deeply. His throat felt bruised. "He confessed."

Michaud grunted. "Took a long time. I broke his story soon enough, but a confession of murder?" He shook his head. "Took all night."

"Broke his story?" Bastian rubbed his face again, almost too exhausted to think.

"His alibi. That he and his father were together."

"How?"

Michaud laughed, a short, flat sound that made Lubon twitch in his sleep. The watch captain raised his tankard. "Ale," he said.

Bastian squinted. "Ale?"

Michaud shrugged with one shoulder. "That was his alibi, that he'd been going over the books with his father, drinking. I didn't ask what.

Ronsard was an alderman. His word should have been good."

Bastian grunted into his tankard.

"When I asked again, their stories differed. Ronsard said they'd been drinking porter. Julien said it was ale."

Bastian put his tankard down on the stained table. "You got a confession because of that?"

"Because of that." Michaud nodded. "It wasn't easy, Bastian. It took all night, and I had Ronsard and the other aldermen yelling at my back." The watch captain's bearded face was serious. "I would have given up, if not for you and that dog of yours."

Bastian picked up the tankard again, uncomfortable with the unspoken thanks. "Where is he?" He nodded at the empty cells. "Desmaures?"

"Julien? Provincial guards took him this morning."

Bastian nodded and drank another mouthful of ale. It was a two-day journey to Desmaures. By tomorrow night, Julien would be in gaol. "Hard labor?"

"For murder? Yes. And Ronsard's off the town council. He'll lose the inn, what with the fine for perjury and payment to the girl's mother."

Bastian felt no sympathy for the man. He deserved to lose his status and his inn, just as he deserved to be in bed with a broken head. "Why did you mention my involvement?" Vague anger stirred in his breast. Endal would have been safe if Michaud had kept his mouth shut.

"I thought it might change people's opinion of you."

Bastian put down his tankard, puzzled. "What do you mean?"

"With the exception of me and that mistress of yours, few people like you. Have you not noticed?"

High and mighty sal Vere. He'd heard the words muttered often enough behind his back. Bastian pushed the tankard away. "Just because I have noble blood in my veins—"

"It's not the *sal*, Bastian."

"What then? The magic?" His laugh was angry. "Because I talk with dogs—"

"It's not that either." Michaud put his tankard down on the table. "Folk are used to magic. And speaking with dogs..." He lifted his shoulders in a shrug. "It's not big magic, Bastian."

Not like being a wraith.

"It's how you treat people."

Bastian snorted. He kept to himself because he didn't want the townsfolk's pity, not because he thought he was better than them. "I don't like charity."

"There's a difference between pride and arrogance, Bastian."

Heat flushed his face. "I am not arrogant," he said stiffly.

"That's not how the people here see it." Michaud leaned back in his chair and clasped his hands over his belly. "I've heard it said that it served you right. The curse."

Bastian pushed up out of his chair, his hands flat on the table. Endal jerked awake, and a shaft of pain sliced through Bastian's head.

Michaud held up a hand, palm out. "Relax," he said.

"Relax!" He shook his head, trying to clear it. "Liana did not deserve that curse! *I* did not deserve that curse!"

"I know," Michaud said mildly. "You don't have to shout at me."

Bastian hissed a breath at him between his teeth. At his feet, Endal whined. He crouched and touched the dog's head lightly, while rage bellowed inside him. He wasn't arrogant. *He was not.*

He'd seen Melke as arrogant, had detested her for it, when all she'd had was the pride not to show her fear. He would detest her still, if Endal hadn't shown him the truth.

Michaud was showing him the truth now.

Had his own pride made him arrogant? He'd not wanted to be sneered at for his poverty, for the copper coins that he counted out so carefully. He'd not wanted pity.

I was like Melke.

The realization made him flush. He stayed crouching, patting Endal, until the hot blood was gone from his face. Then he stood.

Bastian picked up his tankard and drank from it again, not meeting Michaud's eyes. "The curse is broken," he said stiffly.

"I guessed."

The answer pulled his gaze to Michaud. "How?"

"The first thing you did when you arrived this morning was buy a horse and cart."

"How do you know that?" he asked, frowning.

"I'm the watch captain. I know most things that happen in this town."

Bastian lowered his weight into the chair. "Arrogant?"

Michaud shrugged with one shoulder. "Not any longer, I should think. She was a dockside girl, Bastian."

"Helene."

Michaud nodded.

"Her mother? Is she all right?"

"No," Michaud said simply. "The girl was her only child."

She was nothing, Ronsard had yelled. *A dockside slut.* "I'm glad I broke his head," Bastian said, looking down at his bruised knuckles. He flexed his fingers, remembering the flaring satisfaction of punching the man, of seeing blood spill from his mouth.

"She'd like to see you. To say thank you."

He looked up. "The mother?"

Michaud nodded.

"Not today." Bastian reached for his tankard and drained it. "I need to get Endal home."

Michaud nodded again.

Bastian set the tankard down on the table. *Come, Endal. Time to go.*

Endal shakily sat up. He didn't have to tell Bastian that his head ached. He felt the dog's pain, sharp inside his own skull, and winced from it.

Lubon yawned and clambered to his feet, his tail wagging. Bastian patted him. The pup wasn't as thin as he'd been. His ribs were scarcely visible beneath his brindle coat. *Goodbye, little friend.*

The pup understood goodbye. He licked Bastian's hand and nipped at his fingers with needle-sharp teeth. Puppy's teeth. Salamander's teeth. *No*, Bastian told the pup firmly. *Do not bite people.*

Lubon was contrite. He licked Bastian's hand again.

Bastian bent and picked Endal up, grunting as he lifted the dog's weight. "Goodbye."

Michaud nodded farewell.

Let's go, he said to Endal. *Home to Liana.*

And to Melke.

And to whatever decision he was going to make.

CHAPTER FIFTY-SIX

BASTIAN DIDN'T ARRIVE home until late. His face was grim as he shouldered open the kitchen door. He carried Endal in his arms.

Liana stopped slicing potatoes. She laid down the knife.

"Endal's hurt," her brother said. He knelt and laid the dog carefully on the flagstones.

Liana wiped her hands on her apron. "How?"

"Someone hit him."

"What?" She reached down hastily to touch the dog. She felt his pain, the confusion in his head, the underlying nausea. "Why?"

"Because the son of a whore was too cowardly to hit me."

Alarm jerked her head up. "Hit you? Why would someone want to hit you?"

Bastian pulled a chair out from the table and sat. She saw weariness in the way his arms and legs moved. He rubbed a hand across his face. "It's an unpleasant tale."

Liana knelt beside Endal. She examined the gash, sticky with blood. "Tell me."

He told her while she healed the dog, knitting the faint crack in his skull and coaxing the edges of the wound together. The swelling and bruising eased beneath her fingertips like ice melting in sunlight. She chased away the nausea: *shoo, let him be.*

She looked up at Bastian when he was finished. "You did the right thing."

He shrugged with one shoulder. "Ronsard doesn't think so."

"He did this to Endal?"

Bastian nodded. She saw bruises on his knuckles as he rubbed his face again.

"You hit him?"

"Broke his head."

The words shocked her. "Broke his head!"

"He'll live," Bastian said shortly.

Liana bit her lip. What Bastian had done was just. She was foolish to be dismayed by the brutality of it.

She rose to her feet, stiff from kneeling so long.

Bastian's face lost its grimness. He reached down to touch the dog. "Endal's all right?"

Liana nodded. "He'll be fine."

Bastian swallowed. He blinked, but not before she saw the shine of tears in his eyes. He stood and wrapped his arms around her, lifting her off her feet. She smelled sweat and blood on him, felt his warmth, his strength. "Thank you, little one."

She sat at the kitchen table while he ate and Endal slept, stretched out on the flagstones. He talked of the things he'd bought in Thierry, a horse and cart and more provisions. He told her how he'd arranged for fresh slate for the roof and new glass for the windows. His mood was distracted. He didn't answer several of her questions.

She had a feeling that more than the innkeeper troubled him.

Finally he pushed the plate away. "How was your day?"

She wanted to talk with him about Hantje, who'd refused again to let her heal the scar beneath his lower lip, but now wasn't the time. He looked exhausted. "Fine."

Bastian nodded, but she wasn't sure he'd heard her. He rubbed his face. Stubble rasped beneath his hand.

Liana stood. "Go to bed," she said, bending to kiss his cheek.

"I will," he said. But he made no move to stand. When she looked back from the doorway he was staring down at the tabletop, a frown pinching between his eyebrows.

CHAPTER FIFTY-SEVEN

LIANA DREW BACK the curtains in the sick-room. The morning was gray. A fine drizzle fell and tiny drops of moisture flecked the window panes. The sight made her heart lighten.

She heard footsteps in the corridor, slightly irregular, as if the walker limped. Her fingers tightened on the streaked green curtain. She turned her head.

Hantje stepped into the doorway. "Is she awake?"

He wore Bastian's clothes. Their height was similar but he was leaner, still gaunt from his illness. The shirt and trousers hung on him.

"Not yet." The smile on her mouth was unrestrained and glad; she couldn't hold it back. "Come in."

Hantje avoided meeting her eyes as he crossed the room. He didn't come to stand beside her.

Liana released the curtain. She walked back to her chair and sat.

Hantje didn't sit beside her in the second chair. He stood and looked down at Melke. She slept with one hand lying on the coverlet, the fingers loosely curled into her palm. Her breathing was soft and even, her face peaceful. Against the worn linen pillowslip her hair was starkly black.

Liana smoothed the skirt over her knees, aware of how far away Hantje was, how close. She watched as he reached down and took hold of his sister's hand. The movement was slow and careful and achingly gentle, as if Melke was as fragile as the finest porcelain. The tenderness of his touch made Liana's throat tighten.

"I can't thank you enough." Hantje's voice was low, little more than a whisper. He didn't look at her.

"Nor can I thank you."

He glanced at her. "That was different."

She held his eyes, gray eyes, the color of smoke and storm clouds. "What you did for me was far greater than this." She touched Melke's wrist lightly.

Hantje's eyebrows drew together in denial. "You saved her *life*."

"And you saved mine."

Hantje's gaze fell. His cheeks flushed faintly.

The tinge of color gave her courage. Liana looked at the scar beneath his lower lip. "Let me heal it," she said. Thought of touching Hantje made her heart beat slightly faster.

He shook his head, a sharp movement. "No."

It was like a slap across the face, that one word, the flat tone of Hantje's voice as he uttered it, the way his mouth tightened afterward. Liana looked down at her hands.

Hantje had sacrificed his body for her. He'd let the psaaron rape him. Now he didn't want her to touch him.

A week ago his feelings had matched hers. She'd sensed it in him, felt it. A blossoming of something, a beginning full of possibilities. What had changed?

Liana raised her head. "If you wish to thank me, then let me heal you."

Hantje's gaze jerked to her again. His lips parted, but whatever words he wished to say remained unuttered. He closed his mouth, swallowed. She saw clearly that he didn't want her to touch him.

Shame heated her cheeks. She wanted to murmur an apology, to slide out of the chair and hurry from the room. Only pride kept her seated. Pride, and the need to understand what had changed.

Hantje swallowed again. "Very well."

He released Melke's hand and sat on the edge of the bed, awkward and tense. He flinched when her fingertips touched below his mouth. That tiny backwards movement hurt her. Misery clenched in her chest, and then she felt him, felt the complex knot of his emotions: incandescent joy that Melke lived, self-hatred, despair, and—

And she understood why he didn't want her to touch him. She understood why he held himself so rigid, his fingers white-knuckled as he gripped the coverlet.

The shame, the misery, became nothing.

Hantje's feelings *had* changed. There was no confusion in him now. The emotions were deeper and richer, sweeter.

He ached to touch her. It was a fever inside him. And beneath that was love, strong and pure. Hantje loved her. He wanted to share her life. He wanted to be the father of her children, to stand at her side as the seasons changed and the years passed.

He loved her, and he knew he wasn't good enough for her. He was a wraith and a thief. He was penniless.

The touch of her fingers hurt him.

Liana removed her hand. Joy swelled inside her. "Hantje."

She saw him swallow, saw the rapid beat of the pulse at the base of his throat.

"What?" His voice was hoarse.

Liana leaned forward and touched her mouth to his.

CHAPTER FIFTY-EIGHT

H ANTJE PUSHED HER away and scrambled
from the bed. Panic thudded hard in his
chest. "What are you doing!"

Liana stood. Color flushed her cheeks. Her silver-
white hair was as cool and beautiful as moonshine.
"Kissing you."

"Don't!" he said, taking a step back. The floor
swooped beneath his feet.

"Why not?"

"Because I don't want you to."

A smile shone in her eyes. "Liar," she said.

Hantje swallowed. He took another step backwards.

"You want me as much as I want you."

Hantje shook his head, while his heart hammered against his ribs. *I am a wraith.* "No," he
said.

Liana stepped toward him. "Yes."

He flinched as she tried to kiss him again, and stumbled back another pace. "No!"

Her hands fisted in his sleeves. "*You want me,*" she said fiercely.

Hantje unfastened her fingers and pushed her away. "No, I don't!"

Breath hissed between her teeth. She stamped her foot. "I don't care that you're a wraith!"

Time stood still for a long moment. His heart didn't beat. There was no breath, no flow of blood. Just her words.

And in that moment his dream was real, bright and golden, perfect. Liana. A home with children. Watching her sleep at night. Protecting her. His heart began to beat again and blood to flow in his veins... and hope was extinguished.

Liana deserved a man who was worthy of her. Not a wraith, a thief.

"I care," he said, and he turned from her.

She grabbed his arm. "Don't be a fool, Hantje!"

He halted in the middle of the floor. "Let go of me."

"No."

He turned his head and looked at Liana. Her face was determined. She held his gaze and he watched as hope lit her eyes and softened her mouth. "Hantje—"

"No." He cut her off, knowing what he had to say. "It's not I who am the fool, Liana. It's you."

The words were cruel. He wished them unsaid as soon as he'd uttered them. He saw her head jerk back, saw her nostrils flare as she inhaled, saw the color drain from her cheeks.

He left her standing in the middle of the bed-chamber, pale, with Melke asleep in the bed behind her.

It had to be this way.

CHAPTER FIFTY-NINE

BASTIAN LOOKED DOWN at the stream bed. He closed his eyes. All his life this stream had been dry.

The channel that had been choked with silt, the channel that two of his uncles had died trying to open and that no sal Vere had dared clear since, was unblocked. The river had washed the silt away. Now water ran through Vere, as if the stream hadn't been dry for almost forty years.

He should feel joy. Instead, the sight of water brought tight grief to his chest. The stream flowed, and his parents weren't here to witness it.

Bastian opened his eyes and stared down at the water. "I wish you could see this," he whispered.

A useless wish. The past couldn't be altered.

Come, Endal. He turned back toward the farmhouse. The grass was still dead and cracks still gaped in the ground. No birds sang. But there was water in the stream. Vere would come alive slowly. One day there'd be green growth and the soil would be soft beneath his boots and his ears would catch the sound of birds singing.

His children would run through thick grass, laughing. They would play on the beach and build castles in the sand.

Children.

Bastian narrowed his eyes and looked up at the sky. The morning drizzle had lifted, but the clouds were still thick and beautiful and full of water. A cool breeze whispered over his skin.

Clouds. Water in the stream. *What am I going to do?*

He needed to speak to Melke, to thank her. He needed to do it today. To delay any longer would be unforgivable. She'd risked her life, had almost died to save Liana. To save Vere.

To save me?

Bastian trudged back to the farmhouse. The stone he'd stolen from her was in his pocket, small and smooth. Dread slowed his steps. He didn't want to explain his act of theft, but he had to, just as he had to decide what it was that he felt for Melke. And what he was going to do about it.

It was a relief to see Liana sitting hunched on the kitchen doorstep. Bastian pushed aside guilt and dread and indecision. He'd talk to Melke later. Now, Liana needed him.

She had sat like this, hugging her knees with her head bowed, when she'd dropped the cooking pot, spilling soup over the floor and leaving them with only bread for dinner. And when she'd found a nest of baby birds that had starved to death. And when every one of the flowers she'd planted had shrivelled and died before blooming.

Bastian sat down on the doorstep beside her and put his arm around her shoulders. "What's wrong, little one?"

Liana looked up. Her smile was wan.

Bastian hugged her close, feeling how delicate she was, made of fine bones and soft skin. "Tell me," he said. *And whatever it is, I'll make it right.*

"It's Hantje." Her voice was a whisper. He thought he heard tears in it.

Every muscle in Bastian's body clenched. Sudden fury bellowed in his chest. *I'll kill him.*

His arm tightened around her shoulders. "What has he done?" If Hantje had touched her, if he'd *dared*—

"He says he doesn't want me, and he *does*." Liana's voice broke on the last word. She began to weep.

Bastian pulled her closer. "It's all right," he said, while his anger gave way to bafflement.

"He thinks he's not good enough for me, but he is! He *is*." Sobs distorted Liana's words. He hadn't the faintest idea what she was talking about.

"Hush," he said, pressing a kiss into her hair and smelling rosemary. "Don't cry. It'll be all right."

Endal whined and tried to lick Liana's face.

Do you know why she's crying? Bastian asked him. *Something about Hantje?*

I know that she wants to mate with Hantje, Endal said, and succeeded in licking Liana's chin. *And that he wants to mate with her.*

Bastian sat stiffly on the step, hugging Liana. Shock was blank inside him. The noises that he uttered, soothing, were automatic.

What? How do you know?

I can smell it.

Bastian pushed the words away. Impossible. Unbelievable.

But Endal never lied.

You can smell it?

Yes.

Liana and Hantje?

Yes, said Endal, trying to climb onto Liana's lap. *Didn't you know?*

Bastian narrowed his eyes and looked up at the clouds. The sun burned high above them, almost at its zenith. No, he hadn't known. Liana and Hantje. Liana and a wraith.

Endal could smell it?

He listened to Liana's weeping, and to the thud of his own heartbeat. "Hush," he whispered. Sobs shook her body. She wanted to marry Hantje. A wraith, a would-be thief, a man who was braver than he was.

"Tell me," he said, when Liana's tears had slowed and her gulped breaths were steadier.

"Hantje says he doesn't want me." Her voice trembled. She opened her arms for Endal to put his head and forepaws in her lap. "But I can *feel* it. He wants me as much as I want him." She held Endal awkwardly, tightly, burying her face in his black coat.

"How much do you want him?"

Liana's head rose sharply. "I *love* him." Her face was fierce and tear-stained. "And he loves me."

"Liana, love and desire are two different things. Sometimes it's difficult to distinguish between them." He brushed her cheek with light fingers, trying to take the sting from his words.

She shook her head. "Hantje is the only man I'll ever want to marry."

Bastian didn't speak for several seconds. "Are you certain?"

"Yes!"

He envied Liana's certainty. She knew her own heart. "Does Hantje feel the same way?"

"Yes." Fresh tears welled in her eyes. "He does."

"Then why—"

"Because he thinks he's not good enough for me! And he *is*. He's the kindest, nicest..." Her face twisted.

Bastian held her while she wept into Endal's fur. The dog bore it patiently.

"I'll speak with him," he said when her sobs had quieted.

Liana stiffened. "You?" She raised her face and looked at him. Tears streaked her cheeks. "Why?"

"Because I think you should marry him."

He saw hope flare in her eyes. "You do? But I thought you'd... But he's a *wraith*."

Bastian smiled. "I know."

"You want me to marry him? You really do?"

Bastian nodded. "I want whatever makes you happy." And if that was a wraith, so be it.

Her arms were around his neck. "Thank you."

Bastian shut his eyes and held her close. A child no longer.

He opened his eyes and kissed her hair and released her. "Go wash your face, little one, while I find your wraith and talk some sense into him."

Liana smiled. Joy shone through the drying tears. She hugged Endal and pushed him gently from her lap and stood. "Bastian, do you truly think you can persuade him?"

He saw anxiety and hope in the way her hands gripped together, the knuckles whitening. "If he loves you, then yes."

"He does." There was no uncertainty in her voice or eyes.

"Then don't worry."

Her face was tearstained and radiantly beautiful. She bent and pressed a kiss to his cheek. "I love you, Bastian."

"I love you, too," he said, but she was gone, running into the house.

Bastian sat on the doorstep, rubbing his cheek. Liana and Hantje. Liana and a wraith.

It wasn't what he'd wished, but did it truly matter that Hantje was a wraith? Bresse wasn't Stenrik.

He rubbed his cheek and sighed. *You can smell when people want to mate?*

Yes. Endal yawned widely, showing his teeth.

What about me?

You want to mate with Melke.

The bald words brought blood to Bastian's face. He felt it beneath his fingertips, hot. Embarrassment crawled over his skin. He let his hand fall.

You smell that?

Yes. Endal scratched vigorously behind one ear.

And Melke? Do you smell anything from her? Does she wish to mate with anyone?

Endal stopped scratching. His pale eyes fastened on Bastian's face. *You would like to know?*

Bastian cleared his throat. More heat scalded his cheeks. "Yes," he said, aloud.

Very well. Endal shook himself briskly. *I shall smell.*

Bastian looked at him. A dog. A simple creature who liked to chase sticks and bark at lizards, and who knew things that most humans didn't. He could tell when people were afraid and when they lied, and when they desired one another.

Thank you, Endal, he said.

BASTIAN FOUND HANTJE in the sickroom. *No,* he said, catching hold of Endal's thick leather collar. *Don't disturb them.*

It wasn't embarrassment that halted him in the open doorway. He didn't need the dog's senses to know that whatever Melke and Hantje talked about was deeply private.

They sat with their heads bent together. Hantje's face was tight and bitter, his eyes shut. The black hair was bound back at his neck.

Melke's hair hung free, sliding forward over her shoulder. He saw the fineness of her profile, the paleness of her skin, the red of her lips moving as she talked. Her words were too low to hear.

She reached to touch her brother, laying a hand at the nape of his neck.

Hantje flinched. His eyes shut more tightly. His mouth twisted.

The young man hated himself, Bastian realized. It wasn't merely that he thought himself not good enough for Liana. He hated himself.

There was love in the angle of Melke's head, tilting toward her brother, in the touch of her fingers at the nape of his neck. Quiet love, and quiet despair.

Bastian watched her, the movement of her lips and the soft fall of her hair, the elegant lines of nose and cheekbone and jaw, the slender fingers resting on Hantje's neck.

Desire, yes, and something that was more than desire.

He turned away from the open door. *Come, Endal. They want to be alone. We'll wait downstairs.*

"YOU SHOULD HAVE left me there."

"Don't you dare say that." Melke tightened her fingers on Hantje's neck. "Don't you dare *think* it!"

He said nothing. His eyes were still closed, as if he couldn't bear looking at her.

Melke touched her brow to his. "I could never have left you there," she whispered.

"Why don't you hate me?"

"Because you are my brother and I love you."

He shook his head, his forehead moving against hers.

"Yes."

But Hantje made no reply. He sat, stiff and tense, hunched into himself.

"Hantje, please. You must stop this. It will destroy you." *And if it destroys you, then it will destroy me.*

"It's all my fault." His voice was rough. "Everything's my fault."

"No."

"Yes!" Hantje pulled away from her. His eyes opened. She saw his distress, his self-hatred.

"The curse is broken," Melke said quietly.

He made a sharp, dismissive gesture with his hand.

"I am unharmed. Liana is unharm—"

"You almost died!"

"But I didn't die. I'm fine." Her voice was calm, soft.

Hantje's lips twisted. He shook his head.

"And Liana is unharmed, thanks to you." Pain twisted in her chest at thought of what he'd endured, an endless night of brutality. "And Bastian is unharmed."

"None of this would have happened if I'd not—"

Melke laid her hand over his mouth. "Don't, Hantje. Please. You must forgive yourself." But he pulled back from her touch and she saw that he rejected her words. It was in the stiffness of his face and the bitter tightness of his mouth, the hard gray of his eyes.

He pushed the chair back, the sound of wood against wood harsh, and stood. An awkward kiss was pressed into her hair. "Go to sleep," he said roughly, and then he was gone, his gait clumsy, as if he didn't see the floor.

Melke bowed her head and tried to hold the tears back with her fingers. *Don't do this, Hantje. Please.*

CHAPTER SIXTY

BASTIAN CAUGHT THE young man's arm as he pushed past him. "You and I need to talk."

"What?" Hantje pulled away from him. He blinked, and the bitter misery on his face vanished. It was if a mask slid over his features, haughty. His chin lifted.

Bastian experienced an odd pang of familiarity as he watched the transformation. "You're very like your sister."

Hantje's mouth tightened. "She's better than me."

Bastian shrugged. "Maybe. Maybe not."

The young man's eyes narrowed. "She—"

Bastian blew out a breath that was part sigh, part laugh. "You mistake me. I wasn't insulting your sister."

Black eyebrows drew together. "Then what?"

"We need to talk."

Hantje followed the silent invitation of his hand, stalking past him down the corridor and into the unfurnished parlour. Bastian closed the door behind them. The air was stale and musty.

"Well?" Hantje asked. He crossed his arms over his chest, defensive, proud.

"Liana wishes to marry you."

The haughtiness vanished for a fraction of a second, allowing Bastian a brief glimpse of anguish before the mask snapped back into place. "It's merely an infatuation." The young man's voice was stiff. "She'll forget me once I'm gone."

"I doubt it," Bastian said mildly, and watched as Hantje's mouth tightened. "She's very certain."

"You needn't worry." The words were flat. "She's safe from me. I have no intention of taking advantage of her."

"No. So she said."

Hantje's eyelids flickered slightly. There was a moment of silence, broken only by the *clack* of Endal's claws on the wooden floorboards as he explored the empty corners of the room. "Then we understand each other and this discussion is over." Hantje stepped past him and reached for the door handle. "I'll leave as soon as my sister is able to travel."

Bastian caught the young man's arm. "No. This discussion is not over."

He felt Hantje's muscles clench beneath his fingers, saw anger flare on his face.

The young man shook his hand off. "No? What more do you wish to say?" There was a dangerous edge to his voice and fierceness in his eyes.

Endal stopped exploring the room. He came to stand beside Bastian.

Bastian kept his face bland, his voice mild. "What do you know about Liana's gift?"

Hantje's glaring rage faltered. "She heals."

"Yes, she does." Bastian studied the young man's face. Kind, Liana had said. He saw no kindness, only anger and bitterness and a curving scar beneath his lower lip. "And when she heals, she *feels* who her patient is."

"Feels?"

Bastian held Hantje's eyes. "She knows you as well as you know yourself. She knows who you are, she knows what you dream about, and she knows how you feel about her."

The anger drained from Hantje's face. His skin, already pale, became paler. "No." It was a whisper, aghast.

"So let's discuss your marriage."

Hantje turned away, abruptly. His footsteps were loud and sharp as he crossed the room. He stood at one of the tall windows, his back to Bastian. Dust motes spun in the air. "I will not marry her."

Bastian leaned his shoulders against the door and watched him. Endal lay down across his feet, heavy and warm. "She is of an age to be married."

"Not to me."

"Why not?"

"Because I'm a wraith."

"Not exactly what I had in mind, I agree." Bastian touched the red stone in his pocket, turning it between his fingers. "But no reason not to marry Liana."

Hantje turned to face him. "But I'm a *wraith*."

Bastian shrugged. "An uncomfortable gift."

"Uncomfortable!"

Endal sat up. His ears pricked.

The young man's face twisted. "Do you have *any* idea what it means to be a wraith?"

"Your sister told me about your family." Bastian held the stone between his thumb and forefinger, small and hard. "But this isn't Stenrik. The things that happened to your mother will never happen to Liana."

"But if I'm discovered—"

"You will be exiled. Not burned, not... used."

Hantje swallowed. His expression was as bleak as the bare room. "I can't marry her."

Bastian began to lose his patience. "Because you're a wraith? I've already told you—"

"Because I'm a thief!"

Bastian straightened away from the door. He released the stone. "I was under the impression that you had failed to steal anything."

The young man's face flushed. "I *tried*."

"And failed," said Bastian, aware of the stone in his pocket. "Therefore you are not a thief." *Although I am. And your sister, most definitely, is one.*

Hantje's chin lifted. "I had the intention of stealing." Thin daylight fell over his face, adding no color, making his hair blacker and his skin ashen.

"Do you still have the intention?"

Hantje's head jerked back. "Of course not!"

"Then you are no thief."

The young man met his eyes for a long, silent moment. His face was tight, the skin stretched taut over his bones. Recognition teased at the edges of Bastian's memory.

"I can't marry Liana," Hantje said, his voice flat. "It's all my fault, everything. I can't marry her."

Bastian looked at Hantje and saw his father in the young man's face, saw bitterness and despair and guilt. He hadn't known what to say then. He'd been too young, too stricken by grief, too overwhelmed by what had occurred. Now he knew.

"Everything's your fault?" There was a flick of contempt in his voice. "You blame yourself for *everything*?" He made a sound in which laughter and disgust were mingled. "Don't be such a fool!"

Color rose sharply in Hantje's face. His chin lifted. "I started it," he said stiffly.

"The first mistake was yours, yes. But everything else?" Bastian shook his head. "No."

"But—"

"This," he jabbed a finger at Hantje, "*this* is your second mistake."

"I beg your pardon?" Hantje said, cold hauteur in his voice. He looked down his nose at Bastian.

"Punishing yourself. It's the *stupidest*—' Rage surged inside him. He closed his eyes and took a deep breath. "My father did this," he said, opening his eyes and staring at Hantje, holding his gaze. "He blamed himself for my mother's death. He punished himself. And he punished us too. He didn't mean to, but he did. And if you do this, then you'll be punishing your sister and mine."

Hantje's chin lowered.

"The mistake you made is wiped out. Gone." His hand cut through the air, making more dust motes swirl. "What you did for Liana... We can never repay you for that."

Hantje's face tightened slightly, a tiny flinching of his facial muscles. For a brief instant Bastian thought he saw memory of terror and pain in the young man's eyes.

"I deserved it." Hantje's voice was hoarse.

"No. You didn't."

The young man's gaze fell.

"The first mistake was yours," Bastian said quietly. "But the second was mine, and it was worse than yours. I could have stopped this. I could have stopped it all."

Hantje's eyes jerked up. "What do you mean?"

"The salamanders offered me the necklace back."

The young man's brow creased. "I don't understand."

Bastian clenched his hands in his pockets. He cleared his throat. The words still stuck. He had to force them out: "I hadn't the courage to meet their terms."

He couldn't look at Hantje, couldn't meet his gaze.

The young man uttered a sound that was too harsh to be a laugh. "I hadn't the courage either. I chose to steal their gold because I was afraid to earn it."

A tension in his chest that he'd been unaware of, a tight rigidity, eased. Bastian looked up and met the young man's eyes. Gray eyes, steady, not judging him. Hantje's mouth twisted into something that was almost a smile, wry and slightly bitter. "You found your courage."

"So did you."

Again the tiny muscles in Hantje's face flinched.

"I can never thank you enough for what you did," Bastian said quietly. "You saved my sister."

"And you saved mine."

There was little comparison between the minutes he'd spent with the salamander and the hours Hantje had endured with the psaaron, but Bastian had no words to articulate his gratitude for the young man's courage and his regret that it had been necessary. "Just marry Liana," he said gruffly.

Something flared in Hantje's eyes, bright. "You really mean it?"

Bastian nodded.

"But I have no money, nothing to offer."

Bastian looked at the young man's face, proud, and thought of the piles of gold and silver coins on the floor beside his bed. Tomorrow. He'd tackle that hurdle tomorrow. "It will take much work to restore the farm. I'd be grateful for your help."

The young man swallowed. "You do mean that?"

"Yes." He nodded. "Now go and find Liana."

Hantje didn't move. He stood in front of the window, an overcast sky behind him. "And my sister?"

"I hope she'll stay here, too. I hope you'll both think of Vere as your home."

Hope. He did hope it.

Something glittered in Hantje's eyes, as bright as tears. "You truly mean that?"

Bastian nodded again.

A smile lit the young man's face, more brilliant than sunlight. "Thank you."

Bastian shook his head. "Go and find Liana."

"I shall." Hantje crossed the room with long strides, stirring the dust. His grip, when he clasped Bastian's hand, was strong.

"Welcome to Vere," Bastian said.

"Thank you."

He was too thin, too pale, with the marks of illness and injury still etched on his face. An easterner, with hair down to his waist and joy shining in his eyes. A wraith.

Liana has chosen well, Bastian told Endal, as he watched the young man walk down the corridor. *Very well.*

CHAPTER SIXTY-ONE

MELKE EASED HER feet into the soft leather slippers and stood. There was a moment when the room dipped and swayed, when she clutched at the wall, and then everything steadied, ceiling and floor and windows.

She needed to be outside. She needed to feel sunlight on her skin and breathe fresh air into her lungs.

Movement in the mirror caught her eyes. She saw herself, for the first time since she'd come to Vere. The dark skirt was the same, the gray blouse, the black hair, the pale face.

Melke turned her head away. *Wraith*.

She held on to the handrail as she walked down the stairs. The wood was cool beneath her hand.

Hantje's bedroom was empty. The kitchen was empty.

Her legs grew steadier with each step. Sunlight beckoned, dimmed by clouds in the sky, but still sunlight.

Bastian stood outside, in the yard.

Melke shrank back in the doorway. He hadn't seen her. His attention was focussed on Endal. They were silent, standing together at the well, but she knew that they talked, man and hound.

Amusement lit Bastian's face. He laughed, a boyish sound, loud and delighted. Endal uttered a low bark and pranced and wagged his tail.

What had the hound said to make Bastian throw his head back and laugh like that?

Pale wolf-eyes stared at her.

Bastian stopped laughing.

They looked at her, man and hound, and then Endal came bounding toward her. She needed no gift to know that he was pleased to see her. It was in the joyful wriggle of his large body, the sweeping tail, the exuberantly licking tongue.

Bastian crossed the yard more slowly, his hands in his pockets.

She stood in the doorway, stiff and awkward, patting Endal. He had saved her, this man. A Bressen who spoke with short, hissing esses and guttural consonants and who wore his hair cropped so short that the nape of his neck was bare and vulnerable. He'd lain with the adult salamander in payment for her life. She didn't understand how he could have done such a thing, or why.

"Good afternoon." His voice was polite.

Melke swallowed past the tightness in her throat and watched her own hand stroke Endal's black fur. "Good afternoon."

She saw his boots, scarred and dirty, saw the dun-colored trousers, worn soft with use, faded and darned.

"How are you?"

She forced herself to look up and meet his eyes. She was as tall as he was, standing on the doorstep. "I'm fine, thank you."

The laughter that had lightened his face was gone. Stone. She had thought it once before, a face of stone. Not a mercenary, not brutal, but closed and expressionless, giving nothing away.

He had stood before the salamander as he stood before her now. Of course the creature had agreed to the bargain. A strong body and a strong face, handsome and sun-browned, eyes as green as the sea, hair the color of honey, and the eyelashes of a girl, long and curling and tipped with gold.

A prize indeed, this man.

Melke swallowed and raised her chin. "Thank you for saving me."

She saw his mouth tighten fractionally, saw something flicker in his eyes. Surprise?

She clenched her fingers into Endal's thick coat. "Why did you do it?"

He had stripped off his clothes and stood naked, had let the salamander take pleasure from his body. Melke imagined his skin, slick with sweat. She imagined the fear in his eyes.

"Because I had to."

Melke shook her head. "No. You didn't." She lifted her hand from Endal's hair and turned to go inside.

"The curse is broken," Bastian said.

She halted. "Yes."

"Thank you."

Melke stared across the kitchen. The first time she'd crossed this room, she had come to steal. Now Bastian thanked her, when it was *she* who owed the gratitude.

"Don't thank me," she said, turning back to face him. Her voice was flat.

Bastian's eyes narrowed. "Why? Because you're a wraith? Because it's all your fault? Because you *deserve* to suffer?"

The words, the contempt in his voice, stung as if he'd slapped her. Her head jerked back.

"I have just been through this with your brother." His voice was raised, almost a shout. "I thought you had more sense!"

Endal whined. His ears were flat against his skull.

"What do you mean about Hantje?" She spoke through stiff lips.

The fierceness faded from Bastian's face. He held her gaze for several seconds. Anger no longer sparked in his eyes. "I mean that he doesn't hate himself any more," he said quietly. "He'll be all right."

Melke clutched the doorframe to steady herself. Hope was tight in her throat. Her lips parted, but speech was impossible.

Endal pressed against her skirt. He licked her fingers. His tail wagged.

Bastian's boots shuffled on the dirt. He dug into his pocket. "Here. This is yours."

Melke blinked. Her stone lay on his palm, tiny and red, precious. With it came memory of autumn bonfires and gingerbread and Tass barking at the swirling leaves. Mam and Da. "Where did you find it?"

She saw him swallow, saw the muscles work in his throat. "I took it."

Her shock was utter. She stared at him, unable to believe. Not this man, not Bastian. But she saw the truth of his words in his face. Shame flushed his cheeks.

"Take it," he said, his voice rough.

"But... why?"

His eyes slid from hers. "Because I hated you."

It was foolish to feel a stab of pain at the words. His mercenary's face had told her he hated her. She didn't need to hear him say it.

Melke reached to take the stone with trembling fingers. It was warm from his hand. "You didn't have to give it back," she said, cupping the stone in her palm. She could smell gingerbread.

Bastian's eyes met hers. "Yes, I did."

The shame was gone. Instead, there was something else in his gaze, an intensity, a heat. Melke clenched her fingers around the pebble. Awareness of Bastian crawled over her skin. It was suddenly difficult to breathe.

I want this man.

She swallowed. "Thank you," she managed to say, and then she turned and walked fast across the kitchen.

"Melke—"

But she was through the door. Her heart thudded in her chest, fast, and it wasn't because she was running up the stairs. It was because she was a fool.

Bastian didn't follow her, didn't climb the stairs and knock on the closed door. For that, she was thankful.

He had taken her stone and he'd given it back, and she liked him all the more for his honesty and his shame.

She was a fool.

Melke laid the stone on the windowsill. It was absurd to treasure something like this, a common pebble. She touched a fingertip to it. The dead garden lay outside the window, but she didn't see leafless trees and bare flowerbeds and empty fountains. She saw Hantje running through long autumn grass, shrieking with laughter, and Tass barking at swirls of red-gold leaves. She was standing on top of the hill with Da, watching smoke curl up from the chimneys. She was baking gingerbread with Mam, and she was *home*.

Movement in the garden made her blink. The memories vanished.

Hantje was there. Not running through grass, shrieking and laughing, but walking with Liana. Her eyes knew instantly that Bastian was correct; Hantje no longer hated himself. It was in the set of his shoulders and tilt of his head, the openness of his face.

She watched, frozen, as Hantje touched Liana's cheek lightly with his fingertips, as he bent his head and kissed her mouth.

It was a shy kiss, brief and gentle, the kiss of two people newly in love. She saw a blush of joy on Liana's cheeks, saw wonder in Hantje's face. His head bent again, his lips brushed her moon-white hair.

Melke turned away from the window, struggling to breathe. Her chest was tight. Hantje would stay at Vere. She knew it as clearly as if he'd told her.

The air in the bedchamber was as thick as water. She couldn't swallow it, couldn't breathe. Weight pressed down so heavily that her knees almost buckled. *Aloneness.* She gulped air, dragging it into her lungs. It was good that Hantje had Liana—*it was good*—and she had to get out of this house, she had to get out *now*.

Melke went down the stairs blindly, almost stumbling in her haste. She hurried through the kitchen, across the empty yard, away. Dead grass crunched beneath her slippers.

She halted, panting. There was an ache in her ankle where Liana had mended the bone, and an ache in her chest that had nothing to do with her injuries. Hantje would stay and she would go. It was terrifying to think of being alone, almost as terrifying as entering the salamanders' den.

Alone.

Melke turned toward the sea. She was happy for Hantje, *happy*. She'd look at the ocean and let the sea-wind blow through her, and then she'd come back and smile when her brother told her his news. She would not let him see how terrified she was.

The track that led to the beach was thin and rutted, no more than half a mile long, but her legs were trembling when she reached the rising sand dunes.

For a moment it didn't matter that she was alone. Her heart lifted. She smelled the salt-tang of the ocean and heard the whisper of tussock ruffling in the wind, saw waves curling on the white sand and steep cliffs jutting to the west.

Melke sat clumsily on a sloping dune. Tussock pricked through her skirt and gritty grains of sand slid into the leather slippers. She'd walked too far; her legs shook as if she had the palsy. Liana would scold.

Memory came of the girl's face uplifted to meet Hantje's kiss, the soft blush, the shy delight.

Melke hugged her shaking knees and stared at the sea. It was what she'd wished for Hantje, a wife and children, a home. An ordinary life.

But I will be alone.

A gull flew, high above the water. The first bird she'd seen at Vere. Melke watched as it rode the currents of the wind.

The gull didn't mind that it was alone.

The white sand and the white feathers and the glare from the clouds brought tears to her eyes. Melke blinked them back, fiercely.

She would go to Thierry and find employment, and she'd become accustomed to being without Hantje, just as she'd become accustomed to being without Mam and Da.

Or...

She watched as the gull swooped low, skimming the waves. Or she could become what she truly was. A wraith.

She had crossed the line inside herself, not once now but twice. She was a wraith, irrevocably, whether she wanted to be or not.

Her eyes were blind. The gull was a pale blur. *I can be a wraith.* It would be easy. To become unseen, to surrender to her shadow-self, to give in to the shameful, wicked part of her that revelled in her wraithness.

No. Sight returned, and with it, revulsion rising in her throat. *No.* Never a wraith, never again.

"I want to be ordinary," she whispered. But she wasn't ordinary and never could be. Just as she couldn't stay here.

A hot tear slid down her cheek. Melke brushed it angrily away. Tears were as futile as self-pity and as useless. She hadn't asked to be a wraith, but neither had Bastian asked to be born under a curse. He would never be weak enough to pity himself.

Bastian was the reason she couldn't stay at Vere, even if she was asked.

Melke closed her eyes. There were so many things she wanted, so many things she couldn't have. But Thierry she could have, and employment, and the chance to see Hantje from time to time. If she could brave the salamanders' den, she could brave being alone.

Cold wetness against her cheek made her yelp and flinch in terror. "Endal!"

The hound wagged his tail hugely. He licked her chin.

Melke's heart hammered in her chest. She jerked a glance behind her and saw only dry grass and an empty landscape.

Relief and disappointment were equally sharp. Her heart began to beat more normally. "Come here." She opened her arms and let Endal clamber onto her lap, warm and heavy.

She hugged the hound to her, close, and pressed her face into his thick fur. Tussock rustled softly in the breeze and waves whispered on the sand. Endal's breathing was loud. His heart beat faster than hers.

"I'll miss you, Endal."

The hound panted happily, a heavy weight on her legs, uncomfortable. His hock dug sharply into her thigh.

Melke inhaled his hound-scent and rubbed her cheek against the soft roughness of his coat. She didn't want to stop holding him. She sighed and pushed him gently off her lap. "Come, Endal, let's wet our feet and then go back."

The hound loped ahead of her as she walked clumsily down the sand dune, his tail pluming in the wind. He was wolf-like, with his long muzzle and pricked ears and pale eyes. Moon-white eyes, she realized. A handsome creature with his black fur, as handsome as his master. And like his master he could growl and show his teeth and wear a savage face. And like his master, his heart was kind.

Endal ran across the beach. Melke followed slowly, leaving the slippers above the line of twigs and leaves and seaweed that marked high tide. The grains of sand were cool beneath her feet, fine and gritty. She tasted salt on her lips and smelled it, clean and fresh.

Endal rushed at the sea, barking, harrying a wave as it retreated. He lost his loud bravado when another wave hissed up the sand. The sight of the hound backing hurriedly up the beach brought a smile to Melke's lips.

"Don't you like to get wet?" she asked Endal, as he came to stand beside her. She gently pulled one of his ears. It was as soft as velvet. "The sea won't hurt you. Not now. The curse is broken."

Moon-white eyes glanced up at her. A tongue licked her hand.

"You are a handsome beast," she told him, stroking one black ear. "A very handsome beast." *And I am a fool, Endal.*

The hound hesitated at the water's edge while she stepped into the sea, holding the hem of her skirt up. A wave frothed around her ankles, startlingly cool. Endal whined and sidled on the sand, and then he followed her in a rush, splashing water over them both.

The cool seawater dulled the ache in her ankle. Waves swept over her feet and swirled up the beach, foaming. Grains of sand danced in the water.

Melke stood for long minutes, watching the clouds pull back and the sun shine down, watching the sea become blue-green and glittering instead of gray, watching Endal romp through the waves. It was perfect and beautiful, this. A moment, a place.

A glint caught her eye, silver-bright.

Melke bent, holding her skirt up. Water, sand and... a coin.

She straightened and turned the coin over in her fingers, thick and silver. Cold. Wet. Should she keep it, having found it?

Water swirled around her ankles and sea-spray was salty on her lips. She remembered candlelight and Liana's soft voice. *He threw the sal Vere fortune into the sea, all of it, until there was nothing left.*

The coin belonged to Bastian, as surely as the grains of sand on the beach did.

Melke closed her fingers around the coin. A wraith would keep it for herself.

"I am no wraith," she whispered, and the breeze took the words from her lips, lifting them, scattering them, tossing them high over the tussock and the sand dunes. *I am no wraith*.

Melke opened her fingers. The coin twisted as it fell, spinning, glinting. There was a tiny splash as the water swallowed it.

CHAPTER SIXTY-TWO

"**Y**OU COULD HAVE kept it," Bastian said mildly, and watched as Melke jerked around, almost losing her balance. Her eyes were wide. The hem of her skirt dipped into the water.

He saw her swallow, saw her chin lift. "No, I couldn't." A strand of black hair blew across her pale cheek.

Are you certain? he asked, as Endal came out of the water. He saw no desire on her face. On the doorstep he'd thought perhaps... but not now.

Yes. The dog shook himself.

Her face was carved of marble, cold and expressionless, but he trusted Endal.

"There is something I wish to discuss with you."

He thought that Melke stiffened slightly, standing in the sea with her skirt held above her ankles. "Very well."

Bastian relaxed as she stepped from the water. The sea was no longer Vere's enemy, but seeing her with waves washing over her feet had brought sharp fear to his chest.

He caught a glimpse of slender ankles before she lowered the skirt. The hem was dark with water.

"Shall we sit?" He inclined his head at the dunes.

"Very well," she said again. She began to walk up the beach. Her back was straight and her head held high. He thought she limped slightly.

Bastian took her elbow. "You shouldn't have walked so far."

Melke tried to pull away from him. "I am not an invalid." Haughty words, spoken in a haughty tone.

Bastian tightened his grip on her elbow. "Yesterday you were one."

Her lips compressed. She made no further protest. Which told him she was tired and in pain, but wasn't going to admit it.

He'd never walked with a woman like this, side by side with his fingers on her arm. He was conscious of her warmth and the soft fall of long hair, the way blouse and skirt concealed her body yet showed her curves.

He didn't look at Endal. He didn't want to know if the dog smelled his awareness of Melke.

They sat above the high tide mark, where his mother's leather slippers lay neatly on the white sand. Endal stretched out with a contented sigh. Melke smoothed the skirt over her knees. Her feet peeked from beneath the damp hem.

The sight of her toes, shapely and lightly dusted with grains of sand, made faint heat curl beneath Bastian's skin.

He looked away and cleared his throat. "Your brother will be staying at Vere. I hope you will do the same."

"Thank you, but I prefer to live in Thierry." Melke's voice was cool and without inflection.

Her lack of surprise made Bastian blink. He looked sharply at her.

Melke's face matched her voice, expressionless. Her eyes gave nothing away. Only the tight grip of her hands around her knees hinted at emotion.

Bastian cleared his throat again. He loosened the button at his collar. "I would like to apologize to you."

Her brow creased faintly. "I beg your pardon?"

"I said things to you that I shouldn't have. I spat at you, and I shook you, and I pushed you to the ground." He swallowed, tasting shame and something bitter, something that was close to self-hatred. "I apologize."

Melke's eyebrows drew together. She shook her head, a sharp movement. "I stole from you."

"What you did, I would have done too."

"No, you wouldn't." Her voice was flat. She made as if to stand.

Bastian halted her, gripping her arm. "Yes. I would have. For Liana, I would have done everything you did. I would have made the same choices."

She stared at him. Her eyes were wide and dark. He was aware of how brittle she was, as if tiny cracks ran through her.

"I was wrong," Bastian said, holding her gaze. "You have honor. I know you do. I've seen it."

Her answer was silence. Bastian saw how alone she was, how lost and afraid, how vulnerable. She was older than Liana, taller and stronger, and yet she was also more fragile, more easily hurt.

"Don't you think you have honor?" he asked quietly.

Sudden tears filled Melke's eyes. She averted her face and twisted her arm to break his grip.

Bastian tightened his fingers. "Melke," he said. "Look at me."

She shook her head. "Let go of me." Her voice was low and fierce.

"Melke..." There were so many things he wanted to tell her, but he didn't have the words, didn't have the eloquence to explain. He forced open the clenched fingers and pressed a kiss into her palm. He felt the warmth of her skin beneath his lips, smelled sea salt and dog.

Melke became very still.

Bastian raised his mouth. "Look at me," he said softly.

She did. Tears shone in her eyes. "You don't like me." It was a whisper.

The tears and words stabbed at his chest. "I have changed my mind." He kissed her palm again, holding her eyes while his mouth touched her skin. "I would like..." Strange, how hard it was to shape the words with his lips, to move his tongue, to *say* them. Harder than undressing for the salamander. "I would like you to consider staying at Vere. I would like you to consider becoming my wife."

And it was strange how afraid he was of her response, even though he knew that she desired him. Desire and love were two different things.

Sweat was damp on his skin, fear tight in his chest.

Love me.

She was a statue sitting beside him, stiff and still. Her face was bloodless. "Why?"

"Why?" A laugh came from his throat, rough. There were so many reasons why. Her courage and her honor. Her intelligence. Her lustrous black hair. Her pride. "Because I like you."

She shook her head.

Bastian wished for persuasive words, but he had none. He was a farmer, not a poet. "Do you know that Endal can smell when people want each other?" he asked.

A flicker of emotion crossed Melke's face. She glanced at the dog.

"He can smell that I want you. And he can smell that you want me."

Color flared in her cheeks. She turned her head away abruptly and tried to tug her hand from his grip.

Bastian didn't let go. "Marry me," he said. There was an odd sensation in his chest, as if a fist was clenched around his heart. "I promise I won't spit at you or shake you or—"

She stopped pulling away from him. "I know you won't."

The words were almost whispered. They rendered him speechless. Something choked in his throat. She trusted him. Despite everything he'd done, she trusted him.

"You're not afraid of me?"

Melke turned her head. She met his eyes. "No."

"Endal said you were."

She flushed again. Her gaze dropped. "In the beginning. Not now."

Bastian swallowed past the constriction in his throat. *She wasn't afraid of him.* "So you'll stay? You'll marry me?"

Her head lifted. She looked at him. "My bloodline is tainted."

Once he would have seen haughtiness in the angle of her chin, now he saw the shame she tried to hide. "No more or less than mine," he told her. "There's magic in both our families."

Melke shook her head, a frown pinching between her eyebrows. "I'm a *wraith*. My magic is *bad*."

"The ability to become unseen doesn't make a person evil. How they use it does." He held her gaze. *Listen to me. Believe me.* "You're a wraith. You're also the mother I'd like for my children."

The frown was gone. Fresh tears shone in her eyes. He saw the pulse beat in her throat, saw the rise and fall of her breasts as she breathed, saw her fear and her hope. "You truly want that?"

He'd made mistakes during the past month, too many mistakes, but this wasn't one of them. He nodded. "Yes."

Her fingers flexed slightly in his hand. "You want... me?"

"Yes."

Her smile was hesitant and shy.

Bastian smiled back at her. He was aware of a curious sensation in his chest, an odd lightness, a quicksilver shiver of anticipation, a strange sense of...

Joy?

Ivory-white is her skin, and ebony-black her hair,
And her lips, oh, her lips,
As red as rubies, as sweet as honey.
And when she kisses me, oh, when she kisses
me...

He didn't kiss her. She was too fragile, too close to breaking.

The tentative clasp of her fingers was a beginning. Time would come when he'd kiss her, just as time would come when grass grew green on Vere. But not yet, not quite yet. She needed more color in her cheeks. She needed to learn how to laugh again.

Bastian held Melke's hand, while waves hissed on the beach and the wind whispered in the tussock and Endal slept stretched out at their feet. A month ago he'd spat at her, now he asked her to marry him. He imagined lying with her, her body warm and her mouth eager, her eyes laughing.

It was a dream now. But in a few weeks, a few months, it would be reality. Just as rain on Vere was now reality.

Their children would play on this beach.

Bastian tightened his grip on Melke's hand. "Shall we go home?"

A smile was luminous in her eyes. "Yes," said his wraith.

ACKNOWLEDGEMENTS

The words may be mine, but *Thief* wouldn't have made it this far without the help of many people: family and friends, my writing buddies, workmates and bosses, my agent and editors, and first and foremost my father, who showed me how it's done.

Between them they encouraged and supported, pushed and nagged, had confidence in me when I didn't, gave writing advice and feedback, provided motivation and inspiration and wine and chocolate and margaritas, and told me how to kill sheep.

My thanks!

ABOUT THE AUTHOR

Writing runs in Emily's family; her father is a novelist. She loves to travel and has spent time in China, the Middle East, and Scandinavia.

Visit her website at *www.emilygee.com*